BE MY GIRL

A DARK TIDES THRILLER

TONY HUTCHINSON

CHESHIRE CAT BOOKS LTD

The book is published by Cheshire Cat Books Ltd
Suite 50-58 Low Friar Street, Newcastle upon Tyne, NE1 5UD.

ISBN 978-1-9164457-1-0

To Ben and Flynn.
You make me smile every day.

CHAPTER ONE

BREATHE.

The subconscious order flew around her body like a speeding white pinball. Downward pressure on her mouth pushed her head deeper into the pillow, her tongue frantically trying to escape the intrusive synthetic material that tasted new but with a hint of fresh sweat.

Breathe.

Her nose strained to fill bursting lungs, the short snorts only strengthening the pungent smell, a smell alien to her bedroom.

Breathe.

Disorientated, trying to compute the sudden surface from deep sleep, Kelly Jones's terrified eyes blinked rapidly, fighting to focus in the dark.

Breathe.

The pressure…The aching lungs…The smell…

Breathe.

The street lamp sent a dull beam of light through the thin, unlined curtains and her eyes began to adjust.

The hazy blur receded. Her vision returned.

And then she saw them.

1

The eyes staring back at her through the slits of a ski mask.

Her hands shot out of the duvet, grabbing the wrist of the gloved hand on her mouth as she fought for air but the pressure on her mouth increased, forcing her head even deeper into the pillow. She thrashed her legs, arched her back, shook her head, lashed out with her arms; anything to break free, but the hand refused to budge.

Then the blade appeared inches from her face.

She froze, transfixed by the knife.

His speech was controlled, the words spoken in a conversational tone without emotion or excitement.

'Do what I say and I won't hurt you.'

Her body stiffened, rigor mortis like, and her bladder sent a steady trickle of urine on to the white cotton sheet.

Friday – February 2013

Under the fluorescent glow of the tubular light, Detective Chief Inspector Sam Parker swivelled her chair to face the computer and scanned the inbox of her emails for the last time of the day. Her eyes were drawn to one in the middle. Those sent by the higher ranks always caught your attention. Sam looked away from the screen and smiled. Did her emails have that effect on junior officers? She had never thought about it before, but yes, they probably did. Not that she considered herself any different to the person she was in the summer of 2001 when she first collected her uniform.

The cursor hovered over the message from the Assistant Chief Constable and she clicked it open.

From: Trevor Stewart
To: Sam Parker
Subject: Undetected Rape

Sam

I am a little concerned that we still have an undetected intruder stranger rape from November.

I am sure that the CID at Seaton St George has done a thorough job, but I would feel reassured if you and your team had a look at it.

I want you to conduct a review. We can talk resources and terms of reference on Monday. Meanwhile, I have arranged for copies of statements etc to be forwarded to your office.

Enjoy your weekend.
Trevor

Sam Parker turned off the computer, grabbed her coat from the hat stand, and walked towards the door. 7pm. Most of the offices would be empty. Everyone home for the weekend, or at the pub, striving for some sort of work-life balance. Had she not been so tired, she would have stayed another couple of hours doing paperwork. There was always something to do and she hadn't anything to rush home for. Not these days.

The desk phone rang. She hesitated. Answer it? Or keep on walking?

'Sam Parker.'

'Sam. It's Trevor Stewart.'

Shit! Should have kept walking.

'I'm glad I caught you. I'll pop along.'

'Yes, okay. No problem.'

Now what? Another one in no hurry to leave, his rented flat and take-away all he had to look forward to; wife and teenage kids living hundreds of miles away, refusing to traipse around the country as he climbs the promotion ladder. 'Butterfly cops' Ed Whelan called them – landing in one force before flying off to the next.

'Sam. How's things?' he said, walking into her office.

Had she only ever spoken to him on the phone, Trevor Stewart would look as she imagined. The deep, booming voice fit perfectly in the barrel-chested 6' frame.

'Fine. I've just read your email.'

'You look tired. You should try sleeping when you go to bed.'

She maintained eye contact but didn't take the bait, her teeth and lips clamped together. *Slime-ball.*

He dropped into a chair.

Does he have to sit with his legs so far apart?

Trevor Stewart ran his fingers through his sandy hair and smiled at her.

'You've seen my email? Good. We don't want stranger rapes going undetected. It's a bad news story and if we don't sort it, then it's bad news for everybody involved in the investigation. Gives the impression we don't know what we're doing. Three months old. It needs sorting as a priority. We both know he could do another one.'

Sam didn't respond, waiting for him to continue.

'Detecting jobs like this look good on your CV, too. Never does future promotion chances any harm.'

His eyes locked on hers, his voice, quieter, conveyed just a hint of menace. 'But they need detecting fast and I'm not convinced the CID at Seaton have done all they could.'

That's not how your email read, Sam thought. Another police politician – cover your back in writing while saying something else in private. She knew how the game was played, what the stakes were.

'Ed Whelan and myself will look at it on Monday.'

'Good. I'm sure with your experience you'll give it a fresh coat of looking at.' He stood up and checked the creases in his trousers. 'I don't want to keep you. We'll speak Monday. I have every faith in you... but we need a result Sam...and quickly.'

He turned around when he reached the door. 'Let me know if you change your mind about that drink.'

Dream on. Still, she needed to be careful. Trevor Stewart had formed a friendship with a Detective Chief Inspector who made no secret of the fact that he wanted Sam's job.

Through the glass exit doors she could see the fine rain falling, a mist-like vapour highlighted by the orange street lights of the car park. She pulled up the collar of her coat, took a deep breath, and braced herself to get cold and wet.

Weekends were always the worst.

At least the review into the rape would occupy her thoughts until the next job came in and in Sam Parker's world, the next job meant murder.

Sam pulled on to the driveway of her four-bedroom detached house. A number of the lights were on thanks to the ingenuity of plug-in timers. She wasn't fooled by the glow. There would be nobody inside, the house as empty as she was. There would be no easy-going conversation with Tristram, no glass of wine and the inevitable discussion around their shared passion for Burgundy. Tristram had introduced Sam to the joys of the region's acclaimed reds and was always quoting Harry Waugh, the renowned wine merchant and writer… 'The first duty of wine is to be red, the second to be a burgundy'.

These days, none of life's pleasures seemed to matter.

Saturday

'Of course all men are rapists. They have constant sexual urges that they need to satisfy. If they cannot satisfy them with a consenting woman, then they will rape.'

Sitting at the kitchen table, his mouth poised around a cold slice of last night's left-over chilli chicken pizza, he stared at the retro Roberts radio on the windowsill, shaking his head.

Where did the producers of these breakfast radio shows find these women?

'What you need to understand is that if men cannot get the sexual gratification they need, then they will just take what they think is rightfully theirs. Masturbation is no substitution for penetration.'

Letting her words wash over him, he gazed at the ever-growing mountain of pots in the sink, transfixed like a schoolboy staring out of the classroom window on a summer's day. The mugs at the bottom of the mound were now, in all probability, growing their own penicillin; the oven to the left of the sink could double as a photographer's dark room, the encrusted grime on the glass door blocking all incoming light.

As he picked another slice of pizza from the cardboard box, its end drooping as he held the crust between his thumb and index finger, the rising crescendo of the educated and distinctively plummy voice snapped his attention back to the radio.

'Fathers…sons…brothers…husbands…nephews. Every single one of them is capable of rape. The sooner women wake up to the fact that the genteel man next door, the smiling guy on the bus or train, the eloquent charmer in the wine bar, are all potential rapists, the safer they will be. Men use sex to dominate, but rape is not just about domination. It's about dominating when they feel the urge to do so. Their needs are all that matter. All men are rapists in waiting. All men are monsters.'

He tried to picture this woman. Was she one of those professor types? A sour-faced academic with a hatred of men and point to prove? Must be. Probably took her months to come up with that masturbation sound bite. He could see her sitting by the studio microphone, lip curling as she talked about men, despising them but emulating them in the way she dressed…trousers or jeans, brown brogues and baggy T-shirt, and the obligatory short hair and no make-up.

Grabbing the table with both hands, he pushed the chair away from it with his backside and leaped across the floor, the cold on his bare feet feeling as if the outside frost had settled on the terracotta tiles. He grabbed the on-off knob and shut her up with one hard twist. What the fuck did she know? So what if she'd interviewed all those victims. Had she spoken to any so-called rapists? No chance. How did she know what motivated them, what motivated him?

Grabbing the loose-hanging belt on his white, towelled dressing gown, he pulled both ends hard and fast, just a little too tight around his stomach. Stupid cow! Rooted to the spot, he replayed her outburst and asked himself if he was a monster. Inhaling slowly, he decided that depended on your viewpoint. How can I be a monster? I'm gentle with them. I treat them well. Even ask if they've enjoyed it. The muscles in his face relaxed into an ever widening smile, the tightness leaving his arms and shoulders. Loosening the belt, he leaned backwards against the kitchen bench. He planned everything so meticulously; from the moment he selected a woman to making sure he didn't get caught. And domination? What was that about? It wasn't about domination to him.

Taking the stairs two at a time, he bolted into his bedroom. Yanking open his bedside drawer, he dropped on to the bed, sitting upright, staring at the photographs on the driving licences. Licking his dry lips, he looked at each of them, memories flooding from the past and crashing into the present. This wasn't the time to handle the items but, as his breathing slowed, he knew no amount of time would dim the memory of what each licence meant.

Danielle Banks's gloved hand pushed open the door into the town-centre coffee shop. Her dark brown eyes quickly scanned the customers, anxiously looking for her mother's face. She'd already stressed in a text that morning she didn't have much time. Glancing at her TAG Heuer watch, a Christmas present from her parents, she could see her mother was already 10 minutes late. Danielle was late too - but she was working and had an excuse.

Her mother sauntered in, arms filled with designer shopping bags, the ceiling lights bouncing off her bleached blonde hair. Without waiting for a greeting, Danielle barked: 'Mother! I told you I haven't got long.'

'Oh, Danielle.' Donna Banks stretched out her daughter's name as she spoke. 'What's the rush? Sit down. I'll get the coffees.'

'The rush is I've got to be back at work in 20 minutes.' Danielle knew her mother would be deaf to the agitation in her voice.

Donna placed her bags on the light oak table and slowly walked over to the counter, her black Vivienne Westwood woollen coat following the movement of her hips. Always dressed in designer clothes, Donna's toned body still slid easily into a size 10.

By the time she returned with the coffees, Danielle's right foot was tapping up and down like the drummer in a rock band.

'So what's so important that it couldn't wait?' Danielle asked, picking up her skinny latte.

'Nothing's 'so important' as you put it. I was in town and thought it would be nice to have a coffee. I haven't seen you for ages. Are you okay?'

'I'm fine. It's just busy at work and tonight we're stocktaking.'

Leaning across the table, Donna, her dark mascara framing her pale azure eyes, stared at Danielle and said: 'Ditch the job. Work for your father.'

Danielle slammed the tall coffee cup on the table. *Here we go again.*

'Mother, I'm not working in a bloody scrap-yard! We've had this conversation a million times. I didn't get a degree in fashion to work all day in rigger boots.'

Donna pointed her right index finger directly at her daughter's face. 'And we didn't put you through university to waste your time working in a clothes shop for the minimum wage.'

Danielle used a napkin to dab at the foamy coffee she had splashed on the table.

'Look, I haven't got time for this. I'm happy. Okay?'

'Happy? How the hell can you be happy?'

Donna rubbed her face, stared at Danielle and then rested her chin in her hands. 'We worry. Your dad worries. I worry. Especially because you live alone. What was the rush to get your own place after you split with that bastard?'

'Oh Mum,' Danielle sighed, back in her own Groundhog Day. 'We've had this conversation. I'm 25. I want some independence.'

'And why you didn't go to the police after he attacked you is beyond me.'

'I didn't want all the hassle,' Danielle said. 'I've moved on. He was a mistake. I've learned from it.'

'Yes but has he? Has he? I should've let your father have him sorted out. And what the hell are your so-called mates doing letting him know your new address? Are they stupid?'

Donna rummaged in her handbag for her cigarettes then remembered…another victory for the health brigade.

Danielle looked at her mother and softened her tone, more tactic than affection.

'He won't come round. He's too scared of Dad.'

'We just worry, Dan.'

'There's no need. I'm fine.'

Danielle gulped down her coffee and stood up.

'Look I have to go now mum. Stop worrying. I'll come and see you and dad soon.' She leaned forward, kissed her mother on the cheek, and walked away.

'Put some make-up on, Dan. You look so pasty,' Donna shouted as Danielle's long legs, wrapped in thick chocolate-brown leggings, danced past customers queuing for their coffees.

Danielle glanced at her reflection in the coffee shop window as she walked out on to the street. Was she pasty? No, that was her natural complexion. Somehow, after splitting with Duncan, she just didn't want to spend time and effort on looking good. The last thing she wanted at this point in her life was another relationship. If dressing down stopped her getting attention, that suited her just fine.

———

Detective Sergeant Ed Whelan knocked on the door of the three-bedroom semi.

'Ed.' His sister-in-law Jeannie smiled and stepped to the side of the door.

'I should have called first.'

'Don't be daft,' she said, wrapping her arms around his neck and planting a kiss on his cheek. 'Come in, come in.'

Ed put the small box wrapped in silver 'Happy Birthday' paper on the kitchen table. 'Just a little something… how's things?'

'You know. Day to day. Coffee?'

Ed pulled out a chair from under the small circular glass table and sat down.

Jeannie filled the vintage espresso maker. 'I've got this new Kenyan blend.'

Ed watched her shuffle across the kitchen; back stooped, hair all grey streaks, a once beautiful woman now looking 30 years older than she should. 'Sounds nice. So how's things?'

Jeannie closed the door and sat down. 'No change,' she said, shaking her head. 'She doesn't go out. She won't go back to college. She just sits in her room all day watching TV.'

'Any joy with the counselling?'

Jeannie shook her head, her eyes dulled by stress and fatigue.

'She won't go. Says she would have to talk about it and, well, she just can't. God knows what's going on in her head.'

Ed rubbed her arm.

Jeannie scratched her cheek and shouted: 'Jess! Uncle Ed's here.'

Ed gulped when his niece appeared at the doorway. The tops of her arms were as thin as her wrists. Her thighs looked like her calves. The long glossy hair was gone, replaced by short brown greasy tufts. A blind hairdresser with blunt scissors would have done a better job.

'Uncle Ed's brought you a present.'

'Thanks,' Jess said, staring at the floor.

Ed remained in his seat, straining to hear a voice that was barely a whisper.

'Do you want to open it now?' her mother asked.

'No, I'll wait 'til Wednesday. Thanks Uncle Ed.'

Jess turned and walked away, shoulders hunched, head bowed.

Ed licked the inside of his mouth. No hugs, no excitement in her eyes or voice.

Jeannie handed him a coffee. 'It breaks my heart.'

'Mine too. Time's a great healer. We're all here for her.'

Pointless words, Ed knew. He wished he was somewhere else, wished he was in the prison cell with that bastard. Watching Jeannie's tears roll down her gaunt face, he vowed to come face to face with the shit-bag one day, and words would be the last thing on his mind.

Danielle Banks pulled into her bay on the Conifers Estate car park. Stocktaking was never easy and never quick. She sighed as she looked at the digital clock on the dashboard. 7.30pm. The Tarmac already had that pre-frost damp sheen. She slammed the door and her body shuddered in the sudden cold, her ears, nose and fingers numbed in seconds.

She pressed the remote key of the metallic black Mini Cooper S and dashed to her front door, desperate to escape the night.

She darted through the door and turned on the lights, immediately aware that the flat was colder than usual. Her cheeks tingled at a fresh flow of chilled air coming from the kitchen. Had she forgotten to close the kitchen door properly this morning? Where was the draught coming from? Her stomach had the sickening feeling she always got in a fast-falling elevator. Her heart pounded in her chest. She never left a window open, she was on the ground floor, and besides, it was February. Pull yourself together Danielle, are you really so pathetic? Taking her mobile from her coat pocket, her index finger pressed nine three times then rested on the green phone icon. Her right foot kicked the kitchen door open. She lurched towards the wall switch and flicked on the lights. 'Bastard!' she screamed, bringing her clenched fists up to her chest.

CHAPTER TWO

DANIELLE STARED at the broken window over the kitchen bench. Was he ever going to let her get on with her life?

Tiptoeing towards the bedroom, her breathing shallow and fast, she flung open the door and hit the light switch. Her eyes darted around the room. Nothing.

Danielle walked unsteadily back to the kitchen, her knees trembling and the palm of one hand on the wall for support. What had she done so wrong to deserve this? She put the mobile on to the bench and sat down on a wooden high stool, leaning forward to rest her head on her folded arms.

How often had she sat like this since moving in? Maybe her mother was right. What had been the rush to buy a flat? At least at her parents' she would have company, but then again, she couldn't really unload to her mother, a woman who met her husband when she was 16. What did she know about broken relationships?

How long had she kept her head buried in her arms? A minute? Ten? When she did look up, her reddened eyes focussed on a black-and-white photograph hanging on the wall. The photograph showed happier times, Danielle with her three lifelong girlfriends laughing on a night out, all with a drink in their hands. She couldn't recall now who had taken the photograph, but she could remember that it was the week before Duncan assaulted her. As she wiped her eyes, she studied the picture more closely than she had ever done before. Were her clothes too revealing? Was she wearing too much make-up? Were her friends such bad people? And really, what was it with men like Duncan? At first he had been very attentive, always complimenting her clothes and body, but that changed when they moved in together.

'Fucking cock tease! Where d'you think you're going dressed like that? Off out with the slags again? Stick a sign round your neck telling every fucker you're gagging for it.'

There had been so much abuse, so many insults and put downs, she couldn't even begin to recollect them all.

Why is it the very thing that attracts them to you in the first place is the thing they most want to change?

The photograph reminded her that it was those same girlfriends who told her Duncan was suffocating, that he was jealous and too possessive. He had a temper, too, and been in a few drunken fights in the town centre. She had laughed off the warnings. How wrong she was and how she had paid the price…

He had been drinking in the house all afternoon. She was dressed, ready to go out with friends, when he started the argument, asking her over and over to stay at home. She tried to reason with him…it was just a girls' night out; he had nothing to be jealous about. His voice had grown louder and louder until he was screaming obscenities, his nose almost touching hers and eyes blazing with rage. Even now she could smell the lager on his breath. As she turned to walk out of the front door, he had grabbed her wrist and pulled her towards him, spinning her around at the same time. The punch to her cheek had sent her staggering to the floor. Danielle had never been hit in her life and now the memory of the fierce burning sensation in her cheek, that dizzy feeling in her head, sent bile rising in her throat. Had she really seen stars? She recalled his apologies as she stumbled away, tears streaming down her face. Turning around hadn't been an option.

Danielle stared again at the photograph and took a deep breath. Picking up the pieces of shattered glass littered across the windowsill and the kitchen bench, she dropped them in the stainless steel pedal bin, concentrating on not cutting herself. She took a newspaper off the glassed-topped coffee table and used five sheets together to cover the window, sticking Sellotape along the sides of the paper and on to the window frame. She liked the *Sunday Times* and it always took her a week to read. It was also, she realised, much easier covering the broken window with a 'broadsheet' than it would have been with a 'tabloid'. And anyway, she had never liked *The Sun*.

Satisfied the newspaper was blocking out the draught, Danielle stepped back and admired her makeshift repair.

'Dickhead,' she thought as an image of Duncan flashed again in her head.

Her ground floor flat had both a front and back door. She re-checked the locks - how many more times, Danielle? He might be a dickhead, but he wouldn't break in - and made sure the windows were safely shut.

Telephoning her parents would resolve nothing. They would make a fuss and come straight to the flat. The bright green lights on the microwave showed 8.04pm.

In the bedroom, she removed her work clothes and put on a bright yellow vest top and a pair of lemon shorts. The shower could wait until morning. Back downstairs, she flopped on to the floral printed sofa, flicked on the TV and curled her legs underneath her. She scrolled the directory in her mobile and ordered a 'Hot and Spicy Beef Pizza' from Romeo's.

The loud knock at the door 20 minutes later made her jump, the glass just big enough to stop the white wine spilling out of it. She opened the door and her heart sank. *Shit…that creep again.*

The guy, in his early 20s, had scruffy, matted blond hair and was such a skinny six-footer, he could have taken part in one of those 'Mr Muscle' adverts.

He made no effort to hide the lewd look in his eyes and when he licked his lips, she could see his yellowing teeth. The raw emotion of the last hour exploded from her voice. 'What the fuck are you looking at?'

Jerking his head, he glued his eyes to the ground, cheeks on fire, feeling the redness spreading to his neck. She grabbed the box off him and threw a £10 note on to the path. She didn't wait for her change.

His black training shoes made minimal contact with the ground as he rushed back to the safety of the white Ford Fiesta van, the noise of her slamming door vibrating in his ears. He jumped into the driver's seat and grabbed the steering wheel with both hands. He shook it backwards and forwards, so hard it looked like he was trying to snap it from the steering column. 'Bitch!' he screamed, but as her image flashed into his mind, he had to admit that she was a good-looking bitch. His hands loosened their grip as he focussed on her long brown hair, beautiful brown eyes and a body made in heaven for men to drool over; long, slender legs, small waist and big tits, which he's noticed were straining against that yellow top. What he would do to her given the chance. Not that the likes of her would ever look at the likes of him.

He licked his lips again as he remembered going there about three weeks ago with a pizza. There was something wrong with the front door that night, so she shouted he should go to the back but after she opened the back door, she had to go and fetch her purse. He recalled the rush of excitement when he saw the washing basket near the kitchen door, a white thong on top of a pile of clothes. Without a second's hesitation, he had stepped inside, reached across to the basket and by the time she was handing him the money, the thong was safely inside his trouser pocket.

How many times since that night had he enjoyed it in the privacy of his room? The memory was arousing him. He remembered the smell – her smell – and the pleasure he felt as he imagined her wearing the thong or, better still, slowly taking it off. He had been sad to finally burn it but all good things… he smiled. He hoped to get the chance to steal another one, perhaps from her washing line. Then again, that would mean it was clean and that wouldn't be quite the same.

Danielle drank one more glass of wine, ate the pizza, watched a film and was in bed by 11.15. Her friends were coming tomorrow. They would chill together, go out for Sunday lunch, and have a couple of bottles of wine. Climbing into bed, a smile had formed across her face. She had dealt with the broken window and tomorrow would be a good day. She was an independent young woman who deserved to enjoy herself. No man, Duncan or otherwise, was going to ruin her life.

Sunday

He continually scanned the streets and pathways as he jogged to the house. Complacency at this stage would be disastrous. Potential witnesses were everywhere; clubbers heading home; early morning starters on their way to work; and, of course, patrolling police officers. He saw and heard nothing, although he noticed a light shining downstairs in the house opposite hers. He guessed it was about 3.30am.

He slowed to a walking pace, looked around once more, and then sprinted to the back door. He hunched down and shuffled towards the window, a huge grin spreading across his face as he saw the repair.

The knife sliced through the newspaper without making a sound. Intelligent as well as gorgeous, he thought as he let the newspaper fall to the ground. He climbed through the window and crouched on the kitchen bench, eyes straining for anything he could knock over. Lowering himself to the floor, he stood still, senses drum-skin tight, ears straining for any sound, eyes seeking any movement in the darkness. He was doing his best to control his breathing – long, slow, quiet breaths – but his heart was beating so fast, he feared she would hear it. Satisfied there was no movement, and with his vision adjusted, he turned on his infra-red pencil torch, the type sailors use to look at charts in the dark. Licking his dry lips, his tongue inadvertently touched the woollen material of the full-frontal ski mask and he grimaced. He found the key on the kitchen bench and used it to unlock the back door. Taking small steps, stopping after each one, he entered the living room and shone the torch at the front door. He exhaled slowly as he saw the key in the lock. Turning it slowly, he unlocked the door. He froze on the spot. The click of the lock opening sounded like a gunshot. There were only two other doors in the flat – one would be the bathroom, one her bedroom. The ski mask didn't stop his nostrils smelling that faint feminine smell, a smell of light perfume layers and faded flowers. He was now in a state of high sexual arousal. He was already hard. He opened her bedroom door and crept inside. She was fast asleep, her long dark hair lying partially across the smooth white skin of her face. He stood at the side of her bed next to her sleeping body and inhaled, straining to smell her through the mask. He wanted her – ached for her – but he needed to take his time, not rush and ruin something this special. After all, he had waited patiently for his moment. Was this how a boyfriend returning from a night out felt? Just climbing into bed for a cuddle would be bliss. He turned off the torch, put it in his pocket, and opened the locking blade on his Swiss Army knife.

CHAPTER THREE

THE BLACK NIKE training shoes made a rhythmical beat as he pounded the streets an hour later. The mask was rolled up away from his face, transformed into an innocent woollen hat. He sucked in the cold air and watched his breath as he exhaled. The small backpack needed continual adjustment as it slipped and slithered on the shiny material of the black tracksuit. His ears were straining, working overtime to pick up the sound of anything that might spell danger. Safety and anonymity were within reach. Thinking of home caused his memory to conjure up an image of the Roberts radio. He raised his arm like a sportsman signalling a victory to the crowd. What would you make of that, radio bitch? He chuckled at the thought of referring to her as Mrs Roberts.

On the bed, motionless, her wide eyes were staring at a fixed point on the ceiling. Not exactly daddy's little princess now, are you, Danielle? No more than a vessel for someone else's sexual pleasure, one step up from those disgusting blow-up dolls. A living inflatable empty of any humanity, that's all she was. A small pool of excreta gave a clammy, uncomfortable sensation around the small of her back.

His voice had been matter-of-fact but menacing as he was leaving, the order easy to believe.

'Don't move for 20 minutes. Someone's watching.'

Had 20 minutes passed? Was the single guy across the road his accomplice? Was it him who was watching her movements? The wetness of the tears on her cheeks did nothing to bring her back to her senses. She had brought this on herself. Had she stayed with her parents after she split from Duncan, this would never have happened.

A dull fire burned through parts of her body like the dying embers of a barbecue. Her breasts throbbed from his roughness in those coarse gloves. Penetrating her had left her swollen and tender. The sound of his breathing getting quicker and quicker would live with her forever.

How long had he lain there after he finally climbed off her? What had he been saying to her as he caressed her face? Why had he opened her handbag? What had he done to her phone? Questions crowded into her memory, yet there were so many blanks.

'What if he's still in here?' her brain screamed. 'Get out, Danielle! Get out!' She jumped out of bed, ran from the flat, screaming, and hammered on the windows of the first flats she reached. Any window. Any door. Anyone would do.

He leaned his back against the side door to the integral garage and took long, deep breaths. Hidden from prying eyes by the tall leylandii shrubs, his heart rate began to slow. A thread of remorse was already uncoiling in his head but he had enjoyed her and this wasn't the time for reflection. Entering the garage, he walked on to the double bed sheet he had carefully laid down before leaving. He removed his gloves and dropped them on to it before taking off the hat. As it nestled next to the gloves, he wiped his face and placed the backpack on the floor beside the sheet. The backpack had never come into contact with her, and the carrier bag he had strategically placed inside would make sure nothing would contaminate its interior.

He took a clear sandwich bag from his trouser pocket, held it towards the light, and examined its contents; a used condom, its torn wrapper, and a pool of seminal fluid.

Looking made him stir – an involuntary response and movement – and his body shuddered. Understanding the need for total concentration, he bent down and placed the clear plastic bag on the sheet, blocking all images of her from his mind. He stood up, stretched, and allowed himself a smile. He had planned for every eventually. If he was seen on the streets, he was just another jogger. How many joggers wore hats and gloves?

In the unlikely event the police stopped him, they might search his backpack and find the three building bricks.

'*Leg strengthening exercises. Stamina building. Don't the military do it?*'

Only a more thorough search of the bag would reveal two small pieces of rope, a torch and a red Swiss Army knife.

'*Sorry officer. They're from a previous camping trip. I've been looking for that knife. This bag hasn't been opened for months. No need. It's just got my running bricks in.*'

The semen-filled condom in the sandwich bag would surely raise eyebrows and suspicion, but he would say he picked it up off the street rather than leave it for a child to discover in the morning. '*Just as well I had the sandwich bag. Disgusting people, throwing used condoms on the streets. The bag? Oh, I put my energy bar in that before I leave home for my run. I find it easier to open with my gloves on than tearing the wrapper.*'

He knew the police might pat him down, but they wouldn't place their hands inside his tracksuit bottoms.

Sliding his hands inside them, he removed the second sandwich bag he always carried. That bag was carefully placed on an adjoining bench.

Pulling off his training shoes, he pushed down his tracksuit bottoms and kicked them off. He never wore underwear when he was going out on a date.

He removed his tracksuit top and stood there completely

naked. He slapped his stomach and considered losing weight. The girls might appreciate a flatter stomach.

He took the two pieces of rope from the backpack, put them on the sheet, and then rolled up the sheet and put it inside a large polythene bag.

Walking into the downstairs shower room, he caught sight of his grin in the mirror. He opened the blade of the knife, dropped it into the bleach-filled sink, and stepped into the shower. Under the cascading hot water a wave of remorse and revulsion overcame him. It was always the case. She had seemed very nice. As he was leaving her bedroom, she had quietly asked him between stifled sobs, 'why me?'. His reply wasn't contrived; it was a genuine response. 'Because there's no way someone like you would go out with someone like me.'

Of course, remorse and revulsion wouldn't stop him. The time would come when he would need to prove himself again. His encounters weren't borne out of anger against women. He just wanted a relationship with a woman and he had to prove to himself that he could have one. He needed these women. They were his salvation, but salvation could only be achieved by remarkable planning, both before and after his liaisons. They had called him an under-achiever at school but his ability to plan was improving each time. As he lathered himself in an aqua shower gel, he smiled at his bare pubic region; he had carefully shaved before leaving the house. One pubic hair was potentially all the police would need to identify him. They could examine every fibre of her bedclothes and clothing. They would find no hairs. You couldn't leave behind something you hadn't taken in.

CHAPTER FOUR

───────────

ED WHELAN ANSWERED the mobile on his way out of the front door, his mouth a little furry from last night's lager, his head just a little thicker than usual. He was looking forward to the amateur football match, hoping the white frost wouldn't cause a postponement. Standing in the cold for nearly two hours would revitalise him, and then he could enjoy a couple of lunchtime beers by a roaring open fire. His wife and teenage daughter had left yesterday for a weekend in Newcastle, and he was relishing the prospect of a few more hours in male company, watching and talking football. It was a short walk to the football pitch and an even shorter one back home from the pub.

'Sam. Hi. What do I owe this honour on a Sunday morning?'

'Ed, there's been another rape. A girl in her house. Last night. Same MO as the last one I understand. I only got an email from Trevor Stewart on Friday asking us to take a look at the one from November.'

Ed listened, recalling the rape, and the media attention it attracted. To be raped by an intruder in your own home was very unusual.

Sam was speaking again. 'Look, I'm sorry, but can you meet me at the office as soon as?' she asked.

Bollocks, Ed thought. Not often I get let off the leash.

One phrase flashed repeatedly in his head. Same MO. The same *modus operandi*. The same 'method of operation'.

'Okay, I'm on my way. How is she? The victim?'

'He didn't beat her up, thankfully, but she's traumatised, and pretty badly by the sound of it. Who wouldn't be? We're not going to be talking to her at any length today.'

'How old?' Ed asked.

'Not sure yet, but she's in the same range as the first one.'

'Where did it happen?'

'Conifers Estate,' Sam told him. 'She was found at 4.30am. Taken straight to hospital, she was so distraught. Look, I'll brief you at the office. I'm getting into the car now and I don't have a hands-free kit. Don't want to give the Black Rats an opportunity to pull a DCI.'

'Okay. I'm on my way.'

He smiled as the 'black-rat' phrase darted through his mind. After all these years, the traffic department, or Road Policing Unit as they were now known, were still referred to as 'black-rats'. Some even wore 'black-rat' enamel tie-pins, a humorous two-fingered salute to the detectives who coined the phrase way back in police history.

He put the mobile back in his pocket and turned his thoughts to the victim.

Poor kid…raped in her home…in her own bed. Bastard! Prison's too good for them. Castrate them, or better still, put them in a room full of women and lock the doors. How many of these bastards have you interviewed, Ed asked himself? Fuck, I'd have loved to beat the shit out of the lot of them.

Even now, at 55, he still enjoyed that euphoric feeling when they were caught – the look in their eyes. The passing years didn't diminish that feeling.

He would ring Sue later to tell her he had been called out. After 30 years of marriage she was used to 'the job' and the impact it often had on their social lives.

Jesus, where's the car? Did I leave it at the pub last night?

Temporarily disorientated, he remembered Sue had changed her mind at the last minute about getting the train and had taken the VW Golf. He would have to go to work in 'Doris', his lovingly restored 1972 VW bay window camper van.

He opened the electric garage doors, slid on to the white leather driver's seat, and caught sight of his broad shoulders and shaved head in the wing mirror. He took hold of the retro 'Banjo' steering wheel and started her up, marvelling at the musical sound of the air-cooled engine. The drive would take about 15 minutes.

As he drove, the two rapes consumed his thoughts. A second victim, if they were linked, would really ratchet up the local media interest. They wouldn't have been officially told about the latest attack yet but Ed knew the Press – or at least the proper 'operators' – would soon have picked it up. They had their sources.

More importantly, if this rapist has struck twice, it was odds-on he would strike again. He needed to be caught, and caught quickly. Sam Parker would be thinking the same.

Ed winced and wriggled his bum. The upright driving position wasn't the easiest for someone over 6'4' but being behind the wheel of this beautiful classic more than compensated for any discomfort.

So they were due to start a review tomorrow. Not an unusual request. Reviews had been going on for some years now, normally around homicide, and this was just another re-examination of a serious offence. Their job would be to establish if there were any new potential lines of inquiry and whether the lines of inquiry tracked during the initial investigation had been properly followed to their natural conclusion. A second attack would change the perspective of the review. Now they needed to establish if the rapes were linked.

He looked right as he emerged from a junction.

'I despise rapists. Bastards.'

Ed worked well with Sam and knew they would bounce ideas off each other.

The CID at Seaton St George would be handling the initial enquiries into the new attack whilst the Major

Incident Team, headed by Sam, would start to review the first.

He considered the criteria to establish if the two attacks were linked.

What was the age group of the victims? Did they live alone? What was the method of entry? Were weapons used? What words were spoken? But, most importantly, the order everything happened during the attack.

The next batch of questions would follow. Were there other undetected stranger rapes? Had this bastard attacked more than two women?

Slow down, Ed, slow down. Let's see what we've got. Follow the evidence. That phrase should be every investigator's mantra.

Doris's heater and insulation were poor compared to modern vehicles. Ed's feet were so cold he would probably have been warmer outside. He wiped a drop off the end of his nose, glanced out of the side window at the dense housing passing by, and remembered the time when Seaton St George hadn't spread its tentacles of urban sprawl across the once green fields. He had lived in the town, on the North East coast, all his life, and wished he had an aerial photograph from when he was a child to show his daughter the vast changes.

Ed drove into the HQ car park nearest to the Major Incident Team offices. Knowing he wasn't going to be on public display today, he wore the casual clothes he had been wearing to watch the football: blue jeans and a grey jumper, the wellington boots replaced with brown loafers. He presumed Sam would also be in her 'casuals'. It was more important to get to the office quickly than it was to be 'suited and booted'. The Executive – Chief Constable, Deputy Chief, and two Assistant Chiefs – were going to want to know first thing tomorrow morning whether these attacks were linked. In all likelihood, so was the Press pack.

Punching the code into the combination lock, he walked into the office. It was this space, simply referred to as 'the room', that housed all the HOLMES computers and paperwork. HOLMES, a software program, was an abbreviation for Home Office Large Major Enquiry System. It had been refined many times since it was set up following the Yorkshire Ripper case in the mid-1970s and early 1980s.

Ed guessed Sam would come to this long office, where 11 officers could sit in comfort, each with their own computer terminal and each with a specific role in the HOLMES function.

'Hi Sam,' Ed said, smiling.

'Ed,' said Sam, as she stood up, 'thanks for coming out so quickly. Sorry I've ruined your Sunday.'

Ed had guessed correctly, not just about which office Sam would be in but also her wardrobe selection. Sam was one of those women who always looked good. Ed reasoned she would look attractive even when she was blue with cold and shovelling snow in a pair of XL overalls. She was one of nature's beautiful people, a statuesque brunette carrying no excessive weight, looking very attractive now in a clingy white sweater and tight blue jeans tucked inside black leather boots.

A graduate with a keen sense of humour, she had been a DCI for two years, very thorough and with a keen eye for detail. That was all that mattered to Ed. Good investigators who cared. Thorough cops who wanted to catch bad guys. Cops who were prepared to come in on a Sunday at the drop of a hat.

Sitting at a separate desk and nursing a cup of tea, Sam told Ed what she knew of the latest attack.

'Firstly, I haven't called anybody else out yet. Let's see what needs doing. If we need extra staff we can call them later.'

'Yeah, okay,' Ed said, pulling his chair a little closer to the desk.

'Right,' Sam began, tying her shoulder-length hair into a ponytail as she spoke. 'Today's victim is Danielle Banks, 25 years old. She lives alone in a one-bedroom flat at 13, Forestry Gardens, Conifers Estate.'

Ed knew the area and the flats. He had had a school friend who lived close to Forestry Gardens. The flats were built in the early 1980s and were two storeys high. Each flat had its own front door at ground level. The doors opened on to a small hallway or on to a staircase, depending whether you lived on the ground or first floor. The ground floor flats also had a back door giving access to the kitchen. It had been a gated estate when it was built, but the gates had long since been removed and anyone was free to walk around the cluster of flats, which were either owner-occupied or rented from private landlords.

'Danielle's been released from hospital. She's been medically examined and is still sedated. As I said, she was heavily traumatised, understandably. At about 4.30am, Danielle woke up the ground-floor neighbours, banging on their windows and shouting for help. They came out to find her hysterical. She was barefoot and naked from the waist down.'

'Jesus,' Ed said, shaking his head as he raised the mug to his mouth.

'One of the neighbours managed to discover from her that she had been raped. Another got her a blanket. The uniforms and ambulance were called and arrived almost together. A policewoman went to hospital with her in the ambulance. Uniform did a quick, cursory search of the flat just to make sure that no one was inside and then put a cop at the front door to secure and preserve the scene.'

Ed was nodding with approval. The search was good policing. What would be worse than the offender still on the property and not discovered by the police?

'The Crime Scene Investigators are still at the house,' Sam went on. 'They've been there since just after 6am.'

Ed smiled. They all had to get used to calling Scene of Crime Officers 'Crime Scene Investigators' nowadays – or CSIs as they liked to be called – not SOCOs. All those American police shows had a lot to answer for.

'Apparently, there's not a lot of disturbance in the house. We do know the rape happened in the bedroom and that's been the place for the crime scene guys to get started.

'I've told the Detective Sergeant at Seaton to call us if he needs any advice. I've also told his management team if we think there's a link to the other rape, we'll happily take over this investigation.'

Ed nodded again. He liked decision makers. He had worked with plenty over the years in the CID, both in the '80s in his first stint in the force and in the time since his return. Sam was always willing to ask advice from subordinates but never frightened of being the principal decision maker. He had seen first hand what a good Senior Investigating Officer she was. She had led murder investigations, was comfortable with the media, and was well thought of by her senior and junior officers alike. Her gender wasn't an issue to him. It may have been to some of his colleagues back in the day but not to Ed. He had worked with female detectives in the '80s when they were few and far between and had had no issues with them. He certainly didn't have any issues now. He could even remember the name of the first female Assistant Chief Constable in the country and the attention that received. Now there were many women at all ranks.

'What arrangements have been made to interview her?' Ed asked.

'As I said, she's sedated. Her parents have agreed for us to speak to her this afternoon. She never spoke during the journey in the ambulance and the female officer who was with her didn't want to ask her questions given the state she was in.'

Sam told Ed another uniformed officer trained to deal with sexual offences had also gone to the hospital hoping to get some details from Danielle but they were sketchy and both young policewomen had enough about them not to push it.

'What we do know, from what Danielle told the neighbours, is that a masked man raped her in her bedroom after brandishing a knife.'

'Bastard,' Ed said, visibly tensing and straightening in his chair. 'Has the file arrived from the previous attack?'

'All there,' said Sam, pointing at a box full of paperwork on the floor in the corner of the office.

'Let's see what we've got then, shall we?'

CHAPTER FIVE

THE KNIFE HAD BEEN WASHED and bleached and was back in the rucksack with the bricks and two new pieces of rope. The plastic bag and its forensically incriminating contents were now in a large sports hold-all.

The Dralon sofa had seen better days. Purchased by his mother when they had moved into this house, it was now 10 years old. Still, it satisfied his needs. He picked up the game controller, sat down, and started playing *Grand Theft Auto*. Driving the muscle car across the 50' TV screen, he conjured up an image of his mother. She would never have allowed such a huge TV – and her approval had been required for everything. Not once in his entire life had he brought a friend back to the house. Not once. Not that he had any friends. Not at school. Not now. He did tell her about the bullying when it first started, but she had just laughed at him.

'Just like your father. Bloody useless.'

He suffered the daily torment at school in quiet acceptance after that. It was mostly name-calling. He wasn't even deemed worthy of a beating. Sharon Brown had beaten him up once. Beaten up by a girl. God, they'd all loved that.

When he was seven years old, his dad had died of a heart attack. He had been a great father.

The car crashed on the TV as he recalled weekend walks

to the park in the summer and that one, and only, trip to see Newcastle United. The excitement he felt on the train. More people than he had ever seen in one place, a heaving mass of humanity outside St James' Park. The terraces rammed with people, young and old, singing and shouting in unison. Bovril at half-time. The match-day programme, as pristine now as the day his dad bought it, safely tucked away in his bedroom drawer. That drawer housed all his treasured possessions. Occasionally he would flick through the programme and still smell the meaty drink.

Dropping the controller on to the settee, he flopped backwards with closed eyes.

I'm glad you're dead, you cow. Fuckin' bully. Bullied me. Bullied Dad.

She had wanted to move to the new build. He had liked the old house, the one they shared with dad. It was always about what she wanted. Now it was about him. Before her death four months ago, he found nursing her liberating. Helpless, she relied on him for everything; feeding, washing, toilet visits. He enjoyed the power. She was under his control. Before she fell ill, the only time he had any control over his own life was each Tuesday when she went to bingo.

'Good riddance Mother,' he said aloud.

Energised, he jumped up. There was work to do.

The frost crunched under his black hiking boots. The cold, dull morning had left the estate eerily quiet. Who could blame people for staying indoors in this weather? In the five minutes he had been out he hadn't seen one other person. He began to imagine what was going on behind the windows he passed: fathers playing with their children; mothers cooking fried breakfasts or preparing the vegetables for a family Sunday lunch.

Old Mrs Thompson waved at him from the downstairs window of her neat, detached house. His Sunday-morning routine was so set in stone, he reckoned people would be more likely to remember a Sunday when they didn't see him. Routine was good. Routine was akin to being invisible. People were so used to seeing him, he could disappear in plain sight.

The allotment was just over 100 feet long. The piece of land was divided into 12 allotments and surrounded on three sides by houses and by a tennis court on the other. His 'patch' bordered on to the tennis court, not any houses. A communal entry gate was up a small alley. Striding across the frozen ground, he unlocked his shed and turned on the small Primus stove.

'No self-respecting allotment owner would be without a kettle, son,' his father used to say. At least his mother had kept the allotment after his dad had died.

He filled the kettle from a bottle of water in his bag. On the shelf in the shed was an eclectic mix of small hand tools, seed trays, gloves, and plant pots. The peeling paint on the wooden walls reminded him of the day when, as a young boy, he helped his father give the shed a fresh coat, their hands and shoes streaked in green gloss. The laughing had stopped when she tore into them back at home. His eyes narrowed and his face contorted at the memory.

Sitting on the small stool, he exhaled loudly and picked up the tin of paraffin. A quick shake and he knew there was sufficient for his purposes.

The smoke wouldn't be a concern. Nobody was playing tennis and he was too far from the empty gardens of the houses.

Swinging the pickaxe into the frozen ground, his fingers stiffened and the vibrations reverberated through his arms. This would be so much easier in the months to come, once the ground softened.

The cup of tea provided some welcome warmth.

With no sign of the weak winter sun defrosting the ground, it took him another 30 minutes to finish the task. Dropping the plastic bag into the hole, he doused it in paraffin.

What was unusual about a fire on an allotment? Hands in

pockets, he watched the yellow flames, dancing like Ecstasy-fuelled clubbers, destroy any forensic evidence.

Fascinated with forensic science ever since reading the Sherlock Holmes novels as a youngster, his interest had never gone away. Books, TV, newspapers, the Internet… all were sources of information. No need to let librarians, and anyone who asked, know what books you were reading. What had Edmond Locard said? '*Every contact leaves a trace*'? Locard, dubbed the Sherlock Holmes of France and a true pioneer of forensic science, had identified the 'Exchange Principle', the theory that someone committing a crime will bring something to the crime scene and take away something from it. What they inadvertently leave behind or carry away is evidence.

How many times had he read the newspaper or watched the news where forensics had led to some careless fool's arrest? Idiots! But thinkers like him were in a different league. He knew his Locard. He knew scientific examinations could yield a huge amount of evidence.

He would have left fibres on her, on the bedding, in the house, but the police would need his clothing for comparison. His clothing would have brought fibres from her, or her house, out with him. So what? The clothing was burnt and so was any scientific evidence.

He may have left footprint impressions but, with the shoes up in smoke, the trainers couldn't incriminate him.

His semen had left the house with him and as he hadn't taken his gloves off, other than to put on a condom, there were no fingerprints. The mask not only hid his identity but covered his mouth, ensuring he couldn't have sprayed saliva for subsequent DNA comparison.

Fuck you, Mrs Bloody Roberts! Home free.

Kicking the soil over the dying embers, he started to whistle his dad's favourite tune – Louis Armstrong's *What a Wonderful World.*

Ed and Sam spent two hours reading the file on the previous rape.

The victim, Kelly Jones, 26, had woken in her home to find a masked man standing at the side of her bed, dressed in a dark tracksuit and gloves. He rammed his hand down across her mouth and pushed her head into the pillow. Her eyes had been glued on the knife that was swinging like the pendulum of a grandfather clock, millimetres above her face.

'Do what I say and I won't hurt you.' He had spoken quietly, almost softly. Instinctively, she had pulled the duvet up below her chin. He had leaned closer towards her, his voice still quiet and calm.

'Please push the covers off. I want to look at you.'

Tightening her fingers around the duvet, Kelly had yelped as his right hand slapped her in the face.

His voice had not needed to be loud to convey its menace.

'I fuckin' told you, do as you're told and I won't hurt you.'

The stinging sensation in her cheek coupled with the taste of blood had caused her to loosen her grip. The attacker had grabbed the duvet, pulled it away from her and asked her to turn on the bedside light.

He had stroked Kelly's face as he lay next and whispered into her ear: 'Take your nightie off for me. You know you're my babe.'

Cold hatred burned in Ed's eyes as he read through Kelly's witness statement, her unimaginable fear.

Sick bastard!

Kelly had closed her eyes and done as she was told, the man touching her breasts and whispering 'you're beautiful'. She had refused to get on her hands and knees until she felt the knife sticking into her neck.

Each hand had been tied with a single piece of rope to the farthest pole on the headboard. Kelly heard him pull his tracksuit bottoms down and something like a wrapper being torn open. The bed had creaked as he forced himself inside her. When it was over, Kelly was aware of the man doing something to himself, perhaps removing a condom. Still wearing the gloves and mask, he had untied her hands and put the ropes in his pocket. He lay next to her again and she could see the knife in his hand. The words were almost as bad as the attack. 'Did you enjoy that, babe? Was I better than your boyfriend?' Kelly had nodded furiously. 'I'm pleased about that,' the man had said. 'I really enjoyed it as well.'

He had then asked for her purse, which she took from the drawer of the bedside table and handed over. Holding her driving licence, he had stroked her cheek.

'I hope I haven't hurt you, Kelly?'

Hearing him speak her name had almost been too much, but Kelly felt if she could just hold it together, he would leave her alive.

Then he had asked for her mobile. She picked it up off the bedside table and handed it to him. Having pressed a few buttons, he gave it back to her.

'On second thoughts, I won't take your mobile,' he had said. 'Don't ring the police. Don't do anything for 20 minutes. My friend is watching you.'

Kelly Jones believed her attacker had been in her house for over an hour. The police control-room tape showed she called them from her mobile at 4.45am.

Sam and Ed were silent, letting the words in Kelly's statement become a movie reel in their minds, reliving her ordeal.

'In no rush to leave, was he?' Ed said finally. 'He must have known she lived alone. How did he know that?'

'We need to find out,' Sam said. 'What about his voice? Is there anything distinguishing about it?'

Sam picked up the statement again and flicked back through the pages.

'Here it is. Local accent. Nothing unusual. She doesn't say anything about the tone, the pitch.'

'Understandable,' Ed said. 'The bastard's wearing a mask and he's got a knife. That said, if she were to hear it again, I reckon she'd know it was him.'

Sam made a mental note to press Kelly on the voice when they went to speak to her again.

Ed had turned to another detail, a small specific that might play a bigger part in the hunt.

'He tells her to wait 20 minutes and not call the police,' Ed said. 'Why 20 minutes and not 10, or 30? He says an accomplice is watching her.'

'Probably a lie,' Sam slowly shook her head.

'Yep, more than likely. But 20 minutes?'

Sam followed Ed's train of thought, running scenarios through her own head.

'Does it take that long to get home or to his place of safety? Is that just a number he's conjured up? Does he want us to believe he lives 20 minutes away? Maybe it was the first number that came into his head?'

'She does say that after he left there was a spicy smell in the bedroom. Whoever took this statement was on the ball, by the way.'

'Spicy? Curry maybe?' Sam wondered out loud. 'Is he maybe Asian? Or is this just someone who likes spicy food?'

Ed looked up, a small smile on his face.

'So that's most of the population then. Isn't curry our national dish now?'

'Probably. I love it,' Sam said. 'Kelly, on the other hand, says she can't stand spicy food. That's why she she's clear about the smell.'

The language of the initial police report was staccato and impersonal.

Victim lived in a two-bedroom semi-detached house on Bamburgh Way...point of entry believed to be a broken kitchen window... broken window discovered when victim returned from work.

Sam dropped the papers on to her desk and rubbed her eyes.

'Kelly says she contacted her landlord that evening,' Sam said, eyes closed in concentration. 'He said he'd get the window repaired on Saturday morning. He asked her if she'd like him to put a board up for the night but she said she didn't want to spoil his Friday night and that it would wait.'

'Are you thinking what I am?' Ed pushed his chair

backwards, stood up, and put his hands in his trouser pockets. 'The broken window? It might not be a coincidence?'

'I don't like coincidences anymore more than the next detective,' Sam said.

She felt a shiver run through her as she tried to imagine how she would have felt waking to find a stranger in her room.

'You okay, Sam?'

Ed's concerned voice snapped her back to the present.

'I'm fine, Ed. Thanks. Just trying to put myself in Kelly's shoes.'

In reality, Sam knew she'd have to put herself in the shoes of the rapist.

CHAPTER SIX

BAMBURGH WAY, a huge road over a mile in length and with over 300 houses, was part of the sprawling Gull Estate on the north side of Seaton St George. Building had started there just over 10 years ago and houses were still being put up. There were thousands of homes, as varied as the area was vast.

To the south of Gull was the Conifer Estate, which now bordered on to it. If you didn't know otherwise, you would think it was all one estate.

'The forensics from Kelly's house all look up to scratch,' Sam said. 'Numerous fingerprint lifts…some fibres on the bedding that don't match any of the clothes Kelly was wearing.'

'Let's hope he took his gloves off,' Ed said.

'Yeah. And he's still got the clothes he was wearing.'

Both Sam and Ed were acutely aware that every two-bit crook was much more forensically savvy these days. The ever-increasing police dramas on television and the media coverage of all aspects of forensic science had seen to that.

They remained by the desk reading and re-reading the material in front of them, the silence broken only when they had something new to discuss. Other than that, the only sound was the wall-mounted clock ticking away, seconds turning into minutes.

Talking to neighbours had thrown up no investigative leads. No one had seen or heard anything suspicious at the time of the attack. Nobody had seen any unfamiliar vehicles hanging around on the days before. Nothing. A total blank.

An examination of the closed-circuit TV cameras in the area between the hours of 2am and 6am had shown there were very few people or cars to be seen. As usual the quality was poor and those people and vehicles couldn't be identified and subsequently traced.

There had been a media appeal, which had been reported in the local evening newspaper, the *Seaton Post*. The police had released the fact an intruder had entered the home of a 26-year-old female and sexually assaulted her. The Press wasn't told the man was masked, had a knife, wore gloves, or that he tied up the victim. They weren't told how he entered the house, and it wasn't confirmed the victim knew the attacker.

A media strategy was important. Releasing too much information to the Press might mean hard-won confessions being denied in court, with the accused saying he made up the admission based on what he had read in the papers or seen on the news.

The victim's name and address, of course, hadn't been released to protect her identity, but the area where she lived had been made public. That was necessary for the police witness appeal to be effective. Nobody had come forward so far and no police officers on duty had seen anyone or anything suspicious.

There was potentially more positive news from an examination of Kelly's mobile, with confirmation a call had been made during the time of the attack.

'I reckon that he's called his mobile to get her number,' Sam said. 'Kelly is sure he pressed a few buttons on her phone before he told her he wouldn't take it. Her number would show up on his phone as a missed call.'

Open-mouthed, Sam suddenly stopped talking and re-read the paragraph.

'Bloody hell! Look at this!'

She pushed a piece of paper towards Ed and her voice quickened.

'A man claiming he was the rapist called Kelly on the Tuesday after the attack.'

'Number?' Ed asked as he hurriedly scanned the document.

'Whoever it was didn't withhold the number,' Sam said. 'It's the same number her attacker called from her phone.'

'Looks like it's him then,' Ed said. 'What did he say?'

Rummaging through the papers, Sam found Kelly's second statement.

'Here, let's have a look.'

Sam's eyes flashed through the paragraphs.

'Okay. Kelly rang the police immediately after she got the call. It was 7pm on the Tuesday and she was at home with her mother. Kelly couldn't bear to be alone in the house so her mum had temporarily moved in with her after the attack.'

'She could be there for a long time,' Ed interrupted.

Both had interviewed many victims of rape over the years. Most had eventually, outwardly at least, put their attacks behind them but would forever carry the mental scars. Many would never be the same person again.

The woman who had been attacked in the street at night would never again be alone outside in the dark; those who had been assaulted in a multi-storey car park would never use one again; a victim targeted in a park may never be able to take her children there to play. The memory of rape was permanent. It may be locked away in the back of their mind, but it never went away.

'The caller told her he was sorry and hoped he'd not hurt her,' Sam Said. 'Kelly said she was fighting every sinew in her body to hang up, but something inside her was telling her to keep listening. He told her she was beautiful and that he hoped she'd enjoyed their time together as much as he had.'

Ed shook his head. 'What a sick bastard! What else?'

'He said something along the lines of how he hoped they could have gone out together somewhere, but that it was out of the question now she had gone to the police. He said he had seen it in the Press. Kelly remembers he asked her 'why did you do that?' before he hung up.'

Sam paused, thinking about the call and silently saluting Kelly's courage.

'He never raised his voice,' Sam continued. 'He was calm throughout. Kelly thought he had even sounded a little sad when he asked her why she had gone to the police.'

Ed scowled, jaw muscles tensing.

'Sad? He'll be sad alright when we get our hands on him.'

Ed's face reddened and they both fell silent, each thinking through the new information, before the ringing telephone made them jump.

'Jesus,' Ed said.

Sam picked up the receiver. 'Sam Parker.'

She listened and ended the call with a 'thank you'.

Sam replaced the receiver, picked up a pen, and tapped it repeatedly on the desk.

'Ed, we need an interviewer and a level-5 interview adviser. We'll be running this job by tomorrow.'

'Why's that?'

'That was an update from Seaton CID. The crime-scene boys at Danielle's have found a broken kitchen window.'

'So? He had to get in somehow.'

'There are pieces of newspaper stuck to the window frame, some kind of temporary repair. No way Danielle did that after the attack.'

'Coincidence? Forget it. We've got a serial rapist. I'll call them out.'

Sam nodded. 'And Danielle's okay for interview. You make the calls. I'll stick the kettle back on. Oh, and see if you can get hold of Dave Johnson. He can sort out the room.'

He drove to an out-of-town retail park intending to buy identical clothes to the ones he had burnt. If the police ever suspected him, a witness or an image from a CCTV camera could identify his clothing. The new clothes would pass any forensic test – he hadn't been at the scene in them. They were exactly the same clothes, but not *the* clothes.

A self-satisfied smile spread across his face. It was inspired.

He got cash from a machine within walking distance of his house. A future investigation could put him at the retail park that day if he made a withdrawal there. Bank cards, like mobiles, left a forensic trail. From there it would simply be a case of them following the evidence. The CCTV, which seemed to be all over the park, might pick him up going into a sports shop, and the cameras inside might put him at the till buying the identical tracksuit. In no time the police would be building a case, not because they were brilliant detectives, but because of his own carelessness. Likewise, there was no danger of him buying anything on a credit or debit card. Strictly cash only.

The hand movements of the man standing opposite in sweatshirt and joggers were a blur as he pushed and pulled the hangers before taking a black shiny tracksuit from the tubular rack. They looked at each other briefly with an air of recognition, the type where you know the face but can't place it.

He picked the same shiny tracksuit as the man then another in dark blue. On Thursday evening, he would drive to another retail park and buy an identical blue tracksuit. He would use one of them for his next visit, the other he would keep to be handed over to the police if the need ever arose. Conscious that a shop assistant quizzed by police might remember someone buying two tracksuits the same colour – and with the CCTV cameras recording – he used different stores. That said, it seemed to him shop assistants never made eye contact these days and probably couldn't remember anything, which suited him. He wasn't much for eye contact himself. Still, there was no reason to run the risk.

He walked towards the racks of training shoes and tried again to place the face of the other man. *Stop thinking about him and it will come. The harder you try, the less likely you'll remember.*

He turned his thoughts to the police and knew they would

need more luck than a lottery winner to catch him. Only luck had caught Peter Sutcliffe. His capture had nothing to do with all the detectives hunting him. The Yorkshire Ripper was caught by two patrolling uniformed police officers. Pure chance and a million-to-one chance at that.

So long as he wasn't caught at or near the scene, he would be fine. He started to whistle the song as he strolled to the checkouts.

Ed Whelan telephoned a Level-5 interview adviser. The officer would be responsible for producing the strategies and co-ordinating all the interviews with witnesses and suspects. The interview adviser, like the Senior Investigating Officer, didn't interview anyone themselves.

In the sport shop, Jason Stroud's mobile vibrated in his pocket. Answering it, he told Ed he could get to the office within 45 minutes. Jason was delighted to be involved. 'Result,' he thought to himself. He wanted to be on this investigation.

CHAPTER SEVEN

'WHAT ABOUT HIS PHONE?' Ed asked.

Sam found the relevant document. 'Not on a contract. Just a 'pay as you go'. No need for him to hide the number.'

They had been involved in many investigations where mobiles were a central line of inquiry. They knew identifying the owner of a 'pay as you go' phone would be almost impossible. No contracts meant no documentation. Top-up wherever, whenever. Buy the phone and if your name and address were requested, provide a false one. Nobody checks.

Linking it to an individual would be extremely difficult. If the number was listed in the mobiles of friends and associates under a suspect's name, an investigator could begin to show the phone belonged to that suspect.

But it was a long, slow process, and one that always needed a starting point. Anyone criminal who was cautious and smart around planning would keep a separate Subscriber Identity Module card – the SIM – and only use that SIM to contact a victim; no friends or family would ever need to know it existed and there would be no need to hide the number from victims or police.

Ed stood up, frowning, and walked over to the window. He stared at the skyline, his hands resting on the windowsill, and muttered: 'Something else to look for when we search his house.'

Sam leaned back in her chair and stared at the ceiling. 'God, it must have been so much easier in the golden days before mobiles. Getting bills for landlines must have been a piece of cake.'

'Yeah, it was,' Ed said. 'But there was no DNA in those days. Don't hark back, you'll start to sound like a dinosaur like me.'

Their laughter exploded around the room as Jason Stroud walked in and greeted them. Sam picked up her cup of tea, and as her eyes moved to Jason's, he quickly looked away. Had he been staring at her again? Was she imagining it? She had no reason to dislike him but she did think that he was always mentally undressing her. She had seen him sneaking glances at other women in the building. He seemed awkward around women, never meeting their eyes when he was talking to them, but when they weren't looking, he couldn't stop himself staring.

Maybe he was just shy. He was certainly an introvert and therefore by nature not your stereotypical detective. At 29, he had been a cop for 10 years. Similar in size to Sam, he had dark brown hair with a side parting and he wore an ill-fitting double-breasted grey Prince of Wales check suit. It gave the impression he belonged to a bygone age. His black brogue shoes, while undoubtedly expensive, always seemed to be in need of a polish. The yellow or pink ties he always wore, irrespective of the colour of his suit, shirt or shoes, meant he was never going to grace the pages of a fashion magazine. Sam wondered whether the high-street outfitters he visited were actually charity shops.

Jason was, however, a methodical planner, the reason he was such a good interview adviser. He had the knack of reading lots of information and coming up with the right questions.

Ed left Samantha and took Jason into an adjoining office. Alone with her thoughts, she paced the room. Every avenue seemed to have been followed up in relation to the first attack.

Danielle's account would give her a very clear indication whether both attacks were committed by the same man. That said, Sam was already convinced they were. She just wanted a little more confirmation.

She walked to the toilet and began mentally developing the 'lines of inquiry' for the latest attack and some sort of matrix to compare the similarities between both rapes.

One of the first steps was to identify all registered sex offenders living in the area. The skill was deciding how big that 'area' should be. The bigger the area, the more sex offenders, and the greater the number of potential suspects there would be for elimination. With a limited amount of officers at her disposal, the inquiry could grind to a halt running up investigative blind alleys. Meanwhile, the attacker would be free to rape at will.

Ed briefed Jason on both rapes, giving him an overview of each. It was Jason's job to plan the interview with Danielle and liaise with the interviewing officers. He would also identify all areas of questioning for interviewing a suspect, even though one hadn't been identified yet.

Leaving Jason, Ed returned to Sam, who told him she wanted to look at some of the signature traits in the way the rapist – or rapists, she cautioned herself – behaved.

'Okay,' Ed said, as they sat down at a desk opposite each other. 'Lone female in her house at the time. First question… how did he know that?'

Sam considered it, wrapping her pony tail round her fingers.

'Does he already know her?' she said. 'Does he work with her? Has he followed her home? Has he had a conversation with her? A chance encounter where she's mentioned her domestic circumstances?'

'If he works with them, it's a bit dodgy attacking more than one,' Ed said. 'That's if it's the same attacker.'

'Yeah, increases the risk of being identified. Plus, why was she attacked? Why was she selected? Has she somehow come across him? Where does she socialise and who with?'

Jason Stroud popped his head around the door. 'The

interviewer's on her way to see Danielle. I've told her to establish as soon as possible when the window was broken. I just need to pop home if that's okay. I think I've left the oven on. I'll be back in less than an hour and I'll crack on with the stuff for the revisit to Kelly.'

'Yeah, no problem,' Sam said.

She turned to Ed, a look of surprise on her face. 'I never had him down for cooking a Sunday dinner.'

'Me neither, but his wife's just left him.'

Sitting in his front room, he shuffled the driving licences , staring at the beautiful, youthful faces of Kelly, Amber, and, Danielle. Looking at each in turn, he recalled their time together, everything still vividly etched on his brain. He hoped his handwritten notes about Kelly and Amber would let him relive the smallest details of their lovemaking in the years to come.

The small brown moleskin notebook was expensive and pleasant to the touch, just like the girls. In the unlikely event the police ever got on to him, the book would burn easily; recording his thoughts on a computer would leave an electronic trail that he could never be 100% certain had been destroyed by the delete button.

Tonight he would relive his time with Danielle moment by moment. He had enjoyed writing at school, but this was in a different league. At school, his bright imagination had made sure his short stories satisfied his teachers, although there had been one when he was 15, a Miss Joy, who he would have been delighted to satisfy in another way. Was there ever a more aptly named woman, all hair and tits and wiggling that arse in those tight short skirts? She must have known what she was doing to every red-blooded boy in the classroom.

This writing was different, though. This was reality, not fiction He would take hours, not wanting to leave out even the smallest detail. The more he wrote now, the less likely his memory would fade in the future. Examining Kelly's photograph, he reached down and began to touch himself but as his heart rate increased, he reluctantly accepted now wasn't the time.

In the bedroom, like a mother laying down her newborn baby, he placed the notebook and driving licences carefully inside the bedside table drawer. Each licence was face up, each girl looking at him whenever he opened that particular drawer. Neatly, they sat alongside the pen and the Newcastle United programme.

CHAPTER EIGHT

'Do you think Jason is up to this job, Ed?' Sam asked, her legs outstretched as she leaned back in the chair.

'Yeah. Why?'

'It's just that I've known him for 10 years, but I don't really know anything about him. He's quite aloof. Doesn't disclose much of himself. His choice I suppose, as long as he can do the job.'

'He'll be fine,' Ed said. 'He's always done a good job for me, and he was certainly keen enough to get involved.'

'Maybe I'm being unfair. It's just… oh I don't know.'

Sam ran her fingers through her hair, sat up straight, and continued: 'Okay. So. Our two victims lived alone. We know from the first rape the attacker was there for over an hour. Not in a rush to leave. He obviously felt safe in her home. So not only did he know she lived alone, he knew he wouldn't be disturbed. That suggests she was targeted, not a random selection. Agree?'

'Definitely,' Ed nodded. 'He's also taken a knife with him. Kelly couldn't describe it but none of hers had been stolen or moved from the kitchen. Unless he's taken one of her knives, and then replaced it in the drawer, which seems unlikely, then we can assume he's brought his own with him.'

'I don't like assumptions,' Sam said. 'But you're right; if

we believe there's an element of planning, then he's not going to rely on finding a knife at the house, and let's not forget he took the ropes with him too.'

She inhaled deeply. 'I doubt Danielle will be able to describe the knife either. If it's the same person, and he slowly moves the knife across your face, all you'll be looking at is the tip of the blade. That amount of fear? No way you'll be describing the blade or the handle.'

'Natural human reaction,' Ed said. 'And remember, these girls have been woken up in the middle of the night with a masked bastard in their room. They'll have been terrified.'

Ed paused then went on: 'So he knows they live alone. He's taken a knife. He's taken rope. The window in Kelly's case was broken the day of the attack. We know there's also a broken window at Danielle's, but we don't yet know when it was broken. Has he just discovered the broken window at Kelly's or has he done it earlier?'

Ed reflected on what he had just said, pulling his chair closer to the desk, sitting almost to attention.

'Jesus, Sam. He's setting up the entry point in advance.'

'Possibly,' said Sam. 'Very possibly.'

She stood up and tugged at the bottom of her jumper. Creative thinking and logical reasoning always seemed to come easier to her when she paced the room. It was a habit she had discovered during her time at Durham University, often jumping out of bed in the middle of the night and roaming her room until the answer she had been seeking finally flew into her mind.

'Let's take that one step forward, Ed. What if he had broken the window earlier that day? Then he goes out on the night with his mask and knife, but when he gets to the house, the window has been repaired. His attack's blocked.'

'He could break it there and then,' Ed said.

'But if that was the case, why break the window earlier in the day and risk being seen? No, I don't think he'd do that. He doesn't want to break a window in the middle of night and risk waking her up.'

'So, what you saying?'

'I'm not sure what I am saying,' Sam answered. 'What would he have done if the window had been repaired? Gone home? He's all psyched up to rape. Would he really just go home?'

They both paused for thought.

Ed broke the silence. 'Would he risk attacking someone in the street? I doubt it, too many variables.'

Sam started talking with her hands in the style of a modern-day politician.

'Once he's inside, he stands at the side of her bed. He's wearing gloves and the mask. He wakes her and puts a hand over her mouth. He's forensically aware. He's not going to leave prints.'

'But he would have to take his gloves off if he was putting a condom on,' Ed said. 'Christ, when I was younger, I couldn't put the bloody things on for love nor money.'

Sam burst out laughing at a mental picture of a young Ed fighting with a Durex, the moment of passion ebbing away with every failed attempt.

'That's why I stayed married,' Ed said. 'I couldn't bear the thought of trying to pull those bloody things on.'

Still smiling, Sam said: 'Best I don't tell Sue the real reason you recently celebrated your 30th wedding anniversary.'

'Ha ha. Very funny.'

'Okay. Let's agree that he can't put a condom on wearing gloves,' Sam continued. 'Kelly says that at no time when he touched her could she feel his skin. So he must have put his gloves back on once he'd sorted the condom. That must take a hell of a lot of self control. I mean…he's in the house, his victim's compliant. She's tied to the bed and he has her exactly where he wants her. He's ready and yet he still puts his gloves back on. Bloody hell. He's in total control of himself , total control.'

'Kelly doesn't hear the toilet flush at any time when he's in her flat,' Ed said.

Sam, still pacing the room, picked up on that small point.

'He must have taken the condom with him. It's not in her

flat and he hasn't flushed it down the loo. He must have taken it with him, and he's been careful enough to make sure he's not dropped the contents anywhere in the flat. Kelly's bedroom has a laminate floor. Any liquid would easily have been spotted by the CSIs.'

She fiddled with her ponytail. 'More planning. More evidence he's thinking about forensics. What else? The mask?'

Ed said: 'This isn't an opportunist.'

'Agree,' Sam answered. 'Then there's the things he said, telling her he doesn't want to hurt her, then afterwards asking her if he'd been a gentle lover. Calling her his babe.'

'What the bloody hell's that about?' Ed said.

'He wants a relationship with her,' Sam pointed out quietly, her brain processing her own words as she sat down.

'What do you mean?'

'Let's come back to that, if that's okay?' Sam said. 'Let's just continue with what we know.'

'He takes her driving licence. A trophy?' Ed said.

'More a souvenir, I suspect. I'll explain what I'm thinking on that later as well. Then he refers to her by name.'

'Cos he knows it now from the licence?' Ed wondered aloud.

Looking down at the desk, he paused, then added: 'Providing, of course, he didn't already know it.'

Interlocking his fingers, he stretched his arms out in front of him, thinking carefully about his next sentence.

'Cunning and self control. If he already knew her name, he only called her it once he'd seen the licence, giving her, and us, the impression that up to that point, he didn't know it.'

'There's so much going on here, Ed,' Sam said. 'Planning. Control. Victim selection. Ever heard the phrase 'Power Reassurance' rapist?'

'No,' Ed answered, puzzled. His brow contorting, he shuffled in his seat.

Both looked at the door as it opened and Jason Stroud walked in.

'If I'm not interrupting?'

'You're not,' Sam said, smiling.

'A quick update from the interview,' Jason began 'Danielle discovered the broken window in the kitchen when she got back from work late yesterday evening. It hadn't been broken when she'd left the house that morning and she didn't bother reporting it to the police. She thought her ex-boyfriend had done it. She was going to get it fixed this morning.'

'Cheers Jason,' Sam said as he turned and walked out of the office.

Sam continued: 'Kelly in the early hours of a Saturday morning…Danielle in the early hours of a Sunday.'

'Different days, but a weekend nonetheless,' Ed said.

'Ed, we'll need to know everything about these girls… where they socialised, where they worked, what their habits were, who their friends and acquaintances are? That victimology's crucial. It's the amount of planning that concerns me. It's going to make it so much more difficult to catch him.'

Ed's gaze locked on to Sam's. 'We'll get him, Sam. And when we do, it'll be all the sweeter. This bastard's going away for a long time.'

With her elbows on the desk, Sam placed her chin in her cupped hands. The short silence felt longer than it was before she spoke.

'I keep coming back to him returning on the night and finding the window has been boarded up,' Sam said. 'He's all psyched up to rape. What if he had a reserve?'

'Meaning?'

Dropping her arms and pulling the chair closer into the desk, she leaned towards Ed.

'What if he'd broken two windows in two different houses? What if he has second target, in case target one repaired the window?'

'Never thought about that, but it could make sense,' Ed said. 'He's putting in so much planning, it would be stupid to think if plan A is bollocksed, he'd just go home. What you're saying is he might have given himself a second chance.'

'Yes,' Sam said.

'Another possibility is that Kelly and Danielle were reserve targets,' Ed went on.

Sam let that work through her mind.

'Possibly. Let's do some checks on any reports of broken windows on the days Kelly and Danielle were attacked.'

'I'm on it.'

Ed sprang to his feet and walked to one of the desks with a computer.

'They could have come in as criminal damages, or attempt burglaries,' he said. 'Shouldn't take too long. The good thing is single women living alone are more likely to report something like that than blokes who wouldn't be so bothered once they realised nobody had been inside.'

'Let's hope you're right. I need to eat. Do you want a sandwich?' Sam said.

'Cheers. Yeah.'

Turning towards Ed as she reached the door, Sam asked: 'Any preference?'

Without taking his eyes from the screen, Ed said: 'Anything as long as it's got no mayo on.'

'On a diet, are we?'

'No. Just can't stand the stuff.'

'Okay. Won't be long.'

Within 10 minutes he stood up, stretched, and walked slowly towards the window. Staring over the grassed area to the road beyond, he thought about all the information. *I'm going to get you, you bastard and when I do…*

Viewing electronic crime reports, with reams of details, always seemed to strain his eyes quicker than anything else on a computer screen. Standing at the window he grinned, remembering when reports were hand written in triplicate, and how one uniform cop, after three attempts at spelling candelabra, each of them with a line through it, used his artistic talents to draw one on the form.

His mind lost in another era, he jumped as the door crashed open behind him.

'Did I make you jump?' Sam laughed as she bounded into

the office, throwing a small carrier bag on to the desk nearest to the fridge and kettle. 'Dinner's served, master.'

'Only one master in this room and I'm speaking to her.'

Standing next to the fridge, the mood temporarily lightened, Ed allowed himself a wry smile and shook his head, remembering they weren't supposed to have kettles, toasters, or fridges in the office. Health and Safety issue. 'Health and bloody Safety,' he muttered to himself. Didn't everyone use these things everyday at home? What were you supposed to eat and drink when the canteen was closed? When you were called out in the middle of the night? The ones responsible for running the health and safety only ever worked nine to five, Monday to Friday. *Muppets*!

Sam emptied the contents of the carrier bag on to the desk. 'Cheese and pickle for you, prawn mayo for me, two bars of chocolate. Should keep us going. How're you getting on with the windows?'

'Found one reported on the Friday evening before Kelly was raped. Lauren Storey.'

CHAPTER NINE

'I KNEW IT!' Sam shouted, lobbing Ed his sandwich and throwing her arms above her head like a footballer celebrating a goal. 'I love it when a plan comes together. Love it.'

Tearing open her sandwich, she continued: 'Come on then, let's hear it, tell me more.'

'Lauren Storey. Returns home at 5pm. Sees the broken kitchen window and reports it the next day. I've telephoned her. I told her it was just a follow-up call. I didn't mention the rape inquiry.'

Sam nodded, chewing slowly, her mouth full of prawn mayo, eyes fixed on Ed.

'She was able to get it repaired almost immediately…her brother's a glazier. She's 22, lives alone and works in a fashion store. Obviously I couldn't ask her to describe herself, not when I'm only supposed to be interested in a broken window. But there's enough to suspect a connection.'

'Where does she live?' Sam asked.

'Less than 200 yards from Kelly.'

Sam closed her eyes and said: 'She had to be either the prime target or the reserve. Single woman, same age group, same area, a window broken the same day.'

'I agree,' Ed said. 'We'll need to interview her, and tell her what we think. She might have seen someone acting suspicious. We can put a panic button in her house. We need to ask her if we can put some cameras on it as well. If she was a target, he could come back.'

'He could,' Sam agreed. 'We'll need a bigger team tomorrow… there are already loads of lines of inquiry coming together in my head. But for now I'd like someone to visit Lauren. We know she's at home at the moment. She may give us a lead, and I don't want to leave it too long. Imagine how she would feel if we let her spend the night alone when we think she's been singled out to be raped in her own home.'

'Absolutely,' Ed said. 'If she wants any panic buttons or cameras, we'll have to call out the technical guys, and that can't wait until tomorrow. I'll speak with Jason and he can prepare an interview strategy for her. We'll see what she would like before I call out the technical support, but I'll put a call into the supervisor just to put them on standby.'

'Okay. Any other broken windows reported?'

'No, nothing last night. They might not be on the system yet or just never been reported.'

'We may need to put something in the media asking for information about broken windows,' Sam said. 'That could speed things up.'

'Might do,' Ed nodded. 'I'll go and speak to Jason. He's going to need to brief whoever's going to interview Lauren.'

'While you do that, I'll contact control room and ask if anyone else has called in to report a broken window.'

Jason was in the small office next door, working up the strategy for the re-interview of Kelly when Ed walked in. It was a mirror image of the one he had already written up for the interview of Danielle. One of the decisions was to video-record the interviews. The benefits were numerous; as there was no need to write everything down, the interview flowed much more smoothly and was more like a conversation, which in turn helped the victim to relax. The DVD recording also allowed the senior investigators and Crown Prosecution Service lawyers actually see the victim making her statement, her reactions and body language as well as just the bare words.

Interview advisers – few in number – were specifically trained and used in major crime investigations, their skill helping to get the best out of those often reluctant to speak.

Ed updated Jason about Lauren and why she needed to be interviewed today.

'No problem. Ed.'

Sam had the desk phone to her ear, her hand over the mouthpiece. 'Hi Dave,' she said, as Detective Sergeant Dave Johnson walked in. 'Thanks for coming out.'

Wearing a white dress shirt with the sleeves rolled up, and a black-and-white-striped tie, he was a veteran of many major investigations. A good man to have around. Dave had a retirement date to in five months, but it was the last thing he wanted. He felt he could still contribute but after almost 30 years' service, he had been served with a regulation A19 notice. In simple terms, he was being forced out.

At 51, he had no idea what else to do. In reasonable shape, he had a mop of grey hair, which some of the younger female officers thought made him look like Richard Gere. Women of all ages would often look at him admiringly, and blush if he returned their gaze with his piercing blue eyes.

What frustrated Dave even more was that A19 notices had long been consigned to the past, but with all the austerity measures imposed by the Government, shrinking police budgets meant cuts had to be made to officer numbers. It wasn't possible to make police officers redundant, so the forced retirement of those who had completed the maximum pensionable service had again become an attractive option. The cries of 'loss of experience' from the Police Federation had fallen on deaf ears. No one was indispensable.

Sam ended the call.

'No problem,' Dave told her. 'Sundays are always shit days.'

'I didn't know if you had the kids.'

'No. They're older. Got their own mates. You know how it is. What do you want me to do?'

'There's been another rape,' Sam said. 'Looks like it's connected to one back in November. Can you get all the admin and stuff ready for tomorrow?'

'Yeah, no problem.'

Temporarily lost in his own thoughts, he knew that details of the attack would be in the papers tomorrow. The newspaper reports about Kelly were buried in the soil in his allotment. He had felt physically sick when he realised Danielle had called the police. Walking past her house and seeing all those white-suited scientists caused his stomach to heave so badly he thought he was going to vomit in the gutter there and then. As he turned the corner, he bent over double and retched, feeling acid on the walls of his mouth. Why had she called them? Did any woman ever do as they were told? He would have liked to meet up with her, perhaps take her to the cinema, his treat. Wiping his mouth as he stood up, he acknowledged that she was no different to any other woman he had met, just another lying bitch. He'd call her in a few days. He didn't care if that frightened her. That was her problem. He wanted to hear her voice. Shit, if she hadn't called the police, it could have been so different. Who knows where it might have ended?

Breathing in the cold air, contemplating calling Danielle, his mind drifted to those women he'd phoned years ago; girls from school; women whose photographs were in the local paper; women he'd seen working in shops. When they answered the telephone, his first question was what colour knickers were they wearing. He wished he could have seen their faces. Not all of them hung up straight away. Some called him a pervert or shouted obscenities at him. When he told them what he was doing to himself, he hoped they stayed on line long enough to hear him finish.

His calls had more substance to them now. He had had a relationship with them, shared their bed, talked to them afterwards.

His mind veered in another direction. Where the fuck's the mobile? Jerked back into the present, he rubbed his eyes. Where is it? Think! Think!

His second mobile had his victims' numbers in the address book. No other numbers were stored. It was never topped up online or at an ATM. He would travel out of town and buy a top up card for cash at a small local mini-market.

The phone had been bought from an independent retailer in Newcastle, a direct train journey from Seaton St George. Nobody had asked his name and address, and he didn't offer it. He hadn't seen any CCTV in the shop and it didn't look like the kind of place to have a covert system.

That trail was now so cold, it was Arctic.

It must be in the house. It never left his house. Until he was ready to call one of his girls, that is. He always called them miles from home, from some secluded quiet spot. He remembered reading about a kidnap where the police had been able plot the whereabouts of the criminals' phones.

Where had he put it? Convinced it wasn't in its usual place in the tea caddy, he tried to control his panic, telling himself he would look for it as soon as he got home. 'It's not as if I'm a suspect. What evidence could they have? None. Absolutely nothing.'

Sam looked up from her cup of steaming tea as soon as Ed walked in. 'It just keeps getting better,' she said. 'I've just spoken to a Natalie Robson. She contacted control room at 4pm yesterday to report a broken ground-floor toilet window.'

Ed sat down without speaking, not wanting to interrupt.

'She thought it might have just been local kids,' Sam told him. 'Seems she was happy for one of the neighbourhood uniforms to call round sometime today. They've not been yet, which is why it isn't on the system. I've told her we'll get someone round to see her. I kept it vague.'

'To be fair, by the time we call someone else out and they get here, we'll have finished speaking with Lauren,' Ed said.

'We may as well use the same interviewing officer. No need for another briefing, and we'll have some continuity.'

'Yeah that's fine,' Sam agreed. 'Of course, what we do know is that Natalie must have been the reserve. She and Danielle didn't fix their windows. The rapist went to his first choice. There was no need to move on to his second. And by the way, Dave Johnson's out.'

Ed walked to the kettle. 'So enlighten me about this power rapist.'

'Okay,' Sam said, putting her cup down and resting both arms on the desk.

'There are four distinct categories of rapist. I think ours is a 'power reassurance' rapist.'

Leaning against the wall with a freshly made mug of tea in his hand, Ed stared at Sam through squinted eyes. Where did she learn this stuff?

'It's the most common,' Sam went on. 'The behaviour of all rapists during their attack – we're talking stranger rape here – will reflect their everyday personality. This group uses a surprise approach like our attacker, albeit he's sneaking up on the victims in their homes. It's not a blitz attack or a con. This suggests he has a limited social life and he's not happy committing an assault.'

Ed pushed himself off the wall.

'Bloody hell, Sam, what's rape if it's not assault? The worst assault. Jesus, short of killing them…'

He moved towards a chair, the fingers of his right hand tightening around the Newcastle United mug.

'I know that, Ed. What I mean is he's not happy beating someone up. If we're going to use this type of thinking to work out what sort of person he is, we have to try to take emotion out of it. We need to concentrate on the crime and this offender in a way that we can catch him. Being pedantic about particular phrases won't help.'

Ed tried to keep the doubt from his face, not truly convinced but feeling too out of his depth to push back.

'Yeah, okay,' he said. 'Sorry. It's just you said earlier they want a relationship. I can't get my head around that.'

He paused and looked into his mug. 'By the way, where did you learn this stuff?'

Sam allowed herself a quick smile.

'I read a lot. It's fascinating stuff.'

'Go on then. Sounds interesting if nothing else.'

Sam said: 'Look, this guy needs to prove himself to himself. He has low self-esteem. He's demonstrating to himself that he can have a relationship with a woman. In his world, she's a consenting partner. He sees himself as a lover.'

Ed shot up in his seat, tea erupting from his mug and spilling on to his thigh.

'Shit!' he said, rubbing his leg. 'A lover? You sure?'

He shook his head, his jaw hanging open.

'Yes. That's why he asks if he's been gentle, if she's enjoyed it. His fantasy is that this is a relationship. He asked her to undress. That's what you'd expect in a consensual relationship.'

Ed's eyes were locked on Sam.

'He's used minimal force,' Sam told him. 'He threatens her with a knife, but his personality doesn't fit with violence and he has little or no confidence with women.'

Ed's right fist was now tightly held in the palm of his left hand.

'This all sounds well and good, but I've always thought of them as vicious, gutless bastards. I have a wife and a daughter. I'm not sure I can buy into this 'wanting a relationship' school of thought.'

Sam looked at Ed and saw a stubborn anger plenty of 'old school' cops would share, a lifetime in the job setting their approach in stone.

She was patient and pushed on.

'Ed, this is years of research in America. The categorisation has been around since 1977. There must be something in it. We may as well explore it. We've nothing else to go on at the minute. Once we've got Danielle's account we can compare the traits in his behaviour. We already know about the common thread of the broken windows.'

'Yeah, a high level of planning, as we've said.'

'And if I told you this type of rapist uses surveillance techniques on their victims, and may target more than one at once?' Sam left the words hanging in the air.

Ed shook his head slowly and straightened in his chair.

'Maybe there's something in it,' he said. 'Anything that nails the bastard.'

Sam would take that as a victory, albeit a small one.

She went on: 'Our discussion earlier, when I said about him being psyched up – you know, what if the window had been repaired? That's when I remembered reading something about more than one target. I had some notes in my desk. I read them when you were briefing Jason.'

Ed smiled.

'And here was me thinking you were the font of all knowledge,' he said. 'You shouldn't have said anything. You've just shattered my illusions, thinking of you as a combination of brains and beauty.'

'Flattery will get you everywhere,' Sam said grinning, throwing her head back a little.

Then it was back to business, the mood serious once again.

'What about the driving licences?' Ed asked. 'You said they were souvenirs, not trophies.'

'I think that's what they are,' Sam said. 'To him, his victims aren't a conquest so he doesn't need trophies. He wants souvenirs instead, something to remember them by. With a licence, not only does he have their names, he has a photograph.'

She saw a look of bewilderment breaking across Ed's face.

'I'll try to explain.' She paused. 'Did you play sport at school?'

'I was a decent footballer. Played for school, then in the local leagues. Played at a decent standard. I was a bit fitter then. Lighter.'

'You're not too bad these days.'

Ed smiled.

'Okay,' Sam said. 'Did you win anything as a player?'

'A few cups.'

'Did you get individual trophies or medals?'

'Both.'

'Where are they now?'

'Blimey,' Ed rubbed his chin, trying to remember. 'Long gone. Maybe in the loft.'

'They're trophies. They came from a victory. Agreed?'

'Agreed,' said Ed.

'Did you take any photographs of Ellen when she was a child?'

'Of course. Who doesn't photograph their kids? There's loads of them.'

'Are any still on display at home?'

'All over the place…walls, shelves, fireplace…everywhere.'

'They're souvenirs,' Sam told him. 'They remind you of past times. You look at them and they trigger a memory, take you back in time to a place where you once were. You'll probably remember the photographs being taken. They're your souvenirs, Ed. The driving licences are his. Some categories of rapist take trophies. They'll keep them for a short while and then throw them away. You don't know where your trophies are. But the rapist who takes souvenirs, he's different. He keeps them in a safe place. Find him and we'll find his souvenirs.'

CHAPTER TEN

JASON WALKED INTO THE OFFICE. 'Have you got a minute?'

'Carry on,' Sam said, indicating a chair next to Ed.

'Lauren's not been able to give any information. Lives alone; 24 years old. Not seen anyone acting suspiciously near her house. She's not been followed at any time, not that she knows anyway. No issues with former boyfriends. She's not received any nuisance telephone calls. Basically, she can't give us anything.'

Sam nodded. 'Okay.'

'Danielle's description of her attack was strikingly similar to Kelly's, though,' Jason said. 'A masked intruder woke her up. He made her undress, told her she was beautiful, after showing her he had a knife. He told her she was his babe. He wore gloves but she thinks he put on a condom. He raped her after telling her to get on her hands and knees. Afterwards, he lay beside her and asked if he'd been 'gentle' and had she enjoyed it.'

'Same bastard,' Ed said.

Jason told them Danielle had never spoken to the attacker from the moment she woke until the moment he was leaving. She had been too terrified.

'She thought she was going to die,' Jason said. 'She thought he was going to rape her and then kill her. But she did ask 'why me?' as he was leaving. He told her 'because there's no way somebody like you would go out with somebody like me'.'

'Jesus, we need to catch this bastard,' said Ed.

'What else?' Sam asked.

'He took her driving licence. That was in her handbag. She only realised that when we asked her to check. He got her phone and then gave her it back. Two differences, though. He didn't tie her up and after the attack, he asked her if she had any drink in the house. She shook her head to signal she didn't.'

'Bastard,' said Ed.

'He's all of that,' said Sam.

'She's really traumatised,' Jason told them. 'I obviously haven't seen her, but I feel really sorry for her. She's just a nice young woman by all accounts.'

Shaking her head, Sam said quietly: 'Aren't they all?'

'Not tied up, though' Ed observed.

They fell silent, each lost in their own thoughts.

'Okay,' Sam said. 'If he felt there was no likelihood of her escaping, he might have decided not to bother. We know she was so heavily traumatised afterwards, she had to be sedated. She thought she was going to die. She's frozen with terror. She'll have been totally compliant and remember, him not tying Danielle up will fuel his fantasy of her being a partner not a victim.'

Jason took the ringing mobile from his pocket and answered it. Sam and Ed looked at him in silence, waiting for him to end the call.

'Update regarding the interview with Natalie,' he said. 'Like Lauren, Natalie can't give us any leads, but she fits the victim profile…23 and single.'

'Okay. Thanks Jason,' Sam said. 'Get yourself away. Thanks for coming out at such short notice.'

Rising from his seat, Jason added: 'I've arranged panic alarms for both Lauren and Natalie.'

'One last thing, Jason,' Sam said. 'See if Danielle will let us have her phone for a while. He's called Kelly. He might do the same with her.'

He locked the front door behind him, dashed into the kitchen and grabbed the square-shaped blue teapot from the high, light oak shelf alongside the cooker. Pulling it into his chest, the rattle confirmed something was inside before he had yanked off the lid. His puffed cheeks slowly blew out air as his eyes focussed on the mobile and he conceded that his memory was playing tricks on him.

He took the phone and rotated it in his hands, resisting the temptation to turn it on. He felt a sudden need to scroll through the contacts, to see their names and numbers, but discipline was key. Turning it on in the house could come back to haunt him. As it turned through his fingers, he marvelled at its simplicity. While it was a basic, no-frills mobile, it was one of his most prized possessions. He had considered buying one with a camera so he could photograph himself with the girls, but it would have been something else to think about when he was visiting them… something else that could lead to his downfall. It had been so exhilarating speaking with Kelly; the increase in his heart rate, his blood pressure rising quicker than a helium-filled balloon. She made him feel like a small child. Beautiful and exciting, she would have made a perfect girlfriend.

Maybe he would call Danielle on Tuesday. It would be nice to hear her voice.

He returned the teapot and smirked. His mother had collected dozens of them over the years, in all shapes and sizes, and insisted on displaying them all. 'The Rovers Return', 'The Woolpack', and 'The Aidensfield Arms' had been her particular favourites. He had intended throwing them all out when she died, but allowing them to gather dust, uncared for, seemed a more fitting two-fingered salute to his mother.

Upstairs, he took the pen out of the bedside table drawer

and spent a few minutes examining it. Twiddling it between his right thumb and index finger, he admired its sleek silver-coloured lines. It was probably not very expensive, but cost was irrelevant. Provenance was everything. He raised it to his nose, closed his eyes, and sniffed hard. Her scent still lingering in his mind, he collected what was required, walked into the kitchen, and carefully laid everything out on the table.

The doner kebab with extra chilli and garlic sauce was still wrapped in the white paper, a can of Coke next to it, condensation running down its sides. He would eat first and enjoy the kebab while it was hot and the Coke was cold. His fingers scooped doner and salad from the pitta bread with mechanical regularity and in seconds they were a combination of red-and-white stains. His mouth was salivating as he devoured everything and he could feel juices running down his chin. His eyes never wavered from the collection in the middle of the table.

He squirted washing-up liquid on to his hands and cleaned his fingers and chin, his head bent over the kitchen sink as the cold tap jettisoned water. Not wanting to leave stains on anything he was about to touch, watermarks included, he vigorously dried himself with a soiled, musty-smelling tea towel.

Flicking through the cream-coloured pages reminded him of opening the grubby pages of his school exercise books at the start of another lesson. School had been something to be endured, but the imposed discipline of the classroom had at least provided an escape from the taunts. He was such a loner, all of the staff must have known he was ripe for bullying but nobody had cared. Not even Miss Joy. Still, be thankful for small mercies, he told himself; without school he wouldn't be able to write, and his notebook would be as unfulfilled as he was.

He had never opened a school book with excitement and anticipation like this. He rolled Kelly's pen between his finger and thumb, concentrating on his thoughts. The top of the page bore Danielle's name, address, and the make and registration number of her car.

In his spidery script appeared the date he became sure that she lived alone. Subsequent entries showed the dates and times when he had passed the house, and whether any other vehicles were parked outside.

He started to write.

My heart was racing when I went round the back to smash the window. I didn't think anyone saw me. I hid for about five minutes, just in case someone came round. Nobody did. I waited and when I heard a car go past, I smashed the window with a brick. I just tapped the window, but it made a massive noise. It was getting dark. I waited another couple of minutes and then walked down the path. I was shitting myself, but I had done it again. Another window. I walked away and hoped she wouldn't fix it before I came back. I got hard thinking about her. I hoped she would be as good as she looked.

Now came the important part, the narrative of their time together. He needed to recall every detail so his memories would remain as vivid as they were now.

Reaching across to pick up Danielle's driving licence, he smiled at her photograph. Until the girls, he had never put his feelings into words, yet he was at ease with the concept and now the words seemed to flow effortlessly from the pen. Perhaps it was because it was Kelly's?

Words appeared at a blistering rate.

I remember the light on in the house across the road. That put me off at first but I couldn't see anyone. It was cold but I was sweating and my heart was racing. I was so excited when I saw the newspaper over the broken window. I cut through it and climbed inside. I remember the quiet inside the house. I crept into her bedroom. She was laid there. Beautiful. God, I was so hard.

He described waking her, seeing the unblemished skin of her firm body, the long legs, and the softness of her hair. He knew she had enjoyed him. He could feel it. He had been a good lover.

The pen was moving furiously across the paper and the indentations were now visible on the pages beneath.

I wanted to kiss her neck but couldn't because of the mask. I wanted it to last forever but I just knew looking at her I couldn't.

Describing the warm sensation as he came inside her, his pen slowed and the pressure on the notebook eased.

Leaning back in the chair, he stared at the dirty white ceiling and ran his hands across his groin. He would catch his breath before recalling the one-sided conversation.

CHAPTER ELEVEN

SAM SUGGESTED they call it a day. Tomorrow was going to be busy. The Assistant Chief Constable and Chris Shaw, the Head of Crime, would need a briefing and a media strategy would be required. Sam would think about those on the way home.

She had to consider her lines of inquiry and how many staff she would need.

After a final, fruitless check for more reports of broken windows in the last six months, Ed and Sam left the office together.

'Fancy a quick drink?' Sam asked.

'Why not. I didn't get one at dinnertime.'

'Tell you what,' Sam smiled. 'I'll make it up to you. Leave your beloved bus here. I'll drive and drop you off.'

'Sounds like a plan.'

A quick drink had turned into four pints. Time always flew when he was in Sam's company. He lived in a comfortable four-bedroom house in a small village and after 10 years knew many of the residents. The village was a lively place, with a primary school, two pubs, and plenty of community-based activities. He felt at home there.

In the kitchen, he made small talk with his wife and daughter about their trip to Newcastle.

Hugging his daughter, Ellen, he remembered how precious she was to him. It was such a vile world out there, he just wanted to put his arms around her and protect her forever.

He told Sue he had been working on a rape investigation but didn't elaborate. He rarely did. He mentioned his visit to see Jess.

Sue always had food ready for him, even if he came home in the early hours, but he had called her from the office and said he just fancied a couple of chilled beers and a catch-up with the Premier League football on Sky Sports News. He just wanted to switch off, grab some time when his thoughts weren't consumed by the rapist and how they'd find him.

He changed into a tracksuit and stretched himself out on the settee. Sue followed him into the living room and gave him a bottle of ice cold Bierre Moretti.

'Cheers,' Ed thanked her.

'Sam out with you today?'

'Yeah,' Ed said, wiping his mouth and not looking up from the TV. 'She dropped me off.'

'Been out for a drink with her?'

'Yeah. Just a couple.'

'Just the two of you? Very cosy. Didn't think they'd need a DCI for a rape.' Sue was now blocking his view of the TV.

'What?' Ed raised himself on his elbow and tried to peer around her legs. 'I can't see… we're doing a review. I don't choose who's in charge. I went for a pint with her… look, can I just watch the sports? I've had enough of work today. I don't know what your problem is with Sam.'

'My problem is you spend enough time with her at work without going for a drink with her.'

'She's my boss.'

'Not in the pub she isn't.'

'Don't be so ridiculous.' Ed said. 'She's too young to be

interested in me, and even if she was, I'm not interested in her.'

Sue's expression had darkened, anger lines creasing her brow.

'She's lonely, attractive, intelligent, and likes you.'

'She's my boss,' Ed said coldly. 'I get on well with her. End of. Now can I watch the sports?'

Ellen, listening from the hallway, ran upstairs to her room and heard the living room door slam.

Returning to his notebook, he saw the page for Lauren Storey. She had repaired the window when he got there. It hadn't just got a board over it. The glass had been replaced. Pity. She looked a real stunner. Still, Kelly was exciting. He had enjoyed her. A smile broke out across his face. How had he hit on the idea of targeting two women at once? It meant extra planning, of course. Twice as much work to build up the picture of each one but it doubled his chances of getting into a house… doubled his chances of enjoying a woman on any given night.

In fairness, it was Kirsty he had to thank. He had gone to her house and found the window repaired, just like Lauren's, the difference being he had nowhere else to go that night. That was four months ago. The feeling of despair as he left her house was gutting. All that planning and all for nothing.

Running home that night, he vowed through gritted teeth it would never happen again. He decided to refine his preparations, have a choice of two women for any one attack.

He still had his notes on Kirsty and, of course, on Natalie, Lauren, and Emily. In a few months, when the police activity died down, he might find himself in a position to look at them again. He would have to think of a different way in. If the Press ran stories on Danielle, no woman was going to leave broken windows unreported, and certainly not those four.

Even if he waited for summer, single women wouldn't

leave ground-floor windows open; not now, not while he was 'on the loose', as the Press would say. In any case, his planning was too meticulous to count on a British heatwave. He would need to apply himself, come up with a new method. The alternative was approaching them from behind in the open air, but he wouldn't be in control of that environment. He didn't want a confrontation with a hero 'do-gooder' and he certainly didn't want to be disturbed when he was making love.

He closed the notebook. It wouldn't win any literary prizes, but it wasn't for publication. It was strictly for his eyes only. He would begin his search soon. He wouldn't rush, he never did. Opportunists in crime were always caught, sooner or later. Luck never lasted forever. His success was measured by having sex with his chosen partner, escaping the scene, and not getting caught. Planning was fundamental. Finding the right women was all part of the process and gathering intelligence just another part of the hunt. He loved every moment.

Reading the entries about Amber, he became lost in his thoughts again as he remembered her stunning beauty. She had obviously enjoyed herself; she hadn't gone to the police. He should call her again. He had called her since their meeting but she hadn't answered. Perhaps she was busy or her phone was on silent. Maybe she was one of those who won't pick up if they don't recognise the number. The positive was that he'd heard her sweet, sexy voice on her voicemail. He should text her. She might respond to a text.

He carefully replaced everything in the drawer. He might contact Danielle and Amber this week.

He started to whistle that Louis Armstrong song.

***

The temperature in the car had dropped rapidly even though Sam had only been sat on her driveway for a few minutes. She longed for March and the thought of the clocks going forward lightened her mood slightly. She hated going to and from work in the dark. It was almost as depressing as coming home to an empty house. Almost.

She had bought the house three years ago, six months after Tristram was killed. She tried to live in their marital home, the house they had bought together, but it was just too full of memories. She needed a fresh start. Married for two years, she knew Tristram was the one, her soul mate. Life would never be the same without him. She missed the walks by the sea, curling up on the sofa laughing at old Ealing comedy films, a meal in a restaurant, the lazy Sundays with the newspapers and a roast, and the wines of Burgundy. Everything wiped out in an instant. They had talked happily and for hours planning their future... holidays, houses, children, retirement, old age. Their bucket list was continually growing and being refined, their lives together stretching out before them.

Had she known the darkness that lay ahead, that his life clock was counting down at a supersonic speed compared to hers, she would have done more living, less planning. John Lennon said: 'Life's what happens while you are busy making other plans.' How tragically true that was.

The police allowed her to take as much time off as she needed. She was offered any posting she wanted, but she didn't want to leave the CID. When a vacancy arose on the Major Incident Team she successfully applied. Now work was a welcome distraction.

Achievement to Sam didn't mean climbing the ranks. It meant solving crimes, bringing some sort of sense of justice to victims. It also meant getting that true sense of satisfaction when the bad guys were convicted. She liked the feeling of making a difference. To her, that was what policing was all about. Being able to put her head on her pillow, knowing that she had, in some small way, made a difference.

She hurried inside, thankful the central heating had automatically come on.

She turned on some music, crashed into the deep armchair and allowed the sounds of Amy Winehouse to drift over her.

Monday

Startled, Sam looked around to discover where she was. Home. Feeling very cold and with absolutely no idea of the time, her blurry eyes sought out the clock on the living room wall. 2am. The central heating had long since switched itself off.

Dragging herself upstairs, she hurriedly undressed, dropping all of her clothes on the floor. She was in bed within minutes, without brushing her teeth or washing her face. She could concentrate on nothing but sleep.

And yet as soon as her head hit the pillow, her eyes were as wide as dinner plates. Sleep wouldn't come easy, but it was nothing to do with this latest investigation. She had already formulated the lines of inquiry, had a media strategy in mind, and knew how many people she needed.

Sleep would be difficult because she was a woman alone in her home at night. She was only too well aware she was dealing with a serial rapist, a monster who struck in the dead of night, and she knew he would never stop until he was caught.

He was comfortable operating on the Gull and Conifer Estates, so maybe he lived on one of them. Eventually, Sam knew, he would travel further but not yet. It was too soon. His type liked to stay close to home at first, living in the midst of his victims, watching them, learning their habits, establishing when they would be home alone.

Shooting bolt upright, her whole body stiff, she asked herself the question she had been avoiding all day. What if he's watching me? It wouldn't be the last time that night she found herself checking every window in her house. Like a young child with an overactive imagination, she saw shadows and shapes everywhere.

The fact no windows were broken did nothing to ease her anxiety. Wishing she had a German Shepherd police dog, she left the landing light switched on and the wall lights shining above her head. She would sleep at some point, but not now.

The fear she was feeling tonight was going to spread tomorrow. Other single women would feel it when she released carefully chosen details of this latest attack to the media. There was a balancing act between increasing the fear of crime and getting the information they needed to progress the investigation. She needed to warn people to report anything suspicious, and she needed women who lived alone to report broken windows immediately to the police.

While the investigation worked to discover his identity, she had to do her best to thwart any further attacks.

The balancing act would no doubt fail tomorrow.

Ed also tossed and turned in his bed that night. Sue slept soundly next to him, her earlier outburst not affecting her sleep, but his mind was a whirl of thoughts. Not that he was thinking about her words. His mind had a single focus. Waiting for the rapist to make a mistake wasn't an option. Nor was waiting for him to be confronted in a victim's house because a woman wasn't alone on the night he decided to strike. Ed needed to think of a way to catch him, and catch him quickly. Any delay would mean more victims, no question. Forget any potential outrage from the press if the rapist kept offending. There were senior cops who would deal with the media. He just wanted to catch the bastard as soon as possible, and glare into his eyes. He hated these bastards. He knew on a personal level the deep devastation they caused.

CHAPTER TWELVE

Ed rolled over, closed his eyes, and a vision of his niece filled his head. Her whole personality had changed after she was attacked in a town about 26 miles to the west of Seaton St George. That was two years ago. Where did the time go? She was 19 and on her way home from a nightclub. Separated from her friends, she was looking for a taxi. Ed shuddered at the thought of her out there, alone, remembering he too had been at a party enjoying himself that night.

The bastard sprinted up behind her and before she realised what was happening, before she had time to react, he had grabbed her hair, spun her around, and repeatedly punched her in the head and body. Dazed and off balance, she was dragged 10 yards into an alleyway.

Ed could willingly have beaten her attacker senseless at the time. He probably still could. He rolled over again and glanced at Sue, envious of her deep sleep. She always slept well, whether she went to bed on an argument or not.

His niece had told his daughter she felt her attacker's breath on her ear as he spat out the words in a whisper. 'I'm going to give you a good fuckin'.' Her face had been pushed against the alley wall, and she was punched so hard in the ribs that she doubled up, unable to breathe. Her head was rammed down towards her thighs, and holding it there with his right hand, the bastard thrust his left hand up her short summer dress.

She was terrified, semi-conscious, too frightened to scream.

Thankfully, two lads in their early 20s had seen her being dragged into the alleyway and came to her rescue. Two public-spirited, decent young men. *Thank God they had been there.* Both keen boxers, they were part-time doormen at one of the clubs. Not only had they stopped her being raped, they beat the shit out of him, and held on to him until the police arrived.

The bastard had been sentenced to nine years. The crown court judge commended the two young men. His brother's family would be forever in their debt. Ed smiled as he recalled tracking them down to the club where they worked and shaking their hands. He had bought them each a drink and told them his only regret was that he hadn't been with them when they saved his niece. He still felt like that.

Jess had gone from being a bubbly young girl to a recluse. Always full of fun and outgoing, she was transformed now into a tiny timid shell, her sunken eyes telling everyone how much weight she had lost but telling nobody what was going on behind them. Ed shuddered. Yesterday her arms and legs were even skinnier.

He turned on to his stomach, doubled over his pillow, and considered snuggling into Sue. He thought better of it.

He remembered Jess's hair. What a mess. She didn't go out anywhere after dark, and certainly not to pubs and clubs. She barely went out at all. She even had to go through the ordeal of a trial because the bastard had pleaded not guilty. Not guilty! Her face was black and blue, her jaw broken. Who the fuck consented to that?

The defence lawyers were just as bad, putting her through the cross-examination. No better than the shit they defended. *God, I'll never get to sleep if I start thinking about fucking barristers.* He rolled over again, pushing his body just a little closer to Sue.

What the hell was Sam talking about when she said the

rapist wanted a relationship? He was still not totally sold on this categorisation business. That said, they needed to catch him, and Sam seemed to know what she was on about.

Not every girl would be as lucky as Jess. Lucky? What the hell was he saying? She went to a club and was almost raped on her way home. She would have been but for those two lads. How the hell was that lucky? What type of society were we living in when a seasoned detective like him could describe his niece as being lucky because she only had a broken jaw and a few bruises? A just and proper society should have allowed her to walk home at any time in total safety. But, of course, that society doesn't exist. Ed had spoken to many rape victims over the years. Deep down he knew it could have been so much worse for Jess.

He slid out of the bed, glanced at Sue, and went downstairs for a cup of tea.

A busy day lay ahead. He woke early but stood under the hot shower longer than he intended, thinking of each of them in turn. Barely dry when he put on his white dressing gown, he rushed into the bedroom, his wet feet leaving footprints on the green diamond-patterned carpet. He was filled with an overwhelming desire to check on his girls. He flopped on to the bed, rolled on to his stomach, and reached across to the bedside drawer. He handled the licences with the care of an antiquarian book dealer, puckered his lips, and kissed each photograph. Unlike the soldier overseas, he would, in all probability, not be reunited with his absent sweetheart, but the intensity of his longing to see them again was no less fierce.

A self-satisfied smile spread across his face as he read the newly written passages about his time with Danielle.

Were the contents of this drawer his most treasured possessions? The phone was important, but the licences, the pen, and the notebook, were without a shadow of a doubt, his most valued; with the exception of the football programme, they were also the most incriminating.

Ed was at the office for 7am wearing a dark blue Italian suit, a light blue shirt and a red-and-gold-striped tie. There was a time when he couldn't afford so-called labels but now, mortgage free with a reasonable amount of disposal income, he indulged himself.

Walking into the HOLMES room, he saw Sam sitting at a computer terminal, eyes fixed on the keyboard, her two index fingers jumping across the keys. The full mug of tea on the desk suggested she had become so engrossed in what she was doing she had forgotten to drink it.

'Morning, Sam. You're nice and early.'

'Hi Ed. You know the score. This job needs sorting.'

And not because Stewart said it had to be, she thought to herself. She wanted to catch him before others were raped. Then she conceded that Stewart's implied threats were at the back of her mind.

'We've got a briefing at nine with the ACC.'

Sam, like Ed, was much more business-looking today, wearing a light grey pinstripe tailored trouser suit, with black patent leather shoes with a slight heel. At 5'8', Sam didn't need to wear big heels, although Ed had seen her wearing seriously towering stilettos at various functions. Her white blouse looked good against her light-brown skin tone, and the make-up around her brown eyes was as flawless as ever.

'What's with the 'we' Sam?'

'I think it's best we both go. There's a fair amount of information to give them, and two heads are better than one.'

Sam knew Ed would guess why she wanted him to go to the briefing. Over the last few weeks she'd been talking to him about applying for promotion to Inspector. He'd passed the national qualifying exam, so all that stood in his way was the local process. Detective Sergeants didn't get too many opportunities to sit around the table with Assistant Chief

Constables and discuss an ongoing operational matter. Sam was very loyal to those who were loyal to her. She appreciated good investigators who contributed to the investigation process, and believed in doing what she could to help them advance their careers.

She knew Ed was good. She valued his opinion. He had the ability to not only contribute but to bring new thoughts to the discussions. Not wild, off-the-wall thoughts, but the sensible thoughts of a thinker; the thoughts of a problem solver, the thoughts of a good detective. If in some small way she could remind the hierarchy of the existence of Detective Sergeant Ed Whelan, then she would do so. The police needed people like Ed at Inspector rank. Too many of them at that level said the right things in promotion interviews or internal meetings but when it came to making an operational decision, at a critical moment in an unfolding event, many were found wanting. Whether that was a lack of training, or a lack of experience, wasn't her concern. She felt everybody on her team was capable of operating at least one rank above their present one and she would do her best to give her people whatever advantage she could.

'Okay. Thanks,' Ed said. 'What time did you say the briefing is?'

'Nine.'

'That'll give us time to speak with Peter Hunt first.'

'Yeah, we need to formulate a press release with him. I want to appeal for witnesses to the attack on Danielle and remind everyone to report any crime, however small, and that includes broken windows.'

'You're going to be popular with the Crime Managers on the Districts if their reported crime figures start going up,' Ed said.

'I don't care. We need as much information as possible. If that affects the figures, I can live with that and they'll have to. Anyway, don't we want figures that really reflect what's happening out there?'

'Whatever you say, boss,' Ed said with mock seriousness, and for added sarcastic emphasis, he saluted.

Sam laughed. She knew Ed cared for internal politics as little as she did.

Peter Hunt burst into the HOLMES room with a beaming smile and directed a loud 'Morning!' at them. Sam smiled at the dapper, cheerful man, who she held in such high regard. His wispy, brown hair flopped around the wrinkled brow, a brow that was now just three years short of state retirement age.

A lifelong print journalist, Peter had been with the police as Head of Media Services for four years and was a valuable asset to the SIO on major inquiries. He understood the media, their agenda, and was able to advise accordingly.

As far as Sam was concerned, filling media services departments with marketing gurus was fine until a major incident broke, when they were as much use as an ashtray on a motorbike. If the Press was clamouring for information, Sam wanted a Peter Hunt, not someone with a degree in spinning good news and maintaining a nice force website.

Peter sat next to Ed, one leg crossed over the other, pen hovering over the little black notebook, and listened as Sam brought him up to speed on the attack on Danielle Banks.

'Finally, our appeal should seek any witnesses who saw anything suspicious at the time Danielle was attacked, anyone who lives on those estates and has had a window broken in the last six months,' Sam stressed. 'We want anyone who has any information about either attack, anyone who has any suspicions of male family members, friends or neighbours. We should also remind people to keep windows and doors locked and not to leave the door keys in the locks.'

'Are you going to say you believe the assaults have been committed by the same man?' Peter asked.

'No. If that's raised directly, which I am sure it will be, I can only say we are investigating both attacks, but that doesn't mean there's only one offender. I'll tell them we have to keep an open mind. Let's be right, Peter. If there is more than one rapist, and I say that there's only one, I'll look a fool.'

'Do you think it is one person?'

'One hundred percent.'

'You do realise asking people to report their suspicions might lead to an avalanche of names,' Peter said, looking up from his shorthand notes, staring at Sam.

'I do. But to be fair, I'd rather be worrying about setting some parameters around elimination, having been given loads of names, than have no names as I do at the minute.'

'Okay. I'll write something up. Can I log on to one of these terminals?'

'Course you can,' said Ed.

Peter was soon busily typing, but not in the double-digit way of most detectives.

The team would soon be arriving. Ed decided to fill the kettle. Plentiful amounts of tea and coffee were going to be drunk while the detectives waited for their briefing, the room would be filled with conversations about football, soaps, topical news, and police gossip. Everyone would be eager to learn about the new investigation but they were all experienced enough to understand how these things worked. They were used to waiting.

CHAPTER THIRTEEN

As THE ASSISTANT Chief Constable's personal assistant showed them in, Sam and Ed saw that Detective Chief Superintendent Chris Shaw, the Head of Crime, was already there with Trevor Stewart.

The office had a plush, high-quality blue carpet, the type your shoes sank into. The same carpet was fitted in the corridor outside, a silent but powerful psychological indicator of who was occupying the offices in this part of HQ: two Assistant Chief Constables, a Deputy Chief Constable and the Chief Constable. Everywhere else in the building, the corridors were fitted with linoleum.

The ACC, sitting behind his impressive desk, was on the telephone. A long table with four seats either side was pushed up against the desk. Chris Shaw was on one side of the table. Opposite Chris and next to Ed, Sam's eyes scanned the numerous photographs and certificates adorning the walls, and the usual collection of memorabilia from other police forces, both national and international. There were police caps, plaques with police crests on them, and other items, all reminders of past encounters. More souvenirs, Sam thought.

Replacing the receiver, Trevor Stewart smiled and said: 'Morning guys. Thanks for coming. Can I get you a drink? Tea? Coffee?'

Sam and Ed declined.

'Okay,' Stewart continued. 'Tell me what we've got, and what your thoughts are. I did say he would attack again. I just didn't think when I said it he would do it the next night. I hope we haven't missed any opportunities to get him in custody before this latest attack. The Press will have a field day if we could have prevented it.'

Walking to his office, Sam remembered the words of David Greene, the Head of 'CIVITAS', The Institute for the Study of Civil Society, at the time of the London Riots of 2011.

The present generation of police leaders gained promotion by mastering the art of talking about 'issues around' racism or bearing down on hate crime 'going forward'. Learning the management buzz words of the last few years has not produced leaders able to command men in a riot. The injuries sustained by officers show that we have plenty of men and women prepared to be brave when needed, but they are lions led by donkeys who listened a bit too intently to the sociology lectures about 'hate crime' at Bramshill police college.

She was convinced this description applied to many police leaders – if the cap fits and all that – but Trevor Stewart wasn't one of them. A career detective who had scaled the dizzy heights, he was a leader and a decision maker but streetwise, cunning and invariably two steps ahead of everyone else. He looked after number one, and Sam felt he viewed her as inferior to her male counterparts.

She gave an overview of the latest attack, what was known about the first one, and why she thought that the same man had committed both.

Stewart reclined his chair. 'This second attack ups the ante. He needs arresting, soon as, but be careful about placing too much emphasis on behaviour. I'm all for innovation, but sometimes the old ways, checking and doubling checking, are still the best.'

'We're not putting too much emphasis on it, but it's worth exploring,' Sam said.

'That's what they thought years ago on the Wimbledon Common murder,' Stewart said, pushing home his point.

'There's a big difference, Sir. We haven't employed anybody, these are my own thoughts.'

'Just be careful, that's all. Don't get sidetracked. Don't take your eye off the ball.'

Sam outlined the media strategy and what she hoped to achieve. Trevor Stewart agreed that she should perform the role of Senior Investigating Officer on both rapes and asked to be kept updated of any developments, promising her any support she needed with additional resources.

Striding along the corridor, Sam was deep in thought. Stewart gave the impression he had complete faith in her. No hard questions, no investigative interference, only promises of support. That said, she knew she was only as good as her last job. One botched investigation would see her moved sideways to a desk job, joining the ranks of those who separated the green paper clips from the yellow ones. Nobody was indispensable, certainly not someone who blew a major investigation. These investigations received the most media coverage and posed the biggest threat to reputations. Get it wrong and she knew she was out. And his new drinking buddy wanted her job.

'How much smoke and mirrors was going on in there?' Ed asked.

'What do you mean?'

'Chris Shaw never said a word. Stewart's like a smiling assassin. Don't take your eye off the ball. Nice little threat there.'

'We do our job, we'll be okay. Chris Shaw is intimidated by Stewart, and Trevor Stewart's got more faces than the town-hall clock.'

Ed smiled.

Sam flung open the door to the HOLMES room, marched in, back straight, head up, her body language exuding confidence and authority. Ed caught the door before it bounced back off its hinges into his face.

Sam shouted: 'Okay. Listen up.'

Everyone stopped talking, took a seat, or leaned against

the desks as Sam walked to the far wall before turning to face them.

'Jason's briefed you all. We'll be putting a press release out soon. Not only am I interested in anybody coming forward who may have seen anything at the relevant time of the attacks on Kelly and Danielle, I also want anybody who has suspicions about family members, friends or neighbours to come forward. I'll be asking anyone who's had windows broken which they have not reported to the police, to contact us. Dave will run the office.'

Dave Johnson would be the HOLMES room Office Manager making sure everything Sam asked for was done and done properly.

'Check for CCTV cameras in the area, and that includes private shops and houses that may have them fitted. Dave, get me a list of known sex offenders living on the Gull and Conifer estates. I want all of the victims re-interviewed and that includes those who had their windows broken. I want to know their habits, associates, the places they go. I want to know if they know each other. I want to know every detail, however trivial they might think it is.'

Ed looked around. Everyone was staring at Sam. She really did know how to command a room.

'Jason will remain as the interview adviser. I want to establish why these women were targeted? How did the rapist know they lived alone? Find out if these girls had had any unusual visitors or if they've employed any tradesman… plumbers, electricians, whoever. There has to be some sort of common denominator here. Not only did he know they lived alone, he knew that on the night of the attack they would be alone. How? Where is he getting the knowledge?'

She let everyone ponder that last question.

'I want to know what the rapist talked about. How did he smell, what accent, if any, did he have? Did he smell of alcohol? I want to know everything. I think he lives locally. He's visited the victims' houses at least twice, once to break the windows and once to carry out the attacks. He knows the area. He must live close to them.'

Heads nodded around the room.

'Dave, I want door-to-door around the scenes of the rapes and the addresses where the broken windows occurred. Get a trained uniform 'house-to-house' team to do that. Danielle's window was broken on a Saturday. Did any of the neighbours hear the sound of breaking glass?'

Dave Johnson was writing Sam's instructions as fast as he could as her words came firing from her mouth like bullets from a machine gun.

'I want photographs of the two rape victims and the two girls who had their windows broken. I want to know whether the rapist is targeting these girls based on their physical appearance. We'll have a debrief 7pm, but if any of you have any important information, for God's sake don't wait until then. Feed it straight into Dave Johnson.'

Sam was in full flow, focussed and fizzing with raw energy.

'Dave, anything important I want to know about it. And fast. Any questions? No? Right, let's get moving.'

Detectives shuffled back their chairs and rose to their feet. Peter Hunt approached Sam and said the press release had gone out. Local radio and one of the regional TV news stations wanted an interview and could be at the office within 10 minutes.

Sam agreed. She wanted to get her message into the public domain as quickly as possible.

She nipped into the toilets and checked her make-up. She liked to feel feminine, even in the male-dominated environment of Senior Investigating Officers.

Sam did three local radio interviews, two over the telephone and one in her office with a reporter, and a piece to camera for TV outside in the open air. There was nothing difficult about these interviews. As she expected, everyone asked if the attacks were linked and Sam responded self-assuredly that she was keeping an open mind, that it was too early to make the connection, although the fact they had occurred in the victims' homes was some cause for concern.

She asked everybody to be extra vigilant about the security of their houses and urged people with any information or suspicions to contact the police. Sam stressed that it was always best to remove keys from the door locks. She didn't want intruders getting into homes by breaking the glass in a door and reaching through for a key carelessly left in the lock.

He nodded at his Roberts radio and acknowledged that Sam Parker sounded good, but now wasn't the time to dwell or allow himself to be distracted. Buttoning up his coat, he conceded the interview signalled the end of getting in by breaking windows, but he had expected that. Women would be extra vigilant now. They would report broken windows and have them fixed immediately or, even worse, allow the police to hide in their houses, catching him when he returned.

He was well aware he didn't have the nerve to approach a woman in public, control her and the situation, and make her compliant. He had to apply his mind to another way of getting in.

Strolling around the Gull Estate, hands thrust deep into the pockets of the blue reefer coat, cheeks red and tingling, the fleece-lined beanie pulled tight over his ears, his eyes searched for anything that might spark up an idea. The heavy air hadn't dampened his mood and the eerie quiet of the frost-covered streets allowed his mind to process the images he could see.

The white trees, stiffened plants, and frost-covered lawns took him back to winter walks with his dad and his right hand involuntary left his pocket as if to take hold of his father's. His eyes glassed over as he remembered snowball fights and sledging. Walks with Dad were designed purely for fun, but now, in this real world of adults, things were different. He would have fun with the girls, but the serious side had to be attended to first: how to get in?

He saw her pushing the buggy towards him, wrapped up in her red woollen coat, her white knuckles and red fingers on the plastic-coated handles, the young child asleep under the blankets. She walked past, eyes down, without any acknowledgement, even though he had gone to school with her for five years. Hannah Fletcher. She wouldn't remember his name.

The coat concealed the contours of her body, but he had seen her in the summer, wearing a short bright lime-green dress, and she was still worth shagging, kid or no kid. He had never considered seeing someone with a child, but it could work. Too young to shout for help, the kid would provide a good bargaining tool. What delights might be on the cards? How far would she go if she thought he would hurt her precious youngster?

Forty minutes after turning off the radio, he was no further forward with a new method of entry. The sun, more a cape gooseberry than a summer burning orange, was having as much effect on the ground frost as it was on his creativity.

God, this estate is vast. How many single women live here? What a playground, your playground, full of playmates. But you need to get into their bedrooms to play.

His eyes darted between the houses, the driveways, the side roads, the wheelie bins, the phone lines, everything and anything, seeking out that Eureka! moment. One spark. Just one.

Looking upwards, he sighed and turned for home, accepting that today wasn't the day. Forcing the issue could lead to life changing, disastrous, consequences. He would content himself with looking at the licences, reading his notebook, and mentally replaying his time with one of them. The walk back would allow him to ponder which one would have the starring role. The high-pitched siren in the distance warmed his core in a way the winter sun couldn't; he knew the police car wasn't coming for him.

Diagonally across the road, a green Vauxhall Corsa pulled on to a driveway and a hint of recognition made him shorten his stride. Shuffling past the car at a pace normally reserved for funeral processions, he read on the rear nearside panel 'Mrs Muck Out'.

He had seen these vehicles on the estate; cleaning ladies, working in people's homes.

Stopping, he bent down on one knee and pretended to fasten his shoelace. The middle-aged woman, wearing a green smock, got out of the car and his Eureka! moment hit him like an ocean wave crashing on to a falling surfer. She approached the plant pot next to the front door, raised it slightly, and pulled something from underneath. She opened the front door and his breath visibly burst into the air, his hands shaking. Could it really be this easy? Did people really leave the keys to their homes under plant pots in this day and age? Were they so blasé, so stuck in their ways, that crimes being committed didn't stop them leaving their house keys for their cleaners?

He was too isolated, sticking out like a sirloin steak at a vegetarian wedding. He needed a safe place to watch without appearing suspicious. It was irrelevant who lived there. His only concern, the only information he needed, was whether the cleaner replaced the key under the plant pot. He had no idea how long he would have to wait but there was no alternative. An empty bus stop may not be ideal, but at least it provided a reason for his prolonged presence should any prying eyes be watching.

Sixty-five freezing minutes later she left the house. He saw her lock the door and bend down next to the plant pot.

The plan was simple; follow the cleaners and see which houses they went to. His previously compiled and comprehensive list of the names and addresses of single women on the estates would need to be cross-referenced against those the cleaners visited. It would take a lot of time and effort, but the rewards...

He accepted this method would seriously reduce the amount of potential lovers, especially when he eliminated the houses that had alarms fitted, but it would increase his chances of avoiding detection. And that was paramount.

Power-walking through the streets to get the blood circulating, his surveillance mission in the cold had reaped enormous dividends.

What was it his dad used to say?

Always find time to wander, son. It clears the mind and lets the ideas grow.

His mind was his true playground, not this estate. His mind was where he carefully nurtured and tended, a vigneron growing ideas instead of vines. Perhaps he grew more in his mind than in his allotment?

That phrase – 'playmates' – flew into his thoughts. What a great word, just like those models in the Playboy magazines. Looking up, he smiled, hearing Louis Armstrong serenading the visions of his own past playmates.

CHAPTER FOURTEEN

SAM SUGGESTED a cup of tea in the canteen.

Alone at a white Formica-topped table Ed shook his head, bewilderment spreading across his face. Gone was the permanent blue haze of cigarette smoke, a feature of those 70s canteens. Gone were the corned beef or steak pies, gammon steaks and roasts, all served with mash or chips or a combination of both. These days it was like stumbling into a nutritionist convention… printed menus detailing how many calories were in each minuscule portion, herbal teas, and low fat yogurts.

That was the by-product of allowing police support staff to stop supporting and start taking over. What percentage of staff were now non-sworn police officers?

Was it any wonder the majority of detectives went off site to buy food from local bakeries, butchers, and fish and chip shops? They mocked the food of the desk jockeys. They mocked their contribution.

Sam returned with two cups of tea and two oat bars.

'No thanks,' Ed said, as Sam passed him a cereal bar. 'I like to stay fit, but there are some things I draw the line at.'

Sam laughed as she bit into the snack, putting the one Ed had refused into her handbag. He really was a dinosaur.

She broke the silence. 'We need a way to flush him out.'

'You know as well as I do that the best way to do that is for one of our victims to agree to his request for a meet,' Ed said.

Sam nodded, chewing in slow motion. He was out there, somewhere. They just needed to catch him. Fast.

At Sam's suggestion, Ed found himself walking out of the police station towards her car. A drive around the Gull and Conifer estate might explain why these particular victims, in their particular houses, had been selected. Did the houses back on to fields? Were they close to other properties or were they a little distant from their neighbours? Did they have large hedges, giving a degree of 'cover' from passers-by? Did they have a back garden gate, a fence, anything which would make it difficult for witnesses to see? Were they close to a main road along which their man could quickly travel?

In the car park they bumped into PC Louise Smith.

'Hi Louise,' Sam said, smiling broadly. 'How's things?'

'Good. Just coming in for a meeting with Force Intelligence. One of our busy burglars is getting released next week.'

'That's the spirit,' Ed said. 'Get the shite back inside as soon as, before they ruin your crime figures.'

'Yeah, something like that,' Louise smiled, her hair blowing in the wind. 'See you later. Got to dash.'

'I'll give you a ring. Sort out that drink,' Sam shouted.

Louise, who was already at the door, waved her arm in acknowledgement.

'Is Dave Johnson still seeing her?' Ed asked.

'Think so.'

'He needs to watch himself. Her ex-husband's an odd fucker.'

'Really?'

'Quick with the verbals. Bit of a bully by all accounts.'

'She never mentioned it to me.'

Ed opened the passenger door of Sam's recently purchased, bright blue Audi A5 Quattro Sport and lowered himself on to the white leather sports seat. The smell of new leather filled the interior and there wasn't a speck of debris on the black carpet or the factory-fitted mats.

As the engine growled into life, Sam adjusted the heating controls and switched on the electrically heated seats. She felt comfortable cocooned in the cabin of this car.

'Good girl, Louise,' Ed said.

'Should have been promoted years ago, but she's not interested.'

'Bonny girl too… Nice car, Sam. What size engine's in this?'

Happy to drive around in his VW Golf these days, he had in years gone by driven powerful German cars: big BMWs, large Mercs, and an old Porsche or two.

'Four point two V8,' Sam told him as she checked her mirror.

'I'm impressed,' Ed said, meaning it. 'A nice girl like you being a petrol head.'

Sam accelerated away and Ed instinctively grabbed the interior door arm. They both laughed, releasing the tension the investigation was causing.

Too often they found themselves staring into the abyss of human depravity and needed a laugh. Black humour had always played its part in the police.

They had to blow off steam.

When Sam's interview was broadcast on one of the local radio stations through the Audi's Bang and Olufsen speakers, the laughing stopped, both listening intently. It was time to get serious again.

Ten minutes later they were travelling around the estates, visiting the victims' houses in turn.

Ed stared out of the passenger window at the vast spread of suburbia. 'Christ, look at all these houses. Two hundred years ago this town was nothing more than a fishing village around a natural harbour.

'In my time it's expanded beyond all recognition. Houses…the marina…new roads everywhere. Once again we're looking for the proverbial needle in a haystack.'

'Aren't we always?' Sam said, keeping her eyes ahead.

'And failure is not an option.'

Ed turned to face her. 'Yep. Trevor Stewart made that abundantly clear.'

'And as ever, the buck stops with me,' Sam grimaced.

'Pressures of rank. Think of the pension,' Ed smiled.

There was nothing obvious to suggest the location of the properties was paramount in the rapist's selection process.

The loud, ticking clock was approaching 4pm when Dave Johnson walked into Sam's office.

'In the last 25 minutes we've had calls from two women on the Gull Estate. Each has recently had a window broken and both of them live alone.'

'Shit,' said Sam quietly. 'We were right. Any more details Dave?'

'I've sent a crew to each house. Kirsty Sneddon had her window re-glazed that same night. Emily Sharpe had her window repaired the day after.'

'Ages?' Ed asked.

'Can't remember off the top of my head, but early to mid-20s. I'll know more once the detectives get back to me.'

'Keep us posted. Thanks,' Sam said.

Ed was first to break the silence.

'Two more broken windows. Neither of the women attacked, or you would've expected them to have said something when they called in. Or not called in at all.'

'Yeah, I don't doubt that,' Sam nodded in agreement. 'These latest girls, what are their names again?'

Ed looked at his notes. 'Emily Sharpe. Kirsty Sneddon.'

'I've no doubt neither Kirsty or Emily were raped,' Sam said.

Pausing, she leaned back in the black leather captain's chair, her weight causing it to recline slightly. Her voice was noticeably quieter when she spoke again.

'What I do think, though, is that we might have two unreported rapes. We may have two very frightened young women out there, and somehow we've got to get a message to them that it is okay to come to us. That we want to help them.'

CHAPTER FIFTEEN

AMBER DALTON WAS STANDING BAREFOOT, slicing fruit on her kitchen bench as the interview with DCI Parker was broadcast over her laptop. The knife narrowly missed her foot as it crashed to the floor. Amber grabbed the bench with both hands, knocking over the small white breakfast bowl. Feeling the sobs welling up from deep inside, she dropped to the floor, back against one of the units, knees tucked under her chin, arms wrapped around her legs. Her chest heaved and shoulders shook as she breathed with jerky gasps. Her hands clenched into tight fists as she let out a howl. Pummelling her head, she was oblivious to the juice from the freshly cut pineapple dripping slowly and rhythmically from the bench on to her blonde hair.

'Worthless! Dirty! Why didn't you fight back? Why did you let him touch you? Let him have you? You're better off dead. Why haven't the police caught him?'

The stinging in her hands stopped her hitting herself and her arms flopped by her sides. She felt no pain on her head, but knew it would come later. She wanted to confide in someone, but who? She had no family in the North East, having moved to take up a new position in local government last October. She had become friends with a couple of girls in the office but wasn't close enough to tell them about 'him'.

Even if they were best friends, she wasn't convinced she would have said anything. She couldn't even face telling her mother. She was dealing with it alone. Alone. Like she was when 'he' got into her home.

In the three weeks since the attack, she had barely left the house, only to the supermarket for essentials and the doctor's surgery. Out at 9am but back in with all the doors and windows locked an hour later.

Under the impression she was depressed, her GP had no idea about the cause; she hadn't disclosed the rape, instead blaming her anxiety on the new job in a new area. Amber had no idea when she would be able to return to work. Her doctor had recently given her another sick note for two weeks, but she couldn't think that far ahead. Getting through each day was all she could focus on at the moment.

The fist of the devil had punched through her body, and turned her inside out. Her world had changed forever. She was now living in a surreal vacuum, surrounded by normality, but not embraced by it. Sleeping during the day, she fidgeted in the armchair all night, every lamp, ceiling and wall light ablaze in every room, ensuring that darkness never invaded her surroundings.

End it, Amber. Just end it.

He knows where you live, what it's like to have you. What if he wants you again?

Was it him on the phone? Has he got your number?

The call from an unknown number had come three days after the rape. No one ever called her apart from her mother; everyone else sent texts or used social network sites.

She remembered staring at the ringing, vibrating phone, her body shaking, biting her bottom lip until she drew blood. She knew it was 'him'. She hurled the mobile across the room. The back flew off as it hit the wall, narrowly missing the TV, and the battery skidded across the floor. It was still there, mocking her to pick it up and put the battery back in.

She knew nothing about 'him' other than he got into her home, carried a knife, wore a mask and raped her.

Her routine of walking in well-lit streets, sticking to

populated areas at night, using licensed taxis, never having one night stands… none of it had protected her in the one place she should have been safest.

———

Terry Crowther didn't work Mondays. It was the quietest night of the week in the world of pizza deliveries. Crushing the white polystyrene chip tray, he threw it on to the kitchen bench and walked into the bedroom to search for his swimming trunks.

Swimming had become an escape from the taunts; most of the bullies couldn't swim. Now, of course, it wasn't just about the swimming. It provided the opportunity to ogle women wearing not very much.

If his luck was in, and it had to change sometime, he might find one who didn't have a pound coin for a locker. If he was really lucky, and she put her clothes in without locking it, he might get the chance to steal a pair of knickers.

———

Duncan Todd was out of work again. He had been for a run around the Conifers Estate that morning before returning home and watching mindless daytime TV. He didn't run for the pleasure. He ran to maintain his stamina so he could play football on a Sunday morning. Not that he played yesterday morning. He was too tired. He telephoned the coach and told him he was ill, but in reality, he was shattered.

After his run he sat through brain-numbing chat shows for almost two hours before deciding the Internet and porn sites would make better viewing.

Danielle had caught him one afternoon watching porn and gone ballistic. Now he could watch what the hell he wanted without fear of being interrupted. Knowing where Danielle lived was great news, not that there any likelihood of them getting back together. She had made that abundantly clear, but he still harboured hope.

On Saturday night he had seen the pizza delivery guy at her door. Hiding in a doorway under the cover of darkness, he had watched her in those tight shorts chatting to him, no doubt flirting with him, giving him the 'come on'. 'Slag,' he had said to himself. 'You'll fuckin' get yours.'

When he ran past her house in the early hours of that Sunday morning, the house was in darkness.

Ed and Sam knew the 7pm debrief would take about an hour and a half. The numerous new lines of inquiry meant all the detectives would have a lot to contribute, each officer being asked to outline what they had done, what information they had gleaned. They would all play their part in piecing together the overall picture. Teamwork would bring them a result.

Dave Johnson had already started writing on the whiteboard with a black marker. The board was a focal point, a visual reference showing the names and addresses of the women who had been raped, as well as those who had their windows broken. Alongside each name was a photograph. The police photographic department had quickly printed the digital images of Danielle Banks, Kelly Jones, Kirsty Sneddon, Lauren Storey, Natalie Robson, and Emily Sharpe.

'Okay,' Sam shouted, standing next to the whiteboard. 'Let's get started. Six young women, all living alone.'

Seeing the quizzical faces on some of the assembled detectives, she continued without pausing. 'You heard me. Six! Another two have come forward reporting broken windows. Neither was attacked.'

She moved across the whiteboard pointing at each picture individually, naming the women as she did so.

'They are all very similar in age, all in their 20s, ages ranging from 22 to 26. While they're all white, they're not similar in appearance. Our rapist is not attacking a group of women who look alike, so we can probably rule out that he's attacking women who remind him of a previous girlfriend.

Six girls: two blondes, three brunettes, and a redhead, heights ranging from Lauren, who is 5'3', to Danielle at 5'9'. Natalie wore glasses, the others didn't. These girls were targeted not because they had any physical similarities. They were targeted because they were in their mid-20s and because they lived alone.'

She sat on a desk at the front of the room and took a sip from a bottle of sparkling water.

'I believe we may have at least two other rape victims out there. Finding them is now a major line of inquiry. Tomorrow, I'll front another media appeal. This time I'm going to talk in a very general way about the crime of rape itself.'

She planned to talk about the effect rape has on its victims and how the police used officers who were specially trained in the investigation of sexual offences to interview them. She would say how some women found it difficult to report such a hateful crime to the police, but that without the bravery of these victims, the offender would never be caught. She would urge victims to find the courage to come forward.

'I've got have another mobile from the Telecomms Department and tomorrow I'll publicise that number. Anyone calling that number will know they will speak to me.'

Exchanges of information began flying around the room.

A seated detective spoke. 'A cricket ball broke Emily's window. She hung on to it. We've got it now. It's been dusted and they've managed to get a partial print. It looks small so it'll probably belongs to a kid or a woman. Emily picked it up off the floor so the print could even be hers. We've taken her prints for elimination.'

Dave Johnson interjected. 'The other victims didn't know how their windows were broken, although Kirsty thought one of the rocks from her rockery had been moved. Maybe that had been used to break her window.'

The sergeant in charge of the house-to-house team was next to speak.

'A Mr Noble lives directly opposite Danielle. He'd been up most of the night in his front room, reading. He got out of bed about 1am and didn't go back until 5.15am. He's adamant he didn't hear any vehicles during the time he was out of bed.'

'Interesting,' said Sam.

The debriefing highlighted none of the young women had had any unusual visitors in the weeks leading up to their attacks. None of them were known to each other. They didn't go to the same sports clubs, pubs or restaurants.

Bev Summers, a detective who had undergone formal training in the investigation of sexual offences, raised her hand and said she had spent the best part of three hours with Danielle at her parents' house.

'One thing she did tell me was that she had a pizza delivered on the night of the attack. The pizza was from Romeo's. The reason I mention it is that Danielle described this guy as a real creep, someone who makes her feel very uncomfortable. That night she shouted 'what are you looking at?' to him.'

Sam stood up. This sounded very interesting.

All eyes were on Bev Summers.

'She also lost a white thong some time ago, and she's now convinced he stole it. He was stood at the kitchen door with a pizza when she went back inside to get her purse. She was about to put some washing into the machine and the washing basket was near the back door. She remembers the thong being in the basket and she's not seen it since.'

Ed spoke up. 'Before we leave tonight, can we telephone each of our victims and ask if they've ever had a pizza delivered to their homes. If they have, ask where they ordered them from.'

Dave was writing it all down. He looked up. 'There are a total of 13 sex offenders living on the Gull and Poplars estate.'

'Let's reduce that number to only include males aged between 17and 31,' said Sam. 'I believe our rapist will attack women approximately five years either side of his own age. The victims range in age from 22 to 26. That, and the fact that he has to climb through windows, suggests he's reasonably young and fit.'

'Okay,' Dave said, glad of any lessening in the workload. He flicked through his notes and continued: 'We've got a load of CCTV footage from local shops, and one private house. They use VHS tapes, which record on a continuous loop, so not only do the tapes get overused and produce pretty poor images, they record over everything every 24 hours. The tapes will only be of any use in the investigation into Danielle's attack.'

'The usual problems,' Sam said.

Dave nodded. 'We've been to the council's CCTV control centre and asked to see all the relevant digital images.'

Seizing CCTV was easy. The skill came in deciding what the parameters would be, and which images, from which camera, should be viewed first. If Sam and Ed didn't give this careful thought, they could find themselves lost in a mountain of CCTV footage which would take weeks, even months, to examine.

Ten minutes after the debriefing, Sam had some startling answers. Romeo's had delivered to them all. Each described the delivery by a man in his early 20s with blond dirty hair, yellow teeth, and all said he would lewdly stare at them.

Emily Sharpe named him as Terry Crowther. She had gone to school with him.

'Let's do some background checks on Terry Crowther tomorrow,' said Sam.

As everyone was leaving, she walked across to Ed. 'Me and Bev are going for a drink. Fancy one?'

'Would love to, but best not. Need to keep the bride happy.'

CHAPTER SIXTEEN

For two hours Terry Crowther swam in the pool. He saw a couple of tanned beauties, wearing their brightly coloured bikinis, but he was beginning to give up hope. From the water he saw three women chatting by the communal lockers, swimsuits on, but still dry. Good looking, in their early 20s, he watched them walk towards him and the pool. He climbed out of the water. His heart stopped for a fraction of a second, and then began beating faster. One of them had left her locker open. With short, quick steps, not wanting to slip over and attract attention, he went straight to it, walked past the open door and grabbed the pair of white knickers from on top of a pink towel. His stride pattern hadn't altered as he continued walking into the gents' toilets.

The soft lacy material excited him and it took all his effort to keep himself under control. Now wasn't the time. He returned to the pool for two reasons; firstly, he needed to identify which of the three women owned the knickers to enhance his future pleasure, and secondly, if he left the pool after them, he would less likely be accused of theft.

He soon discovered 'Lady Luck' was on his side tonight. His prize belonged to the long-haired athletic blonde with a deep golden tan. He committed her image to memory for future use.

Twenty minutes later, he walked through the leisure centre reception area. No one asked him whether he had seen anything suspicious. He skipped out of the building like a schoolboy enjoying a private joke.

———

Sue had cooked Ed a beef stew with oven-crispy dumplings. He was now slumped in his favourite red leather reclining chair, his feet on the stool, eyes closed, allowing the contentment to envelop him, as it always did when he'd had a hot bath and eaten. Flicking through the TV menu, Sue selected a comedy film, more for her benefit than her husband's. He was already snoring. She fought the urge to wake him and ask about his day with Sam Parker.

———

Sam lay in her bath, her thoughts washing over her brain. She really needed to catch this one before he struck again. Debating with herself what to eat, she considered ordering a pizza, but the thought of some sleazy deliveryman looking her up and down put paid to that idea. She opted for one final security check, a tin of soup and an early night.

Her bed was cold these days. It was always cold. No warm body to snuggle up to. An empty bed in an empty house.

———

He had read, listened and watched every piece of media coverage about Danielle. Her name hadn't been mentioned, of course. Only he, the police and those she had privately told about the rape, knew who she was. He felt like he belonged to some sort of secret society, knowing what the world at large would never suspect.

Sitting on his bed, caressing the moleskin notebook, he was certain there was nothing that could lead the police to his door. The first couple of days were nerve-wracking nevertheless. Questions flashed like lightning strikes through his brain, query after query, each shooting into his head before he had the chance to answer the one before. Had someone seen him running? Had he missed a CCTV camera, one that captured his image and could place him outside at the time? Had someone given his name to the police, although there was no rational reason why they should? Had he left his fingerprints when he removed his gloves to put the condom on?

That reminded him he needed to buy more condoms. He hated doing that. He was convinced all the shop assistants were laughing at him, asking themselves, 'who'd go to bed with you?'. Why were they always girls? Maybe he should buy them from machines in pub toilets? No, that would be worse. In a place like the gents in a pub, the laughing could turn into a kicking. Best to put up with public embarrassment. He would get them on Thursday when he went to buy another dark-blue tracksuit. He also needed to buy a new hat and gloves. It would be easier to buy them off the Internet, but that would leave an electronic money trail.

Had he spilt semen when he was putting the condom in the sandwich bag? No! Stop being stupid! Stop panicking. They've got nothing. Calm down.

Altering his position on the bed, he stretched on his back and replayed the police TV interview in his head, visualising the whole thing. That Sam Parker was a real looker. Older than he would normally go for, but he had to concede that she was fit. How much of a man would he be if he were able to get into her bed? That would be something. To make love with, what did they call her? The Senior Investigator, that's it. To make love to the Senior Investigator who was trying to catch him. Letting out a slow, long whistle, enjoying his own building heat, he could almost smell her. He closed his eyes. How good would it be in her bed? What did her bedroom look like? He had no idea how any of the rooms in her house looked.

But he knew where she lived.

CHAPTER SEVENTEEN

Sam announced the number of the dedicated mobile during every media interview. While it wasn't something she would do on all major investigations, she had used this tactic before with good effect. She was hoping for a twofold result: information about the attacker and giving a helpline for rape victims still too fearful to report.

Of course, there was always a chance she would get an abusive call but it had never happened yet.

With the media interviews complete, Sam and Ed travelled to a scheduled 10am meeting with the Crown Prosecution Service to discuss an impending murder trial.

When it was over, Sam suggested they go for a walk around the marina and clear their heads.

'Good idea,' Ed said. 'Listening to that lot in there, it's a bloody miracle we ever get anyone to court. They want a shed load of work doing.'

'We'll just have to get it done then, won't we?'

'Bloody CPS. They should be called the Criminal Protection Society. Christ, these days they want an eye witness, an admission, and bomb-proof forensics. If it's not nailed on, they won't take it to court. I could flaming well prosecute the cases.'

Sam smiled, teasing him and his endless harking back to his so-called golden age.

'You'll remember the days when the police prosecuted their own cases,' she said.

'Bloody right! Much easier then.'

'No independence, though,' Sam reminded him. 'That's what led to so many miscarriages of justice.'

'Yeah, I know, but still. If they had to run around doing all this work, they might think twice. But no, they just give it to us daft buggers, and tell us to get on with it. And you know as well as me, when we've done what they ask, the defence won't even be arsed to look at it.'

'Are you going to stop moaning, you old goat?'

'Well, it's such a bloody waste of time. No wonder we moan about them.'

'And I'm sure they whinge about us.'

'Probably.'

After two tough hours with the CPS, a walk in the fresh sea air would let them refocus on the rapes.

Seaton St George marina was a purpose-built facility containing yacht berths, shops, bars, restaurants, residential flats, and office units. Within walking distance were a cinema and an array of fast food outlets.

Leaning against the railings, looking across the water, Sam and Ed were taking a battering from the wind, which Sam estimated was blowing a steady, strong Force 6 on the Beaufort scale. Yachts of all sizes were in the water, their masts swaying from side to side, the standing wire rigging rattling in unison, a cacophony of sound. The low-flying squawking seagulls, drowned out by the wind and rigging, were today contributing little more than background noise.

'Could you fancy sailing away into the sunset Ed?' Sam asked, having to raise her voice.

'Not me. I got seasick on a pedalo in Kefalonia. You?'

'Couldn't think of anything better, at least back in the day. Leave everything behind. Just you, the sea, and whoever you invite aboard. Your own world, no outside intrusions. Bliss.'

Pausing, she turned her head to Ed. 'I used to sail with Tris.'

'I know.' Ed looked away.

'Yeah. We did quite a few of the Royal Yachting Association courses. Got some qualifications. You know, navigation and things. We went on a few flotilla sailing holidays. Loved it. We both did. Good times.'

Ed thrust his hands into his pockets and pushed his chin into his chest. 'You should think of going again.'

Sam lowered her head, her voice barely audible. 'Yeah… One day.'

Ed stood still, not wanting to break the temporary silence. His tongue licked the walls of his dry mouth. 'You want to talk about it?'

She shook her head, took a deep breath. 'You don't like the water, then?'

'It's not the water,' Ed said. 'It's the motion of the sea I can't cope with. I've done dinghy sailing in the Lakes, body-board surfing in Cornwall. I enjoyed doing those, but I get really sick out at sea. I learned years ago when I went sea fishing. Sick as a dog all day. I can see the appeal, but it's not for me.'

'Pity. It can be so tranquil.'

'Or not, depending on the weather.'

The blood rushed to his face, his head about to explode. 'Sorry.'

Sam closed her eyes, concentrating on the sounds of the boats and the sea and found herself drifting into foreign waters, Tristram scampering across the deck in shorts and a polo shirt.

A quick sniff stopped her eyes glassing over.

'Right. Back to business,' she said, banging the black railing and standing up straight.

'Okay. Well, I admit I'm still not 100% sold on these categorisations you like so much,' Ed said, leaning on the railings, staring down into the water.

'Any reason in particular?'

'It's the whole 'wanting a relationship' thing I can't get my head around. It just seems, well…' His voice trailed off.

Sam's ears were straining to hear each word as he continued.

'I've never told anyone else this, and I would ask that you don't repeat it.'

'Goes without saying,' Sam reassured him, wondering where this was going.

Ed looked down at the water, his words so quiet that Sam bent down, moved her head closer to his.

'My niece was attacked three years ago.'

'Oh Ed. I'm so sorry. I had no idea.'

His right palm wiped both eyes. 'Bloody wind… No reason why you should. It happened in a different force area. She's my brother's daughter. He and his wife divorced years ago and my niece uses her step-father's name.'

'Was she okay? Is she okay now?'

Sam's genuine concern let his words to tumble out, the momentum in his speech getting ever faster.

'She's changed. She's gone from being a confident girl into a recluse. She wasn't raped as such. Dragged into an alley after being repeatedly punched in the face, her jaw broken in the process. He just came up behind her and punched her. Got her into the alley and punched her in the ribs. Told her what he was going to do to her. Luckily two bouncers saved her. Kept him until our lot arrived.'

He drew breath as he raised his head, and when he spoke his words were much more audible.

'I'd have given him a kicking like he'd never known given half a chance.' Ed turned, looking directly into Sam's eyes. 'So tell me, Sam, does that sound like a guy wanting a relationship?'

She took in the hurt and the hatred and chose her words carefully.

'No. But the man you've just described is a totally different kind of person, a different kind of rapist. Ours is using surprise and serious planning. In your niece's case, he ran up and just started hitting her before she knew what was happening. Even the words he used suggests a lot of anger. He doesn't like women. He wants to punish and degrade. He uses unnecessary force to try and satisfy all that rage. Your niece was in the wrong place at the wrong time.'

She pulled up the collar of her coat, and pushed her hands into her pockets. 'Think about it, Ed. Your niece's attacker was an opportunist, ours is a planner. The type who attacked your niece is referred to as 'Anger Retaliatory'. He's a lone wolf, but not a loner. Our guy's a real loner. Ours will undoubtedly be single, perhaps having been around a domineering female. Your niece's attacker may have been married and was probably openly angry with women in general. He was impulsive but ours isn't. There are differences, Ed, both in the style of attacks, and the type of personality that commit them.'

Ed considered what Sam had said, listing the differences he now saw with clear eyes.

'He did live with someone,' Ed said. 'He was the life and soul according to his barrister. It's just hard to get your head around the fact that according to you, some want a relationship. Jesus. They're still all bastards. Sick bastards, whatever tag you hang on them '

Sam held his eyes. 'As a woman, I know what I would do with them, but as a cop, I have to put that emotion to one side, just as you do Ed. Just as we all do.'

She paused and allowed her hand to lightly touch his forearm.

'Ed, I really hope your niece comes through this. There's lots of counselling out there. Some of it's very good.'

'Thanks.' Ed straightened, rubbing his hands together. 'In some way these girls are linked. They don't know each other, so the rapist is the common denominator. It's him who links them all together. What is it that he knows about them? How does he know it? If we find the link, we find him. It's that simple, Sam. Find the link, catch the bastard.'

'That's why I'm keen to hear at the debrief what we've turned up on Terry Crowther.'

'Terry Crowther,' Ed repeated slowly. 'Might just be our man.'

Sam took a last look at the grey, churning sea.

'Sometimes we just need to get lucky. And I've always believed you make your own.'

Terry Crowther hadn't woken until almost 11am. As soon as he opened his eyes, he reached under his pillow, smiling as his fingers touched soft lace, remembering every curve of her body.

He rolled on to his side, marvelling once again how something so everyday could provide such an instant hit of satisfaction and relief, the type a smoker feels when he draws on that first cigarette outside the airport after a long-haul flight.

He decided to go for a run. He wasn't at work until 5pm.

Selecting one of his tracksuits, he dressed quickly. His training shoes were by the door, and once they were on his feet, he pulled on a woollen hat. Opening the front door, the cold air attacked his throat as he jogged down the path. He turned right, into the wind, his eyes streaming before he had run 10 metres.

It was colder than he expected, wind chill no doubt playing its part, and it wasn't long before he was wishing he had worn his thicker gloves. Increasing his stride, his feet pounding on the pavement, the jog now a run, he knew it wouldn't be long before he forgot about the weather.

Sam was now carrying two mobiles — her everyday one and the one she described to the media as the 'dedicated SIO phone'. It was programmed with a different ringtone so she knew what it was as soon as it rang. She instinctively hurried towards the row of shops where she hoped the buildings would provide some shelter from the buffeting wind.

A female voice spoke to her and the brief conversation ended with Sam saying that she and Ed would be at the caller's house in 20 minutes.

Sam put the phone back into the pocket of her electric-purple Jaeger pea coat. Her face seemed blank, distant before a hardness hit her eyes.

'That was a woman who thinks her husband might have something to do with the rapes.'

'Let's go then,' Ed said, increasing his stride, walking towards the car.

'I said that we'd be there in 20 minutes. Ed. The call. It was from Jason Stroud's estranged wife.'

CHAPTER EIGHTEEN

ED STOPPED WALKING and whipped his head around to face Sam. 'You're joking.'

'Wish I was. That call's the last thing we need.'

'Jesus,' said Ed, shaking his head.

They continued to Ed's car without speaking.

'Where to then?' Ed asked as he clicked the remote and opened the Golf's doors.

'24 Dundee Street.'

'Well at least that's the opposite side of town to the Gull and Conifer estates,' Ed said with relief in his voice.

'As I said, they're estranged. They don't live together. She moved out of the marital home about five months ago. Jason Stroud lives on Alnwick Road. He lives on the Gull estate.'

'Shit. Why does she think it's him? That's one hell of an accusation.'

'Said she'd give us her reasons when we get there. Wants to do it in person. Wouldn't do it on the phone.'

'Jesus,' Ed said, his thoughts flying around like a scrap of paper caught in a gale. How would they play this? How would it pan out? A cop? A cop he knew, albeit not very well. He recalled police officers being convicted of rape, but he had never worked with them. Could Jason really be the bastard they were looking for? No way. Not a chance.

'He's too shy. He hasn't got it in him,' Ed said, his voice quickening with every word. 'I often wondered how he got through his two-year probation. He's not confrontational. Bloody hell, Sam, he's not a rapist. He hasn't got the bottle. Break into their houses wearing a mask, and then rape them? Jason? It just doesn't fit.'

'Think about it,' Sam said. 'That shyness would fit the 'Power Reassurance' profile.'

'Oh, come on, Sam. That doesn't mean he's the one.'

'I agree, but we need to keep an open mind and see what she has to say. Treat this information no differently to any other piece. The fact that he's a cop, and a cop we know, shouldn't cloud our judgement.'

Ed scowled, hands tight on the steering wheel.

'Yeah, you're right. And it won't. But I cannot stomach the thought that this bastard could be one of us. I detest bent cops. They're far worse than criminals as far as I'm concerned. We've both seen more bent cops than we'd have liked. Jesus, I don't want this bastard to be a cop.'

His plan for this morning was simple: identify as many houses as possible where the 'Mrs Muck Out' cleaning ladies visited. He had already seen two of the green Vauxhall Corsas on the estate. Tracking them on foot wasn't going to be easy, but if he followed their general direction, he knew once they were at a house, he would have about an hour to find them. This wasn't an exercise he would complete today. It might take weeks, but time wasn't an issue. Time invested in finding a girlfriend was time well spent.

Assuming the cleaners followed the same routine, he had no interest in the houses they went to after lunch. He needed sufficient time to take the key, get it copied, and replace it. He didn't want to be replacing keys when the schools turned out.

There may still be problems once he had 'borrowed' a key, some unforeseen reason why he couldn't get a copy. Would the key cutter ask for an address? A utility bill as ID? It was good practice to challenge every theory. Challenging, chess-like, each move, be it in the planning or the execution phase, kept him out of prison.

When he had mentally wrestled with how to get the used condoms out of their houses without spilling any of the contents, it had taken a number of false starts before he had come up with the idea of taking a sandwich bag with him. He would put the condom in the bag as soon as he had removed it.

Taking that move to its next logical step, he needed a prepared script to explain the sandwich bag in his pocket in the unlikely event of him being stopped and searched by the police. Trying to think of something to say on the spot would prove disastrous. And lying was impossible, resulting in a tongue-tied stutter, saying whatever came into his head. He couldn't do it at school, and he certainly couldn't do it with his mother.

He repeated the words, which now flowed as easily as a childhood nursery rhyme.

'I picked it up off the street rather than leave it for a child to discover in the morning. We don't want children picking it up. Perhaps throwing it at another kid. Just as well I had the sandwich bag. Disgusting people, throwing used condoms on the streets. The bag? Oh I put my unwrapped energy bar in that before I leave home for my run. I find it easier to open the sandwich bag with my gloves on than I do trying to open the wrapper with them on'

'Fail to plan equals plan to fail' was a sentence continually shouted by Mr Radford, a frightening disciplinarian of a man, whenever someone forgot their homework. Perhaps this teacher would be pleased to know that at least one former pupil applied his maxim so often.

What made the plan around the key so brilliant was that Sam, during her radio appeal, told people not to leave theirs inside the door. Thanks to her, any key he got cut would enter the lock with no resistance from one on the other side. She had done him a huge favour.

What would be worse than getting a key for a house with the right girl inside, only to find you couldn't open the door because another key was already in the lock? He should thank Sam Parker.

Did she have a cleaner? A rich fucker like her must have one? Could he really get away with 'visiting' her? A thought came into his head that triggered a smile. Maybe he could have some fun with her after all.

Turning a corner, he mentally broke out into song, that song, as he saw one of the Corsas parked on a driveway.

CHAPTER NINETEEN

THEY WALKED up the path of the small pre-war terraced house, which would have a back yard leading on to an alley. Years gone by it would have had an outside toilet, what north-easterners often called the 'netty'.

A woman in her late 20s, with blonde shoulder-length hair, opened the door. Sam took in the tight skinny grey jeans, and the loose fitting pale green V-necked cashmere sweater.

Celine Stroud greeted them. 'Hi. Come on in.'

The tiny square hall led straight into a cosy lounge, the walls of which were painted off-white, 'Old English' white was how some of the motor trade referred to it. Fresh cream carnations in a vase were the only distraction on the windowsill and the wall-mounted flat-screen Sony TV allowed sufficient floor space for a pair of dark brown two-seater leather settees. On top of a circular, red Chinese rug stood a square, mahogany occasional table. The room looked newly decorated and the warmth from the gas fire was a welcome relief from the weather outside.

Celine ushered them to a seat. They declined the offer of a hot drink.

Sam introduced herself and Ed. 'How long have you lived here?'

'Oh, it'll be five or six months now.'

Celine clasped her hands together, her fingers continually moving and stroking her knuckles. 'Look, I'm not sure where to begin?'

After a slight pause, she went on. 'I saw you on the TV,' nodding towards Sam, 'and I began to wonder about the rapes. You asked if any woman had any information about men they knew.'

'I did,' Sam replied, slowly nodding her head. 'So what is it about Jason?'

'It may be nothing. It's just a thought. Maybe I shouldn't have interfered. I shouldn't have called. You'll think I'm stupid… Perhaps I am stupid. I'm not sure I believe myself.'

Ed spoke softly, sensing this woman's nerves. 'Let us be the judge of whether it's nothing, and we will certainly not think you stupid. We're glad you called.'

'Will you tell Jason I called you?' Celine said, a noticeable tremor in her voice.

Sam leaned forward in her seat. 'Not at the moment, Celine. Do you mind me calling you Celine?'

Celine shook her head.

'Okay, Celine. Please call me Sam. Let's hear what it is you have to say first.'

Sam and Ed would let her speak without interruption. The secret to police interviewing of a witness, any kind of witness, was to let them speak for as long as they wanted without jumping in with questions. Academics called it 'free recall' and studies had found it to be 90% accurate. The more questions the interviewers asked, the less reliable the answers became. Any questions Sam or Ed might have would come later.

Celine took two large breaths and began. 'I left Jason about five months ago. I couldn't stand it any longer. We'd been married for just under five years. Married 18 months after we met. He was lovely then. Very shy, though. I couldn't believe he was a police officer.'

Sam and Ed remained motionless.

'He started coming into the office where I work after an internal theft was reported. I thought he was nice, but if I'd waited for him to ask me out, I would still be waiting. It was me who asked him out. We started going out and I really liked him. He was very attentive, not like my previous boyfriends.'

She stopped. Sam stared at her. Was she dwelling on those times when everything was new? Thinking of how nice Jason was?

'It's okay, Celine. Carry on,' Sam said quietly.

Celine took another deep breath. 'He didn't want to go to pubs and clubs. He preferred to go to the cinema or stay in. He would come to my house. That was rented just like this is. He lived at home with his mother. I got on well with her and when we decided to get married, she was the one who suggested we move in with her. It seemed a good idea. She'd lived in that house since it was built. We would have no mortgage or rent to pay and as she said, once she died the house was Jason's anyway.'

Celine stopped and ran her fingers through her hair. Sam and Ed sat in silence, waiting for her to speak again. 'I wasn't sure whether Jason wanted to live there, but he never went against his mother. It was obvious to me even then that she was quite the matriarchal figure. Once I moved in, I could see how she all but controlled his life. To escape her, Jason would often go upstairs and sit on his computer or play on his Xbox. How many grown men do you know who buy an Xbox?'

Sam and Ed glanced at each other, their faces expressionless. They were too experienced to project 'non-verbal communications'.

'As I said, I got on with his mother, and when she became ill, I helped look after her. She died not long after I moved out. I know that none of this has anything to with why I called you. I'm just trying to give you an idea of what my life with Jason was like. I was Jason's first and only girlfriend. He wasn't my first sexual partner, and one of my mistakes was telling him that. I told him shortly after we married. I didn't want to lie to him, although on reflection, I should have.'

Sam nodded and gave a look that told Celine she understood.

'He would often ask me to describe how he compared to my previous boyfriends. He became more and more insecure in our relationship. Our sex life became a little weird as a result. I was trying to do things that pleased him in a way that I could demonstrate my love for him. He said he wanted to play games. I agreed and at first I enjoyed them, you know, dressing up, a nurse, a policewoman. It just added a bit of spice and it made Jason happy. When his mother was ill, she was always sedated on an evening, so we knew that she wouldn't disturb us.'

Celine's eyes glazed over and she took another a deep breath. 'One night, the last night, he wanted to have sex with me as if I was a stranger. I was a bit unsure but I agreed. I had to lie in our bed with the lights off, pretending to be asleep. He crept into the bedroom and shone a torch at me. He was wearing a mask. I went crazy. It terrified me. I jumped out of bed and turned on the lights. He had pairs of my tights in his hands, obviously to tie me up. I left him the following day. It was too scary, and I dreaded to think what it would have been next. I wasn't going to stay with him any longer to find out. He said that it was just a bit of fun, but he clearly wanted to act out a rape. What sort of fun is that? It was sickening.'

Neither Sam nor Ed showed any emotion or reaction to Celine's last few sentences. They both understood the potential significance of her words, but neither was going to allow Celine the opportunity to share that significance. They had both been on too many investigative wild goose chases over the years, seen too many so-called positive leads take them nowhere. Celine had given them some information, which may or may not prove useful. What she hadn't given was evidence. Still, now was the time to probe further.

Sam moved forward, sitting on the edge of the sofa, reducing the distance between Celine and herself and spoke in a quiet voice. 'Okay, Celine. Ed and I are going to ask you some questions.'

'Do you mind if I smoke?' asked Celine

'It's your house, Celine, feel free,' said Sam. 'You said that Jason's mother, I'm sorry I don't know her name.'

'Nora, Nora Stroud. I'm sorry, I should have said.'

Celine took out a Richmond from the blue packet on the table, lit it with a disposable lighter, and inhaled deeply.

'It's okay. You described Nora as a matriarch. What did you mean by that?'

'She was very bossy. I noticed that the first time I came to visit. Very outspoken. She would talk to him like he was a dog. Have him fetch and carry for her. If there was something on the news which she had an opinion about, she would scream at Jason if his opinion was different. At times she treated him like a small boy.'

The smoke drifted through her nostrils as she spoke.

'He was a detective, Celine. Could he not stand up for himself?'

Celine glared at Sam, her eyebrows arched. 'Did he stand up for himself at work?'

No one spoke and Celine, sensing that she wasn't going to get a reaction, continued, her voice much quieter. 'Like I said, I didn't believe him when we first met in the office and he said he was a policeman. His mother's word was law. He always kowtowed to her, always.'

'How was she with you?'

'Fine. I don't know whether that was because I was a woman, or whether it was because I wasn't her child, but we got on well together.'

'How old was she?'

'Fifty-eight. No age really.'

'What did she die of?' Sam asked sympathetically.

'Cancer,' replied Celine, adjusting her gaze, staring at the floor, inhaling on the cigarette again.

'You said Jason played on the Xbox. What games did he play?'

Celine looked up. 'I don't know. Football ones. Motor racing. Boys' games I suppose.'

'Do you know what websites he went on?'

'Not porn, if that's what you mean. Not that I knew of anyway.'

'The sex games, Celine, how often did you play them?'

'All the time. Well, whenever we had sex. Certainly the last two years of our relationship. He needed the games to help him get it up. Sorry, to get an erection.'

'Are you okay talking like this, Celine, in front of Ed?'

Celine nodded, took one last deep drag from her cigarette and stubbed it out in an ashtray she retrieved from a sliding drawer in the occasional table. 'I hide the ashtray. Trying to give up. I'm okay talking.'

'The last time you role-played, when Jason wore a mask. What game were you expecting to play when he told you to lie in bed and turn off the lights?'

Celine's response was quiet and measured. 'I don't know… I suppose I thought maybe I was going to be asleep in a hotel room, and he was a guest who had come into the wrong room. Something like that. What I wasn't expecting was for him to be a wearing a mask. It totally freaked me out.' Her eyes filled with tears.

Sam looked at Ed, and the quick movement of her eyes told him to ask any questions he felt relevant.

'Celine, what was the colour of the beam on the torch?' Ed asked, his voice quiet and reassuring.

'Red. Why?'

'Had you seen the torch before?'

She shook her head.

'Is he into any sports?'

'Running. He goes jogging a lot.'

Ed nodded at Sam and as Celine lit another Richmond, they stood up.

Sam told her that they would treat the information with confidence, and asked Celine to contact her if she thought of anything else.

Celine led the way out of the living room, back towards the front door. Before she opened it she turned. 'I hope I've not wasted your time,' she said. 'I hope it's not him. It's just the thought of those poor women.'

Sam and Ed walked out of the house. Celine stood by the open door, smoking her cigarette.

Without breaking stride, Ed turned and said: 'Celine. That night. The last night. What was the mask like?'

'Wool. Like a ski mask. You know, the type that has slits in for the eyes.'

CHAPTER TWENTY

An ANONYMOUS CALL reported an unconscious man lying in the toilets of the Jolly Roger, a town-centre pub which, from when it opened its doors at 9am, was favoured by the unemployed drinking cheap, heavily discounted lager and spirits.

Ambling into the pub, two uniformed officers were greeted by curious stares from some customers, utter indifference from others. The licensee, a man of about 50, black hair greased Elvis-style and a stomach born from a 30-year regime of eight pints a day, waddled towards them, back stooped, black trainers pointed outwards. The strain on his shirt from the enormous beer belly had the cops poised, ready to dodge popping buttons flying towards them like bullets leaving a gun.

'Elvis' pointed them towards the gents' toilets where they found two paramedics kneeling down by a man who was sat on the wet, tiled floor, back against the wall.

His speech was slow and deliberate, a combination of the wound to the back of his head, which a medic was treating to stem the flow of blood, and excessive alcohol. Looking at the cuts and swelling to his face, it was obvious that his injuries were the result of an assault, not a fall.

The door flew open and a drunk, firing nose-twitching

smell-waves of rancid body odour and wearing urine-stained trousers, staggered into the toilets. The younger police officer politely asked him to leave.

'I need a fuckin' piss.'

'Fuck off into the disabled one then,' the older cop said, in no mood for a discussion with a drunk at this time of the day.

The younger officer searched the injured man's pockets with his grunted consent, looking for some identification. In his wallet was a picture of an attractive brown-haired female and a debit card in the name of Duncan Todd.

'Do you know who assaulted you, Duncan?' he asked.

'There were two of them. He sent them.'

'Who did?'

'Brian Banks.'

'THE Brian Banks?' said the older officer.

'Yeah.'

'Why would Brian Banks have you beaten up?'

'I punched his daughter.'

'What the fuck do you expect then?'

The older cop walked to the urinal and unzipped his fly, staring at the white porcelain and the blue disinfectant block. 'You want to make a complaint then?'

'No.'

'Thought not.'

───

Dave Johnson walked to his desk, snatched the report from the top of his 'in-tray' and dropped into his seat. He grabbed the pasty from its paper bag and took a large bite, greasy, flaky pastry dropping on to the document. This looks promising, he thought.

Officer's Report
From: DC Stevens, Intelligence Unit
To: Major Incident Room
Subject: Terry Crowther 24 years 104 Amble Drive Gull Estate

Two convictions for theft (shoplifting) of men's clothing four years ago.
One conviction indecent exposure to a 15-year-old girl (Crowther 17 at the time).
Internet Open Source check – Crowther doesn't appear to use social network sites, doesn't shop online, has no loyalty cards.
Local authority confirms his house has four bedrooms, and he is claiming single-occupancy reduction for purposes of council tax.
House is owner-occupied. No outstanding mortgage.

He looked up and took a smaller bite from the beef and vegetable pasty, the stomach-churning hunger of a few seconds ago reduced. He chewed slowly as his eyes returned to the document.

Saeed Jamal is the owner of Romeo's Kebab and Pizza shop. He is Iraqi, and Crowther is the only non-Iraqi to work there.
Crowther is a good employee. He works every night except Monday, and is paid £6.50 per hour + a free 10" pizza or kebab every night.
Crowther drives a white van when he is at work. It has the pizza shop logo on the van sides.
Crowther owns a black Ford Focus. It's about 10 years old. Registered number yet to be confirmed.

Dave Johnson examined the photograph of Crowther attached to the report. A skinny man standing in between two Arab-looking men, taken inside a take-away food shop, presumably Romeo's.

He stared into Crowther's eyes. Is it you, you twat?

He returned to the report.

Crowther was stopped by the police at 4.30am Saturday – three weeks ago. He was out jogging. Uniform found nothing suspicious about him. The stop-check form shows he wasn't searched.

He stood up and slowly brushed the flakes of pastry off his shirt. Who the hell goes running at 4.30 in the morning?

Sam and Ed were silent as they drove away from Celine Stroud's, reflecting on what they had just been told.

Ed was the first to speak. 'Shit... what did you make of that?'

Sam stared ahead at the road and considered her response. She had been asking herself the same question since they walked out of the house. 'What people get up to within their four walls is a matter for them, but I'll never look at him in the same light again. Neither will Celine. He actually wanted to play out a rape fantasy. How sick's that? Makes my skin crawl.'

Sam shuddered. 'That said, just because you play out a rape fantasy, if that was the intended fantasy, doesn't mean that you'll commit a rape. People fantasise about many things. It's why there is such a variety of porn available on the net.'

'But?' Ed said, knowing from her tone that there was more.

'It was some of the other things she said... the domineering mother, limited sexual experience, loner, playing computer games, jogging. Throw all that together with the close geographical location of his house to the victims, the ski mask... even the bloody red-beamed torch. It could be him. He could be the one. And when she spoke about the rape fantasy...' She paused, rubbing her eyes. 'It was like we were listening to a victim.'

'But she's not,' Ed said. 'She's telling us about Jason's fantasy. As you've just said, people fantasise about many things. It's not an indicator of him being a suspect. There's no evidence that points to him as a suspect.'

'There's not,' Sam agreed. 'But what if we'd just got that info about Crowther?'

'I know. I know. We're going to have to look at him. We have no choice. Not with that information.'

'Ed, we may need to make him a TIE.'

The police acronym for 'Trace', 'Interview', and

'Eliminate' was one step down from a suspect. All TIE's were subject to stringent elimination criteria set by the SIO.

Ed nodded, tension in his eyes.

'I think we need to establish whether we can alibi him out in the first instance,' Sam continued. 'Do it in a way that doesn't get out. If the hierarchy believes that we have a cop who might remotely be a suspect, half of them will want him suspended. Professional Standards will definitely want him suspended. You know what they're like. I don't want to see a guy suspended because he played sex games with his wife, even if they are sick.'

'Me neither,' Ed said. 'But nor do we want this bastard, whoever he is, roaming the streets.'

Sam drew breath, buying time, considering her options.

'Okay. Start off by seeing if Jason was working when the attacks were committed. Maybe he was on annual leave. Hopefully he'll have been away one of the weekends with lots of friends and we can move on.'

'Problem with that Sam is if his wife is to be believed, he hasn't got any friends.'

'I know. Bloody hell. Let's just keep this between me and you at the minute. You check whether he was on leave.'

'Yeah, will do.'

Sam gazed out of the passenger window, the passing houses a blur. When she spoke, her voice was barely audible above the hot air rushing out of the vents.

'The other worrying thing is she said he had trouble getting an erection. He needed the games to help.'

'Why's that worrying?'

'Erectile dysfunction, according to studies, often occurs with the 'Power Reassurance' rapist.'

CHAPTER TWENTY-ONE

SITTING WITH DAVE JOHNSON, Sam and Ed listened as he brought them up to speed with what had happened since they left for their meeting with the CPS.

All the victims had been spoken to again and there wasn't anything distinctive about the odour of the rapist, other than he smelled a little sweaty, and without putting words in mouths, none had picked up the smell of curry or spices. They all described him as having a local accent, none of them recognised his voice, and they were all 100% certain that their attacker wasn't a previous boyfriend or anyone they knew socially. Kelly believed the weapon was something like a big penknife.

None of them had any unusual callers in the weeks leading up to the attacks. During his conversations with them, they now remembered that the rapist asked what they liked to do in their spare time, as well as asking if they enjoyed the sex.

Using the parameters Sam had set down, Dave had reduced the number of sex offenders on the Gull Estate from 13 to four and two officers were conducting background checks into them.

It had been confirmed that it was Emily Sharpe's partial fingerprint on the cricket ball.

'We've got a photograph of Terry Crowther and the checks on him are moving along nicely. He looks promising,' Dave said.

'Why?' Sam asked.

Dave handed her the Officer's Report.

'Interesting. Where did we get the photo from?' Sam asked, passing the report to Ed.

'Confirmed as Romeo's. It was on the wall. It shows him with two other workers.'

'Dave, make some copies of the photo and show it to all our victims. I want to make sure that they're all talking about the same guy.'

'Okay,' Dave replied, dragging the word out.

Sam guessed he was questioning this decision. 'Dave, there's no identification issues here. I want to establish if the girls are talking about the same delivery man. That's not going to compromise any future evidence of identification. If Crowther's our man, we're not showing the victims a photograph of a suspect who they could pick out on an identity parade. There won't be a parade. He's wearing a mask. There's no problem showing them a photograph. I want to make damn sure the person delivering their pizzas is Crowther.'

'And finally,' Dave said, trying to ignore the rebuke, 'Duncan Todd's been detained overnight in hospital for observations with a head injury he received during an assault this afternoon in the Jolly Roger pub.'

'And he is?' Ed asked.

'The ex-boyfriend of Danielle Banks. He didn't want to make a complaint, but he told uniform that his two assailants had been sent by her father, Brian Banks.'

'THE Brian Banks?' Ed asked, eyebrows raised.

'The one and only,' Dave replied.

'Enlighten me,' Sam said.

'Brian Banks,' Ed told her, 'is a successful businessman who made his money in the scrap metal business years ago. Still runs his scrap business, although he got into property developing in the late 80s. Now owns over 200 terraced houses. No criminal convictions, but certainly believed to have been involved in drug trafficking over the years. He also owns a big farm on the edge of town and drives numerous high-powered cars. Been married to Donna for best part of 30 years.'

Ed inhaled slowly before continuing.

'I didn't realise he was Danielle's father. He has the normal contacts you'd expect for someone of his background. There are people who'd do anything for a fee or as a favour to him.'

'Would he have Duncan beaten up if he thought he was responsible for raping his daughter?' Sam ventured.

Ed feigned shock before his mouth twisted into a sneer.

'He would have people seriously beaten up if they passed wind in front of his wife. My view? If he really thought Duncan had raped his daughter, he would've had him killed. It would have been slow and it would have been unpleasant.'

Ed pulled his chair closer to the desk, Sam and Dave waiting for the next instalment.

'People have had their fingers chopped off. Fingers forced around a door frame, with the door part open, and then some heavy kicks the door shut. That would be the type of punishment if they stole from him. The mind boggles at what would happen if he found out who raped his daughter. His cock would probably be cut off, gypsy-style punishment.'

'Then we need to find the rapist before he does,' Sam said calmly.

'Oh, I don't know,' Ed answered with a look in eyes. 'Brian Banks would inflict more pain on him than any court of law could ever do.'

Sam held his eyes for a second, trying to read his expression.

'I know that you don't mean that.'

'Maybe,' Ed said. 'But part of me wouldn't mind Brian Banks or his kind getting to the bastard first. Before his barrister starts telling the court what a sad childhood he had, how he was very remorseful, and how it wasn't his fault.'

Barristers. Even in the dictionary you find them between barracuda and bastard.

'Alright, back to the job in hand,' Sam said. 'Instead of talking vigilantism. Dave, this is a long shot, but can you check the systems for any reports of stolen knickers. I'm just thinking of what Danielle said to Bev Summers. About her thong being stolen. Go back two weeks before the first attack.'

'What are you thinking?' Dave asked.

'If he's stealing knickers when he's not committing rape, which is not unheard of, we may just find a witness who saw him stealing some. It's just a thought. Certainly a long shot, but worth a look.'

'Okay. Will do,' Dave said. He got up and walked out of the office.

Sam had a long soak in a deep, hot bath when she got home and was now curled up on a large white leather settee, the collar of her fluffy pink dressing gown turned up. She could do with an early night and the decision had been made for her when she discovered her two trusted police friends had other arrangements; Bev Summers was going food shopping and Louise Smith was taking her widowed mother out for a meal.

The supermarket ready meal – salmon en croute with rice – had served its purpose. Cooking was a joy when Tristram was alive but since he had gone, she just couldn't summon up the motivation. If it took longer to cook than it did to eat, she wasn't interested. The kitchen clock, in need of a new battery, had stopped working weeks ago but there was no need to use it to co-ordinate a meal. The ping of the microwave was all she needed. Perhaps she should start cooking again after all the revelations about horse meat in supermarket food.

A natural history documentary on the TV provided nothing more than background noise. The table lamp cast enough light for her to read the latest copy of 'Yachting Monthly'. She no longer sailed but couldn't resist reading the magazines. That said, on the small occasional table was a paperback 'Left for Dead'. She hadn't got past the opening chapter of this true account of the 1979 Fastnet yacht race disaster. Some things were too raw.

She was so absorbed in the magazine that she jumped when the dedicated SIO phone rang. She recognised the number, but couldn't place it, and there was no list of contacts programmed into the phone. Was it Ed's? Why would he ring this phone?

'Sam Parker.'

Heavy breathing.

Fuck! Is this him? Is the cheeky fucker ringing me?

Sitting bolt upright, the phone shaking in her hand, she took a deep breath, and muted the TV.

'Sam Parker,' she said again, fighting to keep her voice calm.

The breathing was getting louder, more rapid. *Bloody hell - is he wanking?*

Her mind was racing but she chose her words carefully, her voice quiet, inquisitive.

'What are you imagining us doing?'

The use of 'us' was crucial. If this was the rapist, she was trying to reinforce the fantasy of a relationship, of her being a willing participant. She wanted him to speak. Would she recognise his voice? Was it Crowther? Jason?

'Why won't you speak to me? Tell me what you're doing?'

Was that a muffled laugh, or was it her imagination?

Resisting the urge to tell him to go fuck himself, she ended the call.

Kicking off her mule slippers, she sprinted, hit the landing light switch and took the stairs two at a time, only the tips of her toes coming into contact with the carpet. Without turning on any other lights she ran into the front and rear bedrooms, pulled the curtains open and glanced out of the windows.

Where are you, you twisted fuck? Are you watching?

Stumbling as she ran downstairs, she grabbed the handrail. She slid along the kitchen floor in her plain grey woollen socks, grabbed the back door handle and rattled it up and down. Locked. Like a child in a school obstacle race, she turned and sprinted towards the front door. Her legs were burning as she grabbed the handle. Locked. She collapsed on the settee and tried to convince herself that the breathlessness and increased heart rate were caused by the sudden physical activity. The reality was different. The cause was psychological not physical. Did he know where she lived?

Deep breaths got her heart rate under control. She was his bloody puppet. He was pulling her strings.

'I'll get you, arsehole, and we'll see who's pulling the fucking strings then.'

CHAPTER TWENTY-TWO

THAT CALL WAS EXHILARATING. Sitting in the dark, the driver's seat reclined, his trousers around his ankles, he had seen the landing lights go on and envisaged her checking all the doors and windows. Had he frightened her? Would she guess he was outside? He had seen the curtains upstairs being flung open but she was gone in a second. Total control. Talking to a policewoman. Him! Who would have imagined that? And not just any policewoman. He'd been talking to the one trying to catch him. 'Cosmic,' as *'Only Fools'* Rodney would have said.

It was a pity that she had ended the call before he had finished. He would finish at home, in his own time, thinking of her, imagining her playing with him. He leaned his head back. What had she said? 'Imagine what we are doing.'

Christ, she wants it! He took the newspaper off the passenger seat, stared at her photograph and decided there and then to finish what he had started.

Afterwards, he closed his eyes, his whole body tingling, and decided that on Sunday he would take the press cuttings about the latest attack and put them with the others in the teapot buried in his allotment. He would cut out the photo of Sam Parker and keep it at home. It might not be as good as a driving licence but it would do for now; the press photo and the sound of her voice speaking to him would turn him on again when he got home.

Scrolling through the contacts menu of the mobile, he selected a girl and called her. The phone went straight on to her voicemail.

'Hi, it's Danielle. Sorry I can't take your call, but if you leave a message, I'll get back to you.'

Perhaps she had no signal, or maybe she couldn't get to the phone. He might try again later in the week. For now he would satisfy himself with the memory of the phone call to DCI Parker.

Wednesday

Sam was in the office at 7.30am. A sea fret hovered around Seaton St George and the morning had a damp, cold feel to it.

Ed was in the HOLMES room, standing by the tall beige kettle which had just started to boil, the steam mingling with the heat from the radiators.

'Timed to perfection,' Ed said. 'You must have smelled it.'

Sam smiled, but Ed noticed that she seemed pre-occupied.

With a brief nod of the head he said, 'You alright?'

She looked over her shoulder. 'Can I have a quick word in my office?'

Ed followed her, closing the door behind him, knowing on instinct that something was wrong. He repeated his question.

'He rang. Last night. The rapist. He called the dedicated phone.'

'What? Jesus! Are you okay?'

'I'm fine. It felt kind of spooky, but I'm okay, really.'

Her voice was slow and deliberate and her brown eyes, always capable of transmitting messages to those who knew her well enough to read them, were fixed downwards. As she lowered herself into her chair, Ed sat down opposite.

'What did he say?'

'He never spoke. I could hear him breathing, heavy breathing. I think he may have been masturbating.'

'Dirty bastard. We'll get a panic alarm put in your house today. Fuckin' arsehole!'

'No need to fuss, Ed.'

'I'm not fussing. But we're not taking any chances. We don't know what we're dealing with here. We've put them in other girls' houses, so we're definitely putting one in yours.'

'Okay, okay.'

There was little point in arguing. Ed wouldn't let her go home until one was installed. It was nice, she thought, that he was so caring. A true gentleman was Ed. She looked at him and smiled with an expression that a ditched daughter might give to her father, one of gratitude, one that expressed thanks for understanding.

Ed left her sitting in her office, returning in minutes with two mugs of tea, the dash of milk barely altering the tea's colour.

'Thanks,' Sam said , taking the mug. 'Proper builders' tea.'

'Put hairs on your chest.'

Sam thought she could probably stand a teaspoon inside it. Not that she would want to. Teaspoons in CID offices were usually only washed when they reached the point of needing disinfectant.

'Let's crack on,' she said, her hands around the steaming mug.

'Are you sure you're okay?'

'I'm fine. He wants to think he's in charge, that he is pulling the strings. Let him. Soon enough we'll be pulling his strings.'

'I can't wait to wipe the smile of his face... I still cannot get my head around the fact that the fucker rang you. Cheeky twat.'

Ed was still shaking his head as he read the contents of last night's briefing.

Sam glanced at the wall clock as the SIO mobile rang.

'Is it him again?'

She shook her head. 'Different number.'

'Sam Parker.'

A slight pause was followed by a female voice, a voice so quiet it was almost inaudible.

'He raped me too.'

Sam's hands moved at the speed of an experienced casino croupier, pushing the papers around her desk, searching for a pen. She knocked over her mug, and instinctively pushed her chair backwards as a tsunami of tea covered all before it, before the laws of physics kicked in and the tea resembled an incoming tide creeping across the sand.

Mouthing 'thanks', she took a pen out of Ed's large outstretched hand and searched for a dry scrap of paper before scribbling…

ANOTHER VICTIM KEEP EVERYONE OUT OF OFFICE

Speaking only slightly louder than the victim, she said: 'My name is Sam. Can you tell me your name?'

'Amber. Amber Dalton,' the woman whispered.

'Are you alone, Amber?'

'Yes,' came the response, followed by a series of short, rapid, nasal breaths.

'Would you like me to come and see you?'

A short pause. 'Yes. Yes please.'

'When did this happen, Amber?'

'Three weeks ago. Friday.'

'Where do you live, Amber?' Sam asked, keeping reassurance and calm in her tone. 'I'll be there in 10 minutes.'

Sam was wriggling into her coat before the call even ended. Putting the phone in her pocket, she pulled open the door. Ed was waiting. 'Let's go. I'll explain in the car.'

Within minutes they were in the underground police garage, getting into Ed's car, the passenger foot-well strewn with discarded protein bar wrappers.

'It's like a mobile skip in here,' Sam said, shaking her head.

'It's just a few wrappers. Mind you, I'll need to get rid of them before Sue gets in here. She'll have my life if she sees them and thinks I've had people in here when it looks like a shit-tip.'

Amber Dalton hadn't reported the rape for three weeks and Sam had no idea of her mental state. Getting to her was a priority. The investigation was important but the welfare of this new victim was paramount. Sam was acutely aware that she might be the first person Amber had told. If that was the case, Amber had dealt with this alone for three long weeks.

'Another chance for us to stare into the pit of human depravity,' Sam said as she closed the passenger door.

'Where to?'

'Bamburgh Way. The attack was three weeks ago. A Friday. I don't know if she means early hours of Friday, or early hours of Saturday. Probably the Saturday.'

'If that's the case, it's the same night Crowther was stopped in Bamburgh Way at half four. Friday night to her. Saturday morning to us.'

'Exactly. I'll get Dave Johnson to have the uniform cops who checked him spoken to again. We need to know what he was wearing, why he said he was out at that time, the whole works.'

Sam looked at Ed as he drove and pondered the latest piece of information.

'Ed, if Amber was attacked in the early hours, that was the same night Emily Sharpe had her window broken. Emily didn't have her window repaired and yet she wasn't attacked. Amber was his first choice.'

CHAPTER TWENTY-THREE

13 BAMBURGH WAY was a newly built linked terrace house. Probably two bedrooms, Sam thought as she opened the car door. She would visit Amber alone. Ed would knock on a few doors, talking generally about the previous rapes and his search for suspicious people, vehicles or any other information. He wouldn't even mention the attack on Amber.

Opening the wrought iron black garden gate, Sam walked up the path passing a postage stamp-sized lawn surrounded by winter flowering plants. A small two-seat wooden bench, painted pale blue, rested tight against the wall under the front window, the position ideal for enjoying the sun with the garden facing due south.

The front door opened as Sam's outstretched arm, fist clenched, reached out to knock.

'I saw you coming.'

The barefooted-young woman, wearing a baggy washed out grey velour tracksuit, wore no make-up around her misty blue eyes or on her full, plump lips. Doesn't want to look feminine, Sam thought.

Sam followed her into the house, the front door leading straight into the small living room with an open staircase, bay window, and walls painted in a beige emulsion.

'Please sit down,' Amber said, indicating a red reclining leather chair.

Sam spoke quietly, anxious to show as much empathy as she could muster, while her eyes took in the battery of a mobile lying next to the TV, the body of the phone on the floor nearby.

'Amber, I'm so sorry that I have to meet you under these circumstances. Please understand that I will do everything possible to help you. Have you told anyone what happened?'

'No. I have no family here. No close friends.'

Sam was straining to hear, but understood how difficult this must be for Amber. Asking an emotionally and physically tormented victim to speak up wasn't an option.

Amber sat on a small, cream leather cube-shaped pouffe with her hands clasped on her knees. She was hunched and sat much lower than Sam. Was this a sub-conscious choice? Did she consider herself less worthy? Lower self-esteem?

Sam did her best to put Amber at ease, asking what had brought her to the North East from the South West.

'Is my accent that pronounced?'

Amber explained that she moved to Seaton St George from Bristol in November to take up a new job with the local council. Sam listened, nodding, as Amber told her that she was now on the sick with depression, albeit having lied to the doctor about its cause. She hadn't told anyone about the attack.

'Would you tell me about it, Amber?'

Amber slowly nodded.

'Let's have a cup of tea first,' Sam suggested. 'Shall I do it?'

'No. It's okay. I'll do it. But you can help.'

'Good idea.'

The kitchen was small, spotless, and the black mock-granite workbench held few appliances – a kettle, a juicer, and a small black microwave. Next to the cream-coloured Dualit kettle was a small, brushed stainless steel jar, which contained the teabags.

Waiting for the kettle to boil, Sam learned that Amber

was renting the property, deciding whether she liked living and working in the area before committing to a mortgage.

The milky tea she made was a complete contrast to Ed's industrial effort.

'Shall we sit down and have that chat then?'

Amber nodded, and led the way back into the living room.

'Amber, we have a specialised facility called a 'SARC', which stands for Sexual Assault Referral Centre. In there we have medical facilities, a centre manager, and access to rape crisis counsellors. If you like, I can take you there and we can chat. Or we can stay here.'

'I'd prefer to do it here with you for now.'

'That's fine. If you're able, tell me what happened, and then we can take it from there. Take your time. I've got all the time in the world. Is that okay?'

'Yes.'

Amber bowed her head, revealing a flash of black roots around the centre parting of her other otherwise short, thick blonde hair, and stared at the plain cream carpet, the mug of tea by her feet. Sam may have to gently encourage her through the interview but for now, as much as her heart went out to the young woman, she needed her to plunge into that pool of horror and relive that night, together with all the emotions that went with it.

Sam had undergone specialist sexual offences training years ago but she no longer interviewed people. It was years since she had interviewed a victim.

She would arrange for a written statement to be taken from Amber, and Bev Summers, who Sam trusted implicitly, would take it. For now, though, as Amber had called her, it would be Sam who would be first to hear her story.

Amber's right thumb slowly rubbed the top of the ring on her left hand. Her eyes, staring at the gold, didn't lift when she spoke. Her voice was quiet and slow.

'I feel so ashamed. Why did I not fight back? Why did I let him do it to me?'

Sam shuffled as close to the edge of the reclining chair as she dared.

'Amber, none of this is your fault. I can only try and imagine what you must be going through. You've done nothing wrong here. You're the victim.'

Amber didn't look up, but her voice was suddenly louder, quicker. 'I tried to reason with him, begged him not to, but it was no use. I knew what he wanted and I knew it was going to happen. I was too scared to fight back. Then it was just survival.'

She picked up her mug and sipped on the tea. Sam waited for her to speak again, waited for her to dive back into that pool.

Amber stared at the floor again, her voice once more a whisper. 'It was all about survival. I just felt that if I didn't fight back, he'd do it and then he'd leave me alone. I thought if I fought back, he'd kill me. It was horrible. Horrible.'

Her shoulders shook and she let out a howl. Sam moved out of the chair, knelt down, and put her arm around Amber.

Amber sobbed into Sam's shoulder. 'I should have fought. Let him kill me. Anything's better than this. I just gave in.'

Sam paused.

'Amber, we're all different. Victims of rape react in many different ways, but please believe me when I say many of those victims react in the same way you did. I will do everything I can to help you, but I would like you to help me.'

'How?' Amber asked, moving out of the embrace and raising her watery eyes to look at Sam.

'I need your help to catch the man responsible for the attack. I need you to try and remember as many details as you can. You don't need to do that now. I'll arrange for a specially trained female police officer to help you do that. For now I would just like you to tell me in your words what happened, just so I can establish if it's the same man you heard me talking about on the radio. Can you do that for me please?'

Amber nodded, wiped away the tears that were now trickling down her cheeks and moved back on to the pouffe. 'I'll try.'

Sam believed in allowing rape victims to be involved in the investigative decision-making process. She felt it gave them back a degree of power and control, something that had been ripped from them during their ordeal.

Amber recounted the details of the attack without interruption from Sam, who instinctively knew it was the same man. Now it was three rapes in three months. The worrying trend was that the gap between the first and second was much greater than that between the second and third. With his confidence in evading detection increasing, Sam knew he would strike with increasing regularity.

Amber's attack had occurred in the early hours of the Saturday morning. Her window was broken the same Friday night as Emily Sharpe's. The same night the police stopped Terry Crowther.

Her attacker had worn a mask, brandished a knife, and tied her up.

'When he spoke to me… afterwards.' The mug shook in her hand as she took another sip. 'He called me his babe. Can you imagine what that felt like?'

Sam shook her head.

'Disgusting. That's what it was. I just lay there. I couldn't move and I had to listen to him call me that after what he'd done.'

Amber looked upwards and stared at the ceiling in silence. Thirty seconds passed before she looked at Sam. 'At least I can't catch anything, or be pregnant, thank God.'

She saw the questioning look in Sam's eyes.

'He was wearing a condom.'

'How can you be so sure, Amber?'

'I found the wrapper on the floor, just under my bed, about two days after the attack. I've never had a boyfriend since I moved here. It can only have been from him.'

Sam took a deep breath, forcing herself to ask the next question in the same way she had asked all the others, not wanting to betray her investigative excitement, not wanting to portray the importance of such a small item, not wanting to upset Amber if it had been thrown away, and with it, the forensic opportunities a discarded condom wrapper could yield.

'Do you still have the wrapper?'

'It's in the pedal bin which is now in the shed. I had to get the bin out of the house. I couldn't bear to touch the condom, so I used a pair of tongs to pick it up off the floor.'

Sam could have hugged her.

'The tongs are in there as well. There's some other rubbish in the bin, but it'll still be there. I haven't emptied it. I don't want to touch it, not even to put it in the wheelie bin.'

Sam paused. She had two more questions – phone and pizza.

'Amber, did he try to contact your mobile?'

'I'm not sure. Somebody called it. My mother always rings the house phone and I knew it wasn't her number anyway. When it went off, I just threw it against the wall. The battery flew out. The mobile's not been on since.'

'Can you remember when that call was?'

'About three days after. Maybe the Tuesday.'

'Do you ever have pizzas delivered, Amber?'

'Once. I didn't like the look of the pizza man.'

'Which pizza shop did you order from?'

'Romeo's. Do you know the one I mean?'

'I know it,' Sam said, her expression giving nothing away but her thoughts conjuring up images of Terry Crowther. 'What do you mean you didn't like the look of him?'

'Just the way he looked at me. He made me feel uncomfortable. You know?'

A vacant expression crossed Amber's face. She turned her head away from Sam. When she looked back, her mouth was open and her forehead creased. Again she spoke louder and faster.

'Why do you ask? Oh my God. Was it him?'

'Amber, I'm sorry to say, I don't know who it is. What I will say is this: we might not know who he is at the minute, but we'll catch him. You have my personal assurance of that.'

Tears welled in Amber's eyes.

Sam spoke quietly. 'I want you try to remember any

people who have visited your house lately, or who know that you live alone. Tradesmen, people at work, anybody that comes to mind. You don't have to do it now. Just give it some thought, please.'

Sam spent the next 10 minutes explaining how the police investigation would be conducted. Sam would wait and introduce Bev to Amber, a smooth transition from one police officer to the next.

Once Bev was sat down in the house, introductions complete, Sam stood up. Amber jumped up, flung her arms around Sam and hugged her, pulling her tight into her body. Amber was in no hurry to end the embrace. Had she been, she would have seen the tears in Sam's eyes.

Sam walked towards the car and called Dave Johnson. She asked him to arrange the recovery of the pedal bin. The condom wrapper was the investigation's first forensic opportunity and her main concern was to transform that opportunity into a credible piece of scientific evidence.

She would have a lengthy discussion with a forensic scientist. It was vital that the examination was conducted in such a way that swabbing for DNA didn't remove fingerprints or that the lifting of fingerprints didn't damage any DNA. One scientific examination should never be at the expense of another. There were also other costs to consider. The pressure to get a result didn't exempt her from the cold reality of finance. Every penny spent on a major investigation had to be accounted for – number of officers, how much overtime, hire cars, and the rest. Forensic examinations were just a part of the list.

Amber agreed to hand her mobile to the police. Sam wanted it 'interrogated' by an expert for texts, voicemails, and incoming calls.

Ed was leaning on the bonnet of his car, the door-to-door inquiries fruitless. Too many unanswered knocks. Dave Johnson would need to assign the house-to-house team to return after 6pm.

As Sam put her mobile in her pocket, Ed spoke.

'I got a call from Inspector Wright when you were in the

house. Inspector Never as most of the detectives now call him.'

'What did he want?' Sam asked, opening the passenger door and making no effort to hide the irritation in her voice. 'Oh, let me guess. When can he have his staff back?'

'Right on the money. He'd heard the house-to-house was almost done and reckons he needs his lot back. Local resident groups moaning about not seeing their neighbourhood cop.'

Sam's voice was edged with anger.

'It's about time some of those tossers manned up and told their bloody resident associations that some things take priority over anti-social behaviour and dog shit on the pavements.'

She slammed the car door and settled into the seat. 'Well, whatever he's heard, there's more house-to-house to be done round here now. It's the same attacker. He'll have to manage without them for another couple of days. He's paid to manage his resources, so that's what he'll have to do. If he goes higher up the chain to argue for them back, I'll deal with it and him. Inspector Never. Well named. Never right. Never goes above and beyond. Tosser.'

Ed's elbows were on the wheel, his head resting in his hands. Sam's silence indicated he could now start the car.

'Ed, there's so much information, so many victims and broken windows, we need to keep on top of it all. A nice visual timeline will help everyone. Get an analyst into the HOLMES room to pull together a Sequence of Events. Amber was attacked in the early hours of the Saturday morning. Crowther was out and about that night.'

She looked out of the window, her brain spinning with all the information.

When she turned back to face Ed, he caught sight of the fierce determination in her eyes. Had he not seen it, the tone of her voice would have made it just as clear. 'And I want no mention of Amber to anyone. Not a soul. Lay it on thick with Bev Summers and Dave Johnson. Tell them they are the only people who know about this. I don't want it getting out. If it does, I'll be gunning for them. I've already warned them, but

I want you to reinforce it. The CSI supervisor won't say anything. I've warned him as well. If Jason Stroud is our rapist, and I hope to God he's not, then let him believe that Amber hasn't reported.'

'Okay,' Ed agreed.

'And another thing: we need to bring Terry Crowther in, but we've nothing on him. If he sits and refuses to answer any questions, we'll have to let him go. To say that the circumstantial around the theft of Danielle's knickers is thin is an understatement. Other than that, we've got nothing. It's not a crime to deliver pizzas and eye up the customers. It may not be pleasant and he might be a creep, but it's not an offence. It's not against the law to be out jogging in the early hours, either. We need to get something else. One way or the other we need to eliminate him.'

'Or get him charged,' Ed responded, taking one hand off the wheel and rubbing his eye.

'Absolutely. And what about Duncan Todd? Why did Brian Banks, if Todd's to be believed, have him beaten up? Does Banks know something we don't? Let's have someone pay a visit to Todd. Why doesn't he want to make a complaint? Why does he think Brian Banks was behind it?' Sam asked.

'And Jason Stroud. We know he's got a mask.'

Sam stared ahead, thinking through the implications.

'Jason. I can't get him out of my head either. And how's the rapist getting to and from the scene of the attacks? That Mr Noble, opposite Danielle, is adamant that he heard no vehicle. Is he on foot?'

'Could be,' Ed offered. 'Makes sense. On foot you hear police cars, other vehicles. It's the easiest thing in the world to hide behind a wall. Burglars have been doing it for years. And as you said, Terry Crowther was stop-checked jogging the night Amber was raped.'

'Terry Crowther. Back to him again,' Sam said.

'And we've got the local sex offenders to eliminate,' Ed reminded, exhaling loudly as he pulled away from the traffic lights. 'The problem here is if we're not careful, we'll have detectives running around like terriers in a field full of rabbits.'

'That's where we earn our money,' Sam told him. 'Keeping the whole investigation on track.'

The talking stopped. Sam ran a mental checklist through her head, satisfying herself that she hadn't missed anything obvious. She needed to catch this man.

'He's getting more confident, Ed,' she murmured.

'How do you mean?'

'Kirsty had her window broken four months ago. Three months ago he rapes Kelly. He's waited over two months before attacking Amber but only three weeks before raping Danielle. The gap between attacks is decreasing. He's getting more confident.'

CHAPTER TWENTY-FOUR

SAM LEANED against the headrest and closed her eyes. She knew they had to work fast but she was acutely aware that any procedural mistakes would see the offender walk free from court. Everything had to be lawful. It had to pass the scrutiny of barristers, sitting in chambers or court, far removed from the realities of a fast moving investigation. If a judge ordered an acquittal on the grounds of a procedural breach, the only thing Sam, as the SIO, would be able to look forward to was a sideways shunt into an office job, separating those paper clips, or whatever it was some police officers did.

Sam was a woman in a hurry as she strode through the police station, Ed matching her stride for stride, Sam's words as brisk as her walk.

'Let's hope because Amber's attack's not been in the media, he thinks she's not reported. Until today he would have been right. If it's Jason Stroud, he knows she's not reported. We can use it to our advantage, whoever is responsible. If we decide to ask one of the victims to meet up with him, he's less likely to think it's a trap if he thinks she hasn't reported. That means it must be Amber.'

She stopped and Ed instinctively stopped beside her. Sam turned her head and looked into Ed's eyes. 'God, at times I hate this job. What we ask people to do.'

Sam took a deep breath and started walking again. 'So, we keep it out of the media and away from the team until we've exhausted the possibility of a meet.'

In the HOLMES room, Dave Johnson looked up from his computer and told Sam and Ed of the theft of a pair of ladies knickers from the municipal swimming baths on Monday night.

'Get someone down there to view the CCTV. I know they have it on reception,' Ed said.

'Ahead of you. They're on the way there as we speak.'

'Great,' Sam said. 'I know it's a bit of a long shot but keep us posted. Back to the rapes, get an analyst to do a 'sequence of events' with what we know already. I want it to show dates and times of the attacks, and the broken windows, and cross-ref that with Crowther's known movements. Ed and I will prepare an elimination strategy for those we're going to make TIEs. The usual... forensic elimination, followed by elimination by description, then elimination by alibi provided by someone independent, then alibi by family member, and finally alibi by spouse. You know the score, Dave.'

He spent that morning walking around the Gull Estate and watched a 'Mrs Muck Out' cleaner enter three houses. The third house was exactly what he needed. He knew the woman who lived there, older than he would normally go for, probably mid-30s, but single and fit. A bit posh, always wearing suits, always 'well turned out'.

He watched the cleaner leave the house and drive away. It was a big house, not dissimilar to his own. The mock cobbled driveway led to an integrated garage and the green front door, with high green bushes planted down both sides of the drive providing cover from everyone except those directly opposite the house.

He glanced in all directions, satisfying himself that the street was empty of pedestrians, passing cars, and nosey bastards at their windows. He walked up the drive, bent down by the plant pot next to the front door and found the key underneath. He put the key in his right-hand-side trouser pocket and walked away. The theft had taken less than 15 seconds.

Less than two hours later, he was back. The street was still quiet. He rubbed the key clean of any fingerprints with his handkerchief and replaced it under the plant pot.

He headed back towards the footpath confident that no one had seen him. He put his hand inside the inner pocket of his coat and caressed the copy key. His arousal was instantaneous, forcing him to remove his hand from his pocket. He could sort that later.

Getting the key cut had been simplicity itself. Driving to a North Yorkshire market town about 45 miles south of Seaton St George, he was surprised at how many shops copied keys.

He opted for a market stall, which he hoped would make it much more difficult for the police to trace the transaction, if they ever got to the stage. It had been a bonus for him to discover that the town had a market on the High Street every Wednesday.

He would be in no rush to use the key. Certainly not tonight, perhaps not even the weekend.

What he would do was take every opportunity to build a collection of keys, each one providing entry to their homes, another tangible reminder of past or future conquests, each piece of worthless metal now Midas gold. What was more valuable than intimacy guaranteed?

He grinned. The keys would add another dimension to future sessions of self-pleasure as well.

He returned to his car, retrieved a small bunch of flowers, and stood them up against one of the front doors on the Gull Estate. That would give her something to think about.

Sam and Ed stopped talking as Dave Johnson walked into

Sam's office, immaculate as ever. His suits may not have a designer label, but they were always crisp and neat.

'Great long shot. The results of the CCTV at the swimming baths.'

'Tell me,' Sam said, shuffling in her chair.

'Ten minutes after the victim and her friends leave, Terry Crowther walks out. We're checking to see what time he went in.'

Sliding the chair out from underneath the desk, Sam bounced to her feet.

'Brilliant! Well done. Thanks Dave. Keep us posted.'

As Dave walked away, Sam let out a two-second-long 'Yessss' and shook a raised, clenched right fist.

'Now we can lock him up. Theft. Search his house. Shake the tree and see what apples fall out, so to speak. But first let's see if we can flush him out.'

'Go on,' Ed said, with an idea where this was going.

'Let's see if Amber has had a request for a meet. If she has, let's see if we can talk her into going.'

'That's a big ask, Sam.'

'It is, but it's our best chance at the moment. Amber has said she'll help us as much as she can. I don't like asking any more than you do but it could be a game changer.'

'I think you need to be the one to put it to her. Explain how it will work. And tell her there's a huge chance he won't turn up.'

Sam gave Ed the full power of her gaze.

'You think it's too risky? Another long shot? Too much of a long shot this time?'

Ed met her eye, matching the intensity, as he remembered very different days.

'I'll let you into a secret,' he told Sam. 'It worked for me many years ago. Rapist calls up his victim asking for a meet. At the time I didn't think he would turn up, but the bastard did! Can you believe it? Things have changed now, I know. We have a duty of care towards Amber that was unheard of back in the early '80s. What we did then was very much off the cuff. Now you know the hoops we need to jump through.'

Sam's smile was thin and fleeting .

'Tell me later about yours turning up,' she said. 'Sounds fascinating. But what if this one does, Ed? We'll go through all the hoops, of course. If Amber goes for it, we'll have the surveillance team and we'll choose the meeting place.'

She made no effort to contain the enthusiasm in her voice. She leaned across the desk, bent towards Ed. 'If he turns up, we'll have him. We've probably got Crowther on the knickers at the swimming baths. We've possibly got him going to every victim's house with a pizza, but what we don't have is him connected to them in any other way. We can't put him in their houses. The condom wrapper might do that, but we cannot put everything on hold while we wait for the results. We can't put all our eggs in one basket, but if he turns up, we've got him bang to rights. If someone else turns up, we've eliminated Crowther and still got the rapist.'

She walked away from the desk. Ed stood up.

'It's a potential win-win, Ed.'

'Okay. I'll get in touch with the surveillance team. See what they've got on. Let them pick the meeting place. Let them start to plan it. If he goes for it, we'll need to move quickly, before he gets spooked or bottles it. We should tell him to meet within an hour of us sending the text. That way we pressure him into making a decision. The pressure might make him do something he wouldn't normally do.'

Sam nodded, adrenaline spiking and a picture of the trap closing jumping into her mind.

'Sounds good. I like it. You do that. I'll wait for the results of the examination on Amber's phone. If he has contacted it I'll go and see Amber again.'

'Before I go.' Ed's voice was discernibly quieter. 'I've checked Jason Stroud's hours of work over the last four months. He wasn't at work when any of the attacks took place and he wasn't on annual leave, either. We're going to have to speak to him. Obviously you told Celine our conversation with her was in confidence.'

Sam nodded but didn't interrupt.

'We can't speak to Jason until we tell Celine that we'll have to disclose what she's told us,' said Ed.

'Leave it with me,' Sam said. 'I'll contact her. She came to us in the first place with her concerns so hopefully I'll be able to convince her.'

Ed clenched his fists, his forearms rigid. 'The quicker we eliminate people, the faster we'll catch this bastard.'

CHAPTER TWENTY-FIVE

Brian Banks finished work and was in the Golden Eagle by 6pm. The former coaching inn was in a small village a few miles north of the Gull Estate and had a reputation for its real ales.

Banks looked like a country squire in his light brown highly polished brogues and brown-checked Tweed suit. His ruddy complexion, shaved head, barrel chest, and forearms like Popeye, made him an imposing figure. His booming voice dominated any conversation.

The roaring coal fire pumped smoke up the chimney into cold air above the rooftops, wrapping the village in a damp, musky smell, like a newly opened bag of smoky bacon crisps. The old, stained oak wooden bar top, in need of a new coat of varnish, had an array of hand-pulled beers from both large, long-established, breweries and new micro outfits that had been springing up more and more. Each and every ale was kept in top condition by a landlord who really knew the ropes.

The red, flocked wallpaper displayed old black-and-white photographs of the pub, framed in faded gilt, depicting the occasional motor vehicle from a bygone age.

A dozen people, all known to each other but acquaintances rather than friends and bonded together through their common enjoyment of a pint, stood on a patterned carpet so threadbare not even the oldest local could remember its original colour.

Banks asked who wanted what and bought four pints of Theakston's. He passed the drinks around and joined one of the circles of customers.

As soon as there was lull in the conversation he spoke in a low quiet voice, his gaze moving from one face to another. 'Our Danielle's living back at home. Some bastard broke into her house and raped her.'

A gasp went around the group and then questions were quickly fired, each asked out of concern but asked so rapidly not all were answered or even heard.

When did it happen? How's Danielle? Is she coping? Has she reported it to the police? Have they caught him?

'Yes, she's reported it, but no, they haven't caught anyone. It was Saturday night.'

Banks's body had visibly tensed. His sledgehammer hands were white-knuckled fists and the bulging veins in his neck and forehead looked ready to burst.

The low sound of his voice through clenched teeth carried only simmering hatred and menace.

'If I get my hands on the fuckin' twat, he'll wish he hadn't been born. Twat was wearing a fuckin' ski mask! A fuckin' ski mask! Threatened her with a fuckin' knife! I'll fuckin' kill him, kill him if I get my hands on him, but not before I cut his cock off and stick it down his fuckin' throat! I'll rip his eyes out and piss in the fuckin' sockets.'

The group stood, staring open mouthed. It was the doctor among them who spoke, his soothing quiet voice trying to calm Banks. 'How's Danielle coping Brian?'

Banks shook his head as his fury ebbed.

'How does any girl, any woman, cope with it? No physical injuries to repair, but what must be going on in her head? Jesus Christ. Her mother's doing her best for her, but she's devastated as well.'

Raising his voice and a red flush of anger rising again, he said: 'I thought that fuckin' ex-boyfriend of hers might've had something to do with it. He got what was coming to him, but the missus said Danielle knew it wasn't him. Anyway, Todd needed a kickin' for bloody punching her.'

'Walls have ears, Brian. You shouldn't be talking about beating people up,' one of the group warned. 'Not in public.'

Brian Banks took a deep breath and lowered his voice. 'Yeah, point taken. Anyway I've put the word out. Five grand to anyone who tips the twat up. Then he'll be down the yard. I'll fuckin' sort him. Breaking into her house. Believe me, the twat'll pay for what he did to our Danielle.'

He wrapped his lips around his glass and gulped his way through the pint, not taking his mouth away until he had downed the last drop.

The pub had become a library. No one was under any illusions about what would happen if Banks discovered the identity of the rapist before the police did. Everyone sipped their drinks in silence, each imagining what type of burning and crushing equipment was kept in the scrap yard.

Not that Brian Banks's hands would get dirty. He would be in the company of enough law-abiding citizens, people like them, to provide him with a cast-iron alibi.

Bev Summers had collected Amber's mobile phone. The subsequent forensic examination showed four missed calls and 11 texts from the mobile that belonged to the rapist. Same number used to contact the other girls; same number the rapist called when he used the victims' phones in their homes. He hadn't left a voicemail message, but in all the texts he had asked to meet up. The texts were identical.

'Wood like a meet text me time and place if u fancy'

Bev excitedly notified Sam. 'I'm getting the breakdown of when they were sent.'

'Great!' Sam said.

'He's persistent, though,' Bev went on. 'Plenty of texts. Not just one. And four calls.'

'He is, he certainly is,' Sam said, considering his persistence as she headed to see Amber.

She pulled up outside Amber Dalton's house and stepped into the dark, cold February evening. She walked slowly, contemplating what she was about to ask Amber to do.

Sam knew that throughout the investigation Amber would be riding a seismic wave of emotion full of peaks and troughs, a nightmare journey few people would begin to comprehend. Consider the path the rape victim has to walk… reliving the attack in microscopic detail for the interviewing detective; each second broken down into written sentences to formulate a witness statement; staring at every man, wondering if he was the one; the temporary elation when there was an arrest; the relief if there was a charge but a growing sense of anger and injustice if there was none; the questions she would ask about him and his life, not wanting to know the answers, but with an overwhelming compulsion to ask; the sleepless nights wondering whether he would plead guilty at court, saving her from the ordeal of giving evidence; the terror of being cross-examined; the elation on conviction or the utter devastation if the jury foreman said 'not guilty'; whether to reveal the darkness to a future partner and how much detail to tell.

And it's all down to you, you absolute bastard, Sam thought.

She was aware that once in prison he wouldn't get an easy time from his fellow inmates. Sex offenders never did. Walking up the path, part of Sam hoped that he would get attacked every day; if there was any justice, he would be raped, experiencing the violation and its after effects. Like Ed, she harboured thoughts of brutal vigilante justice, but unlike Ed, she would never speak of them.

'Hi Amber,' Sam said, smiling as the door was opened.

'Hi Sam. Come in. Any news?'

'Not exactly,' Sam answered as she followed Amber into the warm living room, a welcome contrast to the cold outside.

Sam once again sat on the red leather reclining chair, but this time Amber sat on a white settee.

'What we do know is that he has sent a text to your phone

asking to meet.'

Sam didn't want to freak Amber out by saying he had sent 11 texts.

'Is that normal?' Amber asked, her voice quivering and hands shaking.

'It's not unheard of, no. Perhaps it's something we could discuss?'

Sam knew that she would have to be very sensitive and pick her words carefully.

'Amber, we don't have many leads at the moment. We have people we are interested in, but nothing concrete.' She paused and took a deep breath. 'Would you agree to meet him? We would be there to look after you, that I can promise. You would be protected. But if he turns up, we've got him.'

Amber's eyes opened wide in shock as the enormity of what was being asked hit home.

'Me? Oh God, I don't know. I don't know if I could.'

Amber shuffled forward and sat on the edge of the sofa. Sam watched the shroud of vulnerability drop over her.

Looking directly at her, Sam spoke in a soft voice. 'Amber I honestly believe that he'll attack again. This maybe the way to catch him, to get him off the streets before any other girls are attacked. I know it's a lot to ask. I'm not sure even I could do it if I was in your shoes. But I'm not in your shoes. I'm in mine. I desperately want to catch him and at the moment, responding to his text and agreeing to meet him might be our best chance. I'm not for one minute guaranteeing that it will work, because it might not. But I think it's worth a go.'

Amber stared at the floor, reached forward and slowly rubbed her calves, allowing Sam's words to sink in. 'What will happen?'

Sam felt a bubble of relief and excitement, a feeling that Amber was going to find the strength to agree.

'We'll select the location, probably a café but somewhere public. We'll have surveillance officers inside and…'

'Will you be there?' Amber interrupted.

Sam stood and moved slowly towards Amber. She sat next to her, leaned forward and took hold of her hand. 'I couldn't be there, Amber. We have to work on the premise that he has seen me on TV. We'll use people unknown to you, and more importantly unknown to him. If you don't know who they are, you'll not look and acknowledge them. We'll have cameras outside. You'll be perfectly safe. We'll arrange a signal for you to give should he approach you. We don't want to be jumping on someone who has just asked you if they can take a spare chair or the sugar bowl.'

Amber laughed out loud and raised her head, flashing her stunning white teeth. The thought of some poor man getting jumped on by the police for asking to borrow the sugar was hilarious. She hadn't laughed for a long time. This was surreal. She felt she was playing centre stage in a police drama, except that this was true, and in the real world things went wrong. She knew that better than most.

'I want to do it, but I'm scared I'll mess it up...' Amber hesitated, turmoil written all over her face. 'But for the sake of other girls, and those he's already attacked...'

There was silence as she paused. Sam was motionless.

Suddenly Amber stood, looked directly at Sam, and nodded.

'I'll do it. I want him caught as much as you do. Probably more. Let's do it. Let's do it as soon as.'

Sam reached out to touch Amber's arm and let her hand rest gently in a wordless 'thank you'.

'Let's go for Friday. That'll give us enough time to set it up. We'll text him from your phone. We'll set up the meet for Friday afternoon, about two o'clock. I'll have people in the place and outside as well.'

Sam stood. 'I'll ring you and tell you where has been chosen. I can't come here while we're doing this. If he sees me, he'll not show up. Once we text him he might start watching your house.'

Amber nodded and placed her hands in the rear pockets of her jeans.

'You'll be followed all the way. You'll never be out of our sight. Trust me.'

'I do,' Amber said, staring into Sam's eyes. 'I do.'

CHAPTER TWENTY-SIX

ED BRIEFED Sam when she returned. 'The surveillance commander's been told it's on for 2pm Friday, and we've got a partial thumb print on the condom wrapper. First it'll be compared to Terry Crowther's prints, then the three on the sex offenders' register.'

'Let's hope that partial is enough to get a match,' Sam said. 'That'll save us putting Amber through the ordeal of going to the meet.'

'Yeah, let's hope so,' Ed agreed.

Both knew a partial fingerprint may be enough to identify an offender but the icing on the cake would be a DNA profile.

'Eleven text messages to Amber's phone,' Sam said. 'Bev pointed out he was persistent but it's the question of why he's persistent that's key. He wasn't persistent with the others.'

'And the answer is?'

'Staring right us!' Sam said, voice rising with excitement. 'He knew the others had reported. He doesn't think she has.'

Ed nodded. 'Could be. Could be. There must be some reason.'

'He might start to think that she's a potential girlfriend,' Sam went on.

'Jesus… One other thing. What's important to him about Tuesdays?' Ed said.

'Meaning?'

'He rang Kelly on the Tuesday after the attack. Amber thought it was a Tuesday, and the examination has confirmed that the call was definitely a Tuesday. Most of the texts were also sent on a Tuesday. We've checked Danielle's phone and that same number called her phone last night.'

'Same night he rang me.'

'Tuesday.'

Sam ran the fingers of both hands through her hair.

'Don't know. Strange. Maybe there's something in his past. Maybe something eventful or memorable happened on a Tuesday in his past. But it might just be something as daft as there's nothing good on the tele on a Tuesday.'

Ed burst out laughing.

'Yeah, that could be right. Imagine all these psychiatrists suggesting this and that in his childhood when in reality it's just a shit night on the bloody box!'

There was nothing more either could do today.

Walking to his car, Ed reflected on the advances in DNA. He could remember a time when DNA was unheard of…. still a twinkle in some scientist's eye.

He turned the CD player up to a volume more suited to a boy racer, the beat and the lyrics of Queen booming out. *It's a Kind of Magic*.

Cocooned in his car, he was Freddie Mercury, the opening words of the song perfectly summing up his latest hunt. The rapist's mortality would prevent his efforts to remain at large.

'Fuck!' Ed shouted, swerving into a supermarket car park. He fumbled for his phone.

'Hi Jeannie. Just calling to wish Jess 'Happy Birthday'.'

Trevor Stewart appeared outside Sam's office, his uniform epaulettes looking like they belonged on a doll, his shoulders filling the doorway.

'How's it going?'

'Good. We're making good progress. A lot further forward than we were on Monday.'

'Pleased to hear it.'

Stewart sat down. 'I know about the phone call, your phone call.'

Shit. Why am I surprised? He's got spies everywhere, thought Sam.

'Are you okay to continue? Perhaps a change of SIO?'

'I'm fine sir. He's rung a number that I put out into the public domain. It's no big deal. I'm fine.'

'Dave Smithies is willing to take over.'

I just bet he is! Your new drinking mate, the DCI who wants my job. I've got sources too.

'I'm fine, sir. It's not a problem. If anything it drives me harder.'

'Well if it becomes a problem, let me know. I've just got your welfare at heart. Just thinking chummy's not likely to ring a bloke is he.'

'He's just as likely to ring Dave as he is me if his motivation is to taunt the ones trying to catch him.'

Trevor Stewart stood up. 'But he's not likely to be fantasising about sex with Dave Smithies, is he? Keep me updated. Anything you need, let me know.'

Sam slouched back in the chair. Now it was her fault the rapist fantasised about her. Stewart was something else. He couldn't get her into bed but he was reminding her that he could do what he wanted with her career. Bastard.

Sam grabbed her coat.

A sudden snow flurry had Sam reaching to turn on the wiper blades. Great. She hated the snow. Hated it at school when the bullies amused themselves throwing snowballs at anyone who wasn't part of their gang; hated her clothes covered in snow; hated red raw cheeks and wet hair; hated it years later when she fell over chasing a burglar in uniform, watching him escape into the arms of a colleague; hated the piss-taking that followed; even hated her one skiing trip with friends from university.

She turned on to her driveway and despite the snowflakes

clustering the headlamps like moths, the powerful beams lit up the front of the house, shining on a bunch of flowers propped up against her front door.

Who buys me flowers? Someone's got the wrong house.

She dashed to the door, snowflakes invading her mouth and coating her hair like the white top of a Mont Blanc pen. The snow was melting as soon as it hit the ground and it would turn into tiny puddles as soon as she got inside.

She grabbed the flowers, the wet paper disintegrating in her fingers, and darted into the hall, the lamp on the timer providing a dim light. Get into the kitchen, Sam. A wet, tiled floor is preferable to a wet carpet.

The panic alarm didn't ease the memory of last night's call. It was bravado telling Ed she would be fine. It was outrage when she told Stewart she was okay.

She placed the flowers on the bench, a smell like freshly cut wet grass rising from them. She hit the switch on the overhead cooker bulb and an arc of light was thrown across the grey slate floor. She bent down and shook her head over the sink. At the same time she pulled off her jacket and threw it underarm, backwards, in the direction of the table.

More bright light as she opened the fridge door and rummaged around for tonight's microwave ready meal. Lasagne? Or more Salmon en Croute? At least she'd be eating by 8.45.

What was that noise? It didn't belong in her kitchen, but her brain couldn't process its origin. She turned away from the fridge and her legs began to shake. Lurching forward, she grabbed the bench for support. Unable to scream, unable to move, she stood rooted to the spot.

She watched open mouthed, her fingers tightening around the edge of the worktop, as a shiny red cricket ball, the light shining on it like an actor on the boards, inched its way along the black granite bench, before dropping to the tiled floor with a dull thud, rolling a few feet before rattling to rest against the leg of a stool.

Grabbing her phone, her hands trembling and fingers

moving at speed, she flashed through the recent calls memory and hit Ed's number.

He answered it on the second ring.

The words erupted from her mouth, panic oozing from her every pore.

'Ed, he knows where I live. He sent me flowers. They were on my front step. He knows where I live. He knows where I live.'

'Slow down, Sam. What flowers? How do you know they are from him?'

'There's a cricket ball inside them. A red, hard cricket ball. I've never had a pizza delivered. He knows where I live. How does he know? I'm next Ed. He's coming for me. I'm next.'

Dropping the phone, Sam let her head fall on to the bench, fingers now clinging so tight to the granite they turned white. She bent down, slowly, unsteadily, and reached for the phone, aware of Ed's distant shouts coming down the connection.

'Sam! Sam!'

'I'm here,' she said quietly.

'Lock the doors. Make sure that everything's okay with the panic alarm. I'm on my way. I'll ring when I'm outside.'

She lurched away from the worktop, chest still heaving, her legs at first moving slowly then, as an athlete out of the blocks, her thighs were pumping like pistons, carrying her to the light switches by the kitchen door. Dazzling white lights leaped into life around the kitchen. The ceiling spotlights, the fluorescents under the wall-mounted units, the cooker and fridge lights, all engulfing the room in a heavenly white, like the spotlight from a police helicopter. Staring at the window, checking it for damage, she stumbled across the tiled floor and slammed the bolt on the inter-connecting door to the garage.

Running around the room, she flung open the doors of every base unit, dropping into the crouch position like a member of a combat unit, looking into each of them, only convinced he wasn't in the room once she had even peered inside the built-in washing machine.

Her self-preservation gene kicked in and she slumped down, pressing her back against the kitchen door. If he was in the house, he would have to come to her. She wouldn't give him the opportunity of leaping out from behind furniture in another room. The panic alarm could wait.

The kitchen was no longer the centre of domesticity; it was her 'panic room', the type normally the preserve of the rich and famous.

Never before had she considered herself a feeble woman but now, sat on the floor, her whole body shaking, teeth chattering, gasping for breath, knees drawn under her chin, arms wrapped around her shins, she craved the security of a man – her man – in the house.

Finally the mobile danced around the floor as it rang and vibrated. She had probably sat there no more than 10 minutes. Staring at the illuminated screen, she heaved a sigh of relief; Ed's name was displayed. Leaping to her feet, she tore open the door, and sprinted into the hallway.

Ed looked into red, glassy, swollen eyes full of terror and relief.

Resisting the urge to throw her arms around him, Sam was speaking before he had crossed the doorway. 'Ed. Ed. Thank you.'

Putting a big, wet arm around her shoulder, he ushered her inside.

Her words left her mouth so fast they sounded like a vinyl record spinning too quickly on a turntable. 'It was the shock. Sorry. I'm sorry. But he's called me on the phone. He's left flowers. How does he know where I live? How Ed? How?'

His arm was pushing lightly at her back, nudging her towards the bright light, which he presumed was the kitchen. What other rooms project such fierce white light?

'Slow down, Sam. It's okay. Calm down. Look, I'll check the house, but I'm sure everything's fine.'

'I'm coming with you,' she said, almost before he had finished speaking.

'That's fine. C'mon. We'll do it together. No worries.'

A search of every room, albeit with Ed feeling slightly

uncomfortable when he checked inside her wardrobes, satisfied them the house was clear and no windows were broken.

Back at the kitchen, Ed took in the open doors, the lights, and the cricket ball, and grasped the enormity of her fear.

CHAPTER TWENTY-SEVEN

'Okay,' Ed said as he closed the fridge door. 'Let's calm down. He's not here. If it was him, he's certainly a cocky little bastard, I'll give him that. But cocky always equates to fuck-up.'

Reassured by Ed's presence, Sam was white-faced but calmer now.

'Let's hope you're right, but it still doesn't answer how he knows where I live. If he is what links the other girls, how am I linked to him? What links him to me?'

Sitting on a stainless-steel high stool with a black sculptured seat, she put her elbows on the centre island and her head in her hands. 'I'm tired. I'm not thinking straight, but the answer must be obvious. How does he know where the single women live? I suppose he could watch the houses, but how long would that take? Had someone been watching me, or my house, I'm sure I'd have noticed.'

'Okay, Sam, let's switch off for now. We'll have clearer heads tomorrow. The key that unlocks the door of this investigation will present itself to us. One key, that's all we need. Or as Freddie might have said, a kind of magic.'

'Freddie? Freddie who?'

'Never mind. Stick the kettle on. I need the loo.'

In the downstairs toilet, he made a quick call, before

heading back to the kitchen. Sitting on a matching stool he said: 'I've spoken to Sue and it's okay for me to stay here tonight.'

It had been far from okay but he couldn't leave Sam. He would face the consequences tomorrow.

'Ed, there's no need, I'll be fine. Really.'

'I'm sure you will, but I'm staying anyway. I'll sleep on your couch, and get some fresh clothes in the morning.'

'I appreciate it. Thanks. He really spooked me. And now he's taking the piss big time, and that's swearing. Do you fancy a drink? Sorry I've got no beer. A glass of wine?'

'So much for the kettle! Yeah, that'll be good. I could do with a drink. Thanks.'

'Red or white?' Sam asked, smiling for the first time since she'd seen the ball.

'Whatever. I'm not really a wine person.'

Sam walked across the kitchen, more reassured by Ed's presence than she was prepared to admit, to her well-stocked thermo-electric wine cooler. The kitchen was large, modern and spotlessly clean. 'Trevor Stewart wanted to replace me with Dave Smithies.'

'What?'

'Said he was looking after my welfare. You know, after the phone call.'

'I was going to say how does he know that, but he's got eyes and ears everywhere. And Smithies used to have responsibility for the guys with the panic alarms.'

'Well, however they found out, between them they want shot of me.'

'They need a sound reason. And they won't get one. Tossers. Anyway, how do you keep this place so clean working the hours you do?' Ed asked.

'Sorry I can't take the credit. I've got a cleaner. She's been today, hence the reason it looks so spotless,' Sam answered, pulling the cork on a bottle of Vosne-Romanee Domain Jean Grivot, a Premier Cru Burgundy. As the cork came out with a satisfying pop, Sam poured a splash into two large Riedel wine glasses. Ideally she should have opened it to allow it to breathe, but tonight had already been far from ideal.

Sam sat on her stool and passed Ed a glass.

He took a small sip.

'That's delicious.'

Raising the glass to eye level, he stared into it, swirling the contents around. 'Not what you'd get in our house, but I could get used to it. What is it?'

Sam explained to him her love affair with Burgundy wine, how she and Tristram had planned to spend a couple of weeks travelling through some of the vineyards in the region, hoping to visit the small commune of La Romanee in the Cotes de Nuits, watching the French world go by while they overindulged in both the red and white wines that had brought the region its reputation. She decided against telling him that this one bottle was in excess of £70, but she drank it because she liked it, not because she wanted to become a wine boor, telling everyone how expensive it was.

'We'd have brought crates of it back with us, created a little bit of Burgundy on the North East Riviera,' Sam said, grinning.

Ed raised his glass again. 'A Gaelic toast. May the saddest day of your future be no worse than the happiest day of your past.'

'I didn't know you had Irish blood in you,' Sam said, eyebrows arched and a smile parting her lips.

'Of course,' he said, holding the palms of his outstretched hands towards the ceiling. 'The Whelans originate from Cork. Great place. I go back every couple of years or so. I'm sure we've family there but I haven't tracked anyone down. Great-great-granddad came over to Liverpool as a young man looking for a better life, like so many of his generation. Never got further than Merseyside. Unbelievably, he became a cop. A uniform Inspector by the time he retired so I'm told.'

'Fascinating. I'd like to go to over and see that area of Ireland at some time.'

'You'll need to learn to drink the black stuff,' Ed warned with a grin. 'I'm not sure you'll get posh wine like this in the pubs I go to, although a roaring fire, a pint of Guinness, and some good 'craic' takes some beating.'

'Sounds wonderful. But we'll not be going anywhere until we sort this job out.'

'We'll catch him,' Ed said, the smile suddenly gone. 'It's only a matter of time. And don't worry about the likes of Smithies.'

Sam studied her wine.

'It's the time that bothers me. How many more rapes do there have to be before we get our hands on him? And you can't stay here every night until we do.'

'Oh, I don't know. Drinking this every night wouldn't be too difficult.'

They both laughed, the mood lightened again but only for a moment.

'We'll get him Sam,' Ed said. 'The bastard's days are numbered.'

It was Ed who burst the short bubble of reflective silence that followed.

'So, where'd you learn all this stuff about rapists?'

'Being a young widow's not easy. I can't just walk into a pub and sit at the end of a bar like you can. Well I could, but then you get all sorts hitting on you, and I can't be bothered with that crap. All my non-job girlfriends are married, so if I go out to a pub with them, their husbands are convinced that I'm looking for a bloke and will therefore lead them astray. And I can't go out with Bev Summers and Louise Smith all the time. You know what it's like, what'll be said at work, they're my friends so that's why they get the best jobs. It's not fair on them.'

Sam took a sip of wine. 'So I stay in. Most of the TV programmes aren't for me. So I read. And listen to music. I've read all sorts of books on the subject. I find them fascinating. There are books written by British profilers and forensic psychologists but the data pool in America is so much bigger than here. And they've been doing it so much longer, so I read them.'

Ed had never really considered Sam's private life but the

snippets about being a widow had let him see very clearly her lonely existence outside the office.

'And what about you?' Sam asked. 'Why did you have the longest career break in history?'

Ed offered up his glass for a refill.

'Seems a lifetime ago now. I was a young detective when I met Sue. You know, living the life. Her father wanted, no, he insisted, insisted I work in his business. That was the deal if I wanted to marry her. Keep his daughter in the lifestyle she was accustomed to. A life a cop couldn't fund, he said.'

'What happened?'

'Stuck it for 10 years. Walked out the day after his funeral. Let his sons get on with it. Rejoined.'

'Any regrets?'

'Yeah. I'd be retired now if I hadn't met her!'

Sam laughed and reached for the bottle.

One further small glass of wine followed and their conversation was filled not by the man they were hunting but by bickering about who they felt were good superintendents, who were not, and when would Sam be ready for the next step, before the overwhelming need to sleep hit them both.

Sam threw a spare duvet and pillow down the stairs for Ed, who insisted he slept on the living room sofa. Both had forgotten to eat, and by the time they remembered, the need for sleep was greater than the need for food. Detectives often fed off nervous energy, invariably eating when they remembered they were hungry, and more importantly, when they had time.

Upstairs in the warmth of her bed, Sam lay in silence. As she closed her eyes, she imagined Ed walking into the room.

Thursday

Sam shuddered as she walked into the kitchen, already showered and dressed, and looked at the flowers on the bench, the ball on the floor.

They left the house together. Sam went straight to the

office. She would arrange for a CSI to attend her home and have the ball forensically examined.

The chances of getting anything off the wet paper around the flowers were almost zero.

Ed stepped through his front door.

'Sleep well, did you?' Sue asked, standing at the bottom of the stairs, hands on hips, head tilted to one side.

'What was I supposed to do? Leave her to get bloody raped.'

'Oh, spare me the dramatics. She can look after herself that one. And anyway, aren't you the police? No uniforms who could have had a cosy night babysitting?'

'You know there are no spare bodies for that.'

Ed moved forward and put his hands on her shoulders. 'I was looking after a colleague. End of. I love you.' He kissed the top of her head.

She shrugged him off and walked into the kitchen. He decided against asking for breakfast.

Lying in bed, arms behind his head, he stared at the ceiling, mentally running through his agenda. Concentration was difficult as he kept replaying the conversation with the detective. Her words, spoken in that sexy, husky voice, would live with him forever. He could imagine them doing many things, many times.

Jumping out of bed, he rushed into the en-suite bathroom, Sam Parker at the forefront of his mind. Staring into the toilet bowl, struggling to urinate, concentrating on her and not his bladder. He needed a trip to buy a new tracksuit and some condoms. Panicking at the thought of buying condoms, his flow of yellow urine spurted out before dripping on to the white toilet seat, the new drops joining the yellow stains from previous weeks. As he splashed cold water over his face, the word 'condom' was bouncing around his head on a pogo stick, screaming and flashing at him, making him retch. The word was mocking him. Why? Think. Think.

Holding on to the sink, staring into the mirror on the vanity unit, he began frantically searching his memory, writhing mental doors open, slamming them shut. His face was burning. His brain was in overdrive.

There was something else. He knew there was something else. Open the correct drawer. Condom. One small word. One small item. What's its significance?

Beads of sweat sprung up on his forehead, like raindrops on a window. He found the correct drawer, and immediately rammed it shut. He refused to believe its message.

Had he burnt the condom wrapper after the attack on Amber? Not remembering wasn't as devastating as not doing. He couldn't remember burning it. Had he just forgotten? Surely he had. Was his memory toying with him? He was too careful. He must have burnt it because the alternative, the message from the mental filing cabinet, was too disastrous to contemplate. He had left it at her house. That was unthinkable and yet… he needed to satisfy himself, to be absolutely sure. He needed to know if she still had it. She hadn't reported to the police, he knew that much. But would she meet him? He had to send her another text. He had to do it today.

CHAPTER TWENTY-EIGHT

ED WALKED into the office and Sam told him they had a meeting with the surveillance commander in two hours.

'This has got to be spot on, Ed. No fuck-ups.'

Ed threw his jacket over the back of a chair and sat down. *Not like Sam to swear. Pressure's on.*

Sam went on. 'As soon as it's sorted I want to go and see Amber and tell her what we need her to do. Then I want to go and see Celine. I also have to speak to Wright and tell him I want that estate flooding with uniform cops on foot and in cars on Friday and Saturday night. If anyone moves, I want them stopped, and at the slightest suspicion, I want them searched.'

Ed smiled. Wright was going to love this. Far from getting his staff back, 'Never' was now going to be told he would have to commit even more resources to the investigation.

'Do you want me to speak to him? You're going to run out of time,' Ed offered.

'Yeah, okay then. Can you tell him to sort out the operational order? Tell him I want to approve it before it's circulated, and I want it spelled out in simple 'Janet and John' language so everyone knows exactly what's expected of them. If the rapist's out and about, I want him caught.'

Ed leaned back in the chair, concentrating on the instructions as Sam continued.

'Terry Crowther? Do we know what he was doing when he was stopped on the day Amber was attacked?'

'Yeah, we've spoken to the two young cops who stopped him. He was out for a jog. Out for a bloody jog! At half four in the morning! Jesus. And they didn't think it was suspicious. Talk about not being able to detect a bad smell. They never searched him. Anyway, he was wearing a black tracksuit and a woollen hat.'

Sam's eyebrows arched. 'A woollen hat? Or maybe a rolled-up ski mask,' she said.

'They didn't think there was anything unusual or suspicious about him, although they did wonder why he wasn't breathing heavy as he said he'd been running for an hour. Not that they thought to ask. Muppets. Talk about coppers' intuition. It's a joke these days with some of them. They asked him why he was out so early in the morning and he told them he was at work at 7am. That's obviously a lie. And before you ask, of course they didn't ask him where he worked.'

Ed shook his head and continued. 'Talk about just going through the motions. Do they want to catch shit bags? You know, too many these days just don't care enough. Makes you wonder why they joined. Pick up their wages… anyway.'

Sam was also frustrated the uniforms hadn't questioned Crowther much more thoroughly, but dwelling on it now wasn't going to change anything.

'Let's think about it,' she said. 'We've enough to lock him up for the theft of the knickers in the swimming baths. We've also enough to lock him up on suspicion of the theft of knickers at Danielle's. And he was out and about when Amber was attacked.'

Sam stood up and paced the room. 'Let's move the surveillance forward. I want it doing today. That way if he's a no show, we can lock Crowther up at teatime when he's going to work.'

She stared out of the window, her back to Ed. 'Whatever

happens, I want him locking up tonight. Get in touch with the surveillance commander. I want that meeting in 30 minutes. Everything else is on hold.'

She turned and sat down. 'We'll concentrate on the surveillance operation and Crowther. Have Jason draw up a suspect interview plan for Crowther.'

'What about Jason? Do we still want him involved?' Ed asked.

'For now let's just stick to the status quo. If we think that needs to be changed later, so be it. If he is our man, I don't want to do anything that'll give him any idea that we know. If he's not, then we've kept a good cop on the investigation.'

Sam walked back to the window, lost for a moment in her own thoughts.

'My view on him has changed, though,' she said, breaking the short silence. 'I'm calling him a good cop, but I don't mean it.'

'What do you mean?' Ed asked.

Sam turned to face him. 'I can't look at him in the same light. He's making my skin crawl. What if it was him on the phone to me?'

'Oh, come on, Sam. It's a bloody fantasy for God's sake.'

Sam leaped forward, banged her fist on the table, and moved her head closer to Ed's. 'A bloody fantasy about rape!'

Ed slid his chair away from the table, stood up, placed his hands on the desk and leaned forward. Their noses were inches apart. 'So, do you want to leave him on the investigation or not?' he asked quietly.

They each held the other's gaze.

Sam sat down, her voice now quiet and controlled. 'He has to stay. If it's him, I want him close. If it's not him, then I don't want to ruin his career. But when this job's sorted, he's off the team.'

'What?' Ed said, shooting up ramrod straight.

'You heard. He's gone. I'm not working with someone who likes to fantasise about rape.'

'The clue's in the name, Sam... fantasise.'

'Yeah, and what else does he fantasise about? He's off, Ed. No argument.'

Ed pointed the palms of both hands at Sam. 'Okay. Okay. But think about what you've just said. That makes you as much of a manipulator as Stewart and Smithies. You're better than that, Sam.'

She dropped her head.

Ed took two steps backwards. 'I need to crack on. I'll speak to Jason about the interview and sort the surveillance commander. Jason's future's down to you.'

―――

Time was against him, but he had to send a text to Amber. Retrieving the mobile from the tea caddy, he quickly typed out the message,

hi amber fancy that meet

He was so preoccupied with the wrapper, his forefinger was touching the 'send button' when his mind lurched back into the present and he remembered the police could probably locate mobiles. Could they find out where a mobile was when it had made a particular call or sent a particular text? If they could, he had almost brought them straight to his door. Dickhead! Careless! Stupid! Prisons are full of stupid people.

If he had left the condom wrapper at Amber's, he needed to do what he could to get it back, or at least be certain she had got rid of it. He had potentially made a mistake. While he could try to rectify that mistake, he couldn't eradicate it. To make another mistake would be a disaster. One gentle press from his index finger on the keypad could have sent him to prison. He needed to calm down, get back into planning mode, and he needed to do it now.

He would drive to another secluded spot before sending the text. He had never called or texted any of the victims from the same place, always making sure wherever he parked, CCTV cameras didn't cover his car. If the police could triangulate the location of the phone, the first thing they would do would be to check for and view any CCTV. He didn't want his car, or indeed himself, captured on a digital image.

He always drove at least 10 miles away from the last CCTV camera that he saw, to make it impossible for the police to put his car on a particular route, heading in a particular direction, and he never speeded. He wasn't going to gift them his car, in a particular area, at a particular time, because he had been stupid enough to get a speeding ticket.

He wouldn't stop the car to send the text, either. He would simply pick up the mobile and press the 'send' button. If he called a victim, he would always park up, not wanting a patrolling police officer pulling him over for using a mobile while he was driving. That would be another disaster. He was careful never to be parked long enough for anyone to see him, let alone later remember him or his car. The only exception was when he parked up outside Sam Parker's home. He would like them to discover that he was outside her house.

He breathed out slowly and reminded himself he was a planner, too clever for the police. Sam Parker might be good, but he knew he was better. He smiled as he wondered how she had slept last night. What had she thought about the flowers? How had she reacted when she saw the cricket ball? Maybe she would become too preoccupied with her own safety to catch him. Perhaps he could have her. The thought quickly aroused him, and not for the first time that week he fantasised about making love to the woman who was hunting him.

Dave Johnson entered her office to find Sam sitting alone and staring at the wall.

'He's just texted Amber asking for a meet. The timing's perfect.'

'What? Great! That's fantastic.'

Sam was out of her seat, pacing the room for the second time in 30 minutes. 'I'll get on to Amber after the meeting with the surveillance commander. The less time I give her, the less time she has to change her mind. Dave, keep this to yourself. Tell whoever opened the text likewise. I want nothing to get out. I mean nothing. You know the score.'

Dave was walking out as Ed and the surveillance commander, a Detective Sergeant, walked in.

'He's just texted Amber for a meet,' Sam told them. 'But before we tell Amber and respond to the text, I need to know your thoughts.'

The surveillance commander, dressed in blue jeans and a light grey crew-necked sweater, was small in stature, unshaven, and in any room would fade into the background. His appearance and physical presence was as memorable as his bland sweater. Sticking out in a crowd wasn't an option for these people.

Sam knew Gary Ross. He was thorough. There were so many variables in any surveillance it was impossible to plan for every eventuality. The skill was to plan for as many as possible.

Ross looked at the piece of paper on his blue clipboard, looked up at Sam and began. 'Okay. We suggest having the meeting in The Little Coffee Shop on Warkworth Drive. It's in a small row of shops on the outskirts of the Gull Estate. Typical shops on a typical estate.'

Sam nodded. She knew the shops. She listened intently to Ross.

'The advantage here is that the shops are covered by CCTV and there's CCTV in the coffee shop itself. Obviously we don't want to tell anyone inside what we're doing, but I know their system is behind the counter and looks into the shop. We'll need Amber to sit at a table in the window.'

'Okay,' Sam said.

Ross continued. 'Suggest a meet time of 2pm. Get Amber to the shop at 1pm, which will give her time to change tables if necessary. We need her in the window seat.'

Sam picked up a pen and started jotting down the instructions.

'We'll park an unmanned van outside the shop. It has

cameras which we can control remotely, and they'll cover the shop door and the window. There's only one door for customers. We'll have someone in the coffee shop, and they'll change regularly. We'll need to know what Amber is wearing.'

Sam wrote 'clothes' and circled it three times in black biro.

'We'll follow her to the coffee shop. Get her to walk there. It's only 20 minutes. If nothing happens, tell her to leave the shop at 2.30pm and walk straight home. We'll follow her. Tell her from the moment she leaves the front door until she walks back into her house, she'll be in the sight of at least one police officer at all times.'

'Okay. She's bound to look for your people,' Sam said.

'I know. Don't worry, we're used to it. We need a pre-arranged signal if he shows. Something simple. Have her wear a scarf. Have her remove it and put it on the table if he shows.'

'I like that, Gary. You seem to have thought of everything. Well done.'

Ross almost smiled. Almost but not quite.

'Let's hope so. It can still go belly-up. We don't really want to carry out the arrest. We'd rather you do that. No point in identifying our people if we can help it.'

'Yeah, I understand that,' Sam said, turning to face Ed. 'Can you fix that up, Ed? Get two of ours to be the arrest team. Shouldn't take any more than that. Make something up. Tell them we're helping Gary's team out on another job. Keep them out of the area, well out of the way, but close enough to respond.'

'No problem,' Ed said.

Sam continued: 'I also want someone from your team in the CCTV control room, Gary. If he is going to show up, there's a good chance he'll be early to check out it's not a set-up. I want that van on plot and someone monitoring the CCTV before we respond to his text. Will your people be going into the coffee shop solo?'

Ross shook his head.

'No, some will be alone but some will go in pairs. Don't

183

worry, they'll look like customers and customers only. Amber won't know who they are.'

'Bless her,' Sam said, her voice suddenly softer. 'She won't even know if he's there. Her safety is paramount, Gary, even if that does mean compromising some of your people as far as identifying them is concerned.'

Ross nodded. 'Understood. If we need to identify ourselves we will, but hopefully it won't come to that. We'll be in the shop from 12.30pm.'

Sam swept a hand through her hair and puffed out her cheeks.

'Let's get cracking, then. There's no room for mistakes. We'll only get one chance at this.'

'Will do.' Ross stood up and walked out of the office.

'Ed, I'll call Amber. Respond to the text at 12.30pm. Gary's people will be on plot by then. Did you manage to get hold of Wright?'

'He's working it up now, but I'll go and check how he's doing.'

'Was Wright alright, or did he kick off?' asked Sam, a mischievous twinkle in her eye.

'Inspector 'Never' did indeed kick off, but he knows he can't win. No doubt he'll go and whinge to somebody.'

'I want the area flooded with cops tomorrow and Saturday night,' Sam said. 'I want them on foot in plain clothes and I want them on pedal bikes and in cars so they can respond to anything that comes in. We can't rely on catching him today, and we can't bank on it being Crowther. We can cancel it if needs be, but let's have it sorted just in case.'

'Yeah, he knows what's required,' Ed said.

Sam was only too aware how many plates they had spinning. She needed to stay focussed and not allow herself to give more credence to one line of inquiry than another. Today could be the day the case was solved or it could be the day that saw them dumped back to square one. The 'square one' scenario would call for some thought around re-motivating the team. If their man was a no show, and if

Crowther turned out to be in the clear, everyone on the inquiry would feel deflated. Sam's job wasn't just about catching the bad guy but keeping everyone motivated when the investigation took a knock-back. No SIO could ever close any serious case without every member of the investigation team giving 100%.

Sam knew the stakes were high and a sense of foreboding overcame her… a niggling feeling that he wouldn't turn up. Was Crowther too good to be true? Would they get any DNA off the condom wrapper? What if, despite all of her plans, he struck again? The last thought caused her to shiver. She knew it was a real possibility. How does he know where they live? How did he discover where she lived? Would he attack her? Sam picked up the receiver on the cream-coloured desk telephone and quickly punched Amber's number on to the big display. Four rings later and Amber's voice said, 'Hello?'

'Hi Amber. It's Sam.'

'Hi Sam. How are you?'

How am I? Sam never ceased to be amazed by the resilience of victims. After everything Amber had been through, here she was asking how Sam was.

'I'm okay, thanks. Amber, there's been a text received on your phone. It looks like it's from him. He wants to meet you. We'd like to do it this afternoon.'

'I thought we were doing it tomorrow,' Amber spluttered.

'We were, but now that he's texted today, we thought 'strike while the iron's hot' so to speak.'

'What time?'

'We need you to leave home at 12.30pm and walk to The Little Coffee Shop on Warkworth Drive. Do you know it?'

'I do,' Amber said. Sam could hear a level of timidity in her voice.

'Are you still okay to do this?'

'Yes. Yes. It's just a shock doing it today.'

'I know. I'm sorry. I'm sorry I'm discussing this on the telephone and not speaking to you in person, but I can't take the risk of him watching your house.'

'I understand, Sam. How will it work? What do I have to do?'

Sam relayed everything that Amber needed to know… wear a scarf; be in the shop for 1pm; sit in the window; take her scarf off and put it on the table if she was approached.

From experience, Sam knew there were so many things that could go wrong on surveillance, and when a victim was involved, the risk only increased. The more instructions you gave them, the more likely they would be to get it wrong.

'Amber, there'll be undercover police officers in the coffee shop, and undercover police officers following you all the way. I promise your safety is paramount. We'll arrange the meeting for 2pm. If he doesn't turn up, leave the shop at 2.30pm. I know that we're asking you to sit in the shop for over an hour, but we need you there early in case he shows. Is that okay?'

'That's fine. I'll be okay. I hope he turns up. I'd like to see his face.'

'Once you take your scarf off, we'll have someone approach you and say 'hello'. They'll address you by name. Your attacker will probably walk away. We'll get him outside. If he doesn't move, we'll take him in the shop. Can you manage that?'

'I think so. Yes.'

Sam admired Amber's courage. She was adding to her ordeal, but hoped that Amber's bravery would be rewarded with a result.

Once again she reflected on what she was asking of this victim. That phrase, 'what a job', flashed through her mind.

'I'll call you at 12.15pm. I need to know what you're wearing to help our undercover team identify you. You won't know who they are but I promise they will be with you every step of the way. Don't look for them. They'll be there.'

'I know, Sam. Thanks.'

'It's us who should be thanking you, Amber. You are a very brave young woman.'

Sam then spoke more slowly and quietly. 'Amber, remember this. You know that we are going to be there. He doesn't know that we're coming. This is a chance for you to control him. Here's your chance to take the control off him.'

'I'll go and get ready. I'll speak to you at 12.15pm.'

Amber put down the receiver and found she was shaking. Could she do this? She had never considered herself brave. But what was the alternative? Sam was right. This was her chance to have control over him. Holding that thought, she started some deep breathing exercises in an effort to control her trembling.

Breathing under control, she went upstairs and pulled open the wardrobe doors. Sam had said she would ring back and ask what she was wearing. What do you wear to face the monster who raped you?

Amber pushed the coat hangers back and forth along the rail, pulling things out, discarding them, throwing them on to the bed. It was too cold for a dress. Should she wear jeans, or leggings and a short skirt? How short? Which top?

She stepped backward, eyes fixed on the clothes still hanging up, sat on the edge of the bed, and lay back, sinking into the pile of garments.

I can't do this. Her hands covered her face. The shaking returned, more violently than it had been downstairs, and she questioned whether she could even leave the house.

CHAPTER TWENTY-NINE

'Everything okay with Amber?' Ed asked as he returned to Sam's office.

'Think so. All ready with the surveillance team?'

'Yeah. They're all deployed now. They're on their way.'

'Arrest team sorted?'

'Yeah, they're deployed too,' Ed said.

'We just have to wait now then.'

'Always the worst.'

Worse than you think, Ed. He's not coming for you.

Dave Johnson came back in and told them he had just spoken to the Fingerprint Bureau. Whoever the fingerprint on the wrapper belonged to, it didn't belong to Terry Crowther or the three sex offenders.

'Bollocks,' Ed said sourly.

Sam, too, couldn't keep the disappointment from her face but said: 'We still go with Crowther. I accept it's a blow that it's not his prints, but there's all the other stuff with him. Let's get him in as planned if the surveillance turns up nothing.'

Queuing to get into the Warkworth Drive shops car park, the driver of the small, white Peugeot van slammed the palms of both hands on to the top of the shiny, worn-smooth steering wheel.

'Bloody dinner time,' he muttered, shaking his head. 'This should have been done at seven. Less planning, more fuck-ups.'

There were at least three cars in front of him looking for parking spaces and the smells of pies, pasties, and fish and chips filled the air.

He looked out of the driver's window and caught sight of the van's signage reflected in the baker's shop window – 'Peterson's Plumbing Services'.

He hated being rushed. It always led to complications.

He needed the van in position. The longer he sat there, the greater the chances of drawing attention to himself, and the van.

A white-haired, overweight elderly woman in a silk headscarf slid into the driver's seat of a parked Nissan Micra and seemed to take an eternity to start the engine. *How long does it take to put your bloody seatbelt on?* The white reversing lights came on, and the car backed out of the space slower than a silkworm with a hangover.

Driving past the vacant space, he stopped sharply and slammed the gear stick into reverse, passers-by turning to stare as the crunching noise reverberating around the car park.

'Shit. Shit.'

He got the angle all wrong and had to drive back out. He inadvertently slipped the clutch and revved too hard.

'Fuckin' hell.'

With blood pressure rising, he put the van back into reverse, and parked between the white lines. It wasn't ideal. He would have liked the van nearer the coffee shop, but with some adjustment of the cameras, it would do. It would have to do. He couldn't wait any longer. The text message would be sent at 12.30pm.

Convinced that he would be able to alter the cameras and get a visual on the coffee shop, Gary Ross slammed the door shut, pulled the hoodie over his head, stuffed his hands into its side pockets, and walked away from the van with his head down.

Amber was running out of time. She stood in her bra and pants, her hands holding a handful of make-up remover cloths covered in the cosmetics she had applied and then removed.

She took a deep breath, dropped the cloths on the floor, jumped into a pair of faded jeans, and grabbed a top off the bed.

She had been standing by the telephone for ten minutes when it rang. Grabbing it from the cradle before its first ring was complete, she told Sam she was wearing a knee-length blue wool overcoat, blue jeans, a red scarf, a blue hat, and a pair of white Karrimor Alaska trekking boots.

She replaced the handset and stood with her back against the front door, her body over heating – a combination of hot radiators, outdoor clothing, and increasing anxiety. She watched the second hand on her wristwatch, each circuit signalling she was a minute nearer to leaving the house.

Fifteen minutes later, a plain-clothes policewoman jumped from the passenger seat of a battered pale-green Citroen as Amber locked her front door and walked through the gate on to the footpath.

The surveillance team preferred old cars, the kind which could be changed regularly and manufactured by companies not usually associated with supplying police vehicles. Driving around in shiny new Fords, Vauxhalls, BMWs and Land Rovers was a sure way of attracting the attention of the career criminals normally the targets for surveillance.

Amber found it impossible to resist looking around, but everything, and everyone, resembled normality... buses and cars travelling along the road and a few hardy souls walking, braving the elements.

She had never really studied people and considered what their lives were like. She may have looked at them, watched them even, but she never thought about them. Like most, Amber was too wrapped up in her own world to consider anyone else's. Today, walking towards a rendezvous with him, followed by invisible police officers, she saw everybody and, for the first time in her life, wondered what was happening in their worlds.

Were they happy? Were they sad? Were they – like her – victims? Were they being slowly defeated by debt or watching onceloving relationships break down? Had they recently lost a loved one? Were they terminally ill?

She turned up the collar of her coat, thrust her hands deeper into her pockets, and fought the urge to power walk. She had 30 minutes to get there, a walk easily completed in 20.

She hadn't seen anyone resembling police officers. She had to trust Sam and accept that they were following her.

The female surveillance operative followed Amber on foot for about 100 yards, speaking carefully into her body-mounted covert radio. Her long brown hair hid the earpiece. The microphone attached to the jumper under her coat was so small it wouldn't be noticed. At worst she would look like she was talking to herself, or into a concealed mobile on voice mode. Her comments would be brief, and within minutes someone else from the team would take over.

She turned left and walked down another street. Amber walked straight ahead, and was picked up by a male officer on foot on the opposite side of the road. Nothing difficult about this surveillance; they knew exactly where Amber was heading. The unknown factor was whether the rapist was following her.

A young woman hurried down a driveway towards the front door, carrier bags pulling at her arms, her fingers stiff and white after being wrapped around the polythene handles in the cold damp air. Amber watched her place the bags on the floor, fumbling for her house key, and tried to remember the daily routine of her life before he broke in. It was useless. Every waking hour she thought of him.

How old was he? How tall? What did he look like? Where did he work? Why did he do it? Why me?

He consumed her thoughts, this animal who was with her for such a short time, but who in that time had shattered her life, breaking her into a thousand pieces, like a barman dropping a beer glass. He used her for his pleasure, or whatever it was he did it for, without a thought for her. She was a piece of meat – nothing to him, not a human being, not the daughter of devoted parents.

But perhaps Sam was right. Maybe this would give her some control back? Shards of glass were not usually put back together but perhaps she could be.

With each step the constant rubbing on her right calf was becoming more and more irritating, and she berated herself for not having the foresight to wear woollen socks.

The cold steel of the carving knife hidden in her boot was causing far more discomfort than she imagined, scratching away at the same patch of smooth skin above her ankle, the scratch becoming a graze, the graze becoming a cut.

A few cuts were a small but worthwhile, price to pay. Nothing seemed more appropriate than repeatedly thrusting the knife into him, penetrating and violating him, Sheffield's finest as unwelcome an intruder into his body as he had been into hers.

She had to trust Sam, but at no time had there had been any mention of Sam having to trust her.

CHAPTER THIRTY

He bounced up off the driver's seat when the double beep signalled a text message. 12.35pm. How long had he been driving around? He had left the phone switched on in case Amber texted. The 'caller ID' told him it was from Amber. His hand was shaking as he opened the message, trying to drive and read at the same time.

Warkworth drive 2pm the little coffee shop

His heart pounded and his palms began to sweat. Was it a trap? Why did she want to see him? Curiosity? Did she like him? He liked her. Maybe she was the one.

If she had reported the rape to the police, details of the attack would have been released to media, just like the others, but he wasn't totally convinced. You could never be so blasé as to be absolutely, rock-solid sure about anything. But if she had reported, surely it would have been in the press?

He rubbed the sweat off his forehead. He would go, but he wouldn't respond to her text. He needed to get the car home. He needed to be quick. He would get there early, watch her go in, see if she was being followed, see if she spoke to anyone. Would he be able to talk to her? He doubted he would. Asking her about the condom wrapper had seemed a good idea, but if he had left it, as she hadn't reported what he had done, surely she would have thrown it away.

But what if she wanted to meet him? What if she was the one? He would have to make the first move. If he didn't, his chance of seeing her again would vanish. It would be nice to speak to her. Maybe this time she would speak back. That would be even better, a two-way conversation.

He would go into the shop. He could look at her, and then decide whether or not to approach her.

Outside the coffee shop she could feel the acid bile rising in her throat until it filled her mouth, causing her to contort her face and squeeze her eyes tight shut. She forced herself to swallow the warm liquid before opening her mouth and sucking in clean, fresh air. If he was watching, she wasn't going to give him the satisfaction of seeing her vomit in public.

She blew her nose on a used tissue from her pocket.

Breathing deeply and taking small steps, Amber walked into the warm shop, the bell above the door ting-a-linging. The aromatic smell of ground coffee and cinnamon bagels added to her nausea.

She dashed to the toilet, locked the door, and looked at her reflection in the mirror. Running the cold tap, she put the cupped palms of both hands underneath it and threw water over her face, not stopping until her cheeks felt numb.

Pulling open the door, she glanced around and saw a man and a woman sat together drinking coffee, and one man sitting alone reading a tabloid newspaper. Two young women were serving behind the counter.

Was he with the woman? How clever would that be? Was he hiding behind the newspaper? Would he be this early? Why not? She was. He had such an advantage. He knew who she was. She had no idea what he looked like. Any man. It could be any man.

Her shoulders lost their stiffness when she saw a vacant table near the window. She ordered a regular cappuccino and a glass of tap water and sat down. She chose the chair to the side of the table, which gave her a view of the door.

Folding the milky froth into her coffee, her gaze wandered around the café. Small, square wooden tables, adorned with white paper table cloths, and rickety wooden chairs filled the room, while on the metal counter there were cakes, biscuits, and slices as well as a commercial coffee machine.

A typical scene, in a typical coffee shop, in 'Anytown UK'; only today, this one was anything but typical. It wasn't like any other coffee shop. He might come in and buy a coffee.

Gulping down the water, she leaned forward and felt inside her right boot.

Would she be able to do it? Not once in her life had she ever committed a violent act – not even at school, where the girls seemed to fight more than the boys.

At that moment, sitting alone, she knew she couldn't do it, but she hoped that would change once the adrenalin kicked in, when he was next to her, calling her name again. This time she would be ready for him. It would be his turn to experience the explosion of sheer terror.

In the CCTV control room, DC Jimmy Noble watched Amber walk into the coffee shop. He knew two members of the surveillance team were already inside. It was now just a case of making sure the cameras caught as many digital images as possible of people in the vicinity. The attacker might not go into the coffee shop, but he may well be somewhere nearby.

As he sat there, watching the screens, Jimmy remembered some of the lectures he had sat through and the questions that had been posed… how many killers over the years had returned to the crime scene when there was lots of activity to look at? How many killers had spoken to reporters or the TV cameras, saying how terrible it was this type of crime could happen in their community? How many killers had returned to the graves of their victims on the anniversary of their deaths?

Would a rapist turn up for a meet with a victim? He had never been part of any class discussions around the issue, but he felt it was feasible.

If there was the slightest chance the rapist would turn up, he would make damn sure he was caught on camera.

Outside, it had barely risen above zero all day. Stamping his feet, scratching the arms of his reefer coat, he felt like a child waiting for the arrival of a new puppy. Again he glanced at his watch. A combination of the cold, and the hard plastic green seat, had numbed his buttocks in a way that brought back unpleasant memories of sitting on the floor in assembly at primary school.

Five minutes.

The CCTV cameras were pointing down on to the shops, but he didn't think they would deliver an identifiable image of him as he sat in a bus stop on the opposite side of the road.

He rubbed his hands together. Where was she? Was she coming? Had she arrived early? Was she in there?

He could make out the figure of a woman sitting alone near the window, but the condensation on the glass made it impossible to see if it was her. Pulling up the collar of his coat, sinking his neck deep into the rough material, he walked head down, hands in pockets, towards what he hoped was a new relationship. Normally the sex comes after the first date, but this could be the start. Their start. Their first date.

Amber walked to the counter, her legs feeling that they belonged to a Friday night drunk, and ordered another coffee, her eyes fixed on the door. She had lost count of how many times the bicycle-type bell had sounded as the door opened, how often she had jumped, how many times she had tried, but failed, to resist looking at whoever walked in.

The man and woman had left now. At the table they vacated sat a man wearing the type of clothing favoured by builders; dirty jeans, a fleece, and big brown rigger boots. His arms looked too big to belong to her attacker. Was the fleece making them look bigger? The 'builder' had close-cropped stubble across the lower part of his face but she didn't know whether the rapist was clean-shaven or had a full beard.

Maybe the 'builder' was a police officer? Yes, he must be, because if he wasn't, that meant that the lady in the corner, the only other customer, a woman who looked more like a middle-aged school teacher was a police officer, and she didn't look capable of running to anyone's aid.

The doorbell sounded again.

Watching the CCTV, Jimmy Noble slid his chair nearer to the screen, and using the time-honoured expression police reserve for something totally unexpected, muttered, 'What the fuck?'

He punched one number on the speed dial of his phone and called Sam Parker's mobile.

'Sam Parker.'

'Boss. It's Jimmy Noble. I am in the CCTV control room. Does any of your team know about the surveillance?'

'Just myself, Ed and Dave Johnson. Why?'

'Jason Stroud's just walked into the coffee shop.'

Sam's first thought was 'fuck!'.

'Okay. Don't worry, Jimmy, it changes nothing. Just keep monitoring, but thanks for the update. Keep me posted.'

'Okay, Boss. Cheers.'

Sam sank back into her chair, running her hands through her hair. What the bloody hell's going on? Surely it can't be him? Jason Stroud? Coming after her?

CHAPTER THIRTY-ONE

HE ORDERED a hot chocolate and sat down, staring over the rim of the glass cup as he blew on to its steaming contents. He had glanced at the seated middle-aged woman, and the man at the table, but his eyes kept darting back to Amber. She had turned up. Even if she wore no make-up, she looked beautiful, sitting there waiting for him.

Was it a trap? There didn't appear to be any cops outside. Perhaps they were hiding? Were any of the customers cops?

He was desperate to speak to her, but what if she only agreed to the meeting to get a look at him, to describe him to the police and identify him? What if she screamed and the bloke who looked like a builder, who looked like he could handle himself, came to help her?

He blew at the cream again and this time watched it drift from one side of the cup to another.

But then again, what if she wanted him, like he wanted her? She might be sitting waiting for him to make the first move, to introduce himself. She couldn't make the first move. She didn't know what he looked like. But she was here.

His eyes returned to the builder. Was he a builder? He looked familiar? A builder? Think. Think. Don't make a move yet.

Sam's mobile rang again.

'Boss. It's Jimmy Noble again. Jason either didn't buy a coffee, or he's got an asbestos mouth, because he wasn't in there very long.'

'Thanks Jimmy. Anyone else been in who might be interesting?'

'A couple of people coming and going. It's not particularly busy, so we should get good quality stills from the cameras.'

'What about outside?'

'Again, not packed, shouldn't be too difficult to identify people, especially as a lot of them got into vehicles, and we'll have the registration plates on one camera or another.'

'Thanks.'

Ed, answering Sam's call, was with her in her office within two minutes.

'Okay?' he asked.

'Jason Stroud turned up at the coffee shop.'

'What! Fuckin' hell. Sorry. Jesus,' he said, shaking his head as he took a seat.

'He wasn't in long.'

'Maybe he spotted the surveillance team.'

'Possibly. They certainly spotted him. Where's he now?'

'Not sure, but I can find him. What do you think?' Ed asked.

'It might be nothing. Could just be coincidence, albeit a very weird one. He might have just called in for a coffee but we're going to have to talk to him about it. I don't want to knee jerk, but I need an explanation as to why he was there.'

'He might have gone to meet Amber.'

'That's what worries me.'

'Are you going to mention what Celine told us?' Ed asked.

'No. I want to keep that back. We can legitimately ask him what he was doing in the coffee shop but for now let's keep the conversation with Celine between us. I want him to know that we know he was in there. If he's our man, I want him to start feeling a bit of pressure.'

'I'll have him here in 30 minutes. Jesus. Anyway, changing the subject, Duncan Todd doesn't want to make a complaint, but he's adamant that his attack was down to Danielle's dad.'

'Okay. Let's just leave that for now,' Sam said, fiddling with some pieces of paper on her desk, looking at them, but not registering any of the typed words.

'People are also working on the arrest plan for Crowther in readiness for tonight,' Ed told her.

'Good. What about a cuppa? One way or another the surveillance team will be back soon, as will Jason.'

'Good idea. I'll sort one,' Ed said.

Walking out of the office, his thoughts were very much on Jason Stroud.

Amber's left hand was trembling as she finished her second coffee, stood stiffly, and walked out of the shop, disappointed and deflated that he hadn't shown up.

When would she be able to have a normal life again without looking at every man, wondering whether he was the one? Would she ever be able to put him behind her?

The dark grey carpet of cloud was so low she felt if she jumped, she could reach out and touch it. She stopped and stood still. She surveyed the normality around her. What was she doing? What was she thinking? She had just contemplated stabbing someone; killing another human being.

Maybe Sam's suggestion was the way forward. Perhaps she should go and get counselling. Maybe it would help to talk about it. She might even be able to talk to another victim, a woman who understood what she was going through.

She would speak to Sam. She smiled to herself. For the first time since the attack she felt she was taking control in a positive way instead of vigilante-style retribution.

Her stride quickened and her spine straightened. She noticed the gardens with flowers in tubs, radiating colour against the grey backcloth, their hues and tints at the forefront of an otherwise black-and-white photograph.

As the first spots of rain fell, she clenched her fists, declaring to herself her desire to take charge of her own destiny again.

Whether the police caught him or not, she would regain her confidence and her independence. She would no longer let him put her life on hold.

She laughed as the rain increased in intensity, and as she pushed open her garden gate, she realised that she had forgotten about the police officers.

He was so preoccupied as he parked the car, he couldn't recollect the drive to the retail park. She did look beautiful, and he had so wanted to talk to her. Had he missed the opportunity of his life? What if she had wanted to go out with him? He would never know now. What a great girlfriend she would have made.

Slamming the driver's door, he consoled himself knowing that there would be others. Forget her; she's history, a memory of a past relationship. Couples split up every day and ultimately find new lovers. If she had the condom wrapper, it hadn't led the police to him. And of course, he had a door key now.

Buying the tracksuit had been easy. Buying the condoms wasn't. Once more it was a female who served him. He again reasoned that he should buy in bulk and cut down on the visits to the shops, but somehow he felt that would make him look even more ridiculous. What was he, some sort of sex god? If they inwardly laughed at him for buying a packet of three, they would be rolling in the aisles if he bought three or four packs.

Handing her the £10 note, he watched her sway towards the till, all blonde hair, legs, and a pout, her heavily made up eyes never wavering from her older male colleague. Brushing past the man, her big tits straining against her tight, white cotton dress uniform, she seemed magnetically attracted to his hideous multi-coloured tie. Speaking into his ear, just a little too loudly, she said she preferred her condoms flavoured. Fuckin' slut.

His cheeks were on fire when she placed his change into

his outstretched hand. He couldn't bring himself to look at her. He knew that she was laughing at him.

He'd give her flavoured ones, given the chance.

At some time in the future he would have to consider travelling further from home to visit the girls. There was a world of women out there.

CHAPTER THIRTY-TWO

ED RETURNED with the mugs of tea. 'Amber's home safe.
Jason can't get back here yet. He's doing some enquiries, but
he'll be here as soon as he can.'

He placed a plain black mug on the desk within reach
of Sam.

'Thanks. What are you thinking?'

'What am I thinking? I suppose I'm starting to think that
maybe Jason is our man. He lives in the area; he could easily
identify the whereabouts of single women; he went in the
coffee shop at the time the rapist is told to be there; and we
know he fantasises about rape. No hard evidence, okay, but
plenty of circumstantial. If he wasn't a cop, he'd be right
up there.'

Sam said: 'Let's deal with Crowther tonight, and
tomorrow we'll see where we are. Cop or no cop, we need to
sort him. What're your thoughts on him finding out where
single women live?'

Sam raised the mug to her lips, as Ed sat down.

'Not too difficult, is it? All he needs to do is to check the
voters lists. Check crime reports, messages, anything. He'd
easily establish a list of lone females.'

'Not too difficult, I agree,' Sam said. 'Let's not rush
anything, though. See how we get on with Crowther. It could

be Jason, but let's deal with one thing at a time. If he hadn't gone into the coffee shop, we would still be where we were earlier.'

Ed nodded slowly. 'I know, but he did go in.'

'Nothing's ever simple,' Sam said. 'Listen, I need to call Amber now.'

'You do that, and I'll get the surveillance commander to come and see us.'

Staring at the telephone, Sam had the receiver in her right hand, the fingers of her left hovering above the buttons. She knew she had to make the call, but she wasn't relishing it. She had asked too much of Amber and for what? Had he given himself away, it might have been different; the end might have justified the means, but all she had succeeded in doing was expose Amber to more anguish, pile more pressure on her.

She was expecting an emotional outburst, and who could blame Amber if she lost it? Banging the palm of her left hand hard on to the desk, she cursed her decision to go with the surveillance. Too busy trying to nail the rapist, she had taken her eye off the welfare of the victim.

She took a deep breath, and tapped in the numbers on the telephone. Waiting to hear the voice on the other end of the line, her mouth felt like a rag had been stuffed into it. There was never a cold drink on your desk when you needed one, and the tea would still be too hot.

What she didn't expect to hear was Amber talking non-stop, in an excited voice.

No longer was she going to be a victim, she told Sam, leading a life dictated by this a catastrophic experience. She was considering counselling and even talking about helping others who'd gone through a similar nightmare. She wanted to discuss giving up her right to anonymity so she could go public with her own ordeal.

Sam reasoned that it was all, in reality, a long way off, but she was delighted Amber appeared to have had such an epiphany. The resilience of victims never ceased to amaze her, how after such horror they could consider helping others.

As she put the handset back on to its cradle she silently vowed to bring to justice the man who had affected the lives of so many young women. If she needed any further motivation to work tirelessly to catch him, Amber had just been the provider. It had been a long few days, but that conversation had spurred her on to work even longer and harder. Picking up her pen, she started doodling on the desktop blotter while her memory replayed Amber's words.

When her door opened, she jerked her head up. Her jottings featured the word 'puppeteer' countless times. But she promised that she would now be pulling the strings. He would be the puppet.

Dave Johnson and Ed sat down.

'Amber's fine. Really fine,' Sam told them. 'She's talking about being a counsellor herself. She was really upbeat. Not what I expected at all.'

'That's great,' Ed said. 'Just a pity the bastard didn't turn up.'

'We move on,' said Sam, before continuing. 'Dave, I want two detectives outside Romeo's pizza from 4pm. I don't want Crowther getting to work early, and be out on deliveries before we get there. As soon as we have him, I want a search team at his house. You know what we're looking for… tracksuits, trainers, unusual knives, but most importantly, a mobile phone, a SIM card, and the driving licences. Also any female clothing, especially knickers. He might still have those from the swimming baths, or Danielle's.'

Dave was writing furiously as he recorded Sam's instructions.

'I want all diaries, notebooks etcetera recovering. It's not unheard of for a 'Power Reassurance' rapist to write down what he's done, and to keep any press cuttings relating to the attacks. So search for newspaper clippings as well. He may have kept them.'

Dave nodded. Ed admired Sam's decisiveness.

'I want him arrested for the theft of two pairs of knickers, and the rapes of Danielle and Amber. He delivers a pizza to Danielle the night she is raped; he's stop-checked in the area of Amber's house the night she's raped; he's at the swimming baths when a pair of knickers are stolen, and Danielle thinks her knickers were stolen the night he delivered a pizza. There's enough reasonable suspicion there on all counts.'

'Will do. Are we telling everyone about Amber now?' Dave asked.

'Yes. Nothing to lose now. We've tried the meeting. We can't put her through that again. Brief everyone about that rape, please. If anyone asks why the delay in informing them, just tell them to ask me. Nobody will. Let them make up their own rumours.'

'Okay,' Dave said. 'We've already started putting together a briefing sheet for the search team.'

'Great.'

Dave Johnson nodded at Sam and was out of his chair as Gary Ross arrived.

Keep those plates spinning Sam.

'Hi Gary, come in,' Sam said, indicating for him to sit down. 'I've spoken to Amber and she's fine. Can you thank all of your people on my behalf?'

Gary nodded.

Sam went on: 'The fact that he didn't disclose himself to Amber doesn't mean he wasn't there. He may have gone inside. He may have watched from outside. I want stills of everyone in that shop between 12.30pm and 2.30pm, and of everyone outside within those same time parameters. I also want a list from the surveillance log of all registration numbers that were parked in and around the shops.'

It was Gary's turn to write down Sam's requests.

'Okay,' he answered when his pen had stopped moving. 'I'll try and have them to you by tomorrow afternoon.'

'Sooner, if you can, Gary,' Sam said, her tone hinting at a command as opposed to a request.

'I'll try,' Gary said as he stood up. He stopped at the door and turned around to look at Sam and Ed. 'What about Jason Stroud?'

'Probably wrong place, wrong time. I'll keep you posted, but have your team keep that under their hats,' Sam said.

'No problem,' Gary agreed as he walked away.

In fairness, Gary Ross thought, it wouldn't be the first time a police officer had unwittingly walked 'on plot'. He concentrated instead on how he was going to deliver all the stills for Sam.

She was the type who was used to getting what she wanted.

Darkness had fallen like a blanket over the shopping centre, but the neon lighting from the street lamps and the three take-away shops provided all the visibility the two detectives needed.

Terry Crowther got out of his black Ford Focus and started to walk the few short steps across the car park to Romeo's pizza shop, where a couple of early customers were already inside.

Slamming the doors of the pale blue Ford Mondeo, they strode behind him, each step narrowing the gap. He knew exactly who they were the moment he turned around. He hadn't met them before, didn't know their names, but he knew instinctively, from the blue suits, the shiny black shoes, that they were detectives.

The one with the height and shoulders of a heavyweight boxer spoke in a voice that would have sounded threatening in a pulpit.

'Terry Crowther?'

It was obvious that they both knew who he was. How? Nodding, he mumbled: 'Yeah.'

Told that he was being arrested on suspicion of two rapes and the theft of two pair of knickers, he was cautioned, taken by the arm and led to their car. He wasn't handcuffed, but the grip applied to his bicep told him making a run for it wasn't an option.

CHAPTER THIRTY-THREE

HE WAS SHOVED on to the back seat, falling sideways, before straightening himself up. Had they sent the two biggest detectives available?

Following the barked instructions, he scrambled behind the passenger seat, resisting the urge to wipe away the sweat at the back of his neck. Convinced the driver had angled the rear view mirror so he could watch him and not the traffic behind, he tried to control the trembling coursing through his body.

The mobile looked like a small box of matches in the hands of the pugilist, who phoned somebody called Dave.

'Job done, no probs.'

What did that mean? What had they got on him?

The car moved off, and neither of the detectives uttered a word.

What was happening now? Ask me a question?

The detectives didn't even look at each other as the car moved through the streets, both staring out of the windscreen. He turned his head to look out of the side window, shuffling closer to it, making it more difficult for the driver to watch him.

Was the silent treatment a technique they employed?

Were they waiting for him to start talking?

His bursting bladder, increasing heart rate, pulsating temple, and the light-headed dizziness you can feel after a long-distance run were all triggering the involuntary movements of his body. His hands, arm, and legs were shaking, and sweat rashes were everywhere.

They weren't asking questions. Total silence. This was torture.

Would they search his house? Whatever they had now, they would have more if they went to his house. They might not go to his house. What did they have? Why get him going to work? Why not at home? They knew who he was, where he worked. They'd done their homework. They must know where he lives. What else did they know?

Should he just admit it?

No, say nothing until the brief gets there. He knew that he would be putty in their hands. He needed to hold out until he got a solicitor.

Jason Stroud was a man in a hurry as he came into Sam's office. Ed, following, looked on as Jason blurted out that he thought he might have unknowingly stumbled across a surveillance operation. He explained he had gone for a hot chocolate but the second he realised he might be about to 'blow out' a job, he left.

'Did you recognise anyone in the coffee shop?' Sam asked.

'I think there were two people from the surveillance team. Sat at different tables.'

'Anyone else?' asked Sam

'Don't think so.'

'Okay, it's probably nothing. If there's a problem, I've no doubt the surveillance team will be in touch.'

'Cheers,' Jason said, and he walked out of the office.

Sam was happy to leave it at that. If he were to become a suspect, there would be plenty of time to ask questions in a formal interview about 'meeting' Amber. For now, some things were best left unsaid. Jason had been concerned enough to approach her. That alleviated the need for her to ask him why he was there, while still satisfying her need to have him know that she knew he was there.

Patience was always a virtue in any major investigation. Time would tell whether Jason was trying to pull her strings.

'What did he say before you came into the office?' Sam asked.

'He was busting a gut to tell you that he thought he may have stumbled on a job.'

'What did you say?'

'The usual, there's jobs going on all the time. Sometimes we inadvertently walk into them.'

Sam briefly closed her eyes, suddenly weary.

'He might be fishing. If it's him, he knew Amber was going to be there. If he thought a surveillance team was watching her, he'd know that we'd have arranged it. Contact Gary and tell him to brief all his staff not to confirm that surveillance with anyone. We've told him to keep Jason's sighting under wraps, but I don't want anyone even confirming there was surveillance. Let's keep a close eye on Jason Stroud.'

'What about getting another interview adviser?'

'Not at the minute. Monitor his work. We don't want to unnerve him. Let him carry on. Let's not forget he may have nothing to do with this, so just let him carry on doing his job. I don't want to give him any cause for concern. He'll know we're on to him when we want him to.'

'No bother.'

Dave Johnson popped in to tell them that a house near Amber's had CCTV fitted, and on the evening of her attack, the figure of a male was seen nearby at the relevant time. While the images weren't good enough to identify the individual, they clearly showed the male was wearing a tracksuit with the Adidas three stripes on the arm.

Phone calls to the two police officers who stopped Crowther revealed they were 100% certain he wasn't wearing an Adidas top, although they couldn't recall the make of his tracksuit.

Crowther emptied his pockets at the Custody Sergeant's request, and placed his house key, car keys, loose change and wallet on the counter. He watched as his change and wallet were placed in a clear plastic bag, whilst both sets of keys were handed to the boxer, who raised his eyebrows, and allowed his thin lips to part slightly, his gleaming teeth not hiding the menace behind the smile.

Placing the keys in his trouser pocket, the detective said loudly and clearly: 'We'll search his house and car under section 18 of the Police and Criminal Evidence Act, Sarge.'

His eyes never moved away from Crowther, leaving the detainee under no illusions what the police were about to do next.

At the house, the search team co-ordinator drew a rough plan of the ground and upper floors and allocated specific rooms to specific pairs of officers. All six of the search officers had been briefed about what exactly they were looking for, the bonus being that Crowther lived alone.

The integral garage was surprisingly tidy, with very little in it, so that particular search was conducted thoroughly in a relatively short time. Garages full of junk were a search officer's nightmare.

Nothing evidential was found in any of the sparsely furnished downstairs rooms, and the upstairs bedrooms were all empty, with one exception.

That bedroom contained a bed with a black duvet in a heap on top of it and a white sheet, patches of which were as tight and rigid as stone, the dried yellow stains suggesting it hadn't been washed since the day it was bought. The stench of stale sweat swept into the nostrils of the two officers.

'God, I feel like I'm sniffing the insides of a tramp's socks,' the female officer said.

'Make a habit of that, do you?' her male colleague teased deadpan.

'You know what I mean.'

On the bedside table, a lamp, surrounded by a deep

veneer of dust, stood next to a semen-filled condom. Discarded socks and stained white underpants were strewn across the floor, surrounding four empty cans of lager and an empty take-away tin foil container.

'Dirty bastard,' said the male officer.

Wearing thin transparent gloves, the officers removed the duvet, and having searched inside the cover, the woman picked up the only pillow, finding a pair of lacy white knickers underneath. She dropped them into a clear bag which was sealed and had an exhibit label attached, on which was written a description of the item, together with where, when, and by whom the knickers were found.

'Fuckin' perv,' said the female officer.

The search yielded nothing else of evidential value: no driving licences, no additional mobiles, no SIM cards, and no diaries or notes; a pair of black trainers and a black Puma tracksuit were recovered, though.

Thirty minutes after the white knickers had been 'bagged and tagged', Jamie Hampton had identified them as being similar to those that were stolen from her at the swimming baths.

Mass-produced with no singular unique feature, the knickers couldn't be identified as Jamie's to the legal satisfaction of a court, but 'similar' was a good starting point in a police interview.

At the office, Sam and Ed called it a day. Crowther was in custody and would be interviewed tomorrow. Disappointed at the outcome of the searches of his house and car, they hoped for better in the interviews tomorrow.

Stepping out into the dark, cold night, frost already forming on the remaining cars, they shuddered in unison.

'Will you be okay tonight, Sam?'

'I'll be fine,' Sam lied. 'Don't worry. Get home to Sue.'

Turning on the ignition, the bright interior light dimmed,

leaving the car in darkness except for the dashboard lights and their cosy glow.

She answered her mobile.

'Sam. It's Trevor Stewart. Just ringing for an update. I understand you've had a busy day.'

'We've got someone in custody. Early days yet. I'll come and speak with you tomorrow, give you a full briefing.'

'Thanks, I'd appreciate that. Any plans tonight?'

'Early night.'

'Get your PJ's on. Hard frost forecast. Not the weather for anything skimpy.'

'Thanks, but I'm a big girl.'

'It would be remiss of me to comment. See you tomorrow. Goodnight.'

Creep.

Driving home, the 9.30pm news bulletin temporarily diverted her thoughts from the investigation and Slimy Stewart.

Desperate to eat, then sleep, she walked through her front door, locked it, and put the key on the hall table, simultaneously kicking off her shoes. She took a deep breath and pressed her spine against the door.

Maybe she should have told Ed the truth; she was frightened. He would have volunteered to stay again even though she knew it would cause him grief at home. Standing rigid against the door, tears started to drip down her cheeks. *Truth is, I didn't want you in the house again, Ed. I need to keep things professional. I don't want any complications and certainly not with a married man.*

She took another deep breath, marched across the hall and flung open every door, hitting the light switches as soon as she could get her wrist through the gap. With every downstairs light on, she checked every window. Nothing. She checked them all again. Same result.

Thankful for the timer on the boiler, the wall of heat meant the double bed won what was a no-contest over food.

She dragged herself upstairs, and flung open the bedroom

doors. She turned on every light, checked every window. Twice.

She forced herself to go back downstairs and turn all the lights off. Back in her bedroom she stripped, and dropped her underwear into the basket in the en-suite bathroom. Naked, she tied her hair into a ponytail, put on the extra large, powder blue cotton T-shirt she had pulled from under her pillow, and collapsed on to the bed, tugging the duvet under her chin.

Throat parched, stomach tight, legs heavy, head throbbing, she was physically and mentally drained. As her eyes closed, she had a nagging doubt she had forgotten something and through a fog of tiredness, she tried to revisit again in her mind every window, every door.

An anaesthetist's injection would have been slower. She was snoring within seconds.

No part of her brain sounded the alert to reset the panic alarm.

CHAPTER THIRTY-FOUR

HIS STRIDES, like a long-jumper on his run-up, covered the length of the drive in four steps. He pushed his back up against the front door. His tongue ran around the inside of his mouth. Slow deep breaths, he told himself. He looked left and right and listened, like a child obeying the Green Cross Code. Nothing. Where had he read that people were in their deepest sleep around 4am?

He turned the key slowly. Pushing the door, he opened it just enough to step inside then closed it behind him. Slipping the key back in the right-hand side pocket of his blue tracksuit bottoms, he froze, a wax dummy in her hallway. He allowed his eyes to adjust to the dark, waited while his ears took in the silence. He slithered into the kitchen and found what he needed. Back in the hall, his black training shoes were silent on the oatmeal staircase carpet. There would be no warning of his impending arrival.

It was a large bedroom with plenty of room to walk either side of the double bed. The duvet covered her legs, but the flawless skin of her arm was visible. He allowed his eyes to savour the contours of her upper body, the baggy T-shirt not doing justice to her curves. She looked younger; perhaps it was her brown hair tied back in a ponytail?

Laid on her left side, she faced into the middle of the double bed. He inched towards her beautiful back. Breathing through his nose, he could smell lavender. Her soap? Lavender drops on her pillow?

As his right knee touched the side of the bed, she rolled over and bolted upright. She stretched for the bedside lamp and had it on in an instant, the pearlescent bulb illuminating both of them.

'What the fuck?' she screamed.

As if playing the children's game of musical statues, he froze on the spot. Within a split second the 'music' leapt into his head, and he dived on her, knocking her on to her stomach, his weight sending the wind whooshing out of her. His left hand pressed into her shoulder as he pushed himself up and he plunged the knife deep into her right shoulder.

Fire erupted in her flesh as he ripped the blade out, leaving an egg-shaped wound as wide as the hilt of the blade.

Off balance, his body weight shifted, allowing her to force her knees under her stomach, thrusting her back into an arch and flipping him off her. Spinning around, she drove her left knee into his stomach, and as he toppled sideways, groaning, she instinctively rolled to the right, desperate to get off the bed.

Her movements were too sluggish and a searing pain bolted through her scalp as he yanked her ponytail. She squealed but as her head was jerked backwards, the sound was cut off in mid-flow as the moulded steel chef's knife was driven three times between her shoulder blades.

Scrambling for leverage, she stretched and grabbed the side of the bed, and with her hands gripping the underside wooden frame she twisted her upper body and smashed her right foot into the side of his face.

She collapsed to the floor and clawed at the bedside table, heaving herself up into a crouching position. Dizzy, disorientated, her heart pumping blood that was shooting from her body, she toppled backwards, pulling the table towards her, bringing it crashing on to her shins.

The table lamp lurched in mid air, its electric cord still plugged into the wall, before it crashed and shattered, the bulb exploding, throwing the room back into darkness.

The thick hardback book describing the battles of the First World War, which sat on the table, made a dull thud as it hit the floor, unlike the police warrant card, which barely made a sound as it fluttered, confetti like, on to the carpet.

She rolled over and crawled on her hands and knees towards the bottom of the bed, the taste of warm blood flooding her mouth, her blurred vision focussed on a piece of carpet under the windowsill where her mobile was charging in a socket.

Her breathing was shallow but rapid.

Clutching his lower abdomen, staggering, he waited until she emerged from the side of the bed and booted the right side of her rib cage, jerking her upwards, her body acrobatically rolling in mid air. She crashed down with a thud on to her back, her feet scrambling for grip on the carpet, her legs in a bicycle movement, heels scratching at the floor, desperately trying to push herself backwards towards the phone, consciousness shooting from her like steam from a coal-driven train.

She was helpless, an upturned crab. He stood above her. She raised her arms, in one final, futile, effort at self-defence.

Mimicking the wrestler in the ring, he dropped to his knees, ramming the knife into the left side of her chest as he crashed to the floor.

Foam gathered at the corners of his mouth, the veins in his neck pushing against the skin, trying to burst free, his right arm a blur as he knelt next to her, repeatedly thrusting the knife into her chest.

He stabbed and stabbed her lifeless body, a body that twitched involuntarily every time he rammed down the knife.

Gasping for air, his heart feeling as if it might explode, he dropped the knife.

She lay there, motionless, her eyes wide open and

unblinking, a discarded ventriloquist's dummy, staring at her own blood on the ceiling.

Kneeling beside her, as if in prayer, he rubbed his hands up and down his tracksuited thighs. Where had all the blood come from?

He pushed himself on to his feet, grabbed the knife, and stumbled towards the door convinced her eyes were following his every move. His heart was racing.

Her heart would never race again. Never beat again. No amount of electric shock treatment would bring her back. Her heart would remain as silent as the street he was about to step back on to.

Ed was scraping the ice off his windscreen, his ears numb, the thin black socks and leather-soled shoes offering little protection against the crunching frost under his feet.

The engine was running, and the heater was blasting out warm air, locked in a battle with the elements, fighting to warm the interior of the car and defrost both front and rear screens.

If today went according to plan, Crowther would at some stage be arrested for the rape of Kelly and from there the whole investigation could well be 'boxed-off'.

Not wanting to pre-empt anything, he felt Crowther could be their man, so well did he fit the profile of a 'Power Reassurance' rapist as Sam had described. Last night he made a conscious decision to read more about the classification of rapists, and as a ploy to stop chatty strangers turning over on their sun beds to make idle conversation, he thought he might take the books to Skala, his favourite resort on Kefalonia. What holidaymaker wants to chat with someone reading textbooks on sexual offences?

He opened the driver's door. His phone rang, sounding louder than usual in the quiet stillness of the village. What was so important that someone needed to call at 7.30am? He would be in the office within 20 minutes.

Bloody hell. Has Crowther escaped? Topped himself?

'Ed. It's Sam. We've got a job. Meet me at 18 Rothbury Close.'

'What is it?'

'Murder,' she paused. He could hear her taking a deep breath. Her next words were much quieter. 'Ed, the victim.' Another deep breath. 'Louise Smith.'

Ed gripped the top of the open driver's door with his free hand and bowed his head. Louise had worked closely with him in the past. He saw her in the car park on Monday.

He conjured an image of her, picturing her broad smile, a smile that seemed to be drawn permanently on her face, infectious and warming.

He had never heard her speak ill of anyone, and everybody who was anybody knew she was a great girl. What the hell had happened?

'You there, Ed?'

Wiping his eyes, his voice quivered: 'Yeah, yeah. Just a bit stunned. What happened?'

'Multiple stab wounds. Killed in her bedroom.' Her speech quickened. 'Found by her mum. Ed, how did this happen? This is a nightmare. It's all my fault.'

There was a silence as Sam stifled a sob, and took another deep intake of breath, 'Ed, there's a ski mask in the bedroom.'

'Jesus Christ,' Ed whispered, each syllable elongated, as if he was talking in slow motion.

Tears were rolling down Sam's cheeks, her words barely audible over the sobs she could no longer hold back.

'How have I got this so wrong, Ed? Here's me talking about a rapist who wants a relationship, a non-violent individual, and there's poor Louise, my mate, butchered. How could I have been so wrong?'

Ed felt his stomach churning, his forehead going clammy, that sickly feeling he associated with being on boat. His grip on the door tightened as he tried to unscramble his brain, to separate the thoughts of a murdered friend from the investigative ones that he must allow to come to the fore.

One thing was for certain, whatever had happened, it hadn't anything to do with Terry Crowther. He was still in the cells.

'Sam, we don't know that they're linked yet. Let's see what we've got when we get there.'

Sam screamed: 'Ed, are you fucking listening? There's a ski mask there.'

Silence.

Sam, quieter now and breathing quickly in between sniffles, was the first to speak again.

'That's never been put out into the public domain. How many murderers do you know who put a ski mask on? What's the point? If the victim's dead, they can't identify you.'

'Okay. Okay. Let's see what we've got when we get there. I can be there in 15 minutes. Are you alright to drive?'

'I'll be fine. See you there. Let's meet outside,' she said, her tone nasal now, like someone with a heavy cold.

CHAPTER THIRTY-FIVE

INSIDE THE AUDI the only noise came from the windscreen de-mister. If the murder and rapes were linked, everything Sam had ever read must have been wrong. Either that or she had totally misinterpreted his behaviour.

Of course it wasn't unheard of for rapists to become killers, but this type of rapist?

What did I miss? What else could I have done to capture him? Could I have prevented Louise's death? Prevented my friend's death.

Peter Sutcliffe, the infamous Yorkshire Ripper, could have been caught earlier. No detective wants to be forever haunted by their failures; to be one of those SIOs who, had they acted faster, prioritised more effectively, identified the perpetrator sooner, could have saved the lives of innocent victims.

Sam shuddered at the thought. Was she responsible for her friend's murder?

The blast of a car horn made her jump.

'Shit,' she shouted, as she swerved violently to the right, back into the outside lane.

Get a grip Sam.

She slowed down as she approached Louise's house. The last time she parked here was for wine and Italian meatballs; a night with a few of the girls, more bottles of wine than meatballs, and a Sunday morning hangover that stretched into Monday.

A toddler, dressed in pyjamas underneath a blue 'Angry Birds' dressing gown, sat on his tricycle on the footpath, his red-raw hands gripping the handlebars. He looked bemused at all the police cars, tape, and strange people dressed in white paper suits. Behind him stood a group of men and women, no doubt swapping theories on what could have happened to that 'poor girl'. Some were taking photographs on their phones, others were having excited conversations.

She pulled up outside the police cordon with no recollection of the journey, other than almost colliding with that car. Wondering whether the Press would beat Ed, she saw the Crime Scene Investigators' van and a young uniform police officer standing at the front door, clipboard in hand.

Every murder investigation invariably saw the newest member of the response team at the crime scene entrance keeping the log. It was a daunting task for many young officers who had to ask and record the name of everyone entering, often without knowing who they were but knowing they would probably be senior officers.

Sat in the car, Sam spoke into her mobile. There was nobody at the other end. She needed a few minutes, needed to brace herself for what was to come. She inhaled, exhaled, all the time holding the phone to her ear. How many SIOs had she seen on the TV investigating the murder of a police officer? It was the murder they all dreaded.

Approaching the foot-stamping young officer, no doubt cursing his luck and wishing for the warmth of a patrol car, Sam thanked him for keeping the log and took the opportunity to explain its importance. The log recorded everyone who had been into the scene. That list could be invaluable at a later date. A stray hair at a crime scene – neither from suspect or victim - may belong to someone recorded on the log. Without knowing who had been there, identifying the origin of the hair would be nigh on impossible – all a smart defence lawyer would need to raise the spectre of an innocent man in the dock and an undetected offender still at large.

Nothing warmed the toes more than being told you were important.

The senior CSI came from inside the house to the front door and greeted Sam. Julie Trescothick, who had worked closely on a number of murder investigations with Sam, was wearing the regulation white paper suit with a hood, white face mask, and white paper boots.

She went to her van and retrieved two suits and two pairs of paper boots for Sam and Ed. Contrary to TV fictional dramas, nobody, irrespective of rank, ever entered a murder scene without wearing a paper suit.

As they waited for Ed, she gave Sam a brief overview of what had already been done.

Each room had been filmed, including the bedroom where Louise had been found. Still photographs had been taken and large metal plates placed on the floors throughout the house so officers could move about without standing on the carpets and contaminating potential evidence.

Sam thought of the square, metal plates. Cold stainless steel-looking and not much smaller than a paving stone, each about an inch high, set out like stepping stones, leading not across some picturesque stream but to a lifeless mutilated body which only hours before had been a living, breathing friend and colleague.

Sam used her mobile and asked for a Home Office Pathologist to attend, knowing they preferred to come to the scene before the body had been moved. It was important. They could test police theories and get a clearer understanding of what had happened.

Ed pulled up, nodded at everyone but no one in particular, and like Sam, began to fight his way into a paper suit.

'Why are these bloody suits always so fuckin' small?' he muttered, balancing on one leg, trying to force his other foot through a white leg.

The suits acted like the trigger on a starter pistol. In

silence, lost in their own thoughts, unaware of the stares from the neighbours, they both concentrated on pushing their emotions to one side. Now was the moment to let their investigative mindsets take over, to focus on both the scene examination and the scene interpretation.

Telling herself to forget it was a friend, Sam recalled the words of Albert Szent-Gyorgyi, the Nobel-winning Hungarian physiologist, who once said, *'Discovery consists of seeing what everyone else sees, but thinking what no one else has thought.'*

It could have been written for a detective.

'See what everyone else sees, but think what no one else has thought,' she mentally repeated to herself.

Walking towards the front door, they both knew that there would be time later to grieve the senseless killing of a bright, vibrant, young colleague and friend. That time wasn't now. Not in her house.

They needed to be the voice of the victim. Louise Smith couldn't tell them what happened in the last moments of her life, but if they collected the correct pieces, dovetailed them together, the jigsaw would form a picture as vivid as any account Louise could have painted.

No one had to remind them of their responsibilities, or the expectations resting on them from her family and an outraged public.

Nor did they need reminding just how difficult this particular scene was going to be. They both took a deep breath and stepped inside.

Sam blinked hard.

Concentrate.

Louise's voice and laughter played out in her head. She visualised Louise drunk, barefoot, running to answer the door when the hunk across the road dropped off more wine.

Concentrate.

The hallway had a staircase with one turn, and the banister and spindles, painted in gloss white, appeared at first glance to be spotlessly clean. A door on the left led into a small study, which contained a light oak rectangle desk, the type that is delivered flat packed, and a black mock-leather swivel chair. On top of the desk were some letters and papers, and an Apple laptop, the lid closed, which was charging from a four-plug adaptor on the floor. A photograph of Louise, in uniform, with her classmates from training school was hanging on the centre of the wall.

The plain, white door on the right led into a neat lounge with a stone fireplace and a multi-coloured fabric retro settee.

At the bottom of the hall was a large dining kitchen. The kitchen sink and drainer were empty, and the worktops clean with the usual appliances on top. The glass-topped table had six metal framed chairs around it. One window was swinging open, the casement stay banging on the outside of the windowsill.

Nothing downstairs gave any indication whatsoever of the horrors that waited upstairs, with the exception of a missing knife from the block on the workbench.

Sam looked at the block and saw it was the largest knife which had been taken. That always seemed to be the case in domestic homicides. How many people had she interviewed for killing their wife or husband where the weapon was a knife? Every one of them described grabbing the first knife that came to hand but it was always, without fail, the biggest in the block. With total disregard to the law of averages, none of them ever found their hand falling on the potato peeler. Why? Because they all knew exactly which knife they wanted. Choice not chance. It looked like it would be no different here.

Climbing the stairs, Sam chewed the inside of her bottom lip as she saw blood smears on the staircase wall, blood that had undoubtedly come from the clothing, or a body extremity, of the fleeing killer. Scientific tests would establish the origin of the blood.

All the rooms upstairs, with the exception of one, were undisturbed.

Sam walked into Louise's bedroom, looked quickly at what was in front of her, and then fixed her eyes on the window, fighting back the tears.

Ed, close behind, saw his dead colleague laid there and

inhaled deeply, holding the air in his lungs, giving himself a couple of seconds to absorb, and recover from, the wave of sadness.

Each looked at the other and nodded, a silent acknowledgement that it was time to go to work.

Louise's bedroom had become an abattoir. She was on the floor, lying on her back, her lifeless eyes staring at the ceiling, strands of her hair across her face. The carpet around her was heavily bloodstained and there were trails of blood on the floor leading from Louise's body back to the bed.

Carefully walking around the room, stepping on the plates, they both kept their hands in their pockets, even though they were wearing gloves. It was a habit passed on from generation to generation of murder squad detectives.

They could clearly see the sheets strewn over the bed, covered in deep red, almost brown, stains. There was blood on the floor, and on the cream wall, next to the side of the bed furthest from the door, suggesting the attack had continued there, probably as Louise tried to get off the bed and escape.

Julie Trescothick joined them, and pointed out the faint footprint impressions in the carpet, which appeared to be similar to the soles of training shoes. Clearly they didn't belong to the barefoot Louise.

The splattered blood on the ceiling ran from above Louise, back towards the bed, the blood nearer the bed being much less concentrated, the overall pattern similar to paint thrown from a child's brush on to paper. They both knew that for blood to fly off the blade and hit the ceiling in those linear formations needed very fast, very long, up and over arm movements. A forensic scientist would provide expert witness testimony on the Blood Pattern Analysis, but Sam and Ed could see what had happened.

Sam shuddered, and her thoughts turned to Louise's mother. She had met her once, many years ago at some function. To her shame, she couldn't remember her name. From memory, she was older than she expected, giving birth to Louise quite late in life.

What effect had walking into this bloodbath, seeing her beloved daughter lying there carved to pieces, had on her? She would never recover. How could she? That vision would haunt her until her dying day.

'Christ, how many of these do I have to see?' thought Sam. Her mind altered course, a yacht tacking in a new direction, and she thought of her beloved father, and the numbness she had felt when she saw his body in the mortuary. He had been cleaned up before she got there and looked asleep. Only the cold stiffness of his body as she held him in her arms betrayed the fact that he wasn't sleeping. Louise hadn't been 'dressed' for identification by her mother.

Like Sam, Ed had seen these nightmares too many times, and nothing affected any of his senses any longer. His eyes didn't turn away in horror, and the smells of death no longer made his stomach to retch.

Louise had clearly tried to escape but cornered, alone, fighting for her life, she had lost a mismatched battle. That he knew her added to the tragedy before him, but having stared into the abyss of human depravity so many times, he was no longer shocked.

Julie brought them back from their private thoughts by pointing to a front door key, which had been on top of the duvet, caught up in the concertina folds. Near the pillow was a black ski mask.

Sam and Ed stood still in the middle of the bedroom and looked around, their eyes taking in everything before them, their minds trying to process everything they saw and, more importantly, make sense of it. What they were trying to do was interpret the scene, to better understand what had happened.

The pointed blade had entered her body so many times she resembled the spinning wheel of a knife thrower's circus act. There were wounds to her stomach, arms, thighs, and chest.

Sam was first to speak. 'Look at her hands. Her arms. I can't see one obvious defensive wound. Nothing underneath her forearms to suggest she raised her arms to protect herself. No incisions on her hands from grabbing the knife.'

They both knelt next to the body.

'I agree. You'd have expected at least one defensive wound,' Ed said, his mind searching for a scenario where Louise had been helpless to fend off the blows or instinctively reach for the blade.

'These wounds can't all have happened while she was alive,' Sam said. 'Nobody could live through that onslaught. And why kill her anyway? He didn't kill any of the others.'

'His mask's there. Perhaps she got it off him in the struggle. Perhaps she recognised him and this time he used the knife,' Ed suggested.

'Possibly. But was there a struggle? I keep coming back to it… not one single sign of a defence wound, yet look at the ferocity.'

Sam paused, her eyes locked on Louise, and said in a quiet, slow voice, her brain questioning everything: 'And why leave the mask when he's always been so careful, so forensically aware.'

'Panic?' Ed wondered.

'Or total lack of it,' Sam said. 'What if he wants us to believe it's the rapist?'

She rose quickly to her feet. Ed stood up, his left knee clicking as he straightened it.

CHAPTER THIRTY-SIX

'Look, her warrant card's on the floor. Isn't that a better souvenir than a driving licence? Why not take that?' Sam said.

She paused before asking Julie if she had seen Louise's purse.

'Try the handbag over there,' Julie said, pointing at the dressing table.

Sam picked up the handbag, removed a blue patent-leather purse, and flipped it open. 'Look, her licence is still here. It's in the first place you would look. Not taken. Why?'

Ed looked at the purse. 'Same again? Panic?'

Sam's eyes were full of doubt.

'It's possible... but I'm getting the feeling something's not right here, Ed,' she said, her eyes darting around the room.

'Maybe something wasn't right for him this time,' Ed said. 'Maybe she surprised him. Maybe she got his mask off. Things aren't going to plan, the fantasy's falling apart, and yet...' He stopped mid sentence and shook his head slowly. 'I agree,' he said quietly, his gloved right hand slowly rubbing his forehead. 'It's not right. Something's wrong here.'

'Look,' Sam interrupted, speaking quickly, pointing at things as she did so. 'Two photographs on the wall above the bed head. Not disturbed. The bedside table lamp's on the floor, the table's tipped over, but everything in this room above waist height is undisturbed. Everything on the dressing table, undisturbed. Those two pictures and glass ornament on the windowsill, undisturbed. All the blood, with the exception of the blood on the ceiling, is below waist height. I don't think Louise ever stood up. If she never stood up, surely he could have controlled her like he did the others? Could she start fighting from a horizontal position? Would she?'

Ed concentrated, trying to play through those final moments before Louise met the darkness.

'I can't see it,' he said. 'She was a negotiator. If she was in a weak position, she would have talked. No doubt about that. If she got the opportunity, she would have attacked but she was too bright to launch an attack from her bed.'

Sam nodded. 'And if he knew that she was a police officer – and given the way he plans everything he must have done – wouldn't he have been more inclined to tie her up? Louise is a cop. She's not likely to be compliant. None of us know how we would react in that situation but from his point of view, why take the chance? It doesn't add up.'

'So what are you saying?'

'Was she a target of rape?' Sam asked. 'Or was she a target of murder?'

'Okay, Sam. If you're thinking someone wants us to believe it's the rapist, but in fact Louise is a target of murder, and I accept we look at every possibility, what about the mask? Like you said on the phone, we've never put that out into the public domain. If it's not our man, how does the killer know about the ski mask?'

Sam stared at the mask, silent and thinking.

'And that's the crux of it, that's where it all falls apart. But this is just so unlike the others.'

'Maybe he just graduated from rape to sex murder,' Ed suggested.

'Possibly, but it just doesn't fit those rapist typologies we discussed,' Sam said, shaking her head.

'Human behaviour, and all of its subtle individual traits,' Ed said.

'Could be, but then again…'

Their discussions were cut short when Jim Melia, the small, slim, pathologist with the fingers of a concert pianist, came into the bedroom and greeted them. They had worked many murders together and introductions weren't necessary.

Jim knelt down, and Sam's eyes were drawn to the mass of hair in his ears, like the undergrowth in an abandoned garden, something she had never noticed before.

'We'll establish how many wounds at the mortuary, but I would suggest that any one of those to the area of the heart is potentially fatal,' Jim said.

'We can't understand the lack of defence wounds, Jim.'

'Have all the photographs been taken?'

Sam nodded.

Melia leaned forward to study Louise's hands and arms, moving them slowly with an unlikely grace. 'Unusual, not what you would expect… Let's roll her on to her side.'

'Ah! There's your answer,' Melia said, pointing to four large stab wounds in Louise's back, between her shoulders. 'If she was stabbed in the back first, that could explain why there's no defensive wounds. She wouldn't have the strength.'

Sam told him about the series of rapes they were investigating and how each victim described their attacker was wearing a ski mask and brandishing a knife.

'Well, this poor young lady wasn't vaginally raped,' Melia said. 'As you may be able to see, it appears she was menstruating. She has a tampon inside her vagina. That's not to say, of course, she has not been anally raped. Have any of the other victims been anally raped, or was there any attempt to anally rape them?'

'None,' Sam said, already contemplating the implications of the pathologist's findings.

'Well, we'll know more when we get to the office, so to speak,' Melia told them.

Sam and Ed walked outside into the damp air in silence. Sam wriggled out of her suit. Ed started to struggle out of his own.

'What are you thinking?' Sam asked.

'Apart from looking like an idiot in front of that lot?' Ed muttered, his back to the neighbours, pulling his foot out of the suit in an ungainly hop.

Paranoid, like Sam, that someone in the assembled throng could lip read, he kept his head low.

'No apparent rape, not unless he put a tampon inside her afterwards, which is a bit too far-fetched, even for someone who's planning every step. No obvious souvenirs taken. No broken window, so has he been earlier and forced it open? Wouldn't Louise have closed it anyway? Did he close it enough she didn't notice it? Or did he get in some other way? Tell you what, I don't know about you but I'm freezing. Let's get in one of the cars.'

Ed switched on the engine, and turned the heater up to the max. Sam took a tissue from her pocket, blew her nose and then rubbed her hands.

'The key,' Ed said. 'Is there any significance with that? And the knife? Missing from the block. If he took it, why didn't he bring his own? Mask and key left behind. Careless… or deliberate?'

'Agreed,' Sam said. 'Plus a sustained attack… but the mask? You were bang on, we've never put that into the public domain.'

Her voice trailed off.

The heat in the car was stimulating their thoughts in a way the cold could never do.

Sam shifted, turned and faced Ed. 'The way he got in may have been refined. We've put a lot of information out there telling lone females to report broken windows immediately. So breaking a window earlier would just massively reduce his chances of success as a result.'

'Did Louise leave the window open then?' Ed said.

Sam thought about it… would a sharp, highly trained cop take that risk?

'Possibly, but even if she did, I can't see our man leaving that to chance. The window doesn't look forced, but that's not to say it wasn't.'

Ed slid down the seat, splayed his legs underneath the

steering wheel, and looked at the roof lining, concentrating on Sam's words.

'The killer may have opened it on his way out just for our benefit. We know he's a planner so he may have got copy keys, or stolen them. How he's done that, God knows. I agree not bringing a knife with him but using one from the block, if that's how it played, fits more with a killer who's opportunistic rather than premeditated. You go to kill, you go armed. So if we're right about the knife, that's disorganised rather than organised. That's a huge shift in behaviour if it's the same man. Leaving the mask may have been panic. The key may have just dropped out of his pocket, or may have nothing to do with him. But the rest…'

Ed leaned forward and turned down the fan.

'Ifs, buts and maybes. It's messy, Sam. Too many variations.'

'I know. Let's make some calls as soon as we get to the mortuary. It'll be at least half an hour before the undertakers get Louise there. I want a search team doing the drains, gardens, and flat roofs around here to try and find the knife. Check the bins as well.'

'Distances?' Ed asked as he sat up straight and reached to the back seat for his notepad.

'Do it in a half-mile radius using Louise's house as the centre. If we have no luck, we can extend the search later. Get house-to-house to knocking on the doors in the immediate vicinity.'

'Okay.'

'Arrange a meeting with as many of our staff as you can muster after the post-mortem. I'll leave it to you to pick a family liaison officer and have them discuss with Louise's mum whether there was already a knife missing from the block. And re-check everything re that key.'

'Yeah, okay.'

'We'll also need a family liaison officer to visit the ex-husband. I don't want him finding out about Louise's death when I do the media. I'll call Dave Johnson and tell him where we are, and get him to tell everyone this is not necessarily linked to the rapes.'

Sam opened the door and got out. She bent down and put her head back into the car. 'We still need people to interview Crowther, and I want those stills from the surveillance available this afternoon. I'll organise a press conference about Louise's murder after the post-mortem. See you at the mortuary.'

Ed nodded as cold air made his cheeks tingle.

'Now shut the damn door, you're letting the cold in.'

———

The detention officer opened the blue interview-room door. Crowther jumped out of his seat and was speaking before the solicitor walked through it.

'Fuckin' hell, where've you been? Why didn't you come last night? I'm shitting it here.'

'Close the door, Terry, and sit down,' the bespectacled solicitor said in a quiet voice. After years of custody visits, she was used to even the coolest heads reacting badly to the strains of incarceration. 'There was no requirement for me to attend last night. The police told me you wouldn't be interviewed until this morning.'

'Fuckin' hell, have you seen what they're trying to pin on me? I'm no fuckin' rapist.'

'Why don't you tell me all about it, and we can go from there.'

Sitting down, Crowther scowled. 'Couldn't they have sent a bloke? This is embarrassing.'

Jill Carver sighed, removed her teal tortoiseshell Paul Smith glasses and stared into Crowther's sullen face. At 37 years of age, she was 13 years his senior, but hundreds of years from the world he inhabited.

The murder team had, as usual, given her the bare minimum of disclosure but she wanted to hear his account before advising him whether he should answer any questions in the forthcoming interview.

'No, they couldn't. Now, are you going to tell me what this is all about? Two counts of rape. The theft of underwear's insignificant at this stage,' she said, struggling to keep the distaste from her voice.

Jill leaned forward, straining to hear him. Crowther was suddenly fighting back tears, staring down at the table, his voice quivering. The smell of her perfume had his nostrils twitching, and he was unable to resist sneaking a quick look at her cleavage. Old habits…

'I haven't got the bottle to fuckin' rape someone. I've never had any kind of sex.'

Jill kept her expression neutral.

'Terry, the allegations are that you broke into their houses and raped them.'

His head snapped up. 'Are you fuckin' stupid? Are you listening? I've never had sex with anyone. Ever.'

Leaning back in her chair, she spoke quietly and slowly. 'Are you telling me that you are a virgin?'

He couldn't bring himself to maintain eye contact with her attractive round face, framed by deep black shiny hair, fearing that she would be grinning at him.

'Yes. Yes, I fuckin' am.'

Stifling a sob he continued: 'Get them to get a doctor and do a test. I've never had sex.'

Jill told him that wouldn't be necessary, and that the police had recovered a white pair of knickers from his house, which a witness called Jamie Hampton had identified as being similar to the ones she had stolen. The police had CCTV footage from the swimming baths showing him leaving not long after Jamie.

He looked up at her, his face on fire, and began nodding his head before allowing it to drop. His hands were trembling, his shoulders shaking, and he began sliding back and forth on the chair, staring at the floor.

'I steal their knickers and wank into them. I admit that, but I'm not a fuckin' rapist. They'll know about the indecency conviction. Fuck! They'll pin this on me.'

Raising his head, tears welling in his eyes, he stared at the dirty walls.

A rapist? What a joke. Sitting here is the longest I've ever spent with a woman that wasn't related to me. She's got to get them to believe me.

Jill Carver looked at him with a mixture of pity and revulsion. No way was he a rapist. Socially inadequate, no question. A pervert, a creep, absolutely… but a rapist? Not in the proverbial month of Sundays.

Reaching over to her soft leather briefcase on the floor, she pulled out a pad and her Mont Blanc fountain pen, a present from a grateful client, smoothed down the skirt of her dark blue suit, and sat upright.

'Okay, Terry, let's get you out of here. I need to know where you were on the nights of the rapes, and I want you to tell me about the knickers you stole.'

CHAPTER THIRTY-SEVEN

SATISFIED THAT ALL THE 'PLATES' were still spinning, Sam and Ed both put away their phones and went into the small office adjoining the mortuary where notes and tea were made, and began pulling on new paper suits.

Jim Melia, now wearing green overalls and white wellies, his Tweed jacket and black trousers hanging from a hook on the back of the door, sounded almost eager.

'C'mon then. Let's make a start.'

Sam's mobile vibrated. Trevor Stewart's name appeared on the screen.

'I better take this first. Give me a minute. Morning, Sir,' she said, walking out of the room.

'I'm pleased you didn't say 'good', Sam. What have we got, then, apart from the obvious – the tragic loss of a colleague.'

Sam described the scene and the initial actions she had instructed be carried out.

'Ski mask, you say. So our rapist's now graduated to murder.'

'Possibly, sir. We'll see what we've got after the PM which is about to start.'

'Why 'possibly', Sam? What are you thinking? Don't tell me you think this is unconnected?'

'I'm not convinced. Not at this stage. We're exploring all the options.'

Stewart was all cold, pompous authority. No sleaze or smut today.

'We need this sorting quickly. If you think they're unconnected, I'll appoint Dave Smithies to run the murder and you concentrate on the rapes.'

You manipulating bastard.

'There's no need for that, Sir. There are similarities. I suggest for now I run both.'

Stewart was silent and Sam could picture him wanting to bring in his favourite but caught by indecision.

'For now it is, then. I'll review it on Saturday. When's the press conference?'

'After the PM.'

'There'll be a lot of interest, obviously. Make sure you're prepared. If you need extra staff, let me know. Keep me in the loop.' He paused. 'Are you publicly linking the murder with the rapes?'

'I intend to tell them we are keeping an open mind.'

'Do that. Don't link them. They'll have a field day if we link them. It'll be open season on Eastern Police. I hope we don't find ourselves in a position where we could have prevented this.'

'I need to go, Sir.'

He hadn't asked how Louise's friends and colleagues working on the investigation were coping. Not asked about Louise's family. All he was interested in was covering his arse. Maybe she should tell his wife what he's really like.

'Speak to me after the press conference, then.' He ended the call.

'Let's go,' Sam said and followed Jim and Ed into the mortuary and shivered. These places were always freezing. And so dark. No natural light. Well there wouldn't be would there?

The musty smell of death seemed to seep from every part of the building, latching on to you so no matter how many showers you took, how many times your clothes went to the dry cleaners, it clung to you for days.

Like so many times before, Sam saw the concrete floor, the long, metal examining table, the draining hole, the knives and scalpels laid out in sequence, and the hosepipe on the floor ready to send water flowing around the body and down the plug hole, keeping the table free of blood and small matter.

Louise was the difference, her naked body on the table, lying on her back, arms pressing against the raised sides, feet either side of the draining hole. Even the local idiots, stumbling in here accidentally, would be in no doubt where they were.

The mortuary technician had prepared everything, and Sam did wonder how a petite, thirty-something female, ended up doing a job like this. Did they advertise in the Job Centre?

The technician, towards the end of the examination, would use the hand-held power drill with the circular bladed saw to remove the back of the skull. Always the worst sound, thought Sam; a screeching that made her clamp her teeth together, the blade overcoming the resistance of the skull, sending particles of bone dust into the icy air.

Sam tried to view the bodies as nothing more than carcasses, no different to animals in a slaughterhouse, and it was a mindset that generally worked, but in the inevitable silences that occurred during the post-mortem, there was no hiding the fact you were looking at a body that had recently been a living human being. She knew only too well this one was going to be tough. She looked away from Louise's lifeless eyes, and the image of her drunken, barefoot friend flashed through her mind again.

The Crime Scene Investigators were already milling about preparing for the examination. Under the instructions of the pathologist they would photograph each injury from a multitude of angles and label all samples that were taken.

Post-mortems varied in length, but Sam knew this one would take a long time; cataloguing, measuring, and photographing all the injuries during the initial external examination would, in her experience, take over an hour.

Standing less than a metre from the table, Sam swallowed hard and fought to put her emotions to one side. The first flash bounced off the camera. The examination had begun.

———

Manoeuvring her car through the hospital grounds, Sam mulled over the post-mortem.

Four stab wounds to the heart. Thirty-two wounds in total. A rage killing. The killer was in such a hyped-up state, even when Louise was dead and still, the frenzied stabbing continued.

The blood on the bedroom ceiling confirmed the vicious unrelenting nature of the attack, but it was during the post-mortem that the sheer force was brought home. The four wounds to the heart were such the knife had gone clean through and penetrated her back.

Was this the same man, if Louise's killer was a man, who was the rapist? The rapist asked if he had been a good lover. Would removing his mask turn him into a butcher?

There had been no rape this time and no torn tissue suggesting non-consensual anal sex.

The more she replayed the murder scene on her mental DVD player, the more convinced she was that they were hunting two different people.

The Press would no doubt link the murder and the rapes, jumping to conclusions; buzzing about like wasps around the dregs of a pint of a lager. The 24-hour news society of 21st-century Britain was a hungry beast that needed feeding, and if the media sharks weren't fed, they'd feed themselves. Sam knew she needed to manage them.

The so-called 'red tops' would sensationalise the investigation if they sniffed a connection, and more importantly, if they believed there was a lack of progress. Sam would need her wits about her at the press conference if she wanted to avoid a media circus baying for organisational blood.

Walking into the station, the smell of fish and chips rolled down the stairs like mist floating down a hillside. Sam's stomach lurched. When had she last eaten? In the office, detectives were eating as they typed; some had a bread bun on the side, and all had a mug of tea or a can of fizzy pop.

'Alright for some,' Sam said as she walked into the HOLMES room, raising a smile from her colleagues, smiles that quickly vanished. As she walked past a detective who had his mouth crammed with food, she grabbed a couple of chips from his polystyrene tray, regretting it immediately as one of them fell and landed on her blouse.

'Shit,' she said, louder than she intended, causing the whole office to look in her direction. Examining the stain, she cursed her lack of foresight in not having a change of clothes in the office. Thirty minutes to a press conference, and her mind was now focussing on whether the stain would be visible on TV. *Not the ideal preparation, Samantha.*

'How's it going with Crowther?' she asked.

Jason Stroud was stood beside a new board, examining the still photographs provided by the surveillance commander; they had been divided into two categories, those inside the coffee shop, and those outside.

'It's not.'

'No coughs, then?' Sam said, now standing next to Jason.

Jason smiled. 'Some people wouldn't cough if they had bronchitis. He's not one of them. He's like little boy lost. He's gone 'no reply' in the first interview on his brief's say so. She said outside the interview room he'll cough the knickers, but not the rapes. She looks fairly confident.'

'Who's his brief?'

'Carver. Jill Carver.'

'Pretty fit,' said one of the interviewers.

Sam didn't respond to the sexist comment, but her raised eyebrows and steely stare left him under no illusions he was treading on dodgy ground. She turned back to Jason who was on more dodgy ground than he realised.

'Sorry,' Jason said. 'He meant it from the point of view that it's unnerving Crowther. He's keeping his eyes down most of the time during the interview. Can't look at her.'

'Jill Carver,' Ed boomed, walking into the office, looking around to steal a chip.

'Otherwise known as the butcher, because of the cases, and detectives, she's carved to pieces. Watch her, Jason. She's got more faces than the town-hall clock, and she's not averse to flashing those eyes to get what she wants.'

'I gathered that much, but to be fair, watching him in the interview, I don't think he's our man,' Jason said.

Ed waited until he reached them and lowered his voice. 'Well, just be careful with her. The butcher nickname is double sided. When it's to her benefit, she'll happily use her womanly charms and handle some male meat if it will help her cause.'

'Ed!' Sam said, eyes wide and blazing, her voice taut with shock and disgust but without rising above a whisper.

'Sorry, Sam, but it needed to be said. I know lifelong vegetarians that worry about that particular butcher. Forewarned etcetera.'

Ed paused and rubbed his eyes, trying to remember what a decent night's sleep felt like, but when he spoke, his tone was alert.

'You wouldn't get her off the duty solicitor's rota. He must have asked for someone from her practice. Why would someone like Crowther ask for a brief like her? Maybe there's more to him than we think. Where's Dave?'

'We've not seen him this morning,' Jason said. 'Just presumed he was with you.'

'Not with us,' Sam said.

Turning the rest of the room, she shouted to no one in particular: 'Anything on Crowther's computer?'

'Just the usual porn sites. Nothing criminal,' someone piped up.

Sam glanced at the board displaying the surveillance photographs. 'There are more stills than I thought. Any joy yet?'

A seated detective answered: 'Not really. Some identified. Nothing yet. Early days. We'll get them sorted.'

Sam spoke to Ed. 'Find Dave. Make sure he's alright. Whatever his relationship with Louise, the guy's going to be in shock.'

CHAPTER THIRTY-EIGHT

THIRTY MINUTES LATER, make-up reapplied and teeth brushed, Sam, accompanied by the Head of Media Services, Peter Hunt, walked on to the raised platform in the media briefing room and cast her eyes over the assembled print, local radio and regional TV reporters. The nationals were also out in force.

Concentrate Sam.

Silence descended. Eleven sets of eyes watched her sit down behind a table littered with mobiles and digital recorders. Notepads were poised. TV cameras watched impassively from tripods while two photographers were on their feet, flashbulbs lighting up Sam's face.

I hope they can't see that stain.

Sam looked at her prepared statement and began.

'Just after 7am this morning police were called to an address in Rothbury Close where the body of a 34-year-old female was found. She has been identified as Louise Smith, a serving police officer, who lived alone at the address. Louise was separated from her husband.

'June Harker, her mother, discovered Louise this morning. Louise had been stabbed multiple times.

'A Home Office Forensic Pathologist has carried out a post-mortem, and extensive scientific tests are being carried out at Louise's home. Over 40 personnel are actively engaged on this investigation.

'I urge everyone to be vigilant when it comes to the security of their homes, and to contact the police if they notice anything untoward.

'I would ask anyone who has any information, or who saw or heard anything suspicious between 8pm last night and 7am this morning, to contact the incident room. Thank you.'

The reporters looked up, the photographers sat down.

Here we go.

The reporter from Sky got in first.

'Two single women have been sexually assaulted in their homes. Now a single woman has been killed in her home. Is it the same man?'

I knew that was coming.

'These attacks are being investigated separately. It's too early to say if they are connected.'

'Surely you must have some indication,' Sky man pushed.

'As I said, it's too early to be making those investigative conclusions.'

Sam looked at Sky man as she answered his question. He was now in a position of strength. Everyone else was an observer. He was having a conversation with her.

'Was the police officer targeted?' he asked.

'We are following a number of lines of inquiry. That is one of them. The alternative is that she was subject to a random attack. I don't believe that to be the case.'

Sam could sense some hostility in the room. Nobody else could get a word in. Not my problem, she thought to herself.

'Why would a serving police officer be targeted?' he asked.

He's after the terrorism angle.

So-called 'Islamic State' had declared their desire to murder a serving police officer.

'Louise may have been targeted because she was a police officer, but equally, she may have been targeted because she was Louise. As I've said, these are lines of inquiry we are following.'

More likely the latter, Sam thought silently.

Sky man crossed his legs. Others would now get the chance in their media scrum.

'You said the victim had multiple stab wounds. How many?' asked a blonde woman at the front, who Sam knew was a journalist from one of the 'red tops'.

When would the less experienced reporters realise that where you sat was key? Those at the front always dominated the conference.

'As I am sure you can appreciate, there are some details we need to keep back for a suspect interview. Suffice to say that Louise was stabbed multiple times.'

Questions were asked about which room Louise was found in, when she was last seen alive, how her mother was coping, whether she had any children, siblings, and how her colleagues were coping with the news.

It was Darius Simpson from the *Seaton Post* who dropped the bombshell question.

'Any suggestion that the killer was wearing a ski mask like the sex attacker?'

Everybody in the room sat up at the potentially sensational revelation.

How the hell does he know about the ski mask?

Sam felt her face redden.

'I am here today to appeal for information about the murder of Louise Smith, and I repeat, if anyone saw or heard anything suspicious after 8pm last night to contact the incident room.'

'But can you confirm that the previous attacks were committed by a man wearing a ski mask?' Darius asked.

I'm going to kill whoever leaked this.

Sam was relieved to hear calm and steadiness in her voice.

'No, I can't, but while we are talking about the previous attacks, I would urge everyone to be vigilant about their household security, and report anything suspicious to the police.'

Sam had learnt a long time ago that the secret in press conferences was to respond to a question, not answer it. Politicians did it all the time.

The blonde was back, picking up from Darius.

'A masked man represents a serious threat to single women. Are you any nearer to catching him?'

Sam stuck to her 'respond' tactic.

'Every intruder represents a threat. That is why I urge people to be vigilant around their security, and that is why I am keen to seek any information from the public, however small they may deem it to be. With regard to arresting the person or persons responsible, we are following a number of lines of inquiry.'

'Which you have presumably been following since...' the blonde said, looking at her spiral-topped notebook, 'November. What assurances can you give the public that you will catch this man?'

Sam silently thanked Peter Hunt, himself a hack from the old school who had long-ago coached Sam through just these skirmishes. Press cons were battles for control, a fencing duel played out – for the police at least – on a minefield. One careless move…

'Firstly, there may be more than one man. At no time have I said that all these attacks are linked, committed by the same perpetrator. We will leave no stone unturned. We will exhaust all lines of inquiry, but I am here to appeal for information into the murder of Louise Smith. I would reiterate that I am keen to hear from anybody who saw or heard anything suspicious between 8pm last night and 7am this morning.'

Peter Hunt stood up, his timing practised to perfection.

'Thank you, ladies and gents. I will arrange one-on-ones for those of you that are interested.'

The TV and radio preferred to have their own interview with the SIO.

Everyone, including Sam, was on their feet.

Darius Simpson shouted out a further question, throwing the room back into silence, and everyone's attention back on to Sam.

'Do we know if the knife used to kill this victim was the same type as used to threaten the victims of the sex attacks?'

Where's he getting his bloody information?

With her blood pressure rocketing, Sam's response was short and measured.

'As I said earlier, we are not linking the murder of Louise Smith to the sexual assaults at this time.'

Sky man was first to respond.

'Were the other attacks carried out by a man with a knife?'

'Those investigations have not as yet been linked to Louise's murders, and as such I am not going to comment today on the details of those attacks.'

'When will you link them?'

'When – and if – there is evidence to do so.'

Peter Hunt spoke again.

'Thank you, ladies and gents. I have a photograph of Louise available for those who want it.'

Sam was out of her seat. The one-to-one interviews could wait. She walked after Darius.

He stopped and turned around when Sam called his name. They had a mutual respect for each other, based on a professional relationship built up over many investigations, over many years, and neither had ever lied to each other.

'I need a word,' Sam said, taking hold of his arm and ushering him into a corridor with access restricted to police staff.

Turning to face him, she said: 'Darius, how did you know about the ski mask and knife?'

He looked into her eyes, his hands in the pocket of his brown corduroy jacket, his scarf, of varying tones of red and black, hanging loosely around his neck.

'I can't tell you that, Sam. I've got to protect my sources as much as the next guy.'

'Well, in that case,' Sam said, keeping the eye contact, 'as we've never put into the public domain the attacker was wearing a ski mask, it's a fair presumption that your source is the rapist. That means you're obstructing, maybe even conspiring to pervert, the course of justice.'

'Now hang on, Sam,' Darius said, his right hand now out of his pocket and scratching his thick, floppy blond hair.

She moved closer to him, her nose almost touching his, her minty fresh breath invading his personal space, and the sharp authority in her voice thrumming with underlying anger.

'I'm not hanging anywhere, Darius. I trust we both want the same result here, and if I think you are withholding evidence…'

She paused, a great believer in using silences to unnerve people.

Darius's shoulders dropped very slightly, and he bowed his head. Quietly, he answered, his right hand playing with his scarf.

'Fair enough, Sam. Brian Banks was shouting his mouth off in the pub the other night. Everyone who was in there must have heard him. But look, you didn't get that from me.'

Banks. Fucking idiot, she thought.

'Which pub?'

'The Golden Eagle.'

'Time?'

'I can't remember exactly. I went in early doors. Probably around six. He was telling his mates his daughter had been raped, and the guy was wearing a ski mask and had a knife. He's put five grand up for any information.'

'Jesus. Did you know anyone else in there?'

'No. Not by name anyway. I know them by sight. Seem a regular crowd on a Wednesday.'

'Right. I'll keep you posted if we get any breakthroughs.'

'Thanks. And Sam. Really, you didn't get any of this from me. He's a dodgy bastard.'

'Get what?' she said, looking at him over her shoulder, walking away from prying eyes and ears.

She pulled her phone out of her bag and made a call.

'All okay with the Press?' Ed asked, his mobile pressed to his ear.

'No, it bloody wasn't. How well do you know this Brian Banks idiot? He's been shouting his mouth off in the pub about how his daughter was raped by a masked man who got into her home.'

'Fuck! The stupid bastard.'

'I want you to go and see him, and tell him that he is in danger of single-handedly fucking up this investigation.'

She filled Ed in on her conversation with Darius. 'If Darius heard him, others in the pub could have done. After you give him a bollocking – and make it a good one – ask for the names of as many people as he can remember who were there that night. It could even be the killer was in the pub, overheard Banks, and wants us to believe it was our rapist.'

'I'm on it, Sam. Mind you, that would tend to rule Jason out. He knew that we had Crowther locked up.'

'But he doesn't think Crowther is our man, does he? He said it when we were talking about that solicitor. When did that become his opinion? Perhaps he knows Crowther's not our man. Maybe he knows better than any of us.'

CHAPTER THIRTY-NINE

REPORTERS WERE MILLING around chatting when Sam returned to the media briefing room. She survived, did a number of interviews unscathed and 40 minutes later was back in the HOLMES room.

Dave Johnson jumped to his feet and asked if he could speak to her in her office.

She glanced at her watch. 4pm.

'Everything okay?' she asked as she sat down behind her desk. 'We were worried about you this morning.'

He dropped into a seat and Sam spotted the sweat patches under his arms. She had never seen stains on Dave's shirts.

'Fine. I just needed some time out. It was a shock about Louise. Just trying to get my head round it. But listen, the lab's been in touch. We've got the DNA result off the condom wrapper. It's not Crowther's and it's not Amber's.'

'So if the rapist's not Crowther, the rapist could still be the killer.'

'Potentially, yes. It's also possible the DNA just belongs to someone who helped make the thing but that's highly unlikely. Everything is all automated these days. Crowther's admitted stealing the knickers, both pairs. His solicitor's given us a heads-up he's prepared to admit stealing more, but that's as far as it goes. He's having nothing to do with the rapes. Brief says he hasn't got it in him.'

Cupping her right hand around her chin, Sam considered Dave's words carefully before responding.

'It may be he knows we've got him anyway for the knickers from Danielle and the swimming baths and he's ready to chuck in a few other admissions to ingratiate himself, to con us into thinking he's coughing everything.'

Dave nodded, locked his hands behind his head, sweat stains on full show.

'Or it may be he's nothing more than a sleazy loser who steals women's knickers.'

Sam considered Crowther, picturing him in her head.

'We know he lives alone. Parents are dead. He doesn't seem to have had any girlfriends. He appears to all intense and purposes to be a loner.'

Dave nodded. 'I agree boss, but of course we know he was out running the night Amber was attacked.'

Sam shook her head, details darting through her mind.

She said: 'But the uniforms are adamant that he wasn't wearing an Adidas tracksuit, and we know from the CCTV that someone was out that night wearing a three-striped top. And remember, the girls have described the rapist's clothes as Adidas.'

Tilting her head, Sam looked at the ceiling hoping for a flash of inspiration from the dirty white paintwork, but there was nothing.

Keep working the evidence, Sam told herself.

Dave continued: 'The house-to-house teams were approached by a neighbour of Emily's who had just got back from a week in Lanzarote. She didn't know what was going on until yesterday. Seems she heard the sound of breaking glass at Emily's, went outside and the only person she saw was the postman doing his deliveries. She asked him about the noise and he told her he'd seen two boys run past him. One was carrying a cricket bat.'

'Interesting,' Sam said. 'Do we know who he is? At the

very least we'll be able to confirm when the time the window was broken.'

'We've already tracked him down. Bev Summers will see him later.'

'Excellent. When did that come in?'

'Last night.'

Sam wanted another look at the CCTV stills. Her brain was pounding, demanding a breakthrough, any scrap that would advance the investigation.

The February temperatures had done little to freeze the surface mud and water. 'Marvellous,' Ed muttered as he tiptoed like an overweight ballerina, the glossy shine on his black leather shoes vanishing with each step. Why were the offices always at the back of the yard in these places?

Scrap metal seemed to be piled everywhere and the noise from the crusher pounded his ears like a Canary Island dance club. A raised-arm signal from the owner brought down the decibels, but not much, and Ed's ears were still ringing.

'Sergeant Whelan. How can I help you?' Brian Banks shouted.

Wearing a red sleeveless padded jacket, a checked woollen shirt, blue jeans and brown rigger boots, Banks was playing to the crowd of three next to him.

Past caring about his shoes, Ed marched up to Banks, and like a hitch-hiker thumbing a lift, indicated 'the office'. He spoke with just a hint of aggression.

'I need a word. A private word.'

'And good day to you too, Sergeant.'

'Now,' Ed said, marching towards the office, the sniggers of Banks's audience only adding to his anger.

Banks stepped into the office. 'Tea?'

Ed slammed the door shut and his voice erupted.

'You've been shouting your mouth off in The Golden Eagle about the attack on your Danielle.'

Banks stepped toward Ed, the gap between them so small

their toes were almost touching, Banks's eyes were bulging and when he shouted, Ed could see saliva clinging to his lips.

'Don't you dare come in here and accuse me of shouting my fuckin' mouth off. What the fuck are you doing about catching the bastard who attacked Danielle? Fuck all by the look of it.'

Ed matched Banks's volume and aggression. 'For your information, we're working our bollocks off to catch this bastard, but you letting your gob go won't do anything but fuck it up. Now the Press know the bastard who attacked Danielle was wearing a mask. Want to know how? Because someone heard you being the big man on Wednesday night in the fuckin' pub.'

Ed wondered whether Banks's eyes were going to burst.

'I was fuckin' angry, for fuck sake! My daughter's raped in her home by a twat wearing a mask.'

'But we'd deliberately kept that from the Press,' Ed said. 'We'd not released it and I know the girls sure as hell didn't. So it's down to you shouting your fuckin' mouth off.'

Banks walked backwards and sat on the corner of the desk, his arms outstretched, palms facing upwards, and the redness draining fast from his face.

'Look Ed, I was wound up. I'm sorry. I wasn't thinking. I wanted to kill the bastard and I still do. I put out five grand to find him.'

Taking his cue from Banks, Ed lowered his voice.

'I know you have. Look, I understand where you're coming from but you're not helping. The guy that attacked Danielle will be a loner. He's not going to be running around telling the world and his wife what he's done. Your five grand won't sort anything out.'

Ed put his hands in his trouser pockets before continuing. 'There's a guy in custody who stole a pair of Danielle's knickers a few weeks ago.'

Banks shot up off the desk. 'You're fuckin' joking?'

'Before you go jumping to any conclusions, we don't think he attacked Danielle. I don't want to find him beaten up somewhere.'

'I don't even know who the fucker is.'

'I'm sure it wouldn't take too long.'

'Sounds to me like the wanker deserves it. What are you fuckers doing protecting nonces like him?'

Ed held Banks's hate-filled eyes.

'Just leave it, Brian. And while I'm on, having Duncan Todd beaten up wasn't a particularly bright idea either.'

'Duncan Todd? I don't know what you're talking about.'

'Well, we'll leave it at that, then. You know, and now you know I know.'

A temporary silence then Ed made his move to get the man onside.

'Now I want you to do something for me. Something that might actually help catch your Danielle's attacker, not balls it up.'

Banks's eyes narrowed. He spoke slowly. 'Go on.'

'I want you to make a list of everybody you can remember being in the pub that night and what they were wearing as best as you can remember.'

'Yeah, okay, but how will that help?'

'I want to know who overheard you so we can visit them and tell them not to say anything. Call it damage limitation,' Ed lied.

Ed Whelan had only one interest about who was in the pub. If the rapist and the killer weren't one and the same, the killer had to have heard about the ski mask and before Louise's murder, those who overheard Banks in the pub were potentially the only ones apart from police officers to have known about it.

Ed left the yard having told Banks he would telephone him later for the list. Clearly Banks wouldn't remember everyone but visiting those he was able to recall would lead to other names and the domino effect would begin.

In between tears, and protracted silences, June Harker seemed to make endless cups of tea, shuffling from the living room to the kitchen, her red tartan sheepskin-lined zip-up boot slippers never fully lifting off the floor. Her blue, thick cotton dress and white Arran cardigan were immaculately clean but emphasised her frailty in the small, well-kept house, so hot the Family Liaison Officer wondered if the radiators had been pumping out heat since September.

Sitting down, his jacket laid across the arm of the plain green wing-back armchair, waiting for yet another weak, milky tea in a china cup, Paul Adams looked around at the framed photographs of a young Louise playing in the street, noting the cars captured in the background were smaller, more boxy than those today. It was clear the street outside this house had been her playground, a house that had been her childhood home.

A head-and-shoulders photograph of Louise in her police uniform, displayed in a large silver frame, took pride of place on the pine fire surround.

He took the drink and sipped it out of politeness. June seemed to be sitting to attention like old people of a certain background tend to do when they are in the company of so-called authority. Paul listened to her shaking voice, synchronised with the shaking of her cup on her saucer, telling him Louise's first love had been her job.

'Alan Smith loved himself, though. He never liked Louise being in the police. All those men,' June said. 'He kept saying she would have an affair. He was always accusing her if she was late home. Then it was him that had one. Not that it surprised me. And they had only been married three years. So much for his vows! No, I never liked him, but I kept my own counsel. Louise was besotted with him.'

As a vacant look overcame her, Paul gently pushed for more, knowing a devil could be hiding in the detail.

'Do you know where he's living now, June?'

June raised the cup to her lips, fighting back tears. 'Living over the brush with a woman somewhere in Newcastle.'

Paul had an address for Alan Smith, and knew that he had already been told Louise was dead.

'Sorry to ask these questions, June, but I need to establish certain things. Was Alan ever violent towards Louise?'

June stared ahead, thinking hard.

'I don't think so... No. They argued, but I don't think he ever hit her. Most of her friends were police officers. She should have married one of them. He was a brewery rep, so he was always in pubs, talking to women, no doubt. I told Louise to go and meet someone else after he left, but she never did. Now she never will.'

The silent sadness that followed June's sharp intake of breath made the rattling of her cup on the saucer seem deafening. Paul stood and gently took the cup from her, fearing it would fall off the saucer. He put it on the dark occasional table next to her.

'Will someone be going to see Alan?' she asked, looking up at Paul.

'I'll see him later, June. Did Louise ever mention anyone threatening her?'

'No. Everybody loved her. Why would anyone want to hurt her?'

'That's what we'll find out. Detective Chief Inspector Sam Parker will visit you later. She's very good. She knows what she's doing. She's in charge.'

June nodded.

'I'm sorry. I know that this is really hard. Can you tell me if any knives were missing from the block in Louise's kitchen?'

June's face was full of concentration again.

'I don't think so.'

'What about her keys? Were any of those missing?'

'No. There are only the two sets as far as I know. She has one and I have the other. I got Alan's when he left. Louise's key is in the hall, on the table. I used mine to open the door this morning.'

Her voice fell away. Paul could imagine what was replaying in her mind.

'Does anyone else have a key?'

'No. Not even the cleaner. Louise leaves the key under the

plant pot when she comes. I told her not to leave the key there, but she never listened.'

'Do you know the name of the cleaner?'

'It changes. Just depends. They come from an agency. 'Mrs Muck Out' or something liked that.'

'How often?'

'Once a week. Always on a Wednesday. Our Louise said they were very good.'

Paul Adams talked generally about inquests, funerals, and the set-up of the investigation, before June politely asked if he could come back later. She looked exhausted.

'Is there anyone I can call to come and sit with you?' Paul asked.

'No. There's no one. I prefer to be by myself anyway.'

'Tell you what, I'll be back in a couple of hours. Is that okay?'

'Yes. Thank you.'

The single tear that trickled from her right eye slid slowly down her cheek.

Alone in her house, she shuffled into what had been the dining room of her pre-war semi before Louise converted it into a bedroom (*I'm not spending good money on a stair lift our Louise*) and rested her weight on the Zimmer frame she had kept out of sight of the detective. She gripped the metal as tightly as her bony arthritic knuckles would allow and stared at the crucifix on the wall, tears now rolling down her face.

'How did you allow this to happen?' she whispered.

Nothing anyone had ever preached from the pulpit had prepared her for the discovery of her only child's mutilated body.

Her chest heaved, her voice wailed and the sobbing began.

CHAPTER FORTY

THE COLD AIR was a welcome contrast to the stifling heat in the house. Paul Adams walked to the car, relieved the awkward first meeting, a step into the nightmare of another's personal tragedy, was over. He had been there for hours and his only short break was when he walked down June's path to hand a photograph of Louise to another member of the team. Copies would be needed for the press conference.

There would be many more visits, more tears and recriminations, but the first one was over. No introductions would be necessary at the next.

He now had information he could feed into the HOLMES room, information that would be important to build the picture of Louise and her life. He knew Sam Parker would value his contribution to the investigation. 'The more we know about the victim, Paul, the more we know about the killer,' Sam would say, like a mantra.

He wanted to impress her. Sam Parker wielded influence. She could get him on to her team where he would work on high-profile investigations and get noticed, improve his chances of promotion. He would accept the piss-taking by the older detectives on the team. It was part of the game and promotion was everything.

Bev Summers had joined the police at 18, and now 23 years later, had never married. A career detective, she preferred to live alone under her rules rather than living a married life of compromises.

Staring into the glass panel of the door, the internal hall light bounced back her reflection as clear as if she'd been peering into crystal blue water on a sunny day. Her light grey suit and blue-and-white-striped blouse had seen better days; her short blonde hair with its split ends would require Lisa's wizardry when she had time for a trip to the hairdressers. The tight wrinkles around her mouth, the result of a lifelong love affair with cigarettes, were beyond monetary, or human, intervention.

Sam was standing next to her. She wanted to speak to Bev about the phone call and the flowers, confide in a woman, a woman she had known for years. The journey had provided the opportunity.

Bev knocked on the brightly painted green front door, a complete contrast to the rotting window frames, of 19, Felton Drive, a detached house on the Gull Estate.

'You do the talking,' Sam said.

A man in his mid-20s opened the door, his short dark brown hair drawing the eyes to his short, pointed nose.

'Yes?' he said in a quiet, almost timid, voice, showing Bev more of the left side of his face than his eyes.

Bev held forward her warrant card.

'Hi. Mr Spence? Michael Spence? I'm DC Summers. CID. I wonder if I can have a word? Nothing to worry about. It's about a broken window, and you telling a lady that you saw a couple of young lads running away with a cricket bat.'

'Oh. Yes, the boys with the bat. I remember.'

'Can we come in?'

Sam watched him change his stance; right hip pushed against the door frame, left arm touching the other side. Was he blocking their way in? He looked vaguely familiar. She hardly saw her postman – she was at work or still in bed when the post arrived, but a few weeks ago she did sign for a couple of books. Was it him?

'Will it take long?' he asked.

'Not really. Just a couple of details I need,' said Bev.

'Okay. Alright. I'm not sure I can help much.'

They followed him down a long hallway then took the first door on the right into the lounge. A harsh, pungent smell like ripe blue cheese hit them like a punch, the stale odour a physical thing. Sam's mouth twisted in a reflex and Bev's right hand shot up to her nose, her nostrils drawing in the welcome remnants of nicotine from her fingers.

A long, gold faded Dralon settee was against the back wall and two worn matching armchairs were either side of it. The stained, threadbare carpet hinted it had started life as brown a couple of millennia ago. Sun-faded yellow paint covered the woodchip wallpaper, and the ornate wall lights had patches of brass-coloured metal showing through the gold paint. The decor matched the era in which the house was built, the only concessions to modernisation and the movement of time an enormous flat-screen wall-mounted TV, a Sky digibox and an Xbox.

After a quick glance, checking for things they would rather not touch, Sam and Bev sat down on the armchairs, Bev suddenly thankful of her old suit.

'Michael. As I said, I'm investigating the broken window, you know, where you saw some men running away.'

'Yes,' he said shuffling on the settee. 'I was delivering. I work for the post office, as you can probably guess,' indicating his uniform with hands so small they looked as though they should be on the wrists of a child.

Sam couldn't help notice the tramline creases on his shirt and trousers. At least he keeps himself clean, she thought, not like this bloody house.

'I heard the sound of broken glass, and then they ran past me. One of them was carrying a cricket bat.'

'Were they running towards you?'

'Yes.'

'Did you see where they came from?'

'I think they ran down one of the driveways, but I couldn't be sure. I didn't think the CID would be interested in broken windows?'

'We're interested in all crime,' Bev said, her voice light, unthreatening. 'Now, can you describe these men?'

'More like boys, really. About 16, 17, I would say. I can't remember what they looked like. I didn't think it would be important. I thought it was just two lads who'd broken a window playing cricket.'

'Can you remember anything about them?'

'They had tracksuits on. Adidas, I think. Yes. Adidas. Black. Both were black. One lad was ginger, one was dark haired. About my height.'

'Five foot ten?'

'Yeah. About that.'

'Anything else?'

'No, not really. I only saw them for a couple of seconds, and then they were past me.'

He shuffled.

'What about the bat? Can you remember anything about that?'

'Not really no… wait… yes. Yes, I can. It was a Slazenger bat. I remember that now.'

'Did they speak to each other?'

'No, they were just laughing.'

Sam glanced around the room. There was no personal footprint; not one ornament, not one print or poster on the walls, and no family photographs.

'Who do you live here with, Michael?' Sam asked.

'Is that important?' he mumbled, staring at the floor.

'Just making conversation. Typical detective, always asking questions.'

'I live by myself since my mother died. I used to live with her.'

'Do you have any brothers or sisters?'

'No. I'm sorry but I've told you what I know.'

Sam pressed on regardless. Was he getting agitated?

'Michael, do you always deliver on the Gull estate?'

'I do. It's terrible what has been happening there. I mean not being safe in your own house. The papers have been full of it.'

'Yes, it's terrible. But we'll catch him.'

'I hope you do,' said Michael in a quiet voice, his gaze fixed on the floor, his hands, clasped together, resting on his knees.

Staring at the top of his head, Sam said nothing for about 10 seconds and then rose to her feet.

'Did you know any of the girls who've been attacked?'

'I know them by sight. I don't know them, though. Like I said, it's terrible.'

Sam resisted the urge to probe further. How did he know who the victims were? They had never been named. Had he seen the police activity at the houses when he was delivering the post and put two and two together? Did he deliver those books?

He may need to be interviewed again and they could get to the bottom of it.

One thing was already certain: he would know who lived alone. Single women living alone didn't get post addressed to anyone else. Chances are he would have more knowledge about single females than Crowther. He would pass unnoticed in the area during daylight. What was more natural than a postman walking up someone's driveway?

According to the house-to-house team, no one else had seen anyone running away from the broken window. Would he have said anything to anyone had the witness not asked him about it?

Walking through the hallway, Sam looked over her shoulder.

'Do you play cricket, Michael?'

'Can't stand the game.'

'Me neither,' Sam said, stepping outside, filling her mouth, nostrils, and lungs with cold, clean fresh air. Was she imagining her skin itching?

'Michael, did you tell the occupant of the house that you had seen two boys running away?'

'No.'

'Oh. Okay. Thanks then,' and she walked off down the path, Bev following.

'I never see her. She's always at work,' he shouted.

Sam didn't turn around.

In the car, Bev lit a cigarette, put the pink lighter back in her handbag, and blew smoke through the open window, her two-fingered salute to the anti- smoking brigade who had banned smoking in police vehicles. Sam hadn't objected when they were driving here.

Sam ignored the cigarette. Her eyes were fixed on his front door, her mind replaying their conversation.

She had been in the house for a matter of minutes, but there was something not quite right about Michael Spence. He had looked nervous, shifty even. He couldn't really describe what the boys looked like, yet he remembered the make of their clothing. He hated cricket, but in what could have only been a fleeting glance, he recalled the bat was a Slazenger. Two separate pieces of information, each where he remembered the manufacturers. It was almost as if he remembered too much. Too much, and yet nothing he said would lead to an identification of the two youths.

Sam had a niggle, a feeling like an itch she couldn't quite reach.

Had she just been talking to the rapist?

Why had he not told Emily? Was she always at work? Easily checked. It would be great to have Emily signing for something from him after the window was broken.

She smiled to herself. She loved the hunt, and was an ardent believer that if you took everything at face value, trusted everything you were told, nothing would ever be detected.

The 'ABC' of investigations: accept nothing, believe nothing, challenge everything.

Paul Adams leaned against a railing, inhaled deeply on his

cigarette, and gazed over the River Tyne. Alan Smith lived in a two-bedroom apartment on Newcastle's quayside, a converted bonded warehouse, with its large living room and kitchen opening on to a balcony overlooking the river and the quayside's lively bars and restaurants.

The furniture was modern, neutral walls displayed abstract framed prints, while the flowers on the windowsill hinted at a feminine touch.

Alan's heavily pregnant-looking stomach showed a love for his work that was confirmed by the hangdog jowls and the broken veins in his cheeks. At 32, his nose hadn't yet taken on the bulbous, angry red of the hardened drinker, but the facial signposts suggested it wouldn't be long.

Stubbing his cigarette end on the top of a bin, Paul wondered how Alan Smith had ever pulled Louise. He had certainly been punching above his weight, but the world seemed full of fat men with attractive women.

He telephoned Dave Johnson. 'I've seen June. I've just left Alan's, and I'm about to go back to June's.'

'How are they?'

'June's devastated, and Alan's blaming himself, saying if he'd not left her, this wouldn't have happened.'

'A bit late for that now,' Dave said.

'He's going on about visiting June. I'll mention that to her. June has no time for him. Understandable, I suppose.'

He gave Dave Johnson an update of both visits.

June Harker sat alone in her front living room. Was this how it felt when your heart had been ripped out?

Photograph albums covered her thighs and she turned the pages, holding them with the tenderness of a historian handling a precious old book, pausing to look at each photograph of Louise. Her husband had been a keen amateur photographer when he was alive, and the pictures had always given them thousands of memories.

She looked at Louise in school plays, on family holidays,

her teenage birthdays, and her police passing-out parade. Tears flowed down her face. She knew then that her broken heart would never heal.

Coping with the loss of her beloved Jack, who had succumbed to cancer, had been hard enough. But this? Her Louise gone. Taken from her like that? She would never recover. She didn't even feel like she wanted to.

Jack had been 78. She was 73. Louise was a young woman. Why? Not even her faith would provide the emotional crutch she needed to walk this path. Church? What good had come from going there? A life spent being a believer. A believer in what? No God would have left Louise so unprotected, allowed that to happen to her in her own bedroom.

Was suicide a sin? She couldn't remember, and in reality she didn't care. What did she have left to live for now? Her family had been taken from her. Everything she held dear was no longer with her.

The nice young policeman had explained the coroner would look to release Louise's body within 28 days, whether or not anyone was charged with her murder. June knew she wouldn't wait that long. She couldn't go to her own daughter's funeral. She looked at the photograph of Louise on the mantelpiece in her police uniform and vowed that her own funeral would take place before her lovely, beautiful daughter's.

CHAPTER FORTY-ONE

Approaching the police station door, darkness already descending, Ed was aware of someone coming up behind him. Looking over his left hand shoulder, he saw Jason Stroud.

'Can I have a private word?' Jason asked.

Ed stopped, turned around, and walked back into the car park. 'Everything alright?' He looked directly at the detective as he spoke.

Jason spoke so quickly Ed wanted to tell him to stop and breathe.

'I know that you and Sam have spoken with Celine. She's told me what she'd said, and I know she told you about the rape fantasy but whatever it sounded like, I'm not the rapist. You can't think that Ed. Think what you want about me, but I am not the rapist.'

Ed listened. He knew better than to interrupt and start asking questions. The words were speeding from Jason's mouth, like a toddler scampering down a hill, each step more rapid than the last, trying to retain their balance.

'There's a world of difference between fantasy and reality. What two consenting adults do behind closed doors is a matter for them. Other people might not agree with it, but if it's consenting, there's no issue. That's a world away from breaking into someone's house and raping them. Fuckin' hell, Ed, I'd never do that!'

Ed's voice, in contrast to Jason's, was so controlled it was almost hypnotic.

'Jason, believe you me, if we thought you were the rapist, we'd have arrested you. You can thank Sam for not overreacting to what Celine told us. We both know bosses who'd have shit themselves, gone running to someone else to make the decision what to do with you. She didn't. She kept the lid on it.'

Changing to a more assertive tone, Ed continued: 'She'd have arrested you if there was other corroborative evidence, you know that, but there wasn't. Fuckin' hell, Jason, she didn't even take you off the inquiry.'

'I know. I know. I panicked when Celine told me. I could just imagine how it must have sounded. I tried to imagine how I would have reacted if someone told me that about another cop. Not sure what I would have done.'

'Exactly,' Ed said. 'So you've got Sam to thank. It wasn't my decision.'

'I appreciate it, Ed.'

'Don't thank me, thank her.'

'I will. Cheers. It would've destroyed me if that had got out.'

It might still destroy you, Ed thought. You even had my skin crawling.

Ed found Sam in her office, sitting behind her desk but obviously deep in thought.

'You okay?' he asked.

'I'm fine. I'm just trying to put something into perspective about Louise's death. I'm still not sure about the rapist and the killer being the same person.'

Ed nodded, his mind turning over the twists and turns of the investigation, all they knew and everything that remained maddeningly out of reach.

'I've been giving it some thought too,' he said. 'Let's say that they're not the same. If that's the case, we're looking at someone staging a crime scene.'

Sam pursed her lips, fatigue written across her face.

'I know. And we both know that one of the reasons for staging a crime scene is to lead us away from the most logical suspect. So the key is identifying that suspect.'

She paused, and then said: 'How did you get on with Banks?'

'I'll ring him soon,' Ed said. 'He was mad as hell at first but he's going to try to remember as many people as possible. That'll give us a start and we can hopefully identify everyone who was in the pub at the time. I gave him the hard word, told him he was in danger of blowing the whole investigation.'

'Good,' Sam said, picturing the meeting, knowing how Ed would have handled the man.

'Banks didn't tell his mates whether the mask was left behind,' Ed went on. 'He couldn't describe the knife, either. Anyone trying to have us over would have to improvise.'

Sam nodded again.

'And hopefully that'll be their downfall.'

'Absolutely,' Ed said, taking a seat. He knew these moments, bouncing ideas around, were a vital part of any investigation, but he was also aware they could take time.

And time was something they couldn't afford.

'I was coming at it from a different angle,' Sam said. 'I was concentrating on the overkill aspect, all that rage.'

'Okay,' Ed said, letting Sam run.

'Anyone of those stab wounds to the heart would have been fatal. She would have bled to death, no question. Yet the killer kept on stabbing her, as if he couldn't stop.'

Sam stood up and began pacing the room.

'Overkill,' she went on. 'Overkill always, always, means it's personal, an emotional attachment between killer and victim. Could be just an argument and then suddenly something becomes the trigger.

'But I doubt that happened here. Neither of us thinks Louise ever got out of bed. If there'd been an argument before the attack, you would have expected Louise to at least be out of the bed. No, it's something else, something a lot deeper than a row. Like I say, this was personal… emotional.'

'So what you thinking? Family? Friends?'

'We don't have a suspect, or even a cluster of suspects. But I think she knew her killer, and she knew the killer well enough for them to have that emotional attachment.'

Sam sat down, kicked off her shoes, and wriggled her toes. Bliss.

'Whatever the trigger was, it had gone off before she woke up. Has to be. Whether that was before or after he got into the house, it was before she woke.' And with overkill, Sam and Ed both knew, a knife was invariably the weapon of choice.

'We need to find out more about Louise's life,' Sam said. 'That's where he's hiding.'

Sam paused and slid her feet reluctantly back into her shoes – the price you paid for style, she thought for the millionth time.

'How much do we really know about Louise?' she said. 'Has she any skeletons in her cupboard? Really, who hasn't?'

Ed thought about Louise and realised Sam was right.

'I don't know the answer to that,' he said. 'I would have thought the cupboard was clear but I've seen so much over the years nothing surprises me any more. If she has, God bless her, we'll find them.'

'Let's go next door and get a coffee.'

In the HOLMES room and with hands on hips, Sam stared at the surveillance photographs on the board. There were so many, most of them, perhaps all of them, worthless to the investigation, just honest people going about their lives. Sam's scanning eyes fixed on the photograph in the top right corner.

'Bev!' she shouted, looking over her shoulder. 'Come here! Look at that.'

She pointed to the photograph.

'Bloody hell!' Bev said, eyes wide.

'Is this a private conversation or can anyone join in?' Ed appeared beside them.

Sam pointed to the man sat in the coffee shop.

'That's Michael Spence. The postman who delivers on the Gull.'

'The one who saw the lads running away from the broken window?' Ed asked.

'The very same,' Sam said, her heart rate rising for the second time that day, the reflex reaction when there was a potential breakthrough.

'He might have been in the wrong place at the wrong time. Postmen drink coffee like the rest of us,' she said, trying to keep calm and curtail the enthusiasm of everyone, herself included. It was all too easy to make things fit.

Jason joined them at the board and looked at the image. 'Oh shit.'

'What?' Sam demanded.

'Christ, I've just twigged,' Jason said, his voice high with excitement. 'Ed, when you called me out last Sunday, I was buying a tracksuit in a shop at the retail centre. This guy, I don't know how I didn't see it earlier, was opposite me looking at the same tracksuits.'

Jason had reached towards the board and was repeatedly tapping the photograph of Michael Spence.

'What! And you've just realised now?' Sam said, not trying to hide her anger.

'There's that many photographs,' Jason said, his tone laced with embarrassment. 'I just didn't see him.'

'Are you sure it's him?' Ed pushed, his speech deliberately slow and deadpan. Like Sam, he had watched too many false dawns.

'Positive. I recognised him at the time, but I couldn't place him. He's my postman.'

'What tracksuits were you both looking at?' Ed asked, his voice still calm but adrenaline running riot inside.

'Adidas.'

Ed let out is breath slowly but his mind had been ignited by the information. Michael Spence had been looking at Adidas tracksuits the day after the attack on Danielle.

'Jason,' Ed said, 'find Dave Johnson. Tell him to get

271

someone to go to the sports shop. They'll still have the CCTV. Hopefully we can see him paying at the till.'

Back in her office, Sam rocked in her chair and looked up at the ceiling. Spence was in the coffee shop and he was looking at an Adidas tracksuit the day after Danielle was attacked! But take a breath, she told herself. Be calm. First things first. They needed to establish what time he went into the coffee shop. That wouldn't be difficult, not with the digital cameras on a timer. Had he been there before or after Amber?

'So,' Sam said, looking at Ed, 'he says he sees two boys running away after the window's broken. Did he see two boys, or is the broken window down to him? Neither of those lads, if they exist, are the rapist. Our guy's a loner, a loner who wouldn't involve anyone else in his planning and preparation. If Spence's lying about them, then mentioning the cricket bat was a mistake. He knows the window's broken by a cricket ball. How does he know that? Simple – he broke it.'

Ed bit on a thumbnail.

'Maybe he panicked when the neighbour spoke to him, said the first thing that came to into his head? In this case, the truth. He describes them as wearing Adidas tops. Not Nike, or Puma, or any other brand. Adidas. Is he being too clever for his own good?'

Sam put her elbows on the desk.

'The ball's designed to make the victim think the broken window was just a schoolboy accident? The ball's no coincidence. If it was, then why put it in my flowers?'

Sam pushed her chair backwards and jumped to her feet.

'Bastard,' she said. 'He's the one.'

'Okay,' Ed said, following Sam's train of thought, 'let's think about it. We know he lives alone, but we don't know if he's a loner. He said he knew the victims. How does he know who they are? Seen the police activity? Or he knows them because it's down to him.'

Sam had kept her face carefully neutral. She reminded herself again how easy it was to convince yourself the evidence was a neat fit if you jumped to the wrong conclusion.

'Let's lock him up on suspicion,' she said. 'We've enough for that. Get his house searched. Same arrest and search strategies we used for Crowther. Use the same search team. They know what they're looking for. We know he's taken souvenirs. We need to find them.'

Ed scribbled down her instructions.

'Sort out the intelligence picture on him,' Sam said. 'Get Jason to work up an interview strategy. Let's get him in today, but make sure that we get him away from the house. I don't want him getting rid of anything incriminating.'

Ed nodded.

Sam ran her fingers through her hair.

'Use Bev Summers on the arrest team. She knows him. We need to find something, and we need to do it quick. If he panicked when the neighbour confronted him, let's see how much we can get him to panic now.'

Ed stopped writing, pen hovering over the page.

'We might run out of time today,' he said. 'Might be better getting him early doors tomorrow. That said, it's a big risk. If he attacks someone tonight…'

Sam thought about it, weighing up the options and feeling the pressure that was all on her shoulders.

'He's never done two in a week, but that's not to say he won't,' she said. 'We can't afford to lose those souvenirs, though. We can't give him time to burn them or flush them down the loo. If he's got the driving licences in his house, they're not going to take much destroying.'

Ed played through the arrest in his mind, watching it unfold like a movie reel.

'If we go in, it'll need to be a rapid entry,' he said. 'Flushing them down the toilet shouldn't be an issue. Two cops run up the path. One with a sledge hammer, the other with a plastic dustbin. Smash the drainpipe, put the bin underneath it. That'll catch everything flushed down the loo. Burning them is different. That all depends on speed.'

Sam nodded, impressed and thankful she had someone like Ed on her side.

She said: 'It would help if we knew if he smoked. If he does, he's sure to have a lighter or matches and they'll likely be close.'

'Does he smoke?'

'I didn't see him smoking, but I wasn't there long,' Sam said, trying to remember if there was ashtray in that rancid room.

'Chances are if he's a smoker, he'd have had one when you were there, especially if it's him,' Ed said. 'I don't care how in control he thinks he is, his arse would have been nipping.'

'Yeah, I suppose so,' Sam replied, staring at the surveillance photo she'd taken from the wall, her hands raising and lowering it, bringing it closer then further from her face. 'I didn't say anything in the other office… Spence… I've spoken to him in the past. It just clicked when Jason identified him. I got a parcel off him a couple of months ago. He delivered my books.'

Sam allowed the photograph to fall out of her hand and drop on to the desk.

'Are you sure?' Ed asked.

'Absolutely. How in hell didn't I realise earlier?'

'It might just be a coincidence, you know,' Ed said, taking the photograph and staring at the grainy image.

'Coincidence, yeah, that'll be right.' Sam reached again for the still and took it from Ed's hand. 'We don't believe in them, remember. He's the one Ed. It's him.'

CHAPTER FORTY-TWO

JUNE HARKER SAT in the wing-backed armchair, oblivious to everything in the world except her overwhelming sense of grief. How had other parents coped with such a loss? Did they live or just function? What was it like at Christmas and birthdays, those special times? Her heart had been ripped out and it couldn't be any more painful had it been torn from her body in a medieval execution.

Slumped in the chair, she began drifting. Her boot slippers were placed neatly next to her feet. She was wearing the navy blue suit and white blouse she wore to Louise's wedding. In her hands she held the photograph in the silver frame, Louise with a beaming smile underneath her police hat. On the table next to her was a bottle of Cherry Brandy, a leftover from the last Christmas she had shared with her daughter, and seven blister packs of paracetamol. The bottle and packs were both empty.

She felt sorry for the Family Liaison Officer who would find her; he seemed a nice young man, but he would be used to dead bodies, and besides, she wasn't anything to him. Hopefully he wouldn't come back too quickly. She hadn't left a note. Who did she have to read her words? She didn't care who got the money from her savings account, or from the sale of the house. It had all been for Louise.

Perhaps it was true what they said about people drowning. Pictures flashed through her mind of her childhood, of her parents, of her soulmate Jack, and of her precious Louise. She would see them soon. For the first time that day she smiled.

No one would have heard her faint tired voice even if they had been in the next room but to June, the noise reverberated like an exploding volcano.

'Jack, Louise, I'm coming.'

Her eyes closed, her head lolled to one side, and June Harker fell asleep for the last time.

Dave Johnson popped his head around the door.

'You two okay for an update?'

'Of course,' said Sam.

'I've just had the lead CSI on the phone. The key on the bed opens Louise's door.'

'So, do we think that's how the killer got in?' Sam wondered aloud, staring at her computer screen.

Ed thought about it, not 100% convinced.

'It's a good bet but then again, her mum's adamant Louise only had one key.'

'She must be mistaken,' Dave said, taking a seat next to Ed, 'otherwise how did it get on the bed, and how was he able to use it to open the door?'

'Fair point,' Sam conceded, the creases of concentration visible across her forehead. 'Louise could have given anyone a copy key.'

Lifting her eyes from the screen, she looked at Dave.

'Presumably the CSI did all the DNA swabs and fingerprinting before trying the key in the lock?'

'They did,' Dave said.

'Okay. Good.' She sighed. She just needed that one metaphorical key to unlock the door and solve this. 'What else?'

'Nothing from Louise's neighbours. No one heard any

arguments. No one suspicious seen in the area in the last few days. No CCTV covering the area around Louise's house sadly and nothing from the media appeal yet.'

'Any chance of some good news?' Ed said, shaking his head, his eyes locked on the carpet.

Dave gave him a weak, apologetic smile.

'The forensic examination of Louise's house will take another few days,' he said. 'The FLO's on his way back to see June. Alan Smith hasn't been able to give us any potential lines of inquiry. We're still looking for the knife, although a knife matching the ones left in the block has been found in Louise's wheelie bin. It's with forensics.'

'That's a good find, but is it the one we're after?' Sam asked.

'It's got a broken tip and the tip's also in the bin. There doesn't look to be any blood on it. It's possible it got broken and Louise has thrown it away at some point between the last bin collection and going to bed on the night she was killed.'

'Possibly,' Ed agreed, still looking at the floor.

'It's still a good find, even if it just rules it out,' Sam said. 'If the knife wasn't taken from Louise's block, the killer's brought their own. Make sure forensics check for blood trapped between the blade and the handle.'

Dave said he would, although the forensic team knew their job. Sam was just covering every angle.

'They'll continue searching tomorrow within your parameters – drains, bins, flat roofs,' Dave said.

Sam nodded.

'Make sure you thank the search teams, Dave,' she said. 'Always a shitty job.'

'Will do. We're also pulling together a picture of Louise's financial affairs and the techies are having a look at her computer with regards to emails, Internet activity, and social media sites. Same with her mobile.'

Dave stopped talking and blinked a couple of times.

'You look tired. You sure you're alright?' Sam asked.

'I'm fine.'

'Thanks then. Plenty to keep us all busy.'

Dave nodded and stood up.

'Hang on, Dave,' Sam said as he began to walk away. 'There's something else. Me and Ed aren't convinced the rapist and the killer are the same person. There're elements of overkill in the murder and we believe there has been some staging of the crime scene.'

'Not sure about there being no connection,' Dave said, turning to face them. 'There's the mask. The fact a knife's been used. The open window.'

Ed spoke almost before Dave finished.

'But was the window opened to gain entry, or opened afterwards to give us the impression that it was the entry point? It wasn't damaged, so there was no breaking it in advance like the others.'

Dave gave it some thought, head tilted back and eyes briefly closed.

'If he knew she was a cop, he might have thought she would get a broken window fixed straight away. He may have got away with forcing it. How else would he have got in?'

'The key, Dave. We need to sort the key,' Sam said.

Dave stood up, excusing himself as his mobile rang. Seconds later he was back.

'Today just keeps getting worse,' he said. He rubbed his brow.

Sam and Ed looked at him, waiting for him to continue.

'June Harker's dead,' he said quietly, sliding into the seat he had just vacated.

Sam rocked back in her chair and looked upwards.

Ed muttered 'Oh fuck', his hands running over his bald head.

'What's happened?' Sam's voice was soft.

'Looks like suicide. Tablets and brandy. She's wearing different clothes to when Paul left her. She was also holding a photograph of Louise in her police uniform.'

'Shit!' Sam shouted, far louder than she intended. The administrative assistant visibly jumped as she walked past the door.

'Sorry,' Sam called, before continuing. 'Whoever killed

Louise killed June, just as sure as if they'd stabbed her through the heart. Bless her. Finding her own daughter like that. Who can blame her?'

She fell silent, lost in thought. 'We should've done more for her.'

Dave Johnson was first to respond, his voice quiet, his words measured.

'She wouldn't see a doctor. She didn't want neighbours in her house. We can't force people to do things, Sam. This is a tragedy but we couldn't have prevented her death. If it wasn't today, it would have been some other day.'

'He's right,' Ed agreed.

'Still,' Sam said, shaking her head. 'We should have done more.'

'You know, I knew her quite well,' Dave told them. 'Me and Louise went out together, years back, just as friends, but I've met June a few times. She idolised Louise. She was a very headstrong old lady. The FLO is blaming himself for leaving her, but believe you me, if June didn't want to do something, she wouldn't, and if she wanted to be left alone, no one would have been able to tell her otherwise. She'd have been left alone at some point. We can't have FLOs with them day and night.'

'Yeah, I suppose you're right,' Sam said. 'Sorry, I had no idea you and Louise were such good friends. Are you okay? It's not a problem if you want off this one. You could concentrate on the rapes.'

'I'm fine,' Dave said. 'There are no issues with me. You both knew her as well. I don't want to be taken off the team. I want whoever killed Louise bringing to justice. Two women have died. We need to catch this one, and I want to be part of the team that does.'

He took a deep breath and wiped his eyes.

'Yes, I knew Louise, yes, she was a friend, but I won't let that cloud my judgement. I want to stay on this job.'

'Did you still speak to her?' Sam asked.

'I spoke to her a lot until she got married. I didn't like her husband. Once she left him she rang me out of the blue and we kind of rekindled our friendship. I would maybe go out with her once or twice a month…the cinema, a meal, that type of thing.'

'Did she ever mention anything? Enemies? Financial problems?' Sam asked him.

'Her biggest problems were with Smith. He was a twat by the sound of it,' Dave said, his voice suddenly tight with anger as he spat out the word 'twat'.

They were both shocked at Dave's language. Neither of them had ever heard him swear before, and certainly not in front of women or senior officers.

'In what way, Dave?' Ed asked.

'He was a bully. When they were married he would often shout at her. He was never, to my knowledge anyway, violent but emotionally he treated her badly. Being a brewery rep he had carte blanche to stay out late and Louise suspected he had been having affairs before he finally left her for another woman. Louise paid for the house they lived in. He didn't pay a shilling, and no doubt he'll get it now.'

Ed and Sam sat quietly and listened. Dave Johnson was adding to the 'victimology', the picture they needed to paint of Louise's life, the small details as well as the bigger brush strokes.

'Is he capable of killing her?' Sam asked, her voice sympathetic but the question as blunt as she intended.

Dave thought about that, gnawing his bottom lip.

'I've no idea,' he said after a long pause. 'Who knows what goes on in people's heads? Is he capable of walking into her house and brutally killing her? I really don't know. For Louise's sake I really hope not. We all know that at some point during that attack she must have seen her killer, and I dread to think what went through her mind if it was her husband, the man she once loved and married. But… well, he just wasn't a nice bloke.'

'Why didn't you like him?' Ed asked.

Dave paused again but this time only for a moment.

'I only met him a couple of times. I just thought he was a loud-mouthed, arrogant individual. He was always flirting with other women, even if Louise was there. He could be quite obscene, really. Not just flirtatious – you know, pornographic in his innuendos. How Louise put up with it was beyond me. I couldn't believe it when she said they were getting married. I told her she was making a mistake, but she wouldn't listen.'

'Who does when it's about relationships? Who does?' Sam said, scrutinising Dave Johnson in a way she had never done before.

'Listen, I need to get on,' Dave said, standing up and walking out of the office.

Alone again, Ed was trying to read Sam's silent thoughts.

'A potential suspect, the husband?' he asked.

Sam met his eyes.

'Possibly. Let's have an intelligence picture built up of him. The usual stuff…finance, associates, habits. You said he had a temper. After we bumped into Louise in the car park.'

'I just remember her saying that he would shout and ball at her,' Ed said. 'He never hit her, or if he did, she never mentioned it to me. This was ages ago, when we worked on some job or other, but they were still living together.'

'Bad tempered, though,' Sam said. 'Best check if there were ever any reports of domestic violence at Louise's.'

'Okay, will do. Not sure she would have reported even if there were, though. Too embarrassing… Shit! I've forgotten Brian Banks and the list of people in the pub.'

Ed had thrown up his arms and slapped one hand loudly on his forehead.

'Give him a call now, then,' Sam said. 'Once we've got that list we can visit each of them and hopefully they'll recall other people. We need to design a questionnaire so they're all asked the same questions. I don't want to waste time having to go back and ask them something we could have got out of the way on the first visit. And we need a question in there asking if they've told anyone else what they heard. It's not something they're likely to keep to themselves.'

'Will do,' Ed said, scribbling a note. 'And hey, I didn't

know Dave went out with Louise years ago. I thought it was a new thing.'

'Me too. I've never even heard it mentioned on the grapevine. It was news to me.'

'You think they were in a serious relationship now?'

Sam tried to remember what Louise had told her when the red wine was flowing.

'Dave was keener than Louise,' Sam said. 'That's the impression I got from her anyway. The bit about Louise contacting him when she split up wasn't quite right by the way. He rang her, according to Louise.'

'Doesn't he know you and Louise were mates?'

'We're both pretty private people. I never made a song and dance about who my friends were. He might know; he might not. That's why I played dumb about him and Louise.'

'I never found out why he split from his missus,' Ed said.

Sam shrugged her shoulders.

'Who knows? It happens all the time in this job. Anyway, I keep coming back to the crime scene staging. What else could it be? The killer wants us to think it's the rapist. But how does he know about the mask? That's if it is a 'he'. Those people in the pub are potentially the most important line of inquiry we've got.'

'What about June?' Ed asked.

Sam replied: 'I'll contact uniform and see where we are with that. It's almost seven o'clock. We'll leave Spence until tomorrow. Let's get him first thing. We don't know if he's at work, and there's no way of finding out now. Have someone on his house, but use Bev. Like I said, she knows what he looks like.'

Ed was already on his feet as Sam fired off more instructions.

'Get someone to call the post office when it opens. See if he's at work. If he is, we'll get him when he leaves home. If he's not, let's go for the rapid entry.

'Oh and Ed, do me a favour – find out how we're getting on with Crowther?'

Terry Crowther had admitted a total of 11 thefts of knickers over the last 18 months. He had no alibi for the rapes, but there was no evidence to link him to any of the attacks. Jill Carver demanded he be released, assuring Jason Stroud she would be delighted to sue the police for false imprisonment if Crowther continued to be held in detention.

Her threats didn't impress Jason and neither did her arrogant smile. Like most cops, he had little time for the likes of Jill Carver. He had seen it all before with solicitors, trying to intimidate police officers with their huffing and puffing, the same solicitors who, as he was always willing to point out, made a good living out of state-funded legal aid, defending shit bags they knew were guilty but only interested in the money.

Jason told her he would call CPS Direct, the out-of-office-hours arm of the Crown Prosecution Service, to seek the go-ahead to charge and bail Crowther.

'Make it quick.'

'Of course,' Jason said, doing his utmost to convey as much sarcasm as possible, his heels clicking just enough to make her wonder whether he was coming to attention.

Sam was back on the blue carpet, having been summonsed to give Trevor Stewart an update.

He was sat behind his desk wearing a short-sleeved checked shirt. Obviously going straight out, Sam thought.

'You did well with the media, but her mother killing herself adds to the whole sorry state of affairs. How are we getting on?'

Sam told him about Crowther and Spence.

'So, let me get this correct: as we stand, we've got three outstanding rapes, a murder of a police officer, the apparent suicide of the murder victim's elderly mother, and we've managed to arrest someone who steals women's knickers. Not exactly Christmas, is it?'

No shit, Sherlock.

'No. It's not. But Crowther's probably out of the frame, so we've eliminated him. We're going for Spence first thing, so we'll see what tomorrow brings.'

Stewart stood and hitched up his ill-fitting black jeans. 'Update tomorrow it is. Then I'll make a decision as to the SIO on the murder of Louise Smith.'

Sam bit her tongue and swallowed her anger.

'With all due respect, Sir, I've just done the press today. How will it look if I'm taken off it tomorrow? What message does that send out?'

'If that's what happens, we can come up with a script that keeps all concerned happy, reputations intact.'

I just bet you can, Sam thought as she walked away.

Parked on a driveway, courtesy of the householder who thought it terribly exciting to have two undercover police officers 'on a stakeout' of a neighbour's home, Bev Summers had an unobstructed view of the front of Spence's house. She was in radio contact with the two male detectives who had won the toss and were watching Spence's back garden from the warmth of the helpful householder's dining room. The gentleman brewed a decent cuppa, too.

Spence's living room light went out, throwing the downstairs into darkness, the landing light coming on almost simultaneously. Timing switches might be in use, but Bev Summers didn't think Spence was the type. She glanced at her watch. 11.30pm. He was off to bed, she was pretty certain.

Bev remembered how years ago detectives would have just turned up and watched his house. Now thanks to the Regulation of Investigatory Powers Act, commonly referred to as RIPA, a simple static surveillance like this required a huge amount of paperwork, and signatures from various ranks to demonstrate it was legal, necessary and proportionate, in accordance with the Human Rights Act, blah, blah, blah.

Bev smiled. She was sure the police never wanted RIPA and all its bureaucracy, but the civil liberties brigade certainly did. More accountability, they screamed. She sank her head into her fleece hood, pulled the soft material tight around her cheeks, and shuffled in the front passenger seat, trying to get comfortable. Leaning her head on the side window, the cold glass fired a blast of Arctic air into her left temple. She thought of all those left-wing, pious academics talking about the greater good, none of them aware that there were two four o'clocks in the same day, and none of them ever in a position where they were expected to make an instant decision in a fast-moving crisis situation. They couldn't make a decision to save their lives. Not without talking about it for hours. Tossers.

Unable to run the engine for fear of attracting attention, and needing a window open to avoid 'misting up', Bev's fingers and toes were already stiffening despite the gloves and fur-lined boots she had picked up from home. Her backside was going numb, and despite the curry and chips she had eaten en route, her stomach was already starting a series of worryingly loud grumbles.

Whoever thought surveillance was exciting was either deluded or just plain mad. 'Mobile' surveillance invariably meant sitting 'on plot' for hours, waiting for the target to move, while 'static' surveillance, with absolutely no prospects of going anywhere, was mind-numbing in its boredom.

At least tonight the thought of locking up Spence would get her through the hours of tedium that lay ahead. The jackpot prize would be Spence coming out, during the night, carrying his rape kit.

She reached inside the glove box and fumbled for the paperback with its yellowing pages, the back cover barely attached to the rest of the book, the last of the glue stubbornly sticking to the spine; names, addresses, car registration numbers, all handwritten on random pages, in different ink, by different authors, each a reminder of how many surveillances this veteran publication had seen come and go.

Her mobile phone, held against her knees, cast just enough light on to the page she had aimlessly selected. Without taking her head away from the car window, she said aloud: 'Which football club used to play at Vetch Field?'

A quiz was always number one on the 'how to fill in time on a static surveillance'.

CHAPTER FORTY-THREE

BEV BATTLED the overwhelming desire for sleep from 3.30am, when the quiz, a conversation about the state of modern policing, politics, do-gooders, sport, and gossip of the 'who's sleeping with who' variety, was exhausted.

Now, as lights started going on in a few of the houses, Bev pushed her feet against the foot well, her knees cracking as she raised her body up the back of the seat. She wriggled her fingers and toes, and tried to ignore the stiffness in her back. Her nicotine levels were at a dangerously low level, and her body craved the hit of an early morning smoke. A lighted cigarette in a parked car at this time of the morning would give her away to anyone who was looking, and the last person she wanted to tip off was Spence. Not long now though, she thought. The smoke would have to wait.

She picked up her mobile and selected the number for the sorting office, which she had added to the contacts list last night. 6.15am.

'Oh hi. Yes. I wonder if you can help me?' Bev said to the woman who answered. 'Can you tell me if Michael Spence is at work today please? He's my postman. We all know him. Nice guy. Anyway, yesterday he dropped something outside my house, and as I'm in town today I thought I could drop it off for him. Normally I would just wait until he started his deliveries, but I'm going on holiday today, and we'll be at the airport before he gets to our street.'

The woman said she needed a minute to check the rosters. In fact, she needed a good three minutes, by Bev's rough calculation.

'He's in at eight,' the woman said when she finally came back on the line. 'If I could just take your name, and what he dropped, I'll tell him you called.'

The next bit was easy – and fun.

'Hello? Hello? Are you still there? Hello?'

Bev let the woman listen to silence before she ended the call.

She smiled as the little voice in her head said to her: 'Ooh, you little liar, Beverley.'

What would the 'do-gooders' make of that? Not only pretending the signal was lost but saying you'd found his property. Oh my! Tut tut! No conception of the real world those clowns.

She had withheld her number, thwarting any attempt to return her call.

She had what she needed. The woman might ring Spence at home, but it was more likely that she would wait until he got to work. The calculated risk had been worth taking. The rapid-entry team was on stand by, but this way they could get him with no fuss while he was on the street.

His lights went on just after 6.30, and immediately her fingers and toes began to warm, the stiffness in her knees and back began to ease, a welcome reaction to the self-induced injection of adrenalin. She savoured the thrill of the approaching arrest, a hungry wolf salivating at the thought of an animal carcass.

Fifteen minutes later, Spence walked out of his front door and on to the pavement. As soon as she saw him, Bev radioed her colleagues in the neighbour's house, jumped out of the car, and walked towards him, cursing the lack of movement in the joints of her knees. You're getting old Bev, but God, you'll miss this part.

Spence maintained his steady pace towards her, and when they were within five yards of each other, Bev said: 'Remember me?'

He nodded, and Bev immediately told him he was being arrested on suspicion of rape. He stared at the pavement as she ran through his rights and took hold of his arm. He offered no resistance as she led him towards their car.

Spence hadn't spoken one word during the arrest, and he stayed silent during the drive to the police station.

Shuffling into the custody office, head down and shoulders slouched, he stood in front of the Custody Sergeant, his eyes fixed on the black linoleum.

Answering in a barely audible voice, he gave his personal details: name, address, occupation, date of birth. He declined having anyone notified of his arrest.

He was advised to have a legal representative, and as he didn't know any lawyers, he opted for the duty solicitor.

Bev Summers stood next to him, her eyes locked on him, all thoughts of sleep now gone. Was this muttering excuse of a human being capable of breaking into women's homes, terrorising them into compliance, and then asking if they had enjoyed him? Could he really exercise that much control?

Not once protesting his innocence, she questioned whether even a condemned man taking his last walk to the gallows would have appeared any more resigned to his fate.

Nobody noticed her slight shudder. The permanent odour that seemed to cling to the custody office had been replaced by something new, stronger. The sickly sweet aroma drifted towards her, enveloping her like a stale fog. Her stomach heaved. Could she smell his fear, or were her senses playing tricks on her after a freezing night in the car?

She looked downwards at the black floor, and saw tiny swirls of steam rising from the small puddle around his feet. Her eyes searched for confirmation of its source – the wet patch around his ankles that led up to his groin.

She turned away from him and for the second time in 30

minutes, smiled, quite a feat for someone who hated mornings.

'Gotcha!' Bev's mind was shouting.

Sam and Ed met in her office at 7am. They knew the arrest had gone smoothly and were now reviewing the intelligence on Spence.

'No previous. Lives alone, as we knew. Rents a council allotment,' Sam said.

'Allotment?' Ed sounded bemused. 'I didn't know they still had them.'

'If he has an allotment, that'll need searching as well,' Sam said. 'If we have to dig it up, dig it up.'

Dave Johnson hurried into the office, speaking excitedly and without apology for interrupting.

'You might want to get yourselves down to Spence's. The search team's found a diary, and driving licences. We've got him!'

'Fuckin' marvellous,' Ed shouted, automatically punching the air with his right fist, euphoric relief charging through him like electricity. They had the bastard, and if true justice existed, he would soon get what was coming in prison.

Sam rocked backwards in her chair, stretched her legs, put her hands on her head, and allowed the warm, relaxing sensation to run through her body, massaging the stresses from mind and muscles, savouring the almost better-than-sex moment that always swept through her when a major investigation was on the road to conclusion.

How was he going to explain the licences? What was in the diary? Would he confess?

Sam knew the rapes were nailed on. Time would tell whether he was also their killer.

Ed was aware that Dave didn't seem to be sharing in the euphoria, wearing a slightly worried look on his handsome face, a look that said he had more to say and was going to take no pleasure saying it.

'Something else you need to tell us?' Ed asked, looking at Dave standing in the doorway, fidgeting with his blue striped tie.

'There is,' he said, stepping back with hesitation and closing the door. He stood ramrod straight, radiating raw discomfort, a soldier suffering in front of his Commanding Officer.

'Boss, the search team's found a house key.'

'And?' Sam snapped, irritated and impatient. 'Come on, for God's sake. Just spit it out.'

'There's a small brown label attached to the key. Attached with string. The label…'

'Yes?' she said, 'Go on.'

'It's got your name on it.'

CHAPTER FORTY-FOUR

MICHAEL SPENCE SAT in his cell on the wide, wooden bench which masqueraded as a bed, back resting against the wall, knees tucked under his chin, one of his trouser legs stuck to his inner thigh.

This is the end. He knew he'd be interviewed, and while he could stall and deny everything, as soon as they searched his house, they would find his moleskin notebook, and the driving licences. Whatever he said about the licences, they wouldn't believe him. Nobody would. What could he say? I found them. The notebook was better than a confession, written in his handwriting, detailing the planning, and how he felt during his time with them. They would find the mobile phone, and see the only contacts were the girls. And they would find the key with her name on the label.

His head sunk further into his knees as the reality dawned on him. It would be a long time before he would be out. What would happen to his house? His job?

The dirty magnolia cell walls seemed to close in on him with every passing minute, and the stainless-steel toilet in the corner mocked him, daring him to sit on it. Panic pulsated through his veins, like a strobe light in a discotheque, as he contemplated life in prison. He wouldn't get Michael or Mickey in jail. He'd get 'nonce', or 'beast'.

Every prisoner would have carte blanche to attack him, and whoever got to him would be the toast of the prison population, proudly wearing the invisible badge of honour, the badge that proclaimed 'I did the nonce. I sorted the beast'.

What was the slang for prison officers? He couldn't remember. They wouldn't protect him. They'd turn a blind eye. They couldn't 'do' him themselves but they wouldn't lift a finger to stop anyone else. Even if they wanted to protect him, they couldn't keep him safe 24 hours a day. Screws. That's it. That's what they're called.

He'd read books about fellow prisoners spitting in the food of people like him, or throwing scalding hot tea in their face. He could be beaten, stabbed, or slashed. They could get him on the wing or in the showers. He wouldn't survive. They probably wouldn't kill him; but mentally they would break him. Or maybe they would kill him. What would one of those 'lifers' have to lose?

His thoughts turned from one institution to another, from prison to the police. How had they got him? He had been so careful. Another 48 hours and he would have had Parker. Making love to a copper, especially the one hunting him, might have given him some kudos in prison and maybe, just maybe, made his life a little more bearable inside.

On the outside, in the girls' homes, he had been in control, but in there, in jail, he would be powerless. He would be stalked, he would be a victim, and they wouldn't care whether he enjoyed it or not. He had always cared about his girls enjoying it.

The girls had no idea that he was coming, but he knew, in prison, they'd be coming for him, and they'd be coming for him every day. He squeezed his arms around his knees, like the bereaved clinging to a deceased loved one, and started to weep.

What had he done wrong? All he wanted was a girlfriend, to be normal, whatever that was. It wasn't his fault that he was invisible to every woman he came across. He was where he was because of women everywhere. Why couldn't he get a girlfriend? Parker had stopped him. She hadn't been to bed with him but she might have been 'the one'.

He stared at the toilet, and the parallels between him and it were shockingly apparent; the unnaturally low toilet was in the open, in view of anyone who happened to look through the hatch in the cell door. It had no seat, no lid.

Exposed, low, incomplete; it could have been his epitaph.

———

The freezing temperatures combined with patchy fog made driving treacherous, and the airwaves of both police and local radio were full of reports of accidents.

Sam sat in silence in the passenger seat, her mind doing its best to concentrate on anything but Dave's revelation. For a moment she remembered her Royal Yachting Association Day Skipper theory exam, and that this type of fog was known as radiation fog, which unless it was burned off by the sun or blown by a strong wind, would be there all day.

The slight distraction caused by her basic weather knowledge didn't last long.

Ed broke the silence. 'We don't know if it's your key, and even if it is, he can't get to you now.'

Sam was looking straight ahead out of the windscreen. On the verge of tears, she bit her lip, and spoke, once she had killed the sob trying to break from her throat. 'I was on his list, Ed. I might have been next. He could have been coming for me tonight.'

Ed could see the tears flowing down her cheeks from the corner of his left eye, but he didn't turn his head; the last thing either of them needed this morning was a crash.

'I know it's tough, Sam. It's hard to comprehend, but whatever he was, or wasn't going to do, he can't do anything now. We can all think of 'what if' scenarios, but we've got him now.'

He knew he was floundering, a man wading through the syrup of sensitivity, wrestling with his inability to emotionally reach out to her. He recalled doing his best to reassure his niece, but he had been as successful then as he was now. Emotional intelligence wasn't his strongest characteristic, and although he tried, his wife had once told him she had stepped in puddles with more depth. He reverted to what he did best, thinking practically, wondering where Sam could sleep tonight. It was too early to suggest anything to her yet, but he was considering asking her to stay at his house. Perhaps Sue would do a better job of reassuring her than he could. Perhaps Sue would be happier if Sam was in their house, rather than him being at Sam's.

'I could have ended up like Louise,' Sam said, her voice almost childlike.

'Now come on,' Ed responded, his tone admonishing like a parent reprimanding a sulky youngster. 'Neither of us are convinced the rapist and the killer are the same person. I understand what we've been told is shocking, especially for you, but let's not run away with ourselves here. The bottom line is this: even if it is your key, he can't get to you. Yes, you might have been on his list. Yes, he might have been coming for you tonight. But guess what, we got him first! He's locked up, and even if he has a plan of the inside of your house, he's not coming. He'll not be going anywhere for a long time, maybe never.'

He let her digest his words.

'Sam, listen to me. We have to go into his house. We have to look at everything he's got, and I'm sorry, but you need to remember who you are. Everyone in that house will be looking at you to see if there is any reaction. If you ever needed to remind people you have balls of steel, it's now.'

His words pulled her back from the abyss of self-pity. She wiped the tears from her cheeks, sat upright in the passenger seat, and recomposed herself.

'You're right,' she said, turning her head sideways to look at Ed. 'He can't do anything to me now. Let's make sure we nail this bastard. Our motivation should be the victims he terrified. Those poor girls, waking in the dark and he's there in their bedroom.'

Her voice trailed off. She sighed, turned her head, and stared straight ahead.

Ed waited for her to speak.

'You know, at one point I thought he was 'The Puppeteer', pulling our strings. Not now. We're pulling his strings. We're the puppet masters.'

'Too right! Puppeteers, Musketeers!' Ed said as they pulled up outside Spence's house, skin stretching across his protruding knuckles as he squeezed his hands around the steering wheel. 'Too fucking right!'

Sam threw open the door, scrambled out on to the pavement, and slammed the door behind her with such force the passenger side of the car was still vibrating as she marched up the driveway.

Ed closed his door, ran around the bonnet, and walked briskly after her, pointing the vehicle's remote over his shoulder, locking the car.

He followed her into the house, took a deep breath and straightened his tie. This could be difficult. He didn't want Sam breaking down in front of the search team.

They followed the team co-ordinator, a uniform sergeant, into the kitchen.

'How's it going, Ian?' Sam asked.

Ian Robinson was a highly regarded search co-ordinator.

'Good. Look at what we've got so far,' he said, pointing at various bags on the table. 'There might be a bit more at the allotment, but there's plenty here.'

On top of the filthy, chunky, cream painted table, with its thick pine-turned legs, were evidence bags holding items of property recovered from the house.

Sam picked up three clear bags and the faces of Kelly Jones, Amber Dalton, and Danielle Banks stared back at her as she shuffled the bags like a pack of cards, examining each driving licence in turn.

A Swiss Army knife, blades retracted, which had been found in a rucksack in the garage, was now in a toughened plastic cylindrical tube.

The rucksack itself, which Sam and Ed were told

contained an empty carrier bag, was in a brown paper bag, and inside another brown bag was a ski mask recovered from the main bedroom. Anything that might sweat in plastic bags, clothes included, was always put in paper bags, to avoid the potential loss of forensic evidence.

Sam silently acknowledged the professionalism of the search team.

A mobile phone, discovered in a tea caddy in the kitchen, was in special packaging designed to act as a signal inhibitor, ensuring that nothing was received by, or lost from, the phone after its recovery.

The moleskin notebook was in an unsealed clear bag. Ian Robinson suspected the two senior detectives would want to look at it as soon as they arrived.

Sam and Ed stood shoulder to shoulder and put on blue surgical gloves. Ed removed the notebook from the bag.

Bent over the table, Ed could feel Sam's breath on his neck as he turned the pages, pausing on each, reading the title, the name of the victim, and the accompanying text, which contained so much personal information about each victim, demonstrating the extraordinary level of pre-planning undertaken by its author.

The book would be examined in greater detail later, but notwithstanding the evidence it contained, Sam's inability to stand still, like an impatient commuter waiting for a bus, had nothing to do with euphoria or excitement and everything to do with dread.

The only thought in her head – 'am I in it?'

Ed knew what she was thinking. He hoped she didn't appear in the book. He hoped the key had nothing to do with her house, nothing more than the bastard's fantasy, putting her name on a key that would no more open her door, than it would open his camper van. Hoped she didn't have to endure any more shit. Hoped the telephone call, the flowers, her name on a label attached to a key of no significance, was as far as it went.

He flinched as she squeezed his forearm, their eyes focussing on the page.

CHAPTER FORTY-FIVE

Samantha Parker
Tall long legs great arse
Policewoman detective
36 pegswood close green door like mine
Audi A5 4.2 quattro sport bright blue never in garage
Never seen other cars on drive
Doesn't go out at night always in after work
Drinks wine. In big glasses
Mon teatime
saw her on tele and in paper she looks just as sexy as
in real life
sexy voice
got hard looking at her
tried to think what her bedroom looked like
I went upstairs and soon come all over my bed
thinking of her
would <u>LOVE</u> to pull her hair while I am inside her
from behind

ED GRITTED HIS TEETH, feeling his skin redden as Sam's fingers applied more pressure on his arm.

'Look, shall we read this later?' he asked, allowing the hand holding the book to drop to his side.

'No, I'm okay. Let's read the rest.'

'Are you sure? We can do this at the office.'

'Ed,' she said, releasing his arm, the tone of her voice conveying a message he'd heard more times than he could remember from the two women he lived with, the tone where his name was no longer a name, but a galactic word for don't argue. Men are from Mars. He raised the book.

Tues night
drove to Sams sat outside and rang her on special
mobile
sat in car with my trousers down. Started pulling as
soon as her phone rang she answered and I pulled
harder. Her voice so sexy asking me what I was I
thinking of us doing
then she asked me to tell her what I was doing I never
answered just pulled faster saw landing light go on
and saw her at window
come all over steering wheel

'He was outside, then,' Sam said quietly, turning away from Ed. 'Thought so.'

Ed put his hands on her shoulders, gently turned her around to face him, his voice calm. 'He's locked up now, Sam. The piece of shit can write what he wants. The bastard's finished. Look, let's do this later. We've got the gist.'

'No. Let's do it now, read the rest. Let's get it over with. See what else he's written.'

Wed morning
At Sams watched cleaner leave.
found key under pot
Drove to northallerton. The market was on and one
of the stalls copied the key. Drove back and put hers
back under the plant pot. Bought flowers in
northallerton and left them on her step, put cricket
ball in them. That way I knew she would know they

***were off me. Wish I could have seen her face but I
will ask her if she liked them when we are in bed.***

Ed put the notebook back in the bag. 'We've got him.
We've got the bastard. With all that evidence we could get
anyone off the street to interview him.'

Sam shuddered when she thought how easy it had been
for Spence to get a copy of her key, remembering that day she
had left it under a plant pot for her cleaner. Stupid! She
began mentally questioning her habits. How had she been
totally unaware of Spence? He had built up an intelligence
profile of her the police would have been proud of. He must
have watched her. He knew she drank wine; even knew she
drank from large glasses. He had got so close to her. How had
she been so careless? Why had she never sensed or seen him?

Christ, she was supposed to have an eye for detail! She
could understand the other victims not noticing him, but her,
a police officer, trusted with investigating major crime.

She rationalised he was able to watch her because she, like
the majority, thought of home as her safe haven. Most of us
look forward to getting home, Sam reasoned, and our safety
antennae switches to standby mode when we get there. In that
respect she was no different to the other victims, and she
would have to accept her own fallibility, her own
shortcomings.

But never again would she allow that to happen. Never.

Ed suggested two members of the search team go to
Sam's house and try the key in her door, maintaining what
officers knew as 'evidential continuity'. Ian Robinson nodded
his head, raising his vibrating telephone to his ear at the
same time.

Ending the call, he told them a CSI was en route to the
allotment.

'Looks like there might be burnt clothing in the remnants
of a recent fire,' he said. 'They've also found a teapot buried
in the ground containing newspaper cuttings detailing the
attacks.'

'Tremendous,' Ed said. 'But why hide the press cuttings in the allotment yet keep everything else here?'

'No idea,' Sam answered. 'Maybe because he is involved intimately with the stuff here, in a way he's not with the newspapers.'

'Yeah, that could fit. He writes the notes, that's a living document, something always being added to it. He steals the licences, looks at their photos. He needs the phone. But the newspapers, they're other people's thoughts. An archive.'

Sam nodded and started to walk out of the kitchen.

'Come on then. We've seen what we need to here. Thanks Ian,' she said.

Back at the car, they were both lost in their own thoughts. As they opened the doors, Ed spoke, looking at Sam across the roof.

'It's all coming together nicely.'

Sam's face looked drawn, even when the hint of a nervous smile reached her eyes.

'Yeah. He's where he deserves to be. Thank God we've got him, and I don't mean that because it looks like I was next. We needed to stop him because he wasn't going to stop until he was caught. He would have just kept raping at will. Now we just need to find out for sure if he's a killer as well.'

They slid into their seats.

'I was thinking about that walking down the path,' Ed said.

'And?'

'If Spence is our killer, where's the reference to Louise in his notebook?'

'Shit. I never thought of that,' Sam said, slowly tilting her head until it touched the headrest. She closed her eyes and inhaled deeply.

'I was so busy wanting to know if and what he'd written about me, I wasn't thinking like a detective. Thank God you were.' She paused. 'You know I haven't had a cigarette for four years but I could do with one now.'

Ed pursed his lips and nodded.

'I fancy a good drink, but neither of us is going to get what we want. Not today anyway.'

'And we'll be working all weekend,' Sam said before she took another deep breath. 'So who the hell's killed Louise?'

'We'll work it out,' Ed said. 'It might just take us longer than we thought.'

Sam jerked forward and fastened her seat belt.

'If Stewart gets his way, we might not have that time. I promise you one thing, though: you and I are going to get absolutely hammered when this is sorted.'

'Now that does sound like a plan,' Ed grinned. 'And you're paying!'

'You're joking. I'll need a mortgage to buy all your drink.'

They both laughed. The tension had been released; the tension that is always there, suppressed and hidden, out of sight and beneath the surface, but flowing through the arteries like an underground stream. When Louise's killer was in custody, they would blow off steam, a pressure cooker with the valve removed, but until then, that particular valve would remain tightly in place.

'He'll not take you, or us, off this one,' Ed said. 'The rapes are sorted, so it's natural for us all to jump across to the murder, linked or not. Stewart's all piss and wind.'

Sam, Ed, and Dave were all sat in her office. Brian Banks had been able to recall about seven people who were in the bar on the Wednesday night, and Ed was confident the team would eventually identify everyone who was in there.

'Dave, when they're being spoken to, have them all photographed in the clothes they were wearing in the pub,' Ed said.

Dave Johnson's eyebrows came together, and his tanned forehead concertinaed, his face looking older.

'It'll allow us to identify them by their clothing if people don't know their names,' Ed explained. 'You know… 'my view was blocked by a guy in a red sweater'… that type of thing.'

Dave nodded and his brow sprang back, as he took in the relevance of Ed's request.

'Good idea,' Sam said.

Dave looked at his notes. 'The search teams are on their way back to the office with the exhibits. As well as the documents and phone, they've taken possession of three Adidas tracksuits, two blue and one black,' he said.

'The burnt clothing at the allotment,' Ed said. 'If that's what it is, Spence might have been replacing the tracksuits he's worn during the attacks with new ones. They'd be forensically clean if they were seized.'

'He wouldn't be the first to hit on that tactic,' Sam agreed.

'Could be,' Dave said. 'I'm still waiting to hear from the officers who've gone to the sports shop to check the CCTV footage for last Sunday.'

Dave held up a piece of A4 paper.

'I've saved the best 'til last. I've just got this off the techies examining Louise's computer. Obviously there's a lot still to do, but this is significant. It's an email sent to Louise by Smith on the day she was killed.'

He passed it to Sam, and Ed moved from his seat, stood next to Sam's chair, and began reading over her shoulder.

You Fuckin' bitch. That house is half mine so you either sell it or remorgage. I want my share of the profit. You sit there and tell me on the phone that Im not getting anything cos you paid the deposit and morgage. Fuck you I contributed. Im not waiting fuckin' five years for a divorce. I want a divorce now. Julie's 10 times the woman you are. She's good to be with and she is fuckin' great in bed. Get my money you greedy stuck up cow

Sam read the words again and ran a hand through her hair.

'A lot of anger there,' she said, looking up at Ed.

'A lot of motive as well,' he responded.

'Sent yesterday morning,' Sam noticed, weighing up the significance of the timing.

'Are there any more?' She rubbed the paper between her thumb and fingers.

'There might be more, but that's the most recent,' Dave said. 'I told you he's a nasty bastard.'

More swearing, Ed thought.

Looking at Dave, the woman in Sam listened to her intuition. Dave wanted more from the relationship than Louise. Shame, Sam thought. Dave's a really nice guy. Still, you can't force anyone to commit. If it was Smith who'd killed her, Louise might be alive today if had decided to stick with Dave for the long haul.

'He can't spell mortgage either,' Sam said, looking up at the two of them, immediately kicking herself for her insensitivity. It was hardly the time to have a pop at Dave's spelling limitations.

'But there's no disguising the anger and a potential motive in the words,' she said quickly, trying to distract Dave, while the phrase 'overkill' flashed in her head like the blue light on a traffic car.

Overkill - an emotional attachment. The greater the evidence of overkill, the closer the relationship. It certainly ticked the boxes.

'Alan Smith's just elevated himself to the status of 'person of interest',' she said. 'Time will tell whether he'll be elevated to the status of suspect.'

'So, let me get this straight,' Ed said. 'This email is sent after she was killed. If it's down to Smith, why send it to someone who's dead?'

'Throw us off the scent?' Dave wondered aloud. 'If it is him, he could use your very point in an interview. 'Why would I send an email to a dead woman, especially one like that?'

Sam nodded slowly, reading the email again, noting that it was sent before the police had notified Smith of Louise's death.

Jason Stroud, sitting in the HOLMES room, hands cupped

around a steaming mug of black coffee, had been in the office with the interviewing team since 6am. Jacket draped across the back of his chair, top button undone, tie loosened, he felt he could carry his holiday luggage in the bags under his eyes.

He was consumed with one thought: was Spence the killer? He wasn't convinced by Sam and Ed's reasoning. Were they overcomplicating matters? What if Louise had managed to get his mask off him? Had that caused him to erupt?

'All okay with the interview plans?' Sam asked as she walked into the room, Ed close behind her.

'Yeah, fine. Did you know he pissed himself when he was getting booked in? That must be a good sign,' Jason told them, grinning as he looked up at her. 'We've planned out the interviews. Unless he admits everything straight off, we'll have three interviews with him.'

'Any reason for three?' Sam asked, as Ed flicked the switch on the kettle.

'The first one we'll go through each of the attacks. Then we'll have a break. In the second we'll question him about the property the search teams recovered. The third will be the challenge interview,' Jason explained.

'Sounds good,' Sam nodded, taking a mug of tea from Ed and tentatively putting it to her lips. 'Presumably you're geared up in case you get an immediate admission?'

'Absolutely,' Jason said. 'The three of us have spent a long time consolidating our knowledge about the attacks. If he coughs straight away, that won't be a problem.'

Ed smiled as he lowered the mug from his mouth. He could remember, in the days before political correctness, detectives mischievously nicknaming the bad interviewers 'bronchitis' - the only time they got a cough. His particular favourite was calling them 'Tixylix', after the child's cough medicine.

'Can I have a word with you in your office, Boss?' Jason asked.

'Sure,' Sam said, already walking out of the HOLMES room. 'Alright if Ed's there?'

'No problem,' Jason told her.

'What's on your mind?' Sam asked.

'The murder. I've not planned to interview Spence about that yet.'

'That's fine,' Sam told him, switching on her computer, knowing the emails wouldn't stop just because she was in the middle of a major inquiry.

Jason moved his eyes from Sam to Ed before he spoke again.

'I'm just not convinced about the rationale for believing Spence is in the clear on the murder,' Jason said.

Sam took another sip of tea and settled the mug on her desk.

'Yeah, I get that, but I don't think Spence is the killer. A rapist, yes, and one capable of careful planning, but not the killer. That's not to say I'm right. Let's see where we are after the interviews, and then we can decide whether to arrest him for murder.'

'Okay, that's fine,' Jason said. 'I'll keep you posted on how the interviews are going. The solicitor will be here for 9.15. He has no problem with it being monitored so I'll be in an office watching the interviews on a TV.'

As Jason walked towards the door, Ed spoke in a quiet, monotone voice.

'Jason, if Spence's the killer, where are his planning notes on Louise?'

Jason turned and nodded, clearly considering the question as he walked out without saying another word.

CHAPTER FORTY-SIX

MICHAEL SPENCE WAS in a private consultation with his formally suited solicitor, a man whose grandfatherly air was accentuated by blue pinstriped trousers pulled high around his football-shaped stomach.

Sitting on a black plastic seat bolted to the floor and continually shuffling, Spence was still trying to fathom how they had come to arrest him. But one thing that wasn't hard for him to understand was his future. He knew he was finished.

Head bowed, notepad on crossed knee, the solicitor scribbled furiously as the broken man opposite mumbled his confessions in a long monologue.

Spence had his fingers in his mouth, and his hunched shoulders and glassy eyes were a vivid contrast to the masked rapist who crept so confidently into women's homes in the middle of the night.

The solicitor's jaw dropped in astonishment when Spence reached the driving licences and moleskin notebook, and his whole body pushed back into the chair when the flowers and the key took their bow.

After 20 minutes, his aching wrist demanded his pale, podgy fingers drop the pen and notepad on to the light-coloured wood veneer desk. He removed his gold-rimmed spectacles, closed his eyes, pinched his nose between his finger and thumb, and considered the fact opportunities to represent this type of client didn't come along often. It would be a tale worth telling at the next Law Society dinner.

Spence's position was worse than hopeless. It would need a magician to have all the exhibits excluded from the evidence, and that could only happen if the police had made massive breaches in procedure. He knew that was very unlikely on a major investigation.

Not that he would tell Spence that. Everyone was entitled to a defence, even those who were better locked safely away from society. If he gave this sexual predator no hope, Spence might try to take his own life. He made a mental note to pass his concerns to the Custody Sergeant and suggest Spence be placed on 'suicide watch'.

He told Spence his best chance lay in making a full confession at the earliest opportunity, and then entering – or at least indicating – guilty pleas at his first court appearance. The law meant he would have to be given at least some credit and almost certainly a reduced sentence, his small reward for sparing his victims the ordeal of giving evidence and, no less important, saving the system time and money.

Of course, he knew Spence was going to prison for a very long time.

Dave popped his head around the open door.

'Just a quick one, Boss,' he said as Sam looked up. 'I'm sorry, but the key. It opens your front door.'

'We guessed as much, but thanks for letting us know,' Ed said.

Ed looked at Sam, her eyes fixed on the wall, the colour draining from her face, and told her in a quiet, empathetic voice: 'They're only confirming what we already knew. Try and forget it. We've got him now.'

He needed to change the subject, as much for him as for Sam.

'By the way, Sue's asked if you fancy coming to ours tonight? Have some food, maybe a curry, and a drink. She's made up the spare room for you.'

Sue hadn't asked. She was hostile to the idea and had only reluctantly agreed when Ed shouted: 'Jesus Christ, who brings the other woman home for dinner with his bloody wife?'

Sam had expected the key to open her door, but the confirmation still made her throat to go dry, images of a masked man dancing around her mind.

He had been coming for me. Would I have resisted? Been beaten or killed? Would I have capitulated? If he had raped me, I would have been a case study in every police training classroom in the country, forever known as the SIO raped by the rapist she was hunting.

'You alright?' Ed asked.

'Fine. I'd love to. Thanks. Thank Sue as well.'

'Great. I'll let her know.'

Ed stood up, answered his phone, and spoke to the detective who was interviewing the licensee of the Golden Eagle. 'Thanks Jim.'

He put the phone on the desk, sat down, and said: 'Guess who was in the Eagle when Banks was running his mouth off?'

'Surprise me.'

'Alan fucking Smith,' Ed said, rubbing his hands together.

'Are they sure?' Sam replied, her eyes widening as her eyebrows strained to reach the top of her forehead.

'One hundred per cent. He's the brewery rep for that pub. The licensee's known him for years. He was sat at the end of the bar closest to Banks and his cronies. If they could hear Banks, it's a fair guess Smith could earwig as well.'

Sam allowed herself to slide down her chair, and spoke in a slow, thoughtful voice.

'So we have the emails which may show motive, and certainly demonstrate hostility, or as Dave suggested, manufacturing an alibi. We've Smith potentially overhearing the information from Banks. We know that Smith gave his house key to June, but of course we know now, if we didn't already, how easy it is to get a copy.'

She sat up straight, and her voice quickened.

'We need that intelligence picture on him as soon as. If he's our man, we need to get his clothing quickly. One lot of burnt clothing's enough for any investigation.'

'Absolutely,' Ed agreed. 'We need his car as well. If it's Smith, he's had to get here from Newcastle. He's not going to use public transport covered in blood, so he must have driven. We need the car examining for Louise's blood.'

'We do, but if he had the same car when he was still with Louise, he'll be able to explain away any traces of her blood. What we could do with knowing is whether his car was in the Seaton area last night or this morning. That would be a nice piece of corroboration. We need to establish whether any of the ANPRs were operating.'

ANPR, thought Ed. Automatic Number Plate Retrieval. A simple box of electronic tricks that took photographs of the number plates of passing traffic, a souped up version of the system that let supermarkets know whether anyone had stayed too long in the car park.

ANPR was a relatively new addition to the crime-fighting armoury but as ever, Ed knew, it was another technical advance for the far left and civil liberty brigade to moan about.

'What you shaking your head at?' Sam asked him.

'Oh, just the usual,' Ed said, putting his hands behind his head before continuing. 'You know, who do the lefty academics represent? Ask any law-abiding Jill or John and they'll be cheering for DNA databases, CCTV, electronic surveillance, and anything else that helps the good guys. But I suppose the hush-puppy brigade needs a reason to get up in the morning, and they kid themselves what they're doing is for the greater good, like they're superior to us mere mortals, saving the world from state intrusion.'

'And your point is?' Sam asked, never surprised when Ed moved his heart from sleeve to mouth.

'What would happen to their high-and-mighty stance if one their own was murdered, raped or kidnapped; CCTV, ANPR, technical and human surveillance, they would expect the lot! They don't want us to do the so-called dirty stuff, the intrusion into people's lives, but they would expect it like a shot if it was them or one of their family was the victim. Hypocrites. It's all 'human rights' bullshit. What about the victim's human rights? That lot never speak up for the victims, no mileage in that. The 'Big Brother' bollocks doesn't fit with looking after victims.'

Sam could have retired and joined the rich list if she'd pocketed a pound every time she had heard Ed on his favourite soap box. He would never change.

Now she smiled and told him: 'You need to get out more, you'll give yourself a heart attack. Oh, I forgot you need a heart to have a coronary.'

'Ha ha. Very funny,' Ed told her, before slipping back the business at hand.

'I'll get someone on ANPR straight away but if Smith's car is in the area, we'll have to make a decision on what to do with him.'

'I know,' Sam said. 'Do we go for him and look to secure any forensics but tip him off that we are looking at him? Or do we wait and try to get more evidence for the interviews? If there's no forensic in the house and he goes no reply, we haven't got anything.'

Ed nodded: 'See if we can put him in the area and we can decide from there.'

'Agreed,' Sam said. 'There'll be hell on if we lock up the estranged husband and it's not him, so let's be as sure as we can.'

Ed stood up and stretched, putting his arms high above his head and exhaled. 'He's a good bet, though, after reading those emails. If we can place his car in the right place at the right time, I say we take him.'

Sam said: 'You might be right. Let's just see what we've got before we make the decision.'

Jason appeared in the doorway.

'We're about ready to start with the interviews. His brief mentioned to the Custody Sergeant Spence might be a suicide risk. It's recorded on the detention log.'

'Interesting,' Sam answered.

'I think he's going to cough in the first interview,' Jason said, confidence in his voice.

'Let's hope you're right,' Sam told him.

'I'll crack on,' Jason said, turning away from the door.

Sam reached into the top of her in-tray and picked up the brown, tatty internal envelope. Her name was handwritten in box 27. Glancing at the names in boxes 1-26, it was possible to track the sequence of the multiple journeys the envelope had taken across the force. It had been delivered to someone in the Telecommunications Department before her, so she knew what the envelope contained.

'I had the techies knock off a spare copy of the data from Louise's phone,' she said, as she untied the string and took out three sheets of paper. She gazed at each, but lingered on page three.

'Look at this,' she said, as her finger moved down the list. 'Makes and receives a few calls on a daily basis, but gets 14 calls from the same number on the evening she was killed.'

She passed the documents to Ed.

'The number looks familiar. It looks like a job phone,' Sam said.

'Could be,' Ed said, scanning the numbers.

Sam picked up her mobile. 'Shout out the number.'

She punched the numbers, pressed call, and read the name on her screen. Her thumb jabbed end-call so hard a stinging sensation shot through it.

'What is it?' Ed asked, staring at her open mouth.

'It's Dave Johnson's phone.'

'What! Shit!' Ed said, jumping up from his chair. 'Dave's just walked past. How much of that did he hear?'

'Fuck!' Sam muttered under her breath.

Ed hurried to the door and shouted: 'Dave, hang on a minute,' but Dave Johnson, already 20 metres further down the corridor, looked like an Olympic speed walker, long strides, weight switching between heel and toe, forearms parallel to the ground, elbows sticking out. He was headed towards the exit door.

'Dave!' Sam called as she appeared in the corridor, but it was obvious he wasn't going to stop.

They both ran towards the glass door that led to the car park, still swinging after Dave had burst through it, and saw him jump into his car, a plume of thick black smoke shooting out of the exhaust as he accelerated away.

'Shit!' Sam said, throwing open the door. 'Come on, we'll go after him in mine until we get a traffic car on him.'

CHAPTER FORTY-SEVEN

'TRY HIS PHONE,' Sam shouted, tyres squealing as she floored the accelerator, the smell of burning rubber filling Ed's nose as he slammed shut the door.

Speeding out of the car park, she flung the car into a left turn and saw Dave Johnson two cars ahead.

'Straight on to answer phone,' shouted Ed, his voice straining above the sound of the revving engine.

'See if we can get a traffic car to help. We need blues and twos in this weather. Bloody fog.'

The fog had cleared a little, but not much. Sam slammed down on the accelerator, and as Ed watched the rev counter rocket, she shot past the first car. The oncoming driver hit the horn and flashed his lights but Sam was back on her side of the road, avoiding a collision by a swift throw of her wrists to the left. Inches from the rear bumper of the car in front, she waited for an opportunity and then gunned the Audi again, reaching 60mph in an instant, Ed willing himself to ignore the 40 mph signs that filled his vision.

Dave was in the distance and with nothing to slow him down, the gap had grown.

Sam swiftly moved up the gears, hit 70 mph, and started to gain ground.

'Where are the bloody traffic jams when you want them?' she screamed.

She was already gauging the traffic on the fast-approaching roundabout.

'Fucking hell, Dave. What the hell's going on?' she shouted, as she braked hard, flicked the gear stick out of fourth into second, took a sharp left at the roundabout and tore on to the dual carriageway.

Ed held the mobile to his ear. 'Hi Inspector, DS Whelan from the murder team. We need a traffic car to assist in a pursuit of a suspect vehicle. Driving east along Maidenhall Road. We're in an unmarked car, driven by DCI Parker.'

A short pause, a quick glance at Sam, the cars on the opposite carriageway no more than a blur as they passed through her forehead and out of the back of her skull.

'No, no, we're not in pursuit, that was a slip of the tongue,' she heard Ed saying. 'We're following the vehicle.'

They both knew a pursuit would never be authorised at any time in an unmarked car, and with visibility reduced by the fog, the control-room inspector might even baulk at authorising a pursuit in a marked patrol vehicle.

'Where's he going, Ed?' Sam asked, not daring to take her eyes off the road.

'Home maybe? He lives on the sea front. At least he does since he separated.'

The cars sped along the dual carriageway towards the sea, the engine growling as Sam changed down on the approach to another roundabout, the fat tyres sticking to the Tarmac as she hugged the raised kerb before continuing her dash along the outside lane.

They could see him in the same lane, one car in front.

'Not a cat in hell's chance of getting the helicopter to pursue him, not in this fog,' Ed said, as he dialled Dave's number again.

'As you said, we're not pursuing. We're following,' Sam told him as she overtook two cars and a lorry.

Ed glanced at the speedometer. 75 mph.

'Yeah, well let's hope neither us or Dave comes a cropper and we might just get away with that version of events.'

Again Dave's mobile went straight to answer phone.

Ed's ringtone was barely audible above the roar of de-mister, which, despite the inclement conditions, was keeping the screen clear with Teutonic efficiency. 'Cheers Inspector.' He turned to Sam. 'We need to keep following. Traffic's coming from the town centre.'

'Never nearby when you want them, eh?'

'You just keep your eyes on the road, and let's hope he stops soon. That was bordering on dangerous back there.'

'Relax,' she said, turning and winking at him, 'or do women drivers bother you?'

'Never liked overtaking on single-track roads.'

They both knew the road would soon narrow into a stretch of single carriageway and, if the volume increased, a steady stream of oncoming traffic would make overtaking almost impossible.

Dave was ahead, stuck behind a car which was slowly overtaking a transporter HGV.

'He's still heading for the sea,' Sam said.

'The fisherman's cottage has been in his family for generations. He used to rent it out. Maybe he's heading there, but for what I don't know.'

'We'll find out soon enough. Check to see if that traffic car is anywhere near yet.'

Ed pressed redial, spoke briefly, and ended the call with a 'thanks'.

'They've been diverted. Pile-up. Tanker and three cars. Tanker's spilling inflammable stuff all over the road. It's just us for the minute.'

'It never rains,' Sam said. 'But maybe it's a blessing. A traffic car might have spooked him even more.'

'Maybe. Maybe not. We could just do with him stopping.'

'He's got to stop sometime.'

Dave Johnson accelerated on to the next roundabout, narrowly missing a white van. Sam flew over the Give Way markings, forcing a small hatchback coming from her right to brake violently.

'Fuckin' hell, Sam,' Ed shouted, grabbing the door handle.

'I know, I know, but we can't afford to lose him.'

She emerged on to a single-lane road, and ahead, Dave swerved around the car in front and began to overtake, his vehicle sandwiched between the car he was overtaking and the others coming towards him, wing mirrors missing by inches. The air was filled with the noise of blaring horns.

'What's the crazy fucker doing?' Ed shouted. 'We need to back off, Sam. If he hits someone with us tanking after him like this, we'll all be fucked.'

The 30mph limit caused Sam to instinctively slow down. Ed was right. Nothing was worth the risk to innocent people's lives.

The volume of traffic increased on the approach to a series of lights. Dave Johnson, a few cars in front, was now crawling at about 20mph, with little hope of overtaking on the ever-narrowing road. They passed the Sea View Hotel and knew that they were approaching a stretch of road, cut into the cliff, which snaked down towards the sea with tight turns and a 25% gradient.

Sam glanced at Ed.

'Unless he's planning on driving along the coast road, this leads to the car park next to the pier,' she said.

'Or his cottage,' Ed told her.

The descent down to the sea was too twisting to take at speed and Sam, still a couple of cars behind Dave, was, like all the vehicles in front, moving slowly in second gear.

From their elevated position on the road, Ed looked out of his side window and could see Dave Johnson's car.

The urgency and tension rose in his voice as he tried to make sense of what was unfurling before his eyes.

'He's not stopping at the car park, Sam, he's driving on to the pedestrian promenade. Where the fuck's he going?'

Ed watched Dave, as Sam negotiated the final hairpin bend.

'He's out of the car. Shit. He's running on to the pier.'

'Fuck!' shouted Sam, accelerating out of the bend, and with no time to brake, her hands worked in unison, pushing and pulling the steering wheel to the right, the vibrating wheel bashing against her palms, all four tyres fighting for traction as the Audi drifted into the tight entrance for the car park. Sam sped on to the promenade, passing the Ocean View Restaurant and sea-front coffee shops, before screeching under fierce braking and sliding behind Dave's abandoned Ford Focus, its driver's door wide open and engine still running.

Ed flung open his door and was out of the car before Sam brought it to a complete stop.

'Dave! Dave!' he shouted, as he sprinted, arms pumping, his tie flying vertical over his left shoulder.

Dave Johnson dashed along the restored Victorian pier, stretching 150 metres into the fog-bound North Sea, like a pole-vaulter on the runway.

With every stride Ed's leaden legs were getting heavier, his thighs were burning, and the wooden timbers vibrated under his pounding feet.

'For fuck's sake, Dave, slow down!' he shouted, trying to make himself heard above the blasts of the lighthouse foghorn, his chest heaving, gasping for breath. As he glanced over his shoulder, he saw Sam, barefoot and running after him.

An elderly couple, strolling back along the pier, looked stunned as one suited man ran past them pursued by another, with a well-dressed woman, shoes in her hand, chasing them both.

'Police!' shouted Sam as she approached them. 'Don't let anyone else on the pier.'

The elderly couple nodded, in shock, not in agreement.

Dave Johnson reached the end of the pier and came to an abrupt halt, turned, and screamed: 'Don't come any closer!'

'Dave, what the fuck's going on?' Ed shouted, skidding to a stop about 20 metres away.

Back pressed against the waist-high, white painted metal

railings, Dave took a quick look over his shoulder, and saw that the wooden running planks they were standing on continued about six inches beyond the railings.

Sam was now next to Ed, bent over catching her breath. She raised her head, body still bent, hands on her knees, and looked directly at Dave.

'Dave,' she implored, 'what's going on?'

'Keep away. Don't move another step closer.'

His voice was trembling. 'If you move any nearer, I'll jump. I mean it. I'm going to climb the railings and stand on the other side. If you move towards me, I'll jump. Talk as much as you want when I get over.'

'Why not just talk where you are Dave?'

'I'm in fucking control of this Sam, not you!' he shouted, his face bright red.

He turned side-on to face Sam and Ed and put his right foot on the bottom rung of the railings. Ed moved forward slightly, but froze when Dave shouted. 'I mean it, Ed. Move towards me and I'll just jump straight into the sea!'

Ed had no idea how far it was to the water below, but thought it would be the equivalent of jumping off the roof of a house.

The fog had turned the sea flat calm but Sam knew it was high tide, and the tidal stream would flow south south-east at a speed of almost two knots. If Dave went in, he would be swept away, flat calm or not.

'Dave, don't climb over the railings. We can talk here.'

Sam and Ed were edging closer, taking small steps, narrowing the distance between them.

'Don't fucking move!' Dave screamed. 'I've said I'm climbing them.'

Their instincts told them to let him climb. They had narrowed the distance to 10 metres, nowhere near close enough to cover the ground and stop him placing two hands on the railings and vaulting into the sea.

'Okay, okay, Dave. Climb the railings,' Sam said, knowing her options were zero. She wasn't trained in hostage negotiation but she knew keeping Dave calm and her voice soothing was her best tactic.

Keep him talking, Sam. Keep him talking.

Dave climbed the railings and stood on one of the protruding pieces of timber, no more than nine inches wide, one foot in front of the other.

'Sit down!' he shouted, pointing to a small wrought iron bench seat near to where they were standing.

'Dave, I just need to make a call first, if that's okay?' Ed said.

'Do what you want, but if you're not back here within one minute, I'm jumping.'

Ed walked backwards, his strides long, slow, and deliberate, never taking his eyes off Dave. He quickly brought the control-room inspector up to speed, fighting to hear and be heard over the foghorn, and asked for a hostage negotiator as well as uniforms, coastguard and the lifeboat to come to the pier.

His steps were short as he walked back towards Sam and sat next to her.

'Dave, what's going on? What's this about?' Sam was saying.

'You know what it's about Sam. It's Louise.'

'What about her?'

His voice was trembling, tears rolling down his cheeks. He took one hand off the railing and rubbed his face. 'It was me. I killed her.'

Sam knew she needed to sound sympathetic.

'Why Dave?' She fought to hide her emotions, to keep her mind from the image of Louise lying eyes-open and lifeless.

Keep him talking. Sam. You know what Ed will have made sure is on the way but if he jumps now, he'll be dead before they get here.

'Climb back over Dave and let's talk about it.'

His response was loud and aggressive. 'Any talking, we do it here, Sam. I already told you that.'

Silently calculating the distance he would have to cover from the seat, Ed knew he still had no chance of making a grab for him.

'Why Dave? Why?' Sam was asking again, her voice controlled but her mind scrambling for understanding. Someone had once told her in murder investigations never try applying rational thought to what was often an irrational act.

'I thought we were going to make a go of it,' Dave said, his voice shaking. 'Then she told me she didn't see me in that way. I couldn't believe it. We'd had sex recently, just once, but she told me it was a mistake.'

He bent forward and placed his forehead on the railing, his breathing shallower, more rapid.

Ed saw his chance and sprang forward.

Dave jerked his head upwards, a wild smile suddenly on his face.

'You're too far away, Ed. You won't make it.'

Ed stopped. Dave was right. He would be dropping into the sea before Ed had even reached the railings.

Sam tried again, desperate to keep him talking, to buy precious time.

'Dave, just come back to this side. We can sort this out.'

The laugh was high and ragged and ended with a cry that seemed to come from the soul of the man.

'How, Sam? How?' His eyes were wild, his face contorted. 'She's dead. I killed her. I'm not going to prison for the next 20 years. I can't do that. A cop. In fucking prison.'

'The emails? The ones from Smith?' Sam tried to distract him, steady his emotions on a straight fact.

'I wrote them,' roared his broken voice, the fire to Sam's ice.

'You? How?'

Keep him talking. Just keep him talking.

Now Dave spoke quietly, exhausted resignation heavy in his voice.

'I hacked into his account. Louise mentioned his passwords ages ago. He used the same one for everything. He hadn't changed it for years. I just remotely accessed his emails and sent one from his account to Louise, once it was obvious you weren't linking the murder to the rapist.'

'What about the key?'

'I just stole June's and copied it.'

'The knife, Dave? Where's the knife?'

'Down one of the drains miles away.'

Sam saw Ed move two small, tentative steps closer.

'What brought this all on, Dave?'

Looking up to the heavens, his speech was cracked and shallow.

'I thought we'd be happy but she broke my heart. She broke it years ago when she married that twat. Then she broke it again. We argued on the day I killed her. Then she wouldn't answer my calls. I had the key.'

Had he paused for the foghorn, or was he going to jump?

'You know sometimes I would sit in her house when she was at work, imagining her coming home to me.' He took a deep breath. 'If I couldn't have her, nobody was going to.'

Looking upwards, he shouted: 'Why did you do this to me?'

Sam was happy to listen and buy more time, telling herself over and over to stay calm, to convince him she was the friendly shoulder to cry on, someone who wasn't there to judge.

'When I found out she was finally leaving Smith, I knew I had to leave Sally. Seeing the kids just every other weekend kills me, but I wanted Louise in my life and I thought she felt the same.'

'Come down, Dave,' Sam said, wishing she could remember the names of his children. 'Think of your kids.'

Dave smiled his haunted smile.

'It's too late. Too late for anything now. It's over. I'm sorry.'

A sudden push against the railings and he plummeted backwards towards the waters waiting below, arms and legs thrashing like a beetle on its back.

'No!' Sam screamed. She sprang from her seat and ran to the railings, leaning out over the mist-covered sea.

Ed tore off his jacket, hurled it to the ground, and leapt on to the bottom railing.

'Don't even think about it,' Sam shouted, grabbing his arm.

Ed shook her off and climbed on to the second railing: 'I've got to do something.'

She held his eyes. *Control him, Sam. It's what you do, what you've always done.*

'It's too late, Ed. You know it's too late. It was over when he walked past the door. Bad timing.'

She saw hesitation slide across Ed's face.

And she knew the moment was gone.

'Get on the phone to the control room. Update the RNLI. Tell them he's in the sea,' Sam said, her hand again on Ed's right arm.

'You jump and we'll have another dead body and I for one am not telling Sue. There've been enough deaths this week.'

In slow motion, Ed stepped down from the railings, taking his phone from his trouser pocket. Head bowed, chin pressed tight against his chest, he made the call.

Sam placed both arms on the railings, bent her back, and stared into the sea below, letting the tears come.

Ed was back beside her and together they looked down to the water, ears straining for the sound of the lifeboat above the noise of the foghorn, oblivious to the closing sirens wailing behind them. Slowly they shook their heads in tandem.

'I'd never thought of looking within, Ed,' Sam said. 'We were so focussed on Banks shouting his mouth off we never considered one of our own.'

'And why would we?' Ed turned to face her. 'I thought he was sound, but let's not beat around the bush, he was happy for Spence to take the fall, and when that plan wasn't working, he tried to put Smith in the frame. Unfortunately for Smith, he was in the pub when Banks was talking. Dave couldn't have known that. At least I don't think he could. June's dead, and so is poor Louise.'

Ed dropped his gaze back to the sea and the fog turning lazily above the water.

'Maybe the lifeboat guys can save him,' Ed said. 'I hope so anyway. I don't want him cheating justice, getting the easy way out.'

Sam inhaled deeply and filled her lungs with the cold sea air. She sighed and thrust her hands into her pockets.

'What a waste. Those poor kids. The signs were there I suppose, that emotional attachment to Louise. Leaving his wife…living alone… the 'Job' forcing him to retire…'

They stood in silence, looking out to the misty horizon, the gentle lapping of the waves against the old timbers audible between the foghorn blasts. Anyone watching would think they were in a trance, motionless and watching something only they could see.

Sam's phone broke the spell, the call over in seconds, Sam muttering a 'thank-you' born of obligation not elation.

'Jason,' she said softly, searching for the horizon in the fog. 'Spence's going to cough the rapes.'

Still looking out to sea, Ed gave a barely visible nod.

Sam saw a tractor towing a fishing coble across the sands, an old man in oilskins and a Breton cap aboard the open boat.

'Where you going?' Ed asked as Sam started walking away.

She pointed towards the boat.

'On that coble.' She was running now, head back and hair flying. 'At least we can say we did everything we could when Stewart and the IPCC ask.'

Sprinting back along the pier and down on to the beach, she waved her arms and shouted at the fisherman.

The blue-and-white coble was in the water by the shore when Sam reached it. Panting, bent over, hands on her knees, she told the skipper about Dave Johnson. He was sea-testing his new diesel engine, happy, obliged even, to help in the search.

Sam waded into the water, threw an arm and a leg across the side and heaved herself onboard. She crashed on to the bottom of the boat, her right shoulder taking the impact, her clothes soaking up the dirty bilge water.

Standing close to the bow, she'd forgotten how much a boat rocked, even in a calm sea. Gripping the side, a clammy feeling spread across her body. Light-headed, she screwed her eyes shut as the recurring nightmare began to play again in her imagination like a sepia, silent movie, the noiseless splash and sinking cold taking her back to the place where her fear waited in the deep. She hadn't wanted to return to the water like this, not a search and possible rescue. Man overboard drills were an essential part of her RYA training, but this was real.

Her nose twitched, senses recalibrating after one had shut down; now she was on the water, the sea and floating seaweed smelled stronger, saltier and more fishy, and she had completely forgotten the sharp tang of marine diesel.

She opened her eyes and willed herself to look down. The sea was murky and foreboding. *If they couldn't find him in the crystal-clear waters of the Caribbean, what chance have I got in the North Sea?*

And Sam knew the North Sea was tidal.

Fine spray hit her face. It was a sensation she once loved, a feeling like no other, a feeling of freedom and adventure and a future. Now it reminded her of everything that was wrong with the sea. She hated it, despised its power and cold indifference.

And she hated Dave Johnson for drawing her on to the blue-and-white coble, back to the water and the weight of her grief.

She guessed she had been fighting her demons for only minutes when the lifeboat came into view but to Sam, every second had stretched. Her teeth were chattering, her clothing totally inadequate for the sea, but the tears streaming down her cheeks had nothing to do with the cold, nothing to do with her eyes straining to see through the fog, nothing to do with Dave Johnson's likely death. In truth, the eyes fixed on the impassive water had seen nothing but memories and a moment.

When she spoke, her voice was a low, hurting whisper.

'Where are you? Where are you Tris?'

ACKNOWLEDGMENTS

No work of fiction is ever completed without the help and guidance of a great team of people.

I am indebted to Cheshire Cat Books for having the faith to publish.

Paul Jones, Head of Publishing, has a great critical eye and the unerring natural ability to succinctly highlight weaknesses in the narrative.

Every author needs a great editor (megastar Ann Cleeves' words not mine) and Garry Willey perfectly reflects that mantra. His skill with the written word and jovial encouragement helped make this book what it is.

Thanks also to my mate Trevor Wood for his feedback at various stages of the process.

My thanks go to my son, Ben, for providing the cover photograph and Laura Swaddle for designing the cover.

I doff my cap to all the great police officers, both uniform and CID, who I worked with for 30 years. We might not have always got it right, but I believe we always did our best.

And my final thanks are to you, the reader. A book that is not read is just words on a page.

Sadly I encountered many victims of rape and their courage in dealing with the abhorrent crime committed against them never ceased to amaze me. Your bravery is an example to us all. There are now so many wonderful organisations helping survivors I would encourage anyone who is violated to seek their help. Please remember, you are not alone.

Printed in Great Britain
by Amazon